Jenny Holmes has been writing fiction for children and adults since her early twenties, having had series of children's books adapted for both the BBC and ITV.

Jenny was born and brought up in Yorkshire. After living in the Midlands and travelling widely in America, she returned to Yorkshire and brought up her two daughters with a spectacular view of the moors and a sense of belonging to the special, still undiscovered corners of the Yorkshire Dales.

One of three children brought up in Harrogate, Jenny's links with Yorkshire stretch back through many generations via a mother who served in the Land Army during the Second World War and pharmacist and shop-worker aunts, back to a maternal grandfather who worked as a village blacksmith and pub landlord. Her great aunts worked in Edwardian times as seamstresses, milliners and upholsterers. All told stories of life lived with little material wealth but with great spirit and independence, where a sense of community and family loyalty were fierce – sometimes uncomfortable but never to be ignored. Theirs are the voices that echo down the years, and the author's hope is that their strength is brought back to life in many of the characters represented in these pages.

Also by Jenny Holmes

The Mill Girls of Albion Lane

and published by Corgi Books

THE SHOP GIRLS OF CHAPEL STREET

Jenny Holmes

CORGI BOOKS

TRANSWORLD PUBLISHERS
61–63 Uxbridge Road, London W5 5SA
www.transworldbooks.co.uk

Transworld is part of the Penguin Random House group of companies
whose addresses can be found at global.penguinrandomhouse.com

First published in Great Britain in 2016 by Corgi Books
an imprint of Transworld Publishers

A CIP catalogue record for this book
is available from the British Library.

ISBN
9780552171502

Typeset in 11½/14pt New Baskerville by Kestrel Data, Exeter, Devon.
Printed and bound by Clays Ltd, Bungay, Suffolk.

Penguin Random House is committed to a sustainable future
for our business, our readers and our planet. This book is
made from Forest Stewardship Council® certified paper.

9 10 8

For my father, Jim Lyne, who took me on unforgettable motorbike jaunts into the beautiful Yorkshire Dales

CHAPTER ONE

Violet Wheeler posed in front of the full-length mirror set up in a side office at Timothy Thornley's brewery on the corner of Chapel Street.

'Well, what do you think?' she asked her Aunty Winnie, a knot of nervous excitement tightening in her stomach. It wouldn't be long now before she had to face the crowd.

'Not bad,' came Winnie's studied reply.

'Is that all?' A crestfallen Violet turned this way and that. She'd banked on looking better than 'not bad' this day of all days.

Her aunt stole up behind her. Short and stout, she had to stand on tiptoe to peer over her willowy, eighteen-year-old niece's shoulder. 'No, love, I'm only kidding,' she murmured. 'You look smashing.'

Violet wasn't sure. 'Does the shade of the shoes match the dress? They're not from the market – I had to go all the way into town.'

'And it was worth it.' Winnie met Violet's gaze in their reflection in the mirror and nodded her head. Here, in Thornley's dusty office, surrounded by ledgers and order books and with the smell of fermenting hops in their nostrils, she couldn't have been prouder of her niece.

Despite her nerves, Violet soon grew more confident about what she saw. Her sleeveless dress in cream rayon silk wasn't your usual Gala Queen creation of pink chiffon. No, Violet's Whitsuntide gown was altogether sleeker and more *à la mode*, as she liked to term it, with its V-neck, nipped-in waist and draped handkerchief hemline below which her trim ankles and satin shoes could just be glimpsed. The outfit was topped off with long cream gloves and for a headdress, a bold arrangement of silk lilies clipped into her newly bobbed, auburn-tinged hair.

Aunty Winnie relented. 'Don't worry – you're a bobby dazzler in anybody's books.' She had one eye on the scene outside the window. Wilf Fullerton was in shirtsleeves, hitching a pair of grey Clydesdales to the decorated brewery float – the horses done up in shiny brasses and patriotic red, white and blue rosettes. The cart itself was transformed into a flower-decked arbour for the Gala Queen's slow progress up Chapel Street then across Overcliffe Road onto the Common where the Whit Monday celebration was to take place.

'Should I wear this pearl necklace?' Violet asked.

'No pearls,' Winnie advised. 'There's no need to gild the lily.' Now she could see Wilf helping the

Gala Queen's attendants onto the float – little Mabel and June Clough from Raglan Road in short white dresses, ankle socks and kidskin sandals, with bows in their hair. Then there was eighteen-year-old Kathy Land, Violet's good friend and rival for the Gala Queen crown, who this year had had to make do with chief flower girl. She was already up on the float and looking round for Violet to join her.

'You need to get a move on if you don't want them to set off without you,' Winnie urged. 'Then it'll be *Hamlet* without the prince.'

Violet took one last look in the mirror. She and her aunt had made the dress from a pattern in the latest Butterick catalogue. Oh, the hours they'd spent making sure that the seams were free of pulls and wrinkles across the bust and that the hem hung just so. They'd put everything into it, just for this one short day.

She's on her way! Winnie mouthed through the window at Wilf who, having donned his tweed jacket and brown bowler hat, had climbed into the driving seat and taken up the reins. Hearing the horses stamp and their bridles jingle, she shooed Violet from the room, along the dingy green corridor, and down the stone steps onto the street.

'About time too!' Wilf called. 'Stan, give her a leg-up, there's a good lad.'

On cue and with a wink and an exaggerated bow, Stan Tankard was on hand to lead Violet up the small set of wooden steps at the back of the float.

'Violet, where've you been?' Kathy sighed accusingly from beneath the arbour. 'At this rate I thought I should have to stand in for you.'

'Over my dead body.' With a chirpy smile to disguise her nerves, Violet settled herself onto a faded throne borrowed for the occasion from the props department of the Hadley Players.

'It won't rain, will it?' Winnie asked Wilf, who was raring to go. She looked anxiously at some wispy clouds gathered around the spire of St Luke's church on the brow of the steep hill.

'What am I, a bleeding oracle?' the brewery man grumbled.

'Keep your hair on,' Winnie retorted, dressed for the occasion in her best pale blue crêpe de Chine day dress and straw hat. 'Are you all set?' she called up at Violet, who nodded.

Standing cheek by jowl with Winnie on the crowded pavement, several bystanders issued loud verdicts on this year's Gala Queen.

'Blooming lovely,' one old chap commented to young Stan who had removed the wooden steps. 'If I was your age, I'd be bagging the last waltz with her at the church hall later on tonight.'

'Who says I haven't already?' Stan winked back.

'Young Violet's as pretty as a picture.' A stout, middle-aged neighbour sighed wistfully, no doubt recalling her own glory days.

'If you ask me, she's skimped on material for the dress,' her less charitable friend complained.

'She'll be nithered if the wind gets up.'

A beaming Winnie was deaf to criticism. 'Good luck, love!' she told her niece, as the horses took the strain and moved away from the kerb.

Violet breathed deeply and smiled down at her aunt. Then she raised her gloved hand and gave her first queenly wave of the day.

Despite Winnie Wheeler's fears, the sun shone on the Whit Monday procession as it set off up Chapel Street led by the sturdy Clydesdale horses and the float carrying the Gala Queen and her attendants. It was followed by a Sally Army brass band oompah-ing until the windows rattled in the small terraced houses and shops either side of the narrow, cobbled street. Then, striding out after the band, came a gaggle of Sunday School children in fancy dress for the traditional parade, tripping up over Wee Willie Winkie nightshirts and Little Bo Peep hooped skirts. Hard on their heels were pupils from Lowtown Junior School dressed as rats, capering up the street after a harlequin-clad Pied Piper.

Up the hill they paraded, past Sykes' bakery and Hutchinson's grocery shop to the junction with Overcliffe Road where a breeze swept down from the moors, lifting the delicate hem of the Gala Queen's dress and making the ribbons of the dray horses' rosettes flutter gaily in the breeze.

'Not bad.' Sybil Dacre's comment unknowingly echoed Winnie's teasing put-down of her niece. She and Evie Briggs sheltered from the wind in the

11

doorway to Chapel Street Costumiers. Their special-occasion dress shop had been set up two years earlier by Sybil herself, with Annie Pearson and Evie's oldest sister, Lily. The successful enterprise was situated next to the Wesleyan chapel in what used to be Henshaw's haberdashers, and it was with an expert eye that the two needlewomen took in the details of the Gala Queen's dress. 'That bodice is nicely cut on the bias to show off Violet's figure.'

'I recognize the pattern,' Evie declared as they stepped out of the doorway to follow the float towards the Common. 'It's from this summer season's catalogue.'

'You're right, it is. And I'll bet the rayon is from the market. I spotted something similar on a stall there last month.'

'Violet must have sewn it herself.'

'With back-up from Winnie, I expect.' Sybil knew how much their neighbour from Brewery Road doted on her orphan niece. 'Anyhow, between them they've made a good job of it.'

'Toot-toot, stand back!' Stan honked a horn fixed to the handlebars of his bike as he wove and wobbled through the crowd. He was in a race with his pal, Eddie Thomson, to be first onto the Common, ready to hand Violet and her attendants down from their float.

'May the best man win.' Eddie had accepted the challenge at the bottom of Chapel Street. He'd laughed to see Stan sneak off down a side alley to miss the crowd, only to re-emerge near the top of the street, back into the hurly-burly just a few yards ahead of him.

'Yoo-hoo, Violet!' Stan roared above the Onward Christian Soldiers growl of Sally Army bassoons and the roll of drums. 'Yoo-hoo, Your Majesty!'

The queen for the day made out his smooth dark hair and sharp-featured face flushed from cycling uphill and gave a slow, regal wave. He was a card, was Stan, with his car klaxon and booming voice, wobbling alongside and resting one hand on the side of the float.

'Remember to save me that dance later on!' he called now. 'Waltz, foxtrot, quickstep – whatever you like.'

'And me!' Eddie yelled from further down the road. But his voice was lost in the hullabaloo.

Anyway, it was impossible for Violet to give either Stan or Eddie an answer because with a jolt across the pavement Wilf had turned the horses onto the Common and she was greeted with a loud hurrah from the crowd awaiting her arrival. There were men and women in their Sunday best, a sea of smiling faces under caps and berets, cloche hats and jaunty straw boaters, the men in heavy jackets despite the sunny weather but the women in bright cotton dresses with frilled collars, lace and bows.

'Would you credit it?' A daunted Kathy took in the sight of the people jostling for a view in front of craft stalls, roundabouts, fortune-tellers and coconut shies. 'Here's everyone and his aunt!'

Little June and Mabel Clough turned uncertainly to Violet. June looked as if she might burst into tears.

'Don't be put off.' Violet took a twin in each hand and coaxed them towards a waiting Stan as they made ready to descend the float. 'Look at me – cool as a cucumber, never mind that people are staring at us. Just think like a princess and give them a wave.'

'That's right, Princess June!' Stan swung the little girl to the ground while Eddie came up for her sister. 'You two wait there until we fetch their ladyships.'

'Me first.' Kathy nipped in front of Violet. When the hem of her dress caught in her heel, Kathy let Stan reach up to disentangle it, making sure he got a good view of her ankle and silk-stockinged calf.

'Violet?' Eddie was ready with a steadying hand but she scarcely noticed him, for she'd spied her aunt toiling across the rough grass.

'Yoo-hoo – over here, Aunty Winnie! Where's Uncle Donald? I haven't spotted him.'

'He's here somewhere. At any rate, he should be. He dressed up in his Sunday best to mark the occasion.' Breathless, overheated, but still brimming with pride, Winnie supervised Violet's descent from her arbour. 'That's right, Eddie – careful now. Keep her well away from that horse muck. Don't land her in the puddle, there's a good chap. That's it, take your time.'

'I will, Mrs Wheeler, don't you worry.' As far as Eddie was concerned, he could have spent the whole afternoon lifting Violet down from the float. Then there would have been minutes to enjoy the feel of his hands around her slim waist, hours to breathe in her perfume and face powder as he lowered her to the ground.

But all too soon Kathy spoiled the moment by letting Violet know that the lady mayoress had arrived early. 'Her Ladyship's twiddling her thumbs by the band stand, waiting to plonk the crown on your head.'

Then Stan intervened too – 'Better not keep Madam waiting,' – and Eddie had to step right back.

Violet was gone in her cloud of lily of the valley, attended by Kathy and the little ones – and he, Eddie, was tongue tied and rooted to the spot, condemned to continue his worship from afar.

As it turned out, Violet felt that the crowning ceremony was a bit of a let-down. The lady mayoress, a sour-faced woman wearing a fox fur stole over her navy blue clutch coat and self-importantly sporting her chain of office, performed her VIP role with bad grace – Kathy's description of her 'plonking' the crown on Violet's head was spot on. Then she made a short speech telling everyone how lucky they were to have a town council generous enough to lavish money on the bank holiday celebrations. After all, times were hard – roads still needed sweeping, the ash pits had to be emptied and street lights lit. There was muted, grudging applause as the dignitary had

15

her say then she turned to her chauffeur to engineer an immediate exit.

'It looks like somebody got out of bed the wrong side this morning,' Kathy muttered to Violet as the gleaming limousine carried the mayoress across the Common onto Overcliffe Road.

'Yes, and this crown is heavy and it hurts my head.' Violet would have preferred to stick with the silk lilies but it seemed she had no choice. 'How long do I have to keep it on?' she asked Winnie, who was close at hand as always.

'Until after you've judged the fancy dress,' her aunt insisted, adjusting the bothersome crown.

'But that's ages. The children all have to eat their cakes and orange juice first.'

'Chin up, there's a good girl. Come along, June and Mabel. Line up behind Violet and Kathy.'

'Hey up, Violet – try to look as if you're enjoying it,' Stan advised laughingly as he and Eddie dashed by with fresh sacks of coconuts for the shy. They'd both got rid of their jackets, unfastened the top buttons of their shirts and had the wind in their sails as they delivered the coconuts then sped on to try their skill at the rifle range.

'When can we ride the donkeys?' Mabel tugged at Kathy's skirt as she and June fell into line behind the grown-ups. She cast lingering looks across the Common at school friends hopping into the saddle and kicking their beasts into reluctant action.

'After!' Kathy said crossly.

'After what?' June whined.

'After we've walked round the stalls, listened to the band play and judged the fancy dress – that's what.'

'Smile!' Violet told the girls. Then she reminded herself to wave at her Uncle Donald, head and shoulders above the crowd, unmistakable with his slicked-back grey hair, trim moustache and neat silver tie pin.

Inscrutable as always, he acknowledged his niece's wave with a slight nod of his head.

Was he proud of her or embarrassed about the attention she was drawing to herself? Violet couldn't tell. She walked on with her attendants, past the pie and peas stall, deafened by the Sally Army in the centre of a circle of straw bales set out for people to sit on. There was a green, earthy smell of crushed grass, hot pies, brandy snaps and candyfloss. *Smile*, she told herself. *Chin up and smile!*

'That's more like it!' Stan popped up again, waiting in front of Eddie in the queue for Gypsy Rose Lee.

'Eddie Thomson, you're never going to get your fortune told?' Kathy paused to poke fun.

'It's Stan who wants to do it, not me.' Eddie gave an embarrassed cough then quickly stepped out of the line.

'Eddie Thomson, look no further!' Stan crowed in a high-pitched, mysterious fortune-teller's voice. 'Today, here at the gala, you will meet the girl of your dreams!'

17

'Very funny,' Eddie muttered as he backed away.

'Look where you're going!' a warning voice yelled from behind.

Too late – Eddie had come up against one of the straw bales, lost his balance and only just saved himself from landing on his backside in front of Violet.

Thankfully the Gala Queen and her followers glided on, oblivious.

'What's up, Ed?' Stan joshed. 'You've turned red as a beetroot.'

That was it – Eddie had had enough. A chap could fall out with Stan Tankard at times like this – Stan who was always winking and joking and putting himself first, forever making you feel small in front of people. 'I'm off,' Eddie said, turning on his heel.

'Where to?'

'Just off,' Eddie grunted. Off across the crowded field, past fluttering flags and the ice-cream stall, past lithe gymnasts lining up to do acrobatics in the makeshift arena, out onto Overcliffe Road, down Ada Street for a disgruntled, bank-holiday pint all by himself at the Green Cross.

CHAPTER TWO

Tuesday morning brought Violet back down to earth with a bump. She was already hard at work behind the counter at Hutchinson's, the grocer's on Chapel Street, when Evie Briggs called in for a pound of sugar and a quarter of tea.

'Have you got over yesterday's excitement?' she asked as Violet weighed out the sugar into a blue bag. At sixteen, Evie was yet to put herself forward for Gala Queen but she dared to hope that one day her turn would come. Meanwhile, she was full of admiration for the way the older girl had pulled off the role.

Back in the humdrum real world, Evie worked diligently alongside Sybil at Chapel Street Costumiers. This had been a good arrangement after Evie's eldest sister Lily had left the business to get married and have a baby. In fact, Sybil and Lily's friend Annie had left Chapel Street to start her own family at the same time and so Evie had stepped in to help Sybil sew beaded bolero jackets, jersey-knit two-piece suits and for their more daring customers, the fashionable harem pants worn by stars of the silver screen. She had been there ever since.

'Yes, it all went by in a flash.' Violet tamped down the sugar then folded the top of the bag. 'Still, I revelled in it while I got the chance. A quarter of tea, did you say?'

'Yes, please. I thought you looked lovely,' awe-struck Evie said shyly. 'I've seen the dress pattern in the catalogue. The neckline looked a bit tricky to me.'

'It was,' Violet agreed, glancing round to check that her boss was still busy in the stockroom before plunging into details about interfacing and cutting cloth on the bias. 'I was dead set on wearing some-thing up to date,' she confided in the younger girl. 'I scoured the magazines to find a style that would suit me.'

'And you pulled it off.'

Violet smiled at the memory of some of the high-lights from yesterday that stood out in her mind – riding on the horse-drawn float, watching the brass band and applauding the gymnasts, then dancing the night away with the best-looking lads between here and Overcliffe. 'I'm glad I handed the fancy dress prize to your Arthur.'

'Yes, his little face lit up. We thought that sending him dressed as Mickey Mouse was a bit different to your run-of-the-mill nursery-rhyme characters.'

'It definitely caught my eye.' Pushing the weighed

20

tea across the counter, Violet paused to study Evie's open features and noticed that her fair curls, though cut short, refused to conform to the sleek bob that current fashion demanded. It gave her an innocent look, which was the opposite of the dark sophistication that she herself strove for. 'I could lend you the dress pattern,' she offered in a burst of generosity. 'It doesn't have to be made out of rayon – it could be a nice summer cotton or a light linen.'

Taking charge of her groceries, Evie smiled brightly. 'That would be champion.'

'Drop in tomorrow – I'll have it ready for you.'

'Ta very much. Ta-ta then.'

The shop bell tinkled as Evie left and Violet watched her through the window, following her progress up Chapel Street. She allowed herself a moment to ponder how life might be if, like Evie, she could find work as a seamstress – pinning, cutting and sewing cloth instead of weighing out flour and sugar, cutting cheese and slicing bacon all day long. Violet glanced around at the shelves stacked with cereal packets and biscuits, tins of salmon, sardines and mandarin oranges. *There's no point dreaming*, she told herself as she dusted flour from her dark blue apron. There was no doubt about it – the Whitsuntide Gala Queen of 1934 had her feet firmly back on the ground.

That same afternoon Ben Hutchinson, family grocer and lifelong grumbler, made up the order for Jubilee

Drapers shop. 'Drop this off on your way home and no arguments,' he told Violet in his dry-as-dust voice, which matched his cautious, penny-pinching ways. It was the same routine every Tuesday without fail – an order of digestive biscuits, tea, butter, Wensleydale cheese and Jacob's Cream Crackers to be delivered to Ida Thomson and Muriel Beanland on the corner of Chapel Street and Brewery Lane.

'Remember I'll have to leave five minutes early if I want to catch them before they lock up.'

'Have it your own way.' Her curmudgeonly employer ticked items off a list then thrust the Jubilee box into her arms. 'By rights I should dock your wages – these few minutes add up over the weeks, I'll have you know.'

'Ta, Mr Hutchinson.' Resisting the urge to retaliate and glad of the early release from her humdrum work, Violet left with a spring in her step, carrying the order under one arm.

'Hello, Violet!' Their neighbour, Marjorie Sykes, was busy raising the canvas canopy that shielded her window display of bread and cakes from the sun. 'I saw you up there on the Common yesterday. You did a grand job!'

'Ta. It already seems a long time ago.' *And a world away, worse luck.*

'You did your Aunty Winnie proud.' A low sun cast long shadows down the street as Marjorie leaned her hooked pole against the wall. 'I did laugh about that donkey running off with Stan Tankard,' she went on. 'And the donkey man chasing after the runaway all the way up onto the moor.'

'Who can blame the poor thing?' Violet was eager to get away from the bread shop owner, who had become known as a good gossip since taking over the bakery following the death of her mother three years earlier. In fact, if you were in a hurry, you did your best to avoid catching the eye of the dumpy spinster in the yellow flowered overall.

'You mean you'd run a mile from Stan too?' Marjorie chuckled.

'So would anyone with any common sense. Sorry, Marjorie – I have to dash and catch Muriel and Ida before they close.'

Violet reached the drapers just as Muriel was bringing down the blind and bolting the door. Spying the arrival of their grocery order, she quickly slid back the bolt and made way for Violet to step inside. 'Come in, come in. We were beginning to think you'd got lost.'

'I'm sorry about that, Miss Beanland.'

'Muriel – please.'

'I'm sorry, Muriel. Mr Hutchinson always cuts it fine getting the order ready.'

Entering the multicoloured Aladdin's cave of buttons, bolts of fabric, ribbons and lace, Violet deposited the box on the spotless glass counter.

'Never mind, you're here now and I wasn't in any hurry.' Unruffled as always, the co-owner of the drapery shop put Violet at her ease. 'You can help me unpack these new embroidery silks if you've got time.'

'Ooh, I like those!' Violet took several of the small skeins from Muriel and laid them across her palm. The colours of the silk thread shone like emeralds, sapphires and rubies. 'Can I take a couple for Aunty Winnie and pay you at the end of the week?'

'By all means. Let me wrap them in tissue paper.' Muriel bent to her task with precise, careful movements, her small hands folding and tucking neatly, fair hair falling forward to hide her refined features. She was still single at thirty and despite her delicate good looks, was considered a settled spinster who devoted her time to good causes such as the St John Ambulance and the Red Cross. She ran the business she shared with Ida Thomson with quiet confidence. 'How is Winnie – plodding on as usual?' she asked Violet, whose attention had wandered to the array of zipped fasteners on display in the rack by the window.

'Yes, she's doing nicely, thanks.'

'What do you think of the zips?'

'I say they beat hooks and eyes or press studs any day.'

'You're right, they do, though putting them in takes practice. You need a special foot for your sewing machine. Come upstairs and I'll show you.'

Eagerly following Muriel up some narrow stairs at the back of the shop and along a first-floor landing, Violet was already planning to insert the newfangled fastener into an apple-green summer dress she was making. They went up a second flight of stairs to a small mending and alteration room where they found Ida hard at work.

It was the first time Violet had been invited behind the scenes at Jubilee and she was intrigued by what she saw. The white-painted room had bare floorboards and sloping ceilings with a dormer window that overlooked a back lane running parallel to Chapel Street from Brewery Road up to Linton Park. It contained two long tables laid out with garments, scissors and thread, plus a treadle sewing machine pushed back into the alcove formed by the dormer. It was here that Ida sat, a picture of concentration as she worked the treadle with her foot and eased silky fabric under the pounding needle to accomplish a perfectly straight seam.

'Show Violet the foot you need to use for zip fasteners,' Muriel instructed Ida before hurrying back downstairs to answer a loud knock on the door.

'I'll bet you anything that's Mrs Barlow,' Ida guessed. 'She'll be after stockings or such like. Something she can't do without.'

'Doesn't she know you're closed?' Violet wondered, paying attention to the small metal contraption that Ida was showing her.

'Shop hours mean nothing to the likes of Alice Barlow. She drops by regardless, knowing we can't afford to turn away custom. See, you unscrew the normal foot then insert this new one, like so. Then you're ready to sew in the zip fastener.'

Caught up in the ins and outs of the exciting innovation, Violet drew closer. 'But you have to tack in the zip beforehand?'

'To make a proper job of it, yes you do.' Ida smiled up at her. Considered less stiff and starchy than Muriel, Ida's dark brown eyes were lively and intelligent and she gave off the air of someone who took an interest in everything and everyone around her. 'When's your next day off?' she asked. 'I could show you exactly how it's done.'

'Chance would be a fine thing,' Violet countered. Days off from Hutchinson's were rare as hens' teeth, and anyway her uncle constantly reminded her that she should jump at any chance of overtime because the household needed every penny she could earn.

Ida raised an eyebrow. 'The old slave driver keeps you chained to the till, does he? Well, I'm here until half six most days so why not call in on your way home one evening? Oh, except Wednesdays – I leave early then because that's my night with the Players. We've started rehearsing a new play – a murder mystery, very modern.'

It didn't take much imagination for Violet to picture Ida treading the boards. At twenty-five, she had a slim, almost boyish figure, a mass of fair, wavy hair and a way of claiming your attention in whatever she did. Not that she was what you would call a show-off. It just happened naturally due to her quick, athletic grace and a genuine lack of awareness that people liked to look at her.

'You should come along some time,' she suggested, as if the idea had suddenly struck her. 'We need extra people for the smaller speaking parts.'

'Don't look at me.' Violet grimaced. Much as she'd enjoyed her turn as Gala Queen, she didn't fancy getting onstage and being gawped at. 'I don't think Uncle Donald would like it,' she offered by way of excuse.

Ida overrode her objections. 'Well, my young man, Harold Gibson, he takes me over to Hadley on his motorbike but you know my brother, Eddie – he'll give you a lift on his Norton if I ask him nicely.'

'No, ta.' As Violet shook her head in some alarm, she heard footsteps taking the stairs two at a time and blushed to see that it was Eddie himself who burst through the door.

'Talk of the devil,' Ida said and grinned. 'Eddie, I was just telling Violet that you'd be happy to give her a lift to rehearsal tomorrow night.'

'No, I said I wouldn't, thanks,' Violet interjected. She felt her face go red under Eddie's gaze.

'What's up, Eddie? Has the cat got your tongue?' Ida, who had an inkling about Eddie's long-held but secret feelings for Violet, delighted in teasing her brother.

'No. Sorry, I didn't know you were busy up here,'

he told them. Finding this particular visitor in the workroom had come as a surprise and now he was forced to stumble his way through a conversation without giving away the fact that, despite his best efforts to steady himself, his throat was dry and his heart was thumping against his ribcage.

'What did you want, Eddie?' Deciding to call it a day, Ida folded up the dress she was altering and turned off the electric lamp.

'Just to tell you I went after that job as a projectionist,' he mumbled awkwardly.

'The one at the Victory Picture House? How did you get on?'

'I reckon I managed not to put my foot in it but I don't have an answer yet. They said they'd let me know before the end of the week. Meanwhile, I've got plenty on my hands, helping Dad.'

As the brother and sister talked, Violet did her best to fade into the background. From what she knew of the Thomson family, both Ida and Eddie still lived at home with their parents. The house was on Valley Road, out on the edge of town – the only one in the short row that had been given a fresh lick of paint in recent years because their father was a painter and decorator by trade and it was important for them to put on a good show.

She'd known the family since she was small but never played with them or joined the same gang – partly because they were both a few years older than her, and partly because Aunty Winnie, with the best of intentions, had a tendency to shelter Violet and had taken her along to grown-up events rather than leave her to play in the street. This had set her apart from other children – something that both Winnie and Violet now regretted.

'Violet was taking an interest in the alteration work I'm doing,' Ida explained to Eddie, drawing Violet back in to the conversation. 'By the way, Violet, I hear you've got hidden talents in the sewing department. Now, don't be modest – everyone was saying how well you looked yesterday, weren't they, Eddie? And that you made the dress yourself?'

'Yes, well then, I'll be off,' Eddie said hurriedly. At over six feet tall, and broad shouldered, he felt cramped by the sloping ceilings and out of place amongst the female paraphernalia. And given Violet's reluctance to catch his gaze, she was obviously as embarrassed as he was by the situation. He wasn't surprised – she'd never shown any interest in him in all the years he'd known her, and despite acting decisively when the occasion demanded it, he didn't have Stan's brash confidence to push himself forward.

'No need, I'm on my way myself. Ta-ta!' Violet was nearest the door and able to slip out before Ida or Eddie could protest. She was already down on the first-floor landing when Ida caught up with her to thrust a printed leaflet into her hand. 'It's advertising our play,' she explained. 'Derek King's *Mistaken Identity*. I mean it – why not give it a go?'

'I'll think about it,' Violet said as she fled downstairs into the shop, past Muriel laying out the latest Lastex girdles for her tardy customer and sidestepping Eddie's motorbike, which he'd parked bang across the pavement, almost blocking her way.

CHAPTER THREE

'Slow down – you'll give yourself heartburn,' Winnie remonstrated as Violet bolted down her poached eggs on toast.

The table in the back kitchen of their home on Brewery Road was laid out with the linen cloth that Violet's aunt always insisted on with knives and forks, blue and white plates, a brown earthenware teapot and matching milk jug.

'Where's the salt?' Uncle Donald demanded as he sat down, just in from shutting his barber's shop directly across the street. He brought with him a whiff of Brylcreem and shaving soap and the permanent impression that any stray strand of hair or unruly whisker would receive short shrift.

'There it is, right under your nose.' Winnie hovered behind him, ready to refill the teapot from the kettle simmering on the gas cooker in the corner. 'I've baked scones if you've still got room,' she told her niece. 'And don't tell me you're watching your figure.'

'No time for scones.' Violet was up and on the

move before her uncle had a chance to have a go at her as usual – Violet, where's your manners; take your elbows off the table; don't talk with your mouth full. She knew he didn't mean anything by it – it was just the way he was.

Slow, steady Uncle Donald, the methodical Methodist barber had been married to Aunty Winnie since before the Great War, though the two were chalk and cheese. Where she was cheery and friendly, he was dour and determined to see the worst in people. She was stout, whereas he was wiry and gaunt. Each evening she would chat, chat, chat as she knitted or sewed while he stuck his head in a newspaper and never said a word.

Their marriage was a mystery to Violet, as it was to the whole neighbourhood, and once, during her early teenage years, when Violet had overheard a series of arguments and ventured to ask her aunt what kept the two of them together, Winnie, with tears in her eyes, had squeezed her hand and whispered three little words: 'You, love – you!'

Violet had considered this answer and convinced herself that she understood. After all, her aunt and uncle had stepped into the breach left by both her parents passing away in quick succession. First her mother, Florence, had died giving birth to Violet and in the same year her father, Joe, had been lost in battle, scrapping with the enemy for a few yards of mud in a Flanders field. Donald was Joe's brother and it must have seemed the right thing to do for him and Winnie to step in and give a home to the poor orphaned baby.

'I loved you the minute I clapped eyes on you,' Winnie would often tell Violet during the years of her growing up. 'Who could help it? You were such a bonny, magical little thing.'

To the best of Violet's knowledge, the word 'love' hadn't once crossed her Uncle Donald's lips. 'We did our Christian duty,' he would tell people in his upright way, as if he ranked the care of a child alongside the meticulous shaving of his customers and the conscientious saying of prayers in chapel.

'Don't mind him,' was Winnie's advice to Violet whenever her uncle seemed too severe. 'It's not that he enjoys coming down hard on you. He does it for your own good.'

And it was apparently for Violet's good that the ill-matched pair had stayed together, keeping a roof over her head through the worst of times, putting a meal on the table even when Donald had fallen out of work as a clerk in the office at the local mine and onto the dole when Violet was a little girl. Winnie had immediately taken a part-time job in the spinning shed at Kingsley's Mill and Donald had rented an allotment on the edge of the Common to save the cost of buying vegetables by growing everything himself. Then he'd taken up scissors and razor and taught himself the skills needed to become a barber. Countless short back and sides and sticks of shaving soap later, here was Donald Wheeler at the age of fifty-two, nicely set up in rented premises, snipping and clipping hair and trimming moustaches all day long. Meanwhile Winnie, long ago accepting that she would never have children of her own, had cut back her hours at Kingsley's to wash and iron, cook and bake and generally dote on precious, pretty little Violet, the centre of her world.

'What's the rush?' Donald asked as Violet reached for the scarlet felt hat hanging from a hook on the back of the kitchen door. A sunny evening meant that the window overlooking the back yard was open, letting in the sounds of boys playing cricket in the alley between Brewery Road and Chapel Street. Cries of 'Howz'at!' and the solid chuck of leather ball against willow bat interspersed the short interrogation beginning inside the house.

'I want to catch the seven o'clock session at Brinkley Baths.'

'Ah, gadding off, as per usual?'

'I'm not gadding, Uncle Donald. Swimming is good for you.'

'Is that what they say? You can never sit still – that's your trouble.'

Setting her hat at a jaunty angle and taking up the bag containing her swimming costume, rubber cap and towel, Violet blew her aunt a kiss and fled.

'If you see Emily, tell her she still owes me that tanner she borrowed for her tram fare a week last Wednesday,' Winnie called after her from the top step.

34

'Emily Thomson? You mean Ida and Eddie's mother?'

'Yes. She's found herself a new job taking entrance money for the swimming baths. Tell her I haven't forgotten.'

'I will do, Aunty. Now I have to dash.'

At somewhere between a walk and a run, Violet crossed Brewery Road and threaded her way down back alleys, between rows of shabby terraced houses, down steep, moss-covered stone steps until she came to the canal. From here she hurried on along Canal Road, past the tall, oppressive walls of Kingsley's woollen mill then Barlow's chemist's shop and finally the brightly lit Victory Picture House until, at seven o'clock on the dot, she came to the green-tiled entrance of Brinkley Corporation Baths.

'Hello, Violet. Fancy meeting you here!' were the words that greeted her from the lips of Stan Tankard as she stepped inside to join the short queue of women waiting to purchase a ticket. He stood beside the box office with a rolled towel under his arm, wearing grey flannel trousers, canvas deck shoes and a white shirt but no jacket.

'Hello, Stan,' Violet answered with a hint of reserve. Even though they'd danced together after the gala, Stan needn't think that he'd laid claim to her in any way. Yes, he was funny and you could have a lark, and yes, he had a certain way of flattering a girl and making her feel special, but for some reason she wasn't that keen on him. 'What brings you here?'

'What, aren't I allowed to practise my breaststroke along with everyone else?' he said with a wink at the woman in front of Violet.

'Of course you are, but I thought this was a ladies-only session.'

'It is, but I'm the new lifeguard, so I'll be looking after you lovely girls, seeing that you don't come to any harm.'

It was Violet's turn to pay and recognizing Emily Thomson's long, serious face behind the desk, she quietly passed on Winnie's message about the sixpence. With that done and clutching her ticket, she headed for the changing room without taking any more notice of Stan. Five minutes later she emerged from her cubicle and followed the smell of chlorine through the tiled archway containing the footbath out onto the side of the pool.

She found to her satisfaction that there was plenty of room for her to dive in at the deep end and swim some steady lengths. Plunging in head first, she enjoyed the buoyancy of the clean water, the feel of her limbs pushing and kicking, the cool splash against her face. Lost in the pleasant sensations, she came to the shallow end and was about to turn when Stan called down to her. He was standing on the wet tiles directly above her, legs wide apart and wearing his lifeguard's swimming trunks, with a whistle dangling down his bare chest.

'Now then, Violet, don't forget to let me know if you get into difficulties then I can blow my whistle and put my life-saving certificate to good use.'

'Do I look as if I need saving?' she countered, pushing off strongly and aware that he was walking along the length of the pool, keeping pace with her.

Honestly, Stan was slow to take the hint, which annoyed her, but at the same time she couldn't help being flattered. And when she caught sight of him out of the corner of her eye, she couldn't ignore the fact that his recent short stint in the army had helped him to develop a broad chest and shoulders, that his legs were long and shapely, and that his thick, dark hair and twinkling eyes made up for the fact that both his nose and Adam's apple were that little bit too big.

'Nicely does it,' he called again as she reached the shallow end once more. 'Now let me see your back stroke.'

'Leave me alone, Stan,' she grumbled, surging away at a diagonal.

'Yes, Stan, leave the poor girl alone,' a fellow swimmer echoed. The woman, who was older and up for a joke, flailed her arms and thrashed her legs to create a splash. 'Help!' she cried. 'Never mind about Violet, Stan – it's me you have to save!'

Violet smiled to herself and swam on. After half an hour she finished her lengths and got out of the pool, deliberately dodging her would-be admirer as she went to get changed back into her cotton dress. She would have slipped past him again on her way out, only he spotted her as he stood in his swimming things with his towel around his shoulders, talking to Emily Thomson.

Evidently Stan was now in a more serious mood. 'I hope you didn't take umbrage earlier,' he said quietly as he stepped out in front of Violet. 'It was only a bit of fun.'

'No offence taken,' she replied, chin up and sounding chirpy. Her short, damp hair was combed back from her scrubbed face, her eyelashes still wet from her swim.

'Good, that's all right then. Because I was wondering if you might fancy a night out at the flicks with me some time?'

'Oh!' The surprise invitation left Violet lost for words.

'Maybe tomorrow night?'

Violet's instinct was to hurry away without framing a proper reply. 'I don't know about that, Stan, but thanks for asking.'

'The Fay Wray picture is back on at the Victory. Or Greta Garbo's on at the new Odeon in town if you'd prefer. We could really push the boat out,' he persisted.

'I'm sorry but I've just remembered I've got something else on tomorrow.'

Aware that Emily was eavesdropping, Violet kept one eye on the exit. 'I promised Ida that I'd audition for the new murder mystery that the Players are putting on.' Goodness, how did that slip out? It wasn't a downright lie, but as good as.

38

'Never mind. Another time maybe.' Crestfallen for once, Stan shrugged and beat a retreat.

Emily opened the glass partition of her box office and leaned out of her ticket booth to speak to Violet. 'Shall I tell Eddie that you'll be needing a lift over to Hadley?' she asked in her weary, dispirited way.

Violet shook her head and made her escape. 'No, ta. I'll make my own way there,' she called over her shoulder as she stepped out into the street.

Back home on Brewery Road and sitting on the edge of her bed in the silent house, Violet knew that she'd got herself into a fix.

Her curtains were open and she could see the sky turning fiery red as the sun went down behind the grey slate roofs and sentinel chimneys of the houses opposite. She was barefoot and still in her white petticoat, able to see her reflection in the old-fashioned mirror resting on the mantelpiece of the cast-iron fireplace across the room. Tugging impatiently at her fringe to take out the kinks caused by her tight-fitting swimming cap, she frowned at her reflection.

You should have told Stan no, pure and simple, she chided herself. *Then you wouldn't have had to pretend you were joining the Players.*

But then again, did she really want to put him off for good? After all, she could try going out with Stan Tankard just to see. She might like him better than she imagined. Only, he was so full of himself and thought he was a better catch than he actually was, with his whistling and singing and generally drawing attention to himself . . .

Violet sighed and turned back her sheets. She made a fist and thumped her pillow into shape, ready to get into bed. The point was, she was eighteen years old, without many friends other than Kathy, and it was high time she found a nice young man to go out with. Eighteen and grubbing along as a grocery shop assistant, sweeping floors and stacking shelves, wiping down counters and slicing bacon for a boss who never smiled at her or praised her but grudgingly paid her a paltry weekly wage. Often, as Mr Hutchinson handed over her hard-earned pounds, shillings and pence, he made a point of telling her she was lucky to have a job at all, considering men all over the country were going on hunger marches to protest against the government's Means Test. 'And never forget that your aunt and uncle had the Christian charity to take you in as a baby where many wouldn't have. I should count my blessings if I were you.'

Almost nineteen and still single: if she wasn't careful she would end up left on the shelf like Muriel Beanland. She would be one of those spinsters without a family, forced to spend her spare time in the library, reading books or else doing good works.

I should have said yes to Stan, she decided as she drew the curtains and got into bed. *And maybe I still will. As it is, I have to get all the way over to Hadley tomorrow night, and I have only myself to blame.*

*

Though Violet liked to see herself as someone who could rise to a challenge, she approached the Hadley Institute building with butterflies in her stomach. Fresh from the five-mile bus journey over Overcliffe Moor, and with her head down against the usual stiff breeze blowing straight down the main street of the small mining town, she made a plan for the evening ahead.

She would take a deep breath and step through the oak doors of the Institute into the main body of the building. Picking Ida out from the crowd and making a beeline towards her, she would tell her casually that she'd dropped by to take a look at what the Players got up to but that she only had a few minutes to spare due to the fact that her Aunty Winnie needed her home early tonight. She hadn't got as far as making up a reason for this when she had to step to one side in the yard outside the Institute to allow a motorbike to squeeze into a space between a parked Baby Austin and a red three-wheeler. It was only when the rider had switched off the engine and stepped into the porch at the same time as her that she realized it was Eddie.

'Fancy that – us arriving together after all.' Violet seized her chance to use Eddie as a way of sliding in unnoticed. She would let him go first to distract everyone's attention while she merged into the crowd. 'After you,' she added, gesturing for him to go in ahead of her.

41

He hesitated. Taking off his leather gauntlets and unbuttoning his tweed jacket, he was once more put off his stride by everything about Violet Wheeler – her flushed face, shining brown eyes that he could only compare with the colour of hazelnuts, soft lips, slender figure in its apple-green dress – everything.

'I didn't have you down as a matinée idol, Eddie.'

'I'm not,' he said, ignoring her offer and holding the door open for her. 'I'm more the outdoors type. But Ida's roped me in to painting the scenery, that's all.'

'Ah, I see.' Through the door and inside the big hall Violet glimpsed a dozen or so people grouped together in small knots. At the far end was a raised platform with a proscenium arch and faded crimson curtains. Near to the stage there was an upright piano and running around the perimeter of the somewhat dusty, shabby space was a thick metal pipe which brought hot water to ornate cast-iron radiators set against the walls. 'I mean it – I'll follow you,' she told Eddie, the butterflies positively swarming.

'No – ladies first,' he insisted.

So she stepped in and immediately felt everyone's eyes on her, which flustered her and left her unable to pick out the one person she wanted – Eddie's sister, Ida.

'If it isn't Monday's Gala Queen!' Someone over by the piano recognized Violet and came quickly towards her. It was Kathy, accompanied by Evie and her friend Peggy Bainbridge. So Violet needn't have worried – she did know people who would make her feel at home after all.

'Welcome to the Hadley Players, Your Majesty!' Kathy greeted her with a playful smile.

'Hello, Kathy. I didn't know you were a member here.'

'We three joined for the Christmas pantomime last year. We must be gluttons for punishment, mustn't we, girls?'

Peggy and Evie agreed. 'It was *Cinderella*. I only had three lines and on the opening night I forgot each and every one of them,' Peggy admitted.

'I was in the chorus so I didn't have any lines to learn, thank heavens.' As she spoke, Evie bowed her head and looked up from under thick lashes in a way that was reminiscent of the shy but clever schoolgirl that she'd once been. However, Violet could tell that she was blossoming into a more confident young woman, most likely under the encouragement of Sybil, her seamstress employer. She dressed well, of course – tonight in a jade-green dress with a square neckline and crossover skirt. 'Ta for the dress pattern, by the way. I hope you didn't get into bother with Mr Hutchinson.'

It was true, Violet's boss had been his usual sour self when Evie had dropped by that afternoon, tapping his pocket watch and letting Violet know that he disapproved of any interruption to her work.

'Don't worry, he's never happy unless he finds something to harp on about,' she informed Evie.

'What part will you go up for?' Kathy wanted to know. Ever since she'd come second to Violet in the Gala Queen contest, she'd started to view her erstwhile school pal as a potential rival, though they were opposites in the looks department: Kathy was fair haired with soft, small features and a fuller, more curvaceous figure than Violet. 'I play the girl who goes to the races with the villain and gets herself killed. I'm going to wear a big hat and long gloves.'

'Ida mentioned something about me having a small speaking part.' At last Violet spotted Eddie's sister and excused herself. Despite her nerves, she started to take an interest in what was going on around her, noticing an elderly lady arranging sheet music at the piano and Eddie and another man, up on the stage with their backs towards her, laying out dust sheets and mixing a pot of blue paint.

'You found us all right?' Ida spoke to Violet above the general buzz of conversation. She carried a sheaf of dog-eared, closely typed pages and had a blue pencil tucked behind one ear. 'Did I mention that they made me the director for this production? I'm in charge of the actors, music, costumes, scenery – the whole bang lot. If it all goes wrong they can blame it on me!'

'You're pluckier than I am,' Violet acknowledged. 'I've never even stepped onstage before.'

'You'll be fine,' Ida insisted as she went round introducing Violet to the other Players and then to the tall, pleasant-looking man helping Eddie with the scenery. 'Harold, this is Violet Wheeler. Violet, meet my young man, Harold Gibson.'

'Hello,' Violet said, registering her first, favourable impression of Harold and feeling a twinge of envy that Ida had bagged herself such a handsome suitor.

He smiled down at her before dipping his brush into the pot then slapping paint onto the canvas backdrop.

'Anyway,' Ida went on, 'if your nerves do get the better of you up there on the stage, at least you'll be a dab hand at making costumes for us. Eddie, tell Violet you don't have to be Douglas Fairbanks or Joan Blondell to make yourself useful around here.'

'That's true,' her brother acknowledged from halfway up a ladder, brush in hand. The unfinished backdrop behind him consisted of an outdoor scene with the white rails of a race track set against green hills and trees. 'I can't act to save my life.'

Violet's heart went out to a fellow sufferer. 'I'm surprised you let your sister railroad you into this,' she said as a busy Ida bustled off to rehearse lines with one of the lead actors.

'You shouldn't be,' he grumbled, coming down the ladder to change paint pots. 'I'm not saying Ida's a bossy boots but when she wants you to do something she has a knack of getting her own way, doesn't she, Harold?'

His fellow scene painter gave a wry nod of agreement.

'Ta, I'll remember that. I like the scene you're painting, by the way.' Keeping Eddie talking seemed to Violet like a good way of putting off the moment when she would actually have to audition. Meanwhile, the pianist had begun to run through some melodies and other people, including Kathy, Peggy and Evie, were playing out scenes in various corners of the hall.

Eddie took a crumpled photograph out of the bib-pocket of his white overalls. 'We copied it from this picture of the course at Ascot.'

As Eddie came close and squatted at the edge of the stage to show her the picture, Violet breathed in a strong smell of wet paint and saw that his face was speckled blue. She resisted the urge to reach up and wipe away the flecks of paint, wondering for the first time why she hadn't paid much attention to Eddie Thomson in the past. After all, he had the same lithe, loose-limbed physique as Ida, only taller and stronger, and his hair was darker. She put it down to the fact that whereas Ida's confidence drew you to her like a magnet, Eddie preferred to stay in the background.

'Rightio, Ida will be on the war path if I don't get cracking,' he said when Violet had studied the picture and handed it back.

'I'm on the war path anyway,' his sister interrupted, seizing Violet by the hand and dragging her off to join Peggy, Evie and Kathy. 'Violet, I'd like you to read for the part of the dead girl's sister. She's the one who first suspects that the death wasn't an accident. We're on page twenty-two, Act Two, Scene Four.'

How did I land myself in this mess? Violet stood alone at the bus stop waiting for the number 15 to take her back to the top of Chapel Street. After an audition during which her nerves had been torn to shreds, she had managed to walk away with a significant speaking part. Peering down the straight main street in the gathering dusk but seeing no sign of the last bus home, she bemoaned her fate. *I'll have to learn lines and everything. And on top of which I got roped into making costumes. Ah well, at least it means I won't be cooped up at home during these fine summer evenings. And there's Stan's invitation to consider, plus my regular visits to the baths for some exercise, so things aren't looking too bad, considering.*

The sound of a motorbike pulled her out of her reverie. It was Eddie, emerging onto the street in gauntlets, cap and goggles. Spotting her at the bus stop, he drew up to the kerb. 'Hop on,' he invited. 'I'll give you a lift home.'

Violet hesitated, but this time only for a second. 'Are you sure, Eddie?'

Nodding, he steadied the bike. 'Hold tight,' he told her as she stepped onto the foot rest and climbed aboard.

See, he told himself. *All you had to do was spot the girl of your dreams waiting for a bus and offer her a lift without thinking about it. Eureka – it was as simple as that!*

'What do I hold on to?' she asked as she perched nervously on the back seat.

'You wrap your arms around my waist,' Eddie instructed cheekily as he edged away from the kerb. 'Hang onto your hat, Violet. Here we go.'

CHAPTER FOUR

Violet held on for all she was worth as Eddie's Norton CS1 swerved around bends and crested hills on the winding moor road. It felt as though they were on top of the world, looking down at the towns in the valleys below, climbing and swooping, buffeted by winds.

She clasped him tight and sheltered behind his broad back, watching the sun sink in the west and holding her breath as the horizon darkened. Then, as Eddie leaned the bike into a bend, he braked suddenly to avoid three sheep loose in the road.

'Are you all right back there?' he asked, slowing almost to a halt.

The sheep meandered ahead of them until they took it into their heads to step skittishly onto the verge at the far side. 'Silly things,' Violet muttered.

'We nearly had mutton chops for tea,' Eddie laughed, opening up the throttle again and sailing on.

'Good job I was hanging on tight like you said,'

she called above the roar of the engine. It was her first time riding pillion and she loved it, sheep or no sheep. The speed was thrilling, the wind bracing and best of all she had a sense of freedom, just like a bird must feel when it took to the wing.

'Don't worry, you're safe with me,' he yelled back, knowing that the journey would soon reach an end after this last descent onto Overcliffe Road. 'There's always stray sheep on this moor road so I was ready for them.'

Down they went along a bumpy lane bordered by dry-stone walls, rushing past a farm with untidy barns and wisps of straw blowing across the farm-yard. Then Eddie slowed for a narrow humped bridge over the canal and they reached the part where street lamps began.

'You're not too cold?' he checked with Violet as he avoided the tramlines on Overcliffe Road and fell in behind a Bentley travelling at a stately pace towards town. 'It can feel a bit chilly at this time of night.'

'I don't mind, it was worth it.' She smiled, thinking how different everything felt from the back of a bike, how quickly they got past Linton Park and the people standing at the tram stop, how loud the engine sounded as they turned down Ada Street and how strongly the smells of cigarette smoke and beer came at you from the pubs after the clean, fresh air of the moor.

All too soon they came to Brewery Road and Eddie

pulled up outside her house. 'No lights on,' he commented.

'No. Aunty Winnie and Uncle Donald always go to bed early.' She dismounted, feeling breathless and wobbly as she stood on the pavement and looked up at the house.

'Hang on a second while you get your sea legs.' Gallantly Eddie parked the bike and offered Violet his hand to lead her up the steps to the front door. 'All right now?'

She nodded then looked him in the eye as she raised her free hand to pat her windswept hair. 'Ta for the lift.'

'Have you got your key?'

'In my pocket.'

An urge to kiss her came and went before he had time to act on it.

'Thanks again, Eddie,' Violet said, putting her key in the lock. 'You saved me my bus fare home even if you did nearly make mincemeat of those poor sheep.'

She was through the door and closing it behind her, when it struck him that she'd only taken the lift because it had saved her three pence.

More fool me for thinking any different, he told himself as with a heavy heart he kick-started the Norton and headed for home.

'Who was that who brought you back on a motorbike last night?' Winnie asked as she wielded the bread knife at the breakfast table next morning, making 'motorbike' sound like the devil's work.

'Eddie Thomson. I'm sorry if we woke you up.'

'I was still awake. You know I never get to sleep until I'm sure you're back home and safely tucked up in bed.' Winnie sliced the bread and put a piece on a plate for Violet. 'You did wake your uncle, though.'

'I expect I'm in for it, then.' Violet sighed, one eye on the mantel clock and glad that Donald had already crossed the street to open his barber's shop.

'Let's hope he'll have forgotten about it by tonight.'

Violet quickly changed the subject away from Eddie and his bike. 'Ida gave me a part in the play.'

'Did she now? And what will your Uncle Donald think to that?'

'Oh, it's nothing to worry about. There'll be no larking about. This is a serious play about a murder. Kathy is in it, and a few other girls I know. Anyway, I'll tell him it was Ida's idea and everyone knows you can't say no to Ida Thomson.'

Eating and talking at the same time, Violet soon finished breakfast and was eager to be on her way. 'I'll be late for work if I'm not careful.'

'Bring back three slices of pork pie for tea,' Winnie called after her, still with knife in hand and shaking her head at carefree Violet's non-stop energy. *That's youth for you*, she told herself, *always on the go*. It made her tired just to think about it.

Poached eggs on Tuesday, cheese on toast on Wednesday, pork pie on Thursday. Out on the street, Violet smiled at the way her aunt stuck religiously to the same routine. Hurrying up the alley onto Chapel Street, she waved at Ida, just unlocking the door to Jubilee. 'Can't stop – I'm in a rush,' she said. But Ida's rejoinder brought her up short.

'Whatever did you say to poor Eddie last night? We couldn't get a peep out of him after he got in.'

'Nothing. I didn't say anything!' The memory of their bike ride came back so vividly that Violet had to stop and draw breath. She relived its soaring freedom before they reached the outskirts of the town with its sooty chimneys, snaking canal and towering mill walls, then she remembered the care Eddie had taken to make sure she was safely delivered to her doorstep. 'Tell him again – it was very nice of him to bring me home.'

'Tell him yourself next time you see him,' Ida said, with a wink. *There's none so blind*, she thought as she opened the shop door and picked up the letters lying on the mat. Violet was a bright, beautiful girl but she was naïve if she couldn't see the effect she had on Eddie. *That's what comes of being brought up by Methodists*, Ida thought. *Straight-laced, grim-faced teetotallers, the lot of them.*

For the next week or so, Violet didn't see much of Eddie. She was busy at work as usual and in the evenings either she stayed at home to finish a skirt she was making or else she paid one of her regular visits to Brinkley Baths. It was during one of these swimming sessions that she'd finally said yes to a persistent Stan.

'Very well,' she'd agreed when he'd waylaid her on the Thursday evening outside the baths. 'I'll come to the flicks with you.'

'Tickety-boo!' A grinning Stan had quickly arranged the time and place.

'Tomorrow outside the Victory, half six on the dot!'

She eventually heard of Eddie again through Ida, when on the Friday afternoon Violet called in at Jubilee Drapers to buy a zipper for her skirt.

'Eddie got that job as a projectionist at the Victory.' Ida dropped his name into the conversation as she wrote out a receipt for Violet. 'Part time, of course. But you know what they say – every little helps.'

'Lucky him. Now he'll be able to see the latest flicks without paying a penny.'

'That's true. It means you might not get your lift home from rehearsal next Wednesday, though – not if Eddie's working.'

The conversation would have drifted on, with Ida dropping hints and Violet giving no clue as to her feelings about Eddie had it not been for the ding-a-ling of the doorbell and the sweeping entrance of Alice Barlow into the shop.

'White shoelaces!' she announced without pre-liminaries, looking around with an imperious air. 'I'm sure you must have them tucked away some-where.'

Ida stopped writing the receipt and Violet stepped to one side. Mrs Barlow had left her chauffeur at the wheel of the maroon Daimler parked outside and was evidently in a hurry. Dressed in a pale pink jacket with a deep rose-pink dress and in white high-heeled sandals with matching gloves and bag, Alice Barlow could have stepped straight out of the pages of *Vogue* magazine. The trouble with women like Alice Barlow, though, and what stopped you admiring her, was that she let you know just how superior she felt.

'I have plenty of black and brown shoelaces – I'm not sure about white.' Ida pulled out a shallow drawer and sorted through her stock.

'That's no good to me. Colin specifically asked me to buy white ones for his cricket boots.' Noticing Violet and choosing to ignore her, Alice took off her gloves then pulled out a silver compact from her bag, flipped it open and began to powder her nose.

Violet pursed her lips. She resented snootiness, especially from a woman who, according to her Aunty Winnie, had been the oldest daughter of a make-do-and-mend family living above a Chinese laundry at the top of Westgate Road. It was by luck that she'd met and married Colin Barlow whose father owned five chemists in West Yorkshire. In this way she had pulled herself up in the world to the point where she had a chauffeur-driven car waiting for her and an unpleasant way of ignoring people who were of no use to her in her climb up the greasy pole.

'Ah, here we are.' Ida unearthed the desired colour. While she popped the shoelaces into a paper bag, Alice clicked the compact shut and slipped it back into her handbag.

The rose-pink dress was designed to flatter its wearer's slightly plump figure, Violet noted. And she made the most of herself in other ways. Her fair hair was immaculately waved and a dark brown pencil emphasized her arched eyebrows. She wore rouge and a coral lipstick, with nail varnish to match.

'I almost forgot – I'd like you to alter the hem on a dress I had made for me,' she told Ida. 'It's a delicate fabric. Do you think you can do it without spoiling the look of it?'

'We'll do our best, Mrs Barlow,' Ida promised.

'Then I'll send my chauffeur in with it on Monday morning. I'd like it done by the next day if you can manage it. I intend to wear it to a tea dance at the Royal Baths in Harrogate on Wednesday.'

'Yes, Mrs Barlow. I'm sure we can do that for you.' A deadpan Ida gave nothing away but as soon as the doorbell tinkled and her customer was safely ensconced inside the Daimler, she let out a loud sigh. 'See what a good actress I am,' she told Violet. '"Yes, Mrs Barlow; no, Mrs Barlow; three bags full, Mrs Barlow!"'

Violet grinned. 'I know what you mean. We get hoity-toity customers like that in our shop, telling you how to slice the bacon and cut the cheese then taking you to task about how you wrap it. I suppose

56

we shop girls just have to grin and bear it.'

'But wouldn't you like to get your hands round a woman like that's neck and throttle those airs and graces out of her?'

'I would,' Violet agreed. She left the drapers with the feeling that she liked Ida Thomson more and more as she got to know her – even if she did keep on clumsily dropping her brother Eddie's name into the conversation.

The next evening, Violet presented herself to Winnie for inspection before she left to meet Stan. The blue skirt was finished and fitted Violet perfectly and she matched it with a white linen blouse.

'And don't say "not bad" or I'll crown you,' she joked.

'You'll pass muster,' Winnie conceded, folding the tablecloth and putting away the tea things. 'But who have you gone to all this effort for? That's what I'd like to know.'

'Never you mind.' Violet wasn't letting on about her assignation with Stan and a glance at her watch told her that she was cutting it fine. 'Ta-ta, I have to dash.'

Donald sat behind his newspaper, letting silence demonstrate his disapproval of Violet's flibberti-gibbet ways.

Winnie waited for the door to click shut then she leaned forward to rest both hands on the table.

'You look worn out,' Donald said without glancing

up. 'Why don't you sit down and put your feet up?'

'Me? I've got too much to do,' she replied. 'After I've finished this pile of ironing I've got sheets with holes in them that won't mend themselves.'

'I was just saying – you look like you should take it easy.'

Winnie sighed. Violet was gone in a cloud of flowery perfume and now the house was lifeless without her. She had just Donald for company and the fact was that the two of them had run out of things to say to one another years ago.

Stan waited nervously for Violet outside the Victory. Unusually for him, he felt ill at ease in his dark blue blazer with the wide shoulder pads and the high-waisted twill trousers held up by braces – altogether more formal than his usual outfit of tweed jacket and open-necked shirt. Still, he was sure that Violet Wheeler was worth making the effort for.

She was late, though. He watched couples walking arm in arm down Canal Road and into the shiny foyer of the picture house, trying in vain to pick out her slim figure. Instead, Eddie drew up to the kerb and parked his bike outside the entrance.

'Hello, Stan, what are you hanging about out here for?' Eddie asked, in a hurry to get inside. 'Did someone stand you up?'

'I might ask you the same question, only a little bird tells me they've been daft enough to put you in charge of the projector. Can that be right?'

'Ha ha, Stan.' As his pal shoulder-shoved him and shunted him into the wall, Eddie caught sight of Violet hurrying towards them. He felt a moment of nerve-tautening uncertainty until Stan spotted her too and immediately straightened his tie and cleared his throat.

'Wish me luck, Eddie,' Stan muttered.

'You . . . and Violet?' Eddie was slow to understand but when he did an angry shock ran through him – not irritation with Stan but with himself for being too slow off the mark. He hid it by hurrying on across the foyer and through a door marked 'Staff Only'.

'Here she comes, her royal highness!' Stan greeted Violet with a joke which he knew had worn thin since Whit Monday but he was so bowled over by her appearance that it was the best he could come up with. Her brown eyes were bright, her mouth soft and full. Not to mention the rest of her, shown off to advantage in her slim skirt and close-fitting blouse. She was a looker, was Violet, and it was a miracle she hadn't been snapped up long ago.

'Hello, Stan. Sorry I'm late.' She thought he looked smart and spruce, though the whiff of Brylcreem was overpowering as he offered her his arm. *This is only the flicks*, she told herself. *It's an hour and a half of Fay Wray being carried up a skyscraper by a giant ape. It still doesn't mean that Stan and I are officially walking out, not by a long stretch of the imagination.*

*

59

'I can't work her out,' Stan confessed to Eddie the following night.

The two friends had met in the Green Cross after a day's work.

Eddie emptied his glass and tried to change the subject. 'Honestly, Marjorie can talk the hind leg off a donkey.' He'd helped his dad that day with a decorating job above Marjorie's bakery. 'Mind you, she keeps us well supplied with tea and sponge cake while we work.'

'I'm telling you, I was on my best behaviour with Violet,' Stan went on, ignoring him. 'I sat next to her good as gold. I never laid a finger on her until the scene where the monkey climbs the Empire State Building.'

'Don't tell me – I don't want to hear about it,' Eddie muttered.

'Even then, I only held her hand. I was banking on her being scared by the gorilla and burying her face in my chest like the other girls, but trust Violet to be different – she never did.'

'Honestly, Stan, I'm not interested in your love life.' *Especially if it concerns Violet Wheeler*, he thought to himself.

His friend, who was dressed in greasy brown overalls, with his dark hair hanging lank over his forehead, struck a pose. 'Look at me – how could anyone resist?'

Eddie had the grace to laugh and order them two more pints.

'I'm not letting it put me off,' Stan vowed, confidence undented. 'Mark my words – I plan on taking another crack at Violet Wheeler as soon as ever I get the chance.'

CHAPTER FIVE

'I decided to call in and collect our order for a change.' Muriel stood patiently waiting for Ben Hutchinson to make up the usual Tuesday list for Jubilee. She turned to Violet who was up a stepladder tidying shelves. 'It's been one of those days. We had to rush to finish a sewing job on that dress for Mrs Barlow then we found that she couldn't come in to collect it herself so we had to ask Eddie to break off from his job at Sykes' and ride all the way out to Bilton Grange with it. But did he get any thanks? Not one word, I assure you.'

'No, I can imagine,' Violet sympathized.

'But she helps us pay the bills.' Muriel's gaze ranged along the shelf stacked with boxes of cereals. 'I'll take some porridge oats, please, Mr Hutchinson. And a jar of marmalade.'

Taking a pencil from behind his ear and with no glimmer of a smile breaking through his permanent frown, the middle-aged grocer added items to the list then barked at Violet to fetch them. When the order was complete, he took Muriel's money and rang it up on the till. 'Would you like little miss to carry it down the street for you?' he asked.

'No ta – I can manage.' Muriel took the box and left the shop with a cheerful goodbye.

'Say what you like about Muriel Beanland,' Hutchinson commented as he wiped down an already spotless counter and Violet carried the step-ladder into the stockroom at the back of the shop, 'she's had her fair share of troubles but she never lets things get her down.'

'What troubles?' Violet wondered aloud.

Hutchinson tapped the side of his nose. 'Never you mind.'

That's just like you, Violet thought, emerging from the stockroom. *Lead a person on then clam up on them. I'll ask Aunty Winnie. She'll tell me what things Muriel has risen above in her seemingly neat and orderly life.*

Violet's curiosity about Muriel Beanland's past couldn't be immediately satisfied, however, because it was Uncle Donald and not Aunty Winnie who greeted her when she got home.

'What's this I hear about you joining the Hadley Players?' he demanded as soon as she got through the door. He was in shirtsleeves and waistcoat, but immaculately groomed as always.

Violet adopted the careless tone she used when-ever her uncle came down hard on her. 'What if I did? It's not a crime, so far as I know.'

'Less of your cheek,' he snapped. 'I only got to

hear of it through Eddie Thomson when he came in for a haircut first thing this morning. You kept it quiet, though I expect Winnie was in on it. You two are always hugger-mugger.'

Violet drew a deep breath. 'We kept it quiet because we knew how you'd react. And sure enough, we were right.'

Filling a kettle at the kitchen sink, Donald set it to boil on the gas cooker that he'd recently had installed, after years of nagging from Winnie.

'Entering the contest for Gala Queen is one thing,' he grumbled, 'but prancing about on a stage in front of every Tom, Dick and Harry is different. It's not something I hold with.'

Violet sighed and sat at the table. Suddenly the kitchen seemed small and dark, full of antiquated objects like the pair of white china dogs on the mantelpiece, the ticking wall clock and the heavy flat iron resting on its stand next to the fire grate. Her uncle was old-fashioned too – thirty years out of date and miserable with it. Whereas Violet thought of herself as a sort of Cinderella, dreaming of her prince but always prevented from going to the ball.

'Are you listening to me?' Donald asked. 'I get to know everything in the end, as long as I keep my ear to the ground. It was Eddie who gave you the lift back after the rehearsal, wasn't it? And I expect it was him you went to the pictures with on Saturday night.'

'No, Uncle, it wasn't. It was Stan Tankard.' Violet

ignored his startled expression and let a sullen silence develop between them. She was weary of it all – the dogs, the clock, the ashes in the grate and Uncle Donald's attempts to make her conform to his joyless view of life.

'In any case, I want you to stay in more and help your aunt,' he went on with a heavy-handed switch of subjects. The kettle boiled and he warmed the tea-pot then put in two spoonfuls of tea. He poured in the water and waited for the leaves to mash. 'She's not as young as she was.'

Violet considered this a blow below the belt, intended to give her a guilty conscience. 'Honestly, Uncle Donald! That won't work with me and you know it – Aunty Winnie is fit as a fiddle.'

'I knew my ears were burning,' Winnie declared as she opened the front door and set down her shopping bag full of vegetables from Clifton Street market. She smiled her way through what she could sense was the build-up to a serious argument. 'And yes, here I am – fit as a fiddle, just as Violet says!'

'No, sir – I did not know that my sister had gone to the races on the day she died.' Violet read carefully from the script that Ida had given her. 'I believed she had gone to work as usual.'

'Put a bit more life into it,' Ida urged. 'Not so flat and stiff. Try again.'

Violet sighed and caught sight of Kathy and Peggy rehearsing their parts in a different corner of the hall, while Harold was painting scenery on the stage. So far there was no sign of Eddie. She repeated the line again, trying to follow Ida's advice.

'Better,' Ida told her. 'Try to show that you're nervous and upset. You have to pretend I'm a nasty policeman intent on tripping you up.'

What have I let myself in for? Violet wondered. It turned out she wasn't a natural when it came to acting and the more she tried to get it right the more self-conscious she became.

For more than an hour she had tried to master the part of the murder victim's sister, taking tips from the director and concentrating on getting it right. When they broke for tea and biscuits, she drifted towards Kathy for advice.

'The trick is to forget that anyone's looking at you.' Kathy sat on the edge of the stage, legs dangling. Her hair was pinned up to show the nape of her neck and she wore a pair of trousers with turn-ups, giving her the air of a fashionable girl-about-town.

'Rather you than me,' Harold commented. He perched on a stepladder, drinking tea and smoking a cigarette. Broad-faced, with even features and wavy hair combed back from his forehead, he had an air of permanent cheerfulness, which made him easy to like.

'I'll feel such a fool if I can't get it right,' Violet complained. 'But the thing is, Uncle Donald is dead set against me doing this and I want to prove him wrong.'

'Don't worry, you'll soon pick it up,' Ida said as she breezed by. She too was in trousers with a neat cream-coloured blouse tucked into a high waistband. Violet decided it was the look to copy in future; her own calf-length skirt and short-sleeved jumper felt dowdy in comparison.

'Has anyone seen Eddie?' Harold asked from his onstage perch. 'Or do you expect me to roll up my sleeves and finish this backdrop all by myself?'

'He's working at the Victory tonight,' Ida told him before rushing everyone to finish their tea.

Hearing this made Violet realize how much she'd been looking forward to seeing Eddie, and perhaps even another ride home on his motorbike.

'Oh, now someone's down in the dumps!' Kathy noticed Violet's disappointment and teased her for it.

She blushed then protested, 'Don't be daft, Kathy. It's none of my business what Eddie gets up to.'

'Oh no, that's right. A little bird tells me that it's Stan you're interested in these days,' Kathy smirked.

'What makes you say that?' With a toss of her head, Violet went back to her corner of the hall to carry on rehearsing. For another hour she concentrated so hard that she didn't notice Eddie slip in through the side door and it wasn't until Ida called it a day that she realized he was up on the stage lending Harold a hand as before.

'Aren't you glad? There's your lift home, after all.' Kathy winked as she, Peggy and Evie put on their coats, ready to leave.

'No. I'll catch the bus with you.' Eddie was busy clearing dust sheets and washing brushes and Violet decided it would look wrong for her to hang around waiting for him. She was out in the yard, following the others to the stop when she heard a voice call her name and she turned to see Eddie standing by the side door of the Institute.

'Don't you want a lift?' he asked.

The simple question flustered her. 'No, it's all right thanks, Eddie. I can catch the bus.'

'I'll only be five minutes.'

'Oh, in that case . . . Are you sure?'

'Course I'm sure. Wait there, I'll be with you in a jiffy.'

She felt a small thrill of excitement run through her. After all, Eddie had made a point of coming after her, which meant more than last week's casual, chance offer. He'd seemed shy, as if expecting her to say no, but determined in spite of that. *Perhaps he likes me*, was the thought that dawned on her and made her heart flutter.

Before long Eddie appeared in the main doorway. He put on his goggles and gauntlets in a businesslike way, sat astride his bike and kick-started the engine. 'You know the routine,' he told Violet, winking at her as she stepped up on to the foot rest.

Soon she was on the bike, her arms clasped around Eddie's waist. He eased out of the Institute yard and rode slowly along the main street of terraced houses, passing the bus stop.

'I thought you were meant to be working,' she mentioned.

'I was. I got off at eight o'clock then came straight over to help Harold. Ida would've had my guts for garters otherwise.'

'Yoo-hoo, Violet!' Kathy nudged Peggy and Evie and they all waved.

'Hold tight,' Eddie said, picking up speed. They left the town then passed through fields and climbed towards the outcrop of boulders and cliffs strewn across rough moorland – a landmark known locally as Little Brimstone. The moors stretched out ahead, while the darkening sky held a herringbone pattern of fluffy clouds coloured pink and gold.

'All right back there?' Eddie called over his shoulder.

'Yes, ta. Just keep a lookout for sheep!' she replied. Her heart soared in all this space and beauty and she thrilled once more to the roaring speed of the bike. She was surprised when they came to the top of a hill and Eddie slowed almost to a halt.

He turned and spoke above the idling speed of the engine. 'We could get off and stretch our legs if you're not in a rush.'

Violet nodded and he pulled off the road onto a grass verge. 'How about sitting on that rock?' She pointed and went on ahead to a smooth boulder overlooking a narrow, shaded valley with thorn trees and a cascading waterfall.

Eddie joined her and they sat looking down at

the rushing water. 'This little glen is where I used to cycle to when I was a kid,' he confided. 'You're well hidden once you're down there amongst the trees. That's what I liked about it.'

Violet glanced at him. He sat with hands clasped around his knees, staring intently into the darkness, his profile in shadow, his eye glinting in the last of the light.

'I was never allowed,' she told him. 'I always had to play close to the house where they could keep an eye on me.'

'Don't get me wrong – I enjoyed larking about with the other lads – cricket and football, the usual kick-about stuff. But once in a while I liked to get away.' He stopped short and glanced at her, wondering if he was boring her with his talk.

'You and Ida – you're not alike.' Violet settled into the conversation, soothed by the peacefulness of their surroundings. 'She's not backwards in coming forwards for a start.'

Eddie grinned. 'You can say that again.'

'I like her, though. And she's doing well for herself. I wish I had her get up and go.'

'She and Harold are saving up to get married. She's got a list of things she reckons they need – table and chairs, bedroom suite and everything. It all adds up to fifty quid, give or take.' There he went – rabbiting on again because he wanted to avoid any silence that would give Violet the chance to suggest moving on.

'I meant Ida and Muriel's shop. I'd love to be running a place like that.' Violet reached forward to brush her hand over the harebells growing in a nearby crevice. 'How did they get set up in the first place?'

'It was after Muriel's chap let her down,' Eddie told her. 'I don't know the ins and outs of it – only that she was due to be married but it never happened. That's when Ida left her job in the mending department at Kingsley's and set up shop with Muriel, using the nest egg Muriel had saved for the wedding.'

The surprise information gave Violet pause for thought.

'Muriel's the one with a head for figures. Ida's more involved in the sewing and altering side. Anyway, why are we talking about them? I want to know more about what you get up to.'

'There's nothing to know.' Not wanting to give too much away too soon, she drew back from making confessions. 'Honestly, there's nothing special about me.'

'I'd say there was.' For once Eddie took a risk. Maybe it was the idea that if he didn't jump in with both feet, Stan would make his next move on Violet and it would definitely be too late. Or perhaps it was simply the right place, the right time.

Violet picked a harebell and turned it between her fingers. She held her breath, waiting for Eddie to speak again.

'I'm not talking about the way you look,' he tried

to explain. 'Sorry – that didn't come out the way I meant it to. You look lovely, of course you do. But it's more than that.'

She sniffed the flower and stared ahead, slow to believe what she heard. She wanted the moment to last – the sunset, the peaty smell of the soil, the waterfall. Eddie by her side.

'Stop me if I'm stepping out of line. It might be Stan you're interested in, for all I know.'

'No, it's not Stan,' she whispered. 'We went to the pictures together, that's all.'

'Even so.'

Violet turned towards Eddie. His head was tilted forward and he looked earnestly at her from under lowered brows. She felt a surge of tenderness.

'Stan's not my type,' she insisted. 'You are.'

Her lips when he moved to kiss her were soft and warm, her face cool and smooth as silk. He put his arms around her.

Violet kissed him back. She closed her eyes and softened into his embrace. There was the sound of tumbling water and the feel of his kiss and in that moment nothing else mattered.

Night had fallen by the time Eddie and Violet reached town and the street lights were on.

'Drop me here,' she said when they reached the top of Chapel Street. 'That way we won't wake anyone up with the sound of your bike.' By 'anyone' she meant, of course, her Uncle Donald, who would no doubt be gunning for her as usual.

'Ta-ta then,' Eddie said when she'd got off the bike.

Violet hovered on the pavement, not wanting to leave but knowing she must.

Eddie leaned sideways and kissed her on the cheek. 'I'm working again tomorrow night but we could go dancing at the Assembly Rooms this weekend if you'd like?'

'That's right, we could,' she teased, a smile playing on her lips.

'Or we could go to the flicks?'

'The flicks,' she decided, to put him out of his misery.

A grin lit up his face. 'The flicks it is. I'll pick you up at six o'clock on Saturday. We'll go to the new Odeon – my treat.'

Violet smiled and nodded, raising a hand to wave as Eddie revved his engine and coasted off along Overcliffe Road. The smile lasted all the way down Chapel Street and onto Brewery Road where she finally pulled herself together, took out her key and unlocked the door to number 11.

Inside the house she found the lights on and Uncle Donald in his dressing gown standing white as a sheet at the kitchen window.

'What's the matter?' Violet asked, a sudden fear clutching at her heart. 'You look as though you've seen a ghost.'

'The doctor's upstairs with Winnie,' he told her,

steadying himself against the sink as if he'd been dealt a deadly blow.

Violet didn't wait to hear more. She was up the stairs in a flash, dashing into the front bedroom to find her view of the iron bedstead blocked by the tall figure of Dr Moss.

'Who's there?' Winnie asked from the bed, her voice low and strained. 'Is that you, Violet?'

The doctor stood to one side and Violet rushed forward. 'Aunty Winnie, what's wrong? Are you poorly?'

'Hush,' Winnie said. Her hand trembled as she grasped Violet's hand. Her voice still sounded as if it came from a long way away. 'There, there, love.'

'What's wrong with her?' Violet asked the doctor. She held her aunt's shaking hand between both of hers.

'I'm afraid it's her heart. I've sent for an ambulance to take her to hospital.'

'You hear that, Aunty Winnie?' Violet held her hand tighter still. 'You're going to the hospital. The doctors will soon find out what's wrong and make you better.' As the words spilled out into the hush of the room with its spartan furnishings, even Violet realized how childlike she sounded. She knew with certainty as she looked into Winnie's unfocused eyes that they were untrue.

'No, love,' came the faint response. Winnie lifted Violet's clasped hands to her cheek and let them rest there. 'I was hanging on until you came home, that's all.'

'Aunty Winnie, no!' Violet whispered fervently.

'Hush. I only wanted to say goodbye.'

'No, that's not fair!' The words were torn from Violet's chest, irrational and childlike.

Winnie loosened her hold. Her eyes fluttered shut. 'Look after her, Doctor. God bless, Violet.'

'Come away now.' Dr Moss moved in and put his arm around Violet's shoulders to lead her to the door. He called down the stairs for Donald to come up.

Outside on the street the ambulance arrived and two uniformed men rushed into the house. They passed Violet and Donald in the narrow hallway, intent on getting the patient to the King Edward's without delay.

'It's not fair,' Violet cried again.

Donald shook his head then his legs gave way and he had to sit down on the bottom step. Up in the bedroom they sensed the urgency subside then heard the slow, heavy tread of Dr Moss as he descended the stairs. 'I'm sorry,' he said in a grave voice, his stethoscope still dangling from his neck. 'We did our best but in the end there was nothing anyone could do.'

CHAPTER SIX

Exactly what was so unfair in Violet's mind was hard to explain. As the black-coated funeral men moved in to carry out the smooth and silent business of death, she sat in her bedroom choking back tears but unable to order her thoughts. *It isn't right,* she told herself repeatedly. *Aunty Winnie didn't show any signs of being ill. She's been her usual self, perhaps a bit tired lately, but never less than cheerful. She's fifty years old, which is nothing these days – stout and capable, always well turned out, the sort who goes on and on – everyone says so. And complaints never pass her lips.*

But maybe that had been the problem, Violet concluded. She never said, 'I've an ache in my back or a pain in my chest', rarely visited the doctor but instead relied on home remedies – treacle and sulphur for rashes and heat lumps; monastery herbs for stomach upsets, comfrey for sprains. Anything more serious she must have kept to herself.

She insisted she was fit as a fiddle – her own words said in a breezy way that brooked no argument.

It was typical of Aunty Winnie to keep it to herself, but I should have noticed she was breathless when she came in with the shopping, Violet thought in silent misery. *It was my fault. Uncle Donald said that she needed more help and I flatly denied it. That was me being selfish.* She felt an almost unbearable pang of shame and regret.

Goodbye and God bless. A faltering, faraway voice. A life well spent drawing to an end. But still Violet's chaotic heart and mind protested that it was all too soon and too sudden, like stitches being dropped or knitting unravelling. Winnie should still be here to tut and smile, to keep Violet's feet on the ground, to glow with pride. *But she isn't,* Violet realized. *And now she won't see the rest of my life, which is the one she made for me as truly as any natural mother on this earth. She won't see her Cinderella go to the ball, if and when that happens. She won't see me married with children.*

Sorrow overwhelmed Violet and she sat on her bed and wept.

One of the unexpected things that Violet noticed was that, amid all the arrangements – the notifying of neighbours and the issuing of certificates, commiserations and explanations, the setting of dates – Donald Wheeler refused to speak with the minister from the chapel at the top of the street.

'I'd like to set a time for the funeral of eleven o'clock next Thursday,' Minister Frank Bielby told Violet after he'd knocked on the door and she'd

77

invited him into the cool, clean front room at number 11. 'I take it your uncle will agree?'

'He's out at the moment, but I'm sure he will.'

The minister sat on the edge of the black horse-hair sofa. He was a tweed-suited bald-headed man who wore a stiff, shiny collar, silver-rimmed spectacles and sturdy brown shoes. 'Is there anything in particular that you'd like me to include in the service?' he asked gently. 'I know plenty about Winnie, of course. So I won't be stuck for something to say.'

Hands resting in her lap and sitting on a chair by the window, Violet simply nodded.

Bielby moved smoothly on. 'And how is your Uncle Donald?'

'He's at work.' Violet avoided the question. How *was* Uncle Donald? The truthful answer was he hadn't spoken a word since the funeral men had carried Winnie from the house into the hearse. He'd locked and bolted the door and gone upstairs and she'd not heard a sound until he'd gone down the next morning, out of the house and across the street to open his shop. She'd registered the coming and going of customers all day until her uncle's return at teatime.

'What will you have to eat?' she'd asked, intending to break the atmosphere between them, so heavy that you could almost touch it.

He'd washed his hands at the sink and gone upstairs without a word. The same thing this morning – up and out without food or drink.

'You'll let your uncle know that I'm at hand any time he wishes to speak to me.' A small frown appeared on Minister Bielby's face as he sensed that all was not as it should be. 'And please hand on my sincere condolences during this difficult time.'

Ah yes – those were the phrases. Condolences . . . a difficult time. Nothing specific to Winnie and Donald who had been regular chapel-goers all their lives, whom Frank Bielby had known through countless whist drives and charabanc outings, weekend bring-and-buys and evening lectures. 'I'll tell him,' Violet said with quiet finality.

'It must be the shock,' Ida decided. She'd waited until after the weekend for things to settle down, but now on the Tuesday she called in at Hutchinson's to see how Violet was coping. Violet, pale faced and with her hair pushed back behind her ears, had told Ida that her uncle was maintaining his mysterious vow of silence and that it was driving her round the bend. 'He'll come round. You just have to give him time.'

'We have the funeral on Thursday so I won't come to rehearsal tomorrow evening,' Violet reminded her in a subdued voice.

'No, of course – I realize that.' Ida trod carefully through the conversation with none of her usual vivacity on show. She'd walked up from Jubilee without a coat, in only a yellow cotton day dress with orange panels set into the bodice and skirt. 'Muriel and I would like to come. What time should we be at Chapel?'

'The service will be at eleven. I'm only hoping I can get Uncle Donald to leave his precious shop for an hour or two.'

'He'll be there, of course he will,' Ida murmured.

'Yes, even if I have to drag him kicking and screaming all the way up the street.'

'Try not to worry. Grief hits people in different ways. Keeping the barber's shop going is probably Donald's way of coping.'

'But he doesn't speak to me when we're in the house together – not a word. It's as if I'm not there. Or rather, he glares at me as if – well, as if he *wishes* I wasn't there.'

'I'm sure that's not true, Violet. By the way, Eddie feels very bad for you after what happened. He asked me to tell you that if there's anything you need . . .'

'There isn't, ta.' Right now Violet didn't have room inside her head for Eddie or the secret glen or the kiss. All that had taken place when Winnie's heart had been failing and her life had been ebbing away. *I'm ashamed of myself*, Violet had decided as she'd heard the hooves of the funeral men's horses strike the cobbled street. *I don't deserve to be happy – not now, not for a long time.*

'Eddie wants to help but doesn't know what he can do,' Ida said gently.

Violet shook her head. 'Tell him I said ta very much, but no, there's nothing.' She must put aside happiness of the kind she'd felt with him; Aunty Winnie must be mourned properly in Violet's own version of sackcloth and ashes.

Ida nodded and drew her purse from her pocket. She took out a sixpence. 'Mother said to give you this,' she said sadly, her eyes full of tears. 'She's more sorry than she can say that she didn't pay it back to Winnie in time.'

The hearse that came down Brewery Road and turned up Chapel Street that Thursday led a very different procession to the Whitsuntide festivities that Violet had revelled in only a few weeks before. It was pulled by two plumed horses and driven by the funeral director in top hat and black coat. Winnie's coffin was visible through its gleaming glass sides.

Donald and Violet, the only two family mourners, also in black, walked behind, their hands clasped in front of them, faces drained of emotion. Friends and neighbours followed in silence, looking straight ahead. As they passed Thornley's Brewery, Wilf Fullerton and his fellow workers stood outside and doffed their caps.

In the doorway of Chapel Street Costumiers, Sybil Dacre, Evie Briggs and Annie Drummond (Annie Pearson as was) stood with Annie's little boy. Evie's sisters, Lily and Margie, had joined them too. The colourful little group stood out as a contrast to the dark, stiff-limbed march of the mourners.

'It's Violet I feel sorry for,' Evie told Sybil with a sigh. 'She's the one who'll feel it most.'

Sybil chose to disagree. 'No, it'll be Donald who goes to pieces – you'll see.'

'I admire the way Winnie took Violet in when she was a baby,' Annie Drummond said. 'We all do. What age is Violet now, Evie?'

'Two or three years older than me, that's all.' Evie's young spirits were dragged down by the solemnity of the occasion but she took heart in the presence of her two sisters and their young daughters, Rhoda and Nancy.

True to their word, Muriel and Ida closed their shop and joined the procession, as did an unusually silent Marjorie Sykes and even Ben Hutchinson, determined to pay his respects despite the impact on his daily takings. For Winnie Wheeler had worked and sung, baked, sewed and knitted her way through life and was a much-loved figure in the close-knit neighbourhood and people were sorry that she'd died early and without warning.

The procession passed on up the street until it reached the wide stone steps of the Methodist chapel at the top of the hill, where it stopped and the coffin bearers alighted from the carriage.

Violet waited beside her uncle while the men manoeuvred the coffin up the steps. She felt detached from her surroundings and had to be prompted to move forward, to take her seat inside the enormous white space of the chapel, to stand and sing then

82

kneel and pray. She listened without emotion to the minister's eulogy, noticing instead the way the light streamed in through the tall, clear windows.

What now? she thought when the last strains of 'Lead Us, Heavenly Father' had died away and people began to file out. *Or is there nothing else? Is this it? Do we go home now to an empty house and go on as before?*

But no – there was tea and sandwiches provided in a back room by the women from Winnie's sewing group. There were people to thank for coming, compliments to listen to – she was the salt of the earth; you could rely on Winnie always to help you out; never a cross word.

The dingy room didn't get the sun. It smelled damp even in summer. Paint flaked from the walls. This was what Violet saw.

Now do we go home? She looked at her uncle, pinned in a corner, taking tea and sympathy with misery etched into his gaunt features.

'Well done, love. You did well.'

Violet turned with a grateful smile towards the speaker – Muriel in her green hat and coat, taking her hand and giving it a squeeze, standing next to Ida and Eddie.

'If there's anything you need, you only have to ask,' Ida assured her. 'I mean it – anything at all.'

Eddie said nothing but he stayed almost until last, helping the caretaker to clear trestle tables and chairs after everyone had dispersed, making sure that Violet knew that he too was on hand if she needed him.

I hope he doesn't say anything nice to me, Violet thought. *I won't get through this without crying if Eddie is kind.*

He departed quietly, and then there was no one. Uncle Donald had already left and gone who knew where. After Minister Bielby had led her out onto the doorstep and solemnly shaken her hand, Violet walked down Chapel Street alone.

She went into the house but of course her aunt wasn't there – only her ghost. She looked at the linen cloth on the table that Winnie had washed in the peggy tub, dipped in Reckitt's Blue then starched and put through the mangle twice. The white Staffordshire dogs gleamed on the mantelpiece. Winnie's empty shopping bag hung from a hook on the door.

How could absence be so strong that you could reach out and touch it? How could silence shout? Violet trembled from head to foot and had to sit down at the table. She felt altogether alone. Her life seemed empty and she didn't think she could bear the loss.

Days went by and somehow Violet managed. She got up and went to work, took tins of biscuits down from the shelf to serve to customers, polished the brass scales and pulled down the blind at the end of each day. She went home and made the tea, unsure of whether her uncle would be there to eat it.

On the first Sunday after the funeral she roasted a leg of lamb in the gas oven, mashed some potatoes and made gravy. She set the table and waited for Donald to come down from his room.

'Your dinner's going cold,' she called up to him.

There was no reply. Eventually she took a slice of the lamb for herself then put the rest away in the food-safe in the pantry, relieved when Monday came around and the bustle of working in the shop took the place of the heavy silence of the house.

'I didn't see your uncle at chapel yesterday,' Ben Hutchinson mentioned after he'd taken delivery of two sides of bacon, which he suspended from hooks in the storeroom.

'No. Uncle Donald didn't leave his room all day,' Violet replied with a troubled frown. 'I knew he was in there and I kept on knocking on his door but he refused to come out.'

'What's the matter? Is he poorly?'

'I don't think so. He went to work this morning as usual.'

But later that day Marjorie popped in to tell Violet that she'd walked by the barber's shop on Brewery Road and seen the landlord's man up a ladder, taking away the red-and-white striped barber's pole. 'The blind was down and there was no sign of Donald,' she reported. 'I hope nothing's the matter?'

The news startled Violet. She rushed home from work and found her uncle sitting at the kitchen table, hands tightly clasped, staring straight ahead.

'Uncle Donald, what's happened? Why have you closed the shop?'

He blinked then continued to stare into space.

'Marjorie says you have. And I can see for myself that the pole is missing. Talk to me, Uncle Donald. Whatever is the matter?'

At last he turned his head towards her and focused his gaze. 'Nothing's the matter. A man has the right to close down his business if he chooses.'

'Not if he wants to carry on putting food on his table, he doesn't.' Aware that she was in danger of sounding like her Aunty Winnie, Violet sat down opposite and pointed out the obvious. 'That shop is a little goldmine, people coming in and out all day. You've built it up so nicely over the years. Uncle Donald, why stop now?'

'Because,' he said, shrugging, his gaze stony and cold.

Studying him more closely, Violet noticed that he hadn't shaved for a while and there was dirt under his fingernails. 'I know it's hard,' she said softly.

'You know nothing!' he retorted with a contemptuous curl of his lip. 'Not the first little thing about what went on.'

The words seemed heavy with an unspoken secret and Violet's stomach churned – so much so that she refrained from asking any more questions.

Donald got up from the table and went to look out of the window. 'I went along with things all these years for Winnie's sake, but what I do from now on is my own business, do you hear?'

Violet nodded. His bitter mood unsettled her deeply but she thought, like Ida, that in the end he would deal with his grief in his own way and come through. Meanwhile, she would make herself scarce.

So for the rest of that week she tried to set aside her sorrow and put in as many hours as possible in the grocer's shop and in the evenings she either swam at the public baths or went walking on the Common. Once or twice she dropped in at Jubilee for a chat with Muriel and Ida.

'We're thinking of branching out,' Muriel announced when Violet went in with the grocery order on the Tuesday. She was surrounded by new stockpiles of lace hankies and dainty tablecloths, boxes of cotton reels, skeins of knitting wool and big rolls of silk ribbons. 'Ida and I have had a long talk. We've decided there's money to be earned in making clothes from scratch instead of sticking to minor alterations.'

'Like Sybil and Evie further up the street,' Violet pointed out.

'Hush! Not exactly the same as them.' Muriel introduced a note of caution and held her finger to her lips. 'We don't want to set the cat among the pigeons so we wouldn't like this to get out before we're ready.'

'Your secret's safe with me. But if you begin taking orders to make clothes, won't they be upset eventually?' Violet didn't see the difference between this so-called branching out at the drapers and what currently went on at the dressmakers.

'Not if we aim at a different type of customer,' Muriel explained, arranging the hankies into a fan shape for a display that she would prop up on the top of the glass counter. 'Chapel Street Costumiers makes a point of sewing outfits for special occasions. It appeals to the better-off classes with money to burn. We'd be charging less, using simpler materials – cheap cotton poplins, seersucker and suchlike. A girl from Calvert's Mill could save up for a few weeks and be able to afford one of our dresses if she was careful.'

Violet went away with an undeclared interest in what Muriel had told her. She allowed herself a dream. She imagined – whispered it to herself as she took in the evening air instead of heading home to Brewery Road – that Jubilee's new business blossomed and they needed extra help. *Ida and Muriel know you can sew*, her inner voice said. *They might turn to you in small ways at first – a hem here, a piece of smocking for a child's dress there. You would do the work quickly and well . . .*

Heading up Chapel Street onto the Common, Violet crossed Overcliffe Road and sat on a sunny bench watching a group of young boys kick a football around an impromptu pitch marked out by discarded jerseys and jackets.

'How does that sound to you, Aunty Winnie?' she murmured out loud. 'Wouldn't it be smashing if Muriel and Ida were to offer me a job?'

On Friday of that week, clutching her miserly wage packet and heading home from Hutchinson's determined to make more effort with Uncle Donald so that they could avoid another weekend like the last, Violet found the front door open and voices coming from within. She entered quickly to find her uncle listening to a man she recognized as the rent collector, Mr Fisher.

'I'm not leaving here without my money,' a red-faced Fisher insisted. Despite the heat, he wore a navy blue guard's coat and a brown trilby hat as a way of setting himself apart from and retaining the respect of the tweed-jacketed, flat-capped tenants.

'And I'm telling you I've no rent money to give you.' Donald presented the facts defiantly. He didn't acknowledge Violet as she hurried down the corridor and entered the kitchen. 'I've no wage coming in, that's the beginning and the end of it.'

'Well, it won't do.' Fisher stood firm, though he looked embarrassed to be continuing the argument in front of Violet. 'If I go back to the office and tell Mr Gill that you can't pay your rent, how do you think that'll go down?'

'I don't care if your precious Mr Gill blows his top,' Donald retaliated. Mockingly he turned his trouser pockets inside out. 'You can tell him from me that Donald Wheeler of number 11 Brewery Road is skint. He doesn't have the seven and sixpence to give him.'

Fisher pressed ahead. 'But you're a sensible chap

– you have something put by for a rainy day, surely?'

'I did, but that all went to pay for Winnie's funeral. Yes, that took the wind out of your sails!' Donald laughed at the rent man's sudden intake of breath.

'Uncle Donald!' Violet stepped forward, feeling sick with shame. She took the rent book from under the mantel clock then dipped into her wage packet and began to count out the money. It left her too little to get through the week with, but at least the debt would be paid.

Fisher spread his plump palm and took the coins. 'That goes part of the way towards where we need to be,' he said, his face aflame with embarrassment.

'What do you mean?' Violet's stomach twisted again and she gave her uncle a beseeching glance.

'Look in the book and you'll see we owe Mr Fisher three weeks' rent,' Donald said with a nasty sneer. 'I don't suppose you have any more money to spare, Violet? No, I thought not. So Mr Fisher will be forced to go back to the office without it. Then who knows what our lord and master Mr Gill will decide?'

CHAPTER SEVEN

Violet knew that there was no point trying to reason with her uncle after the rent collector's visit. She pictured him as a crumbling castle surrounded by a moat with the drawbridge up and the portcullis firmly down. In fact, the more she thought about it in the following hours, the more she saw that he'd done this on purpose, deliberately stopping work, isolating himself and putting them both in a position where the landlord, Mr Gill, would be within his rights to turf them out.

No, at the moment Uncle Donald was a dead loss and if Violet wanted to keep a roof over their heads, she saw that the only way forward was for her to go out and find the extra rent herself.

So, the following Tuesday, after she'd given Donald his tea of two fried eggs on a slice of fried bread, she took her red hat from its hook, ready to set off and look for work.

With the food uneaten and congealing on his

plate, he broke his silence. 'Where are you off to in such a hurry?'

Violet was surprised and for a split second she felt sorry for him as she thought of him sitting in the house day in, day out – a broken man since Winnie had died. 'I'll explain later, Uncle Donald.'

'I always say, the trouble with you is you can't sit still,' he complained and a sly look appeared on his face. 'Don't tell me – you're going to hang around on a street corner, smoking cigarettes and hoping one of your so-called young men shows up.'

'When have I ever hung around on street corners?' she protested. 'And I don't even smoke.' Stung to the quick, her pity for him vanished in an instant. 'Shame on you, Uncle Donald! If you can't say something pleasant, it's better that you don't say anything at all.'

'That suits me,' he muttered, seemingly satisfied at having provoked her. He pushed his plate away and leaned heavily on his elbows, shutting her out as before.

Doing her best not to cry, Violet fled from the house and hurried down the alley to cut off the corner onto Chapel Street. How could Uncle Donald be so mean? she wondered. What exactly had got into him? She shook her head in exasperation and hurried up the hill, noticing Ida and Eddie's dad, Dick, in his painter's overalls, standing outside Sykes' bakery talking to Marjorie. She waved at them and rushed on, hoping that she would find someone still working at the Chapel Street dressmakers.

Forced off the pavement to avoid a couple of boys pushing an old pram loaded with scrap metal who had stopped to tease some girls playing hopscotch, she paused to catch her breath. The girls had tucked their skirts into their knickers, showing off their spindly legs without a care in the world. A housewife at number 20 shook a dusty rug from a bedroom window and at the corner with Overcliffe Road an ice-cream seller with his cart advertised his wares for a penny a pot.

Arriving at the top of the street, Violet plucked up the courage to knock on Sybil Dacre's green-painted door. The shop front was smart with a sign written in gold letters above the window that read 'Chapel Street Costumiers – Outfits for Special Occasions'. Violet peered inside and saw that, luckily for her, Sybil was still hard at work, while Evie stood chatting to her married sister Lily. Evie heard her knock and jumped up from her treadle sewing machine to unbolt the door.

'I came to speak to Sybil,' Violet explained, out of breath from hurrying. 'Can I come in?'

'Of course you can,' Sybil called from the shaded interior. She snipped some thread then set down the rosebud-patterned bodice of a blouse she was working on. 'Well, Violet, what can we do for you?'

Violet relaxed as she took in her surroundings. Behind the sewing machines there were multi-coloured bolts of cloth stacked on a wide shelf and in one corner a tailor's dummy. A work table was laid out with measuring tapes, pinking shears and boxes of dressmaking pins, just like the attic workroom at Jubilee but with more space and without the sloping ceilings. 'I hope you don't think this is brazen of me,' she began. 'Only, I'm in a tight spot. I can't say what – that wouldn't be right – but I need to earn a bit extra this week. Before next Monday, to be exact.'

It took a while for Sybil to cotton on to what their visitor was saying, distracted by the freshness of the vision in front of her. Violet was well named – a lovely wayside flower with a natural beauty that made you pay close attention each time you encountered her. Today she was wearing a simple, short-sleeved pale blue dress with a skirt cut on the bias. Under the brim of her red hat, her delicate face was flushed by the evening sun and there was an apprehensive look in her dark brown eyes. 'If you're asking me for a job, I'm afraid we don't have a vacancy at present,' Sybil told her plainly but not unkindly, while Evie and Lily made sure to stay in the background as the older seamstress put Violet out of her misery.

'No, not a full-time job,' Violet rushed on. 'I'm still working for Mr Hutchinson during the day but I have time on my hands in the evening.'

'I see.' Sybil grasped what she was getting at. 'You want to take on extra work.'

Violet nodded. 'I would go to one of the mills for evening shifts as a comber or a spinner, and I did consider it. Only, everyone knows that Calvert's and Kingsley's are both on short time at present, orders being low as they are. And anyway, I'm not trained for mill work. Sewing is the only thing I'm any good at.'

'I can't see you doing mill work. Can you, Lily?' Sybil remembered all too well the relentless whirring and thumping of the giant weaving machines at Calvert's, and the dust and the grime, the stench of untreated wool, the backbreaking work of apprentice loom cleaners and bobbin liggers.

'I would do it if I could,' Violet broke in, trying to stay bold but suddenly finding herself on the verge of tears.

'I believe you.' Sitting at her machine, Sybil was torn between a hard-headed consideration of the cost of paying out extra wages and her natural tendency to help those in trouble. 'You know that we're only just getting on our feet here,' she explained. 'It's true you're a skilled needlewoman and you've been well taught by your Aunty Winnie – your Gala Queen dress proved that. But you do know we wouldn't be able to pay much for odd jobs here and there?'

'I don't mind,' Violet vowed. 'I could machine-sew buttonholes or put in zips for a few pennies – whatever you like.'

'It would help us to get the garments out to customers sooner.' Lily spoke up, though she knew it was no longer her place to interfere.

'If people see how quick we are, wouldn't that bring in more business?' Evie added.

'I get the picture: you Briggs girls are ganging

up on me. Even you, Evie, and you're a little spring chicken.' Sybil allowed a smile to creep across her face. Though only twenty-six herself, she sounded and sometimes felt much older. She reached for a ledger tucked away in a drawer under the work table. 'I'll tell you what, Violet,' she said after a long consideration of the handwritten order book. 'Right this minute you can take away this blouse I'm sewing and a dress I'm in the middle of making that has fasteners all the way down the back. They both have rows of fiddly buttonholes. If you can do them well and get them back to me by Thursday morning on your way into work, I'll pay you threepence for the blouse and six for the dress. How's that?'

Violet's eyes lit up and she felt a flood of relief that her brazenness, as she called it, had paid off. 'That's smashing!' she told Sybil, already thinking ahead towards putting in a similar request to Ida and Muriel. 'You won't regret this, I promise.'

With the wind in her sails and a package containing the unfinished blouse and dress tucked under her arm, Violet marched straight from Chapel Street towards Valley Road on the edge of town. She knew that it overlooked a stone quarry which in turn faced out towards open moors interspersed with green fields where sheep grazed, but it was unfamiliar territory and she wasn't even sure of the Thomsons' house number until an old man sitting on a bench by the side of the quarry answered her query.

'That'd be number twenty,' he replied, sucking at an empty pipe and ignoring a baleful, upturned gaze from the ancient sheepdog lying at his hobnailed feet.

Violet thanked him and continued her quest, calculating that if she spent half an hour persuading Ida to give her some mending tasks, she would still be home before sunset.

Counting the house numbers, she saw that Ida's family lived at the end of a row of small, terraced houses clinging to the bank of a murky pond, with the raw cliff face of the quarry rising behind them. Most of the homes looked damp and run down, and it was clear that the sun rarely brightened their cramped rooms, confirming Violet's impression that this wasn't a salubrious neighbourhood.

Once again, she had to gather her courage to knock. *Needs must*, she told herself.

Violet was glad when Ida herself opened the door and invited her to step into the living room. She accepted a cup of tea from Emily then sat down with Ida at the kitchen table. She noticed its worn oilcloth covering and saw that the sink was piled high with unwashed dishes.

'What brings you here?' Ida began, while her mother poured a trickle of dark brown liquid into a best cup and saucer. 'I know – don't tell me. You've come to give back word on your part in *Mistaken Identity*.'

Violet frowned. Come to think of it, this was a

good place to begin. 'Yes, I'm so sorry but I won't have time to come to rehearsals any more.'

'No need to apologize,' Ida said hurriedly. 'I can see that it wouldn't look right so soon after . . . Well, so soon at any rate.'

For a moment Violet's shoulders drooped as she felt the weight of her recent loss. In the background, Emily shook her head and gave a sad sigh. 'There's another reason why I can't come,' Violet explained. 'I have to stay at home—'

'To keep an eye on Donald,' Emily interrupted. 'Yes. How is the poor soul?'

'He finds it hard without Aunty Winnie,' Violet answered truthfully. 'But to be honest, from now on my evenings will be taken up doing sewing work to earn extra money, which is the main reason why I'm here.'

'To ask for alteration work?' Ida queried, as though the idea hadn't come completely out of the blue. 'I did notice that Donald had upped sticks and left his barber's shop.'

'Well, I never.' Emily sighed. 'Whatever next?'

'I can work quickly and neatly,' Violet assured her, skimming over the problem at home and getting back to the main topic. She kept her fingers tightly crossed. 'Hemming, putting in zips, whatever you like.'

'Left to myself I'd say yes straight off, but let me talk to Muriel about it first,' Ida decided, her heart going out to Violet, whose hand shook as she set her empty cup in its saucer. Through the front window she noticed her father and Eddie unloading brushes and tins of paint from the panniers on Eddie's motorbike and wondered how Violet would react when she bumped into him. According to Eddie, the course of true love was not running smoothly between him and Violet.

'I did think she was interested in me,' he'd confided to Ida soon after Winnie's funeral. 'At least, I hoped she was. But now I'm not sure.'

'Give her time,' had been Ida's advice. 'The poor girl's just lost Winnie. It'll take her a while to get over that.'

But patience wasn't one of Eddie's virtues. He was more the sort who wanted things to happen fast – a footballer with a great turn of speed, a cricketer who could thump a ball for six, but not someone who could happily wait for a love affair to develop slowly. And this wasn't due to arrogance, but more to shyness and a lack of confidence and experience.

'Drop by at the shop first thing tomorrow,' Ida told Violet now. 'I'll have an answer for you then.'

Thanking her, Violet picked up her parcel and made haste to leave. By this time she too was aware of Dick and Eddie's arrival and her face coloured up as she opened the door and stepped out into the small front yard. 'Hello, Mr Thomson. Hello, Eddie,' she said as cheerily as she could.

Tired and hungry after a hard day's work at the top of a ladder, Dick gave a cursory reply and sidled past Violet. The smell of paint and wallpaper paste followed him into the house.

'I see you're not working at the Victory tonight.' Violet felt awkward and snatched at something to say to Eddie, whose bike blocked her way out of the yard. His face was sunburned and he looked windswept after his ride home.

'Not tonight,' he replied, side-stepping first one way and then the other but only succeeding in staying between Violet and the gate.

'Sorry,' she mumbled.

'No, it's my fault,' he muttered back. Then he clutched at a sudden, hopeful straw wafting by in the wind. 'I tell you what – Ida's asked me to deliver another parcel to the Barlows over at Bilton Grange. I don't suppose you fancy a spin out on the Norton?'

'Now? I don't really have time . . .' Violet began, until she saw the stricken look on Eddie's face. Her answer really seemed to matter to him, she realized. 'How long would it take?' she asked.

'We'd be there and back in well under an hour. What do you say?'

'Then I'd like to come,' she decided, calculating that they could go for the spin together and she could still fit in some sewing before she went to bed. Then, if she got up early she could make up more lost time, sew again in the evening and have everything ready for Sybil by Thursday as planned.

Within seconds Eddie had dashed into the house and picked up the necessary parcel from Ida. 'How about that – she had it ready and waiting,' he reported to Violet as he invited her to hop onto the pillion seat.

There was no time for second thoughts – they were off along Valley Road, with Ida standing at the window, a smile playing on her lips, watching the two lovebirds fly.

Mrs Barlow's parcel was safely carried to Bilton Grange.

'What's this?' Colin Barlow asked as he took delivery and turned over the brown package tied up with string. The owner of the thriving chain of chemist shops didn't bother with niceties unless they suited his purposes. He was tall and slim with wavy fair hair and a trim moustache and this evening he was dressed in fawn slacks and a blue blazer, with a yellow silk cravat that gave him a dandyish, matinée-idol air.

'It's for me!' Alice Barlow trilled, appearing behind her husband in the wide doorway of their elegant, modern house. 'I asked for a jacket to be altered and here it is, right on time!'

'Altered – how?' Colin tussled with Alice as she tried to seize the parcel. He seemed annoyed for a reason that neither Violet nor Eddie could fathom.

'I've had it shortened, Colin – not that it's of any interest to you.' Finally, wresting the jacket from him, she tore at the paper as if taking out her bad mood on it.

'It might fit you better if you'd had it let out at the seams.'

As Colin had intended, his ungallant remark caught his wife off guard and reduced her to instant tears. She rushed across the hallway, out of sight. Lightly stroking his moustache, he raised an eyebrow at Eddie. 'Never criticize a lady's weight,' he advised mockingly before looking Violet up and down. 'Not that it would be necessary in your case,' he added.

Their job done, Eddie and Violet beat a hasty retreat. 'What did you think of Errol Flynn back there?' Eddie said over his shoulder as they left Bilton Grange behind.

'Not a lot,' Violet answered. In fact, she wondered how it was possible for two people to be so obviously miserable, living in a grand house with a Daimler in the drive and flower beds decked out like a public park.

'Me neither.' Once they'd dropped the parcel off and begun their journey home Eddie drove more slowly than usual up onto the moor top, wanting to make their time together last longer. When their route home took them past Little Brimstone, he turned once again to ask if she wanted to stop by what he now thought of as their glen.

Violet smiled and nodded. After all, who cared if she had to stop up past midnight to sew those button-holes? 'You're a bad influence,' she grumbled as they dismounted and made their way to the same smooth rock as before. 'I'm meant to be doing other things at home, not out enjoying myself.'

'You are, though?' he checked tentatively as he sat next to her. 'Enjoying yourself?'

'More than I should be,' she confessed guiltily. 'Considering it's no time at all since we lost Aunty Winnie.'

'Well, I'm glad you came, Violet.' He sat back, legs dangling over the edge of the rock, casting sideways glances at her and soaking up the moment.

'I'm sorry if I've been stand-offish,' she said, catching his eye and smiling briefly. He wasn't talking as much as last time and it fell to her to fill the gaps. 'I've told Ida I'll be forced to back out of *Mistaken Identity*, what with keeping an eye on Uncle Donald and having to earn a bit extra. So I won't be coming to any more rehearsals.'

'Now it's me that's sorry,' he admitted, leaning forward to gaze down at the mossy green rocks and tumbling water of the glen. He gave Violet the space to carry on talking if she wanted to. If she didn't, he felt that very soon he would make a move to put an arm around her shoulder and draw her to him.

Violet was ready to prattle on but then the peace of their surroundings registered with her and she too fell silent. She joined Eddie in gazing at the beauty below them – water drops falling on ferns, glistening spiders' webs stretching from branch to branch of green saplings, the gurgling stream. She felt his hand reach out to clasp hers.

'I've waited a long time for this,' he told her plainly and simply.

'What do you mean?'

'For us to come here again, not having to talk, just sitting.'

That was the exact moment when she fell in love, Violet realized afterwards. Eddie saying there was no need to talk, holding her hand, looking into her eyes. She wanted to tell him how she felt but it seemed too soon and instead he kissed her and held her close.

There was a sliver of silver moon in a clear sky, a breeze that made her shiver.

'Come on, I'll take you home,' Eddie said, offering his hand to help her stand. 'At this rate I'll be getting you into trouble and that's the last thing I want to do.'

CHAPTER EIGHT

I should be in seventh heaven, Violet told herself as she sat at her sewing machine in the front room of number 11, the wireless playing in the background. The long summer evening meant that she didn't need to turn on the gas mantle and instead used the daylight to complete the close work on Sybil's rosebud blouse. Buttonholes were complicated – you had to cut out a small rectangle of material and place it right sides together against the edge of the right front of the garment. The next stage was to machine-stitch a still smaller rectangle that you then cut into with a razor blade before turning the whole thing right side out. Then – eureka! – once you'd ironed it flat you had your finished buttonhole.

'Carefully does it,' Aunty Winnie used to say for a job such as this. 'One little slip-up and the whole thing is ruined.'

As the sun sank and dust mites danced in its last rays, Violet banished a sharp regret that she wasn't at Hadley Institute rehearsing her part for the Players.

She concentrated hard until she'd completed six of the eight buttonholes then paused to look around the room at the bric-a-brac that her aunt had collected – a photograph of Violet as a baby taking pride of place on the mantelpiece, alongside a Minton vase with a pattern of red roses and a clock that no one had bothered to wind since Winnie died.

I am *happy*, she told herself, recalling the soaring feeling she'd had when Eddie took her hand and tenderly kissed her. Floating and drifting, pressing her lips to his, not daring to believe.

But then again it's not right to feel this way – not so soon and not while Uncle Donald is miserable, not to mention the difficulty over paying the rent. It's wrong of me to fill my head with Eddie and his dark brown eyes, thick, long lashes and that way he has of looking up from under his fine straight brows, a slight smile on his lips.

As Violet drifted off once again into her happy memory of last night's kiss while the wireless played a lively jazz tune, she hardly noticed her uncle's footsteps descending the stairs and it was only the opening of the door that brought her crashing back down to earth.

'What the dickens . . . ?' he grumbled, striding across the room and abruptly switching off the wireless. 'The window's open. Do you want the whole world to hear that din?'

Anxious to avoid another pointless argument, Violet bit her tongue and went back to her sewing.

'It's bad enough listening to your contraption rattling on without the wireless belting out that racket,' Donald continued. 'It's giving me a headache.'

'This extra work will help us pay the rent,' Violet explained then continued with short bursts on the machine. 'I'll be finished in half an hour, I promise.'

'Then you'll be gadding off as usual, I expect.' Donald's next step was to go over to the window and slam it shut.

'Could you move out of the way of the light, please?' Violet asked, growing more exasperated but not anticipating the explosion that followed.

'Can't a man go where he likes in his own house?' He turned from the window and advanced on Violet, towering over her. 'I'm asking you a civil question – who are you to stop me standing where I like, doing whatever I like?'

Sitting in his shadow, Violet found herself trembling. Her uncle's face was sunken, the skin pulled taut across his sharp cheekbones, the corners of his mouth downturned beneath his grey moustache and there was a trace of spittle on his bottom lip. Nevertheless she stood up for herself. 'I don't call that a civil question,' she said quietly.

'Don't answer me back,' he snarled. 'I won't have it, not from the likes of you.'

'What do you mean, the likes of me?' It was no good – Violet felt herself drawn in despite her earlier resolution. 'What have I done wrong?'

'Ask anyone on Brewery Road and all the way up Chapel Street what you've done wrong. You'll find plenty of people willing to give it to you chapter and verse.' Donald thumped his fist on the work area surrounding Violet's machine, dislodging a box of pins that fell onto the rug and scattered everywhere. 'There's your carrying on with Stan Tankard for a start.'

Violet stood up. It was his sneering, holier-than-thou tone that angered her more than anything. 'Once and for all, Uncle Donald, can you please tell me what you have against Stan?'

'Oh, so you don't mind having your name dragged into the dirt along with his?'

'A girl can have a lark with him,' Violet insisted. 'What's wrong with that?'

'There's plenty wrong. He's got himself a bad name, the way he struts around reckoning he's cock of the walk. And what is he really? A loom tuner at Kingsley's, that's all.'

'No. Stan's got a job as a lifeguard at Brinkley Baths as well,' Violet said before realizing that this would set the seal on her uncle's bad opinion.

'That's why you're so keen on swimming all of a sudden, is it?' Donald's sneering contempt reached a new peak. 'Those lifeguard costumes are downright indecent, if you ask me . . .'

'No one did ask you,' she muttered.

'Not to mention the skimpy outfits you girls wear these days. It proves what I'm saying – you and Stan

Tankard are heading for the gutter, which is where you both belong.'

Incensed and with trembling hands, Violet put away her sewing things. 'Aunty Winnie must be turning in her grave,' she whispered. 'You'd never dare say such things if she was still alive.'

Donald took a step back and a look of shame flickered in his eyes. Then he cleared his throat. 'Well, she's not,' he declared with renewed bitterness. 'So it's me you have to answer to now, not her.'

'Worse luck,' Violet said after a long pause. She put her scissors into her sewing basket then crouched to pick up the scattered pins from the rug. 'Don't worry, I'll do my best to stay out of your way from now on, Uncle Donald.'

'Good job too,' he said, taken aback by her sudden capitulation.

'It'll be best for both of us.' Her heart felt sore and her head was in a spin as one by one she put the pins back in their box and Donald slammed the door behind him.

'I thought you'd be pleased.' Muriel studied Violet's sad expression when the younger girl called in at Jubilee to collect some mending work during her dinner break next day. 'According to Ida, this is what you've been hankering after – sewing more zips and hems, and such like.'

'It is.' Violet tried to put on a cheerful front, though she'd slept badly and she still felt unhappy after the argument with her uncle. 'I'll do a good job, I promise.'

'Have you got time for a cuppa?' the older woman asked, coming out from behind her counter.

Just being in the shop raised Violet's spirits – surrounded by cards of lace trim, rayon undergarments, racks of embroidery thread, calfskin gloves and packets of silk stockings, she felt in her element. 'Yes, please. I've got fifteen minutes before Mr Hutchinson sends out the troops.'

'Tea and biscuits, it is.' Fashionably neat in her straight grey skirt and a fitted lilac top, with grey leather shoes that had a small heel and a bar across the front, Muriel led the way into a small kitchen at the back of the shop. 'Ida's out getting her hair cut at the new hairdresser's on Canal Road, but I can nip through to serve a customer if I hear the shop bell ring.'

'How's she having it done?'

'Shorter, in an Eton crop. You know Ida – she's daring in that respect.'

'It'll suit her,' Violet predicted. Sitting down to accept her cup of tea, she was startled to feel tears well up and trickle down her cheeks before she could stop them.

'Oh, love, what is it?' Muriel asked.

'I'm sorry, I haven't got a hankie.'

'Take mine.' Muriel's handkerchief was edged with lace, with a blue flower embroidered in one corner. She gave it to her then rested a hand on Violet's shoulder. 'What's the trouble? Would you like to let me in on it?'

'It's Uncle Donald,' Violet sobbed. 'I don't know what's got into him ever since Aunty Winnie died. He's shut his barber's shop and now we're struggling to find the rent. He's coming down on me like a ton of bricks, saying I belong in the gutter and I don't know what else.' Her troubles poured out until at last she blew her nose and pulled herself together. 'I'm sorry, it's just that I don't have anyone to turn to.'

Muriel nodded. 'I know. It can be a lonely life without brothers and sisters. I look at the Briggs girls and what they've been through, especially Margie when she had her baby and there was no father in the picture. That was a bad time for the poor girl – she went to ground at her granddad's house on Ada Street and for a time things looked bleak. But it all turned out perfectly well because she had Lily and Evie to help her. Now Margie is nicely set up in an office job and her little girl is happy playing all day with Lily and Annie's bairns. That's what having a big family does – it pulls you through the hard times.'

Violet blew her nose a second time. 'If I worked in a mill, it might be different. I'd make friends with the other girls, there'd be a big gang to pal up with and go dancing with at a weekend. I sometimes think that's what I should do – get a job at Calvert's or Kingsley's.'

111

'No, don't do that,' Muriel advised. Like Sybil, she was all too aware of the grinding effects of mill work. You only had to look at the worn faces of the women trudging through the entrance to Calvert's at half past seven each morning to know that a life of spinning and weaving was no solution to Violet's problems. But, sorry to see Violet so crushed and unhappy, she made a confession of her own. 'I was by myself when my young man let me down. I was all set to be married – the dress was made, the church was booked. But then at the last minute my fiancé, Ron . . . well, he got cold feet.'

'Did he tell you why?'

'No. I never got a clear explanation from him, not even a note to say where he'd gone. Ron left me high and dry and I never saw him again.'

'That's awful.' Violet looked long and hard at Muriel's calm face. 'What about your family?' she asked.

'Like I said, I was on my own. Mother got diphtheria when I was eight. There were complications and she never got better. She died when I was ten. Father was killed a few years later in the war. After that, it was up to me to see what I could make of my life.'

Violet shook her head as if making space for common sense amongst her muddled emotions. 'And here's me going on about my worries. What must you think of me?'

'I think you're going through a bad patch,' Muriel

sympathized with a soft smile. 'And if you need someone to lean on, you know where to find me.'

Violet said a heartfelt thank-you as she handed back her empty cup and she felt her sadness ease. 'I'll have your mending done by Saturday,' she promised, chin up and ready to go back to work.

Out on Chapel Street the sun shone brightly and strains of 'Night and Day' drifted through the open door of Sykes' bakery.

'You're late,' Ben Hutchinson challenged the moment she walked into the shop.

'No. I'm dead on time,' she countered. 'And don't you dare go on about docking my wages, or else.'

Saturday came and the work for Sybil, Muriel and Ida was finished and returned on time. Muriel and Ida paid Violet on the spot and right there and then offered her more hems to sew, so she was pleased with herself when she went home after work to enter details of her earnings in the back of the rent book kept on the kitchen mantelpiece. She stashed the money away in her sewing box in the front room before escaping again into the fresh air as soon as she heard the sound of her uncle's footsteps coming downstairs.

Where should she go on this fine evening, she wondered, perhaps hoping to bump into Eddie if she made her way up to the Common where a group of pals often got together for a kick-about after the regular Rovers fixture. In fact, she was disappointed not to have heard from him since Tuesday and had begun to wonder if she'd read too much into the situation.

Eddie Thomson kissed you, she reminded herself, enjoying the breeze on her bare arms and legs as she walked up the hill. *He definitely made the first move – I'm not making it up. He admitted he'd waited a long time for us to be together and he looked deep into my eyes.*

So what? A small, doubtful voice wormed its way into her head and set up a dialogue with her hopeful, love-struck self. *What's in a kiss?*

Two kisses, actually.

Once the moment has passed, what's to stop a man changing his mind?

Not Eddie. Eddie doesn't lark about like Stan. He's sincere.

But you never know. Look what happened to Muriel – jilted at the altar, no less. And anyway, the point is – why hasn't he been in touch?

Violet reached Overcliffe Road and her thoughts came full circle. *Because he's been busy, just like me*, she told herself, waiting for a tram to rattle by before she crossed the road.

There, on the Common, she was pleased to make out the usual group of devil-may-care local lads booting a scuffed leather ball over the rough grass. They yelled instructions to each other – 'To, me, Stan!', 'Shoot, Eddie, shoot!', 'Take it down the wing. Now pass to me!' – and raced for goal, roaring with happiness if their side scored or moaning in despair if the shot misfired.

Smiling, Violet kept her distance. She spotted Evie and Kathy on a bench close to the entrance to Linton Park and glad of a chance to have a chat with them both, she joined them.

'We missed you on Wednesday night,' Kathy told her pleasantly as she made room for her to sit.

'I was busy,' Violet replied without going into detail.

'Did Ida tell you that she's given your part of my sister to Evie here?' Kathy went on.

Evie looked embarrassed. 'You can have it back if you like,' she said quickly. 'It wouldn't bother me.'

'No, it's all yours.' Violet settled in to watch the five-a-side match. She saw Stan belt up the wing with the ball, only to be brought down by an opponent and curl up on the ground as if in agony. A concerned Eddie bent down to offer him a hand but Stan rolled and sprang high into the air like a March hare, calling again for the ball.

'Stan's a card.' Kathy grinned. A breeze ruffled her fair hair and she kept the hem of her skirt pinned down with both hands.

'But look at Eddie – he's got the ball now.' Violet watched with admiration as Eddie dribbled towards goal. With the sleeves of his collarless white shirt rolled up and a broad leather belt buckled tight around his slim waist, he cut a dashing figure.

'Look – he's going to score.' Evie held her breath.

'Shoot, Eddie!' Kathy cried.

Eddie let fly with a hefty kick. The ball cannoned past the goalkeeper and shot on towards the hawthorn hedge at the far side of the Common. Someone scrabbled after it, going down on all-fours to retrieve it.

'Now, Eddie on the other hand . . .' Kathy began. She didn't have to say any more for Evie and Violet to know what she meant.

Eddie Thomson was someone you couldn't take your eyes off. He was naturally athletic, moving with good balance and coordination. He ran faster, swerved with more agility, kicked with more force than the rest of his team put together.

'Yes,' Evie and Violet agreed with a sigh.

Eddie's goal drew the impromptu match to a conclusion, it seemed. Once the ball had been rescued, the players shook hands and someone suggested an adjournment to the Green Cross. They picked up their jackets and caps then sauntered towards the bench where the girls sat.

'Now then, Violet,' Stan said as he overtook Eddie and made a beeline towards her. 'Long time, no see.'

'I've been busy,' she replied, putting a hand to her hair to keep it out of her eyes.

'Too busy to drop in and see me at the swimming baths?' he said and winked, at the same time shouldering Eddie to one side. 'Don't you know, I've missed you and your breaststroke!'

Kathy giggled and nudged Violet with her elbow.

'Aren't you boys going to buy us girls a drink of ginger pop?' she challenged.

'You two feel free,' Violet told Evie and Kathy, standing up without giving Stan or Eddie time to reply. 'I won't be joining you. I only came out for a breath of fresh air.'

'Are you sure you won't come?' Eddie said, ignoring more giggles from Kathy and an exaggerated cry of disappointment from Stan. He fell into step beside her.

She smiled up at him as they crossed the road together, noticing that his face was flushed from the recent exercise and his hair was ruffled by the wind. He walked with his jacket slung over one shoulder. 'I'd love to,' she told him, 'but I've taken in more extra sewing work that I have to finish by Monday.'

'Fair enough,' he said, trying not to let his disappointment show. Eddie still wasn't altogether sure where he stood with Violet, who in his eyes looked lovelier than ever in a rose-pink dress made in a wrap-around style which, when the breeze was in the right direction, gave him a glimpse of a shapely calf. 'You're not making excuses?' he checked.

'No, honestly, I'd love to come.' For two pins she'd abandon her plan and follow him to the ends of the earth, did he but know it. 'But the rent's due on Monday so I have to work.'

'So is it all right if I walk you home?'

She nodded and took his arm at the top of Chapel Street, in full view of Kathy, Evie, Stan and the others.

'That's all right, Eddie – no hard feelings!' Stan yelled after them, striking a tragic pose.

Eddie glanced over his shoulder then at Violet who raised her eyebrows.

'Take no notice,' she whispered, though she blushed bright red.

'A chap can see which way the land lies!' Stan wailed. 'It's because I only own a push-bike and Eddie has a 500cc Norton, isn't it?'

Eddie and Violet laughed and walked on. Eddie drew Violet closer to him. 'I don't care what anyone thinks,' he vowed. 'You just say the word, Violet, and I'll take you out on my motorbike any time you like!'

Sewing and daydreaming, Violet got through the weekend. On Monday morning, on the way to work, she delivered more finished items to Ida then went on through the day, doling out sugar and flour, cornflakes and marmalade, cured ham and Cheshire cheese.

'Wakey, wakey!' Ben Hutchinson would bark whenever her mind didn't seem to be on the job – when she spilled sugar onto the counter, for example, or else wiped her hands on her blue calico apron, leaving floury fingerprints on the bib for all to see. Then he would give her the nasty job of climbing the stepladder to bring down a greasy side of bacon from its high hook, ready to be sliced.

'I'm on my last legs,' she confessed to Marjorie, their final customer of the afternoon.

'Ta, love.' The kindly shopkeeper took her packet of tea and put it in her wicker basket. 'Ben, I won't have you working the poor girl's fingers to the bone now that she doesn't have Winnie to look out for her,' she chided. 'She's a little slip of a thing, remember.'

'Mind your own business, Marjorie Sykes,' the charmless grocer snapped back as he drew down the window blind. In retaliation, as if Marjorie's criticism was Violet's fault, he kept her back for a full ten minutes after the shop had shut.

'Drat – now I have to get a move on to be home in time for Mr Fisher,' she grumbled under her breath, speeding down Chapel Street and through the back alley. Sure enough, when she reached home the rent collector was already rat-a-tat-tatting on the door.

'Where is he?' Fisher asked, stepping back and looking up at the front bedroom window. 'If I didn't know better, I'd say Donald Wheeler was up there hiding under the bed.'

'Uncle Donald must have gone out,' Violet said, hastily turning her key in the lock. She foresaw a difficult conversation ahead of her, but hoped that with luck she'd be able to gather her extra earnings together and produce enough money to tide them over until the following week. 'Come in, Mr Fisher. Let's go into the kitchen and I'll put the kettle on for a cup of tea.'

'Never mind about the tea,' he said, taking off his hat and reluctantly stepping over the threshold. This was a touchy matter and privately, he wished it had been Donald Wheeler he was locking horns with rather than the niece. 'You know that you have to pay extra again this week.'

'Yes and I've been doing my best to get together what we owe you.' Taking Fisher straight into the front room, Violet went to her sewing basket to take out both her week's wage and the money she'd earned from her sewing work. 'I don't have the full amount,' she began to explain, 'but I'm sure I can make up what we owe before the end of the month.'

Standing on the worn hearth rug, Fisher turned the brim of his hat between his hands and shuffled his feet. 'My orders are to collect the whole lot in one go,' he stated without expression.

Violet lifted the satin-lined lid of the basket. She put aside reels of cotton and her box of pins, delving deep to draw out the small brown envelope containing her wage from Hutchinson's. 'There's this for a start.'

'The whole lot,' Fisher insisted. 'I'm not to leave with a penny less.'

'Wait a second.' Still hoping to reason with him after she'd produced the extra three shillings and nine pence that she'd hidden away in her old button tin, Violet prised open the lid. That was strange – she couldn't hear any coins rattling and when she did succeed in getting the top off, the tin was empty. Her heart thumped as she went back to the basket and searched again. 'It was in here the last time I looked,' she said amidst rising panic. 'Lord knows what can have happened to it!'

'Look here,' Fisher said, turning his hat this way and that, 'you mustn't try it on with me, young lady. I've seen it all before.'

'Honestly, I'm telling you that I put the extra money in here, every last penny.' Violet's heart raced as she began to draw the only possible conclusion. 'Uncle Donald must have found it and taken it for safe keeping. All we have to do is track him down and get him to hand it over.'

'Three and nine, you say?' Fisher did the calculation in his head. 'That would still leave you a long way short of what you owe.'

'I know but, as I said, I can soon make it up.' Her mind whirling, Violet did her best to believe that things would still work out. After all, surely the stony-faced man standing there in his buttoned-up overcoat had a heart. 'It won't take me long, honestly it won't.'

'*If* you could find the three and nine pence, I might be more willing to believe you,' the rent collector pointed out. 'As it is, I have to stick to the rules. It's the full amount or I'm obliged to serve you notice.'

'Notice of what?' Violet gasped as Fisher dipped one hand into his coat pocket and produced a long buff envelope.

'Eviction,' he said, his facial expression giving nothing away.

'Eviction!' Violet echoed in a faltering voice. It felt

as though a hole had opened up in the floor and she was falling down it.

'You have two days to pack up and hand back your keys,' Fisher explained. The boards beneath his feet creaked as he made his way out into the corridor then through the front door. 'Mr Gill wants you out of here, lock, stock and barrel, by Wednesday tea-time, and that's that.'

CHAPTER NINE

The door slammed and Violet ran upstairs to her uncle's room. She found him sitting on the edge of the bed, shoulders hunched and resting his elbows on his knees, sinewy arms bare and a cigarette hanging from his right hand.

'Where's my money?' she demanded, hardly able to breathe. She rushed at him, inhaling acrid smoke and pushing him with both hands, only to meet a strong resistance from his wiry frame. 'What have you done with it?'

Donald gritted his teeth and let the cigarette drop to the floor where it glowed unheeded on the bare boards. 'Calm down. It's only a few measly shillings,' he sneered.

'You stole it, didn't you?' Furious beyond belief, Violet wanted to shake him until he told her the truth. 'I worked hard for that money. It was meant to keep a roof over our heads.'

'It wouldn't, though, would it?' Donald stood up and went to the window, keeping his back turned.

'We had to stump up the whole amount or we were out on our ear – you heard what Alec Fisher said.'

'You were listening at the keyhole!' If Violet had thought that her fury couldn't get any worse, she was wrong. 'There was I, hunting for my hard-earned cash, which you'd filched from the tin, and even then you didn't let on!' Giving a disgusted sigh, she ran out of words to describe her feelings.

Without looking at her, Donald dipped into his trouser pockets, drew out some coins and scattered them on the floor. They rolled in every direction. A sixpence came to rest at Violet's feet while a three-penny bit lodged itself between the floorboards.

'Why?' Violet asked. The sight of the stolen money on which she'd built her hopes somehow altered her mood. She swung from anger to the edge of sorrowful tears as she raised her gaze from the coins to her uncle silhouetted against the net curtains, then on to the tall mahogany chest of drawers and across the bed with its duck-egg-blue quilt, on again to the solid wardrobe against the far wall. 'Don't you want us to stay here?' she asked tremulously.

With his back stubbornly to her, Donald felt in his shirt pocket for another cigarette. He lit it with a click of his silver lighter, a gift from Winnie to mark his fiftieth birthday.

That was exactly it, Violet realized and a cold shock ran through her. Her Uncle Donald wasn't taking any chances – he'd stolen her money not because he wanted to fritter it away but to make quite sure that they were turned out of Brewery Road.

'That was a wicked thing to do,' she said in a defeated voice.

'It's all settled,' he said in a tone hard as steel. He still refused to look at her, keeping his back turned and staring out through the net curtain, even when Violet broke down and sobbed her heart out. 'From now on we'll have no more to do with one another. We have two days to pack up our things and leave.'

Violet spent the night in desolate confusion. How had it come to this? Just a few short weeks ago her life had been carefree, with only the cut and fit of her Gala Queen dress to worry about and the most important decision on her horizon whether or not to wear a string of pearls to set it off.

Don't gild the lily, Winnie had advised. Now, in the darkness of her bedroom, Violet yearned to hear those no-nonsense tones and to see those eyes gazing fondly at her. What would her aunty have said in a situation like this? What would she have done?

There's no use moping about feeling sorry for yourself would have been her common-sense line. *Worse things happen at sea.*

That's just it, Aunty Winnie. I feel that I'm all at sea and drowning. You don't know how cruel Uncle Donald is to me now. He's shut me out, thrown me overboard and he doesn't care if I sink or swim.

Grieving for lost happiness and afraid of the misery that lay ahead, Violet didn't bother to undress or go to bed. She sat by the window, looking out at the backs of the houses on Chapel Street, at the low stone outhouses and ash pits, the small yards and the back lane running all the way up the hill to Overcliffe Road. She sat through the night, watching clouds scud across the black sky, wishing things could stay as they were, but knowing that they never would, with a cold fear of what tomorrow might bring.

It wasn't by chance that Eddie ran into Violet on her way to work next morning. In fact, he'd planned the meeting down to the last detail. If Violet had to be at Hutchinson's for half past eight, she would have to leave home five minutes beforehand, rounding the corner of Brewery Road onto Chapel Street and passing the doorway of Jubilee with two minutes to spare.

'What are you looking so starry-eyed about?' Ida had challenged Eddie the night before as she sat with Harold on the settee squashed into a corner of the kitchen at Valley Road.

In fact, Eddie had been working out how and when he would intercept Violet and ask her out to the pictures on Friday night, his next night off. 'Nothing. I don't know what you mean,' he'd answered guiltily.

'Oh no, butter wouldn't melt!' Ida had shot him down in flames. 'You're dreaming of a certain somebody, I can tell.'

Eddie had cast a look at Harold that said, *Help me*

out of a tight corner, pal, but the hoped-for back-up hadn't arrived. Instead, Harold had buried his head in his newspaper, reading the reports on Saturday's matches. 'You'd better hurry up and ask her out before someone else we know tries again,' Ida had chivvied as she cosied up to her fiancé.

'All right, I will,' he'd agreed, feeling more confident.

But as he parked his bike and waited, his heart hammered and he ran through the reasons why Violet might turn him down. For a start, he wasn't much of a catch in terms of job and prospects. Although he'd been a bright enough spark at Lowtown Junior School, nerves had got the better of him on the day of his school entrance exam and he'd failed. Painting and decorating brought in steady money, it was true, but he'd climbed onto the back of his dad's business and hadn't struck out by himself the way he should. As for working at the Victory – that was too new for him to know whether or not it would lead anywhere.

'Now then, Eddie.' Marjorie broke into his chain of thought as she cheerfully laboured up the hill. 'What errand has Ida got you lined up for this fine morning?'

His vague answer was lost in a throng of uniformed schoolchildren en route to the grammar school on Westgate Road, and when the pavement cleared there was only Evie and her married sister, Lily, deep in conversation, hurrying by with a smile. Moments later Violet emerged from the alleyway

127

between numbers 10 and 12 and hurried on up the street, head down.

Eddie kicked himself – he should have realized Violet would cut off the corner by using the alley as a short cut. Now he had to run to catch her up. In her pale blue dress and cream cardigan, Violet was a slim, dark-haired figure going against the tide of another group of schoolchildren, hesitating, looking round and finally catching sight of him, stopping to wait.

The moment he saw her face he knew something was badly wrong. She looked pale and when she tried to smile, her large, heavily lashed eyes stayed sad. 'What's up?' he asked without exchanging greetings.

Eddie showing up out of the blue gave Violet a straw to clutch at after a night spent being tugged in all directions by the strong current of her conflicting emotions. She didn't think to question what he was doing there at this time in the morning. 'You won't believe it,' she declared. 'Our landlord has only sent me and Uncle Donald packing. We have to be out of the house by tomorrow night.'

'You don't say.'

'It's true.' Violet gave a short sigh. 'I was hoping Mr Gill would give us a bit of leeway over the rent we owed, but you know what landlords are like – all they think about is having the money in their wallets.'

Slowly Eddie gathered his wits. 'This is a right carry-on. Have you got somewhere to move on to?'

'Not yet. It'll be me by myself, though. Uncle Donald has washed his hands of me.'

'Never.' Again, Eddie found that his words didn't do justice to the disaster facing Violet. 'Why would he do that?'

'You'd have to ask him.' She sighed again. 'All I know is that ever since Aunty Winnie died, he hasn't wanted anything to do with me.'

'I could try to talk him round if you like.' Eddie suggested the first thing that came to mind, but when Violet emphatically shook her head he quickly moved on. 'Or else I can see if anyone has a spare room for you to rent?'

At this Violet brightened a little. 'Yes please, Eddie. That's good of you. And I'll pass the word around myself. Marjorie might know someone for a start, or even Mr Hutchinson if I catch him the right side out.'

'Don't worry, you'll soon find somewhere.'

'Be sure to let people know that I'm no trouble,' she said, raising her head and setting it at a more defiant angle. 'I'll keep the place clean and tidy and I'll guarantee to pay my rent on time.'

Eddie grinned. 'They'll be queuing up to take you,' he assured her, realizing that he hadn't got round to asking Violet out. When he saw Ben Hutchinson step out of his shop onto the pavement and look daggers down the street at the two of them, he knew it was time to go. 'Ta-ta for now, Violet. And try not to worry.'

'Easier said than done,' she said, bracing herself for a day behind the counter with an employer who looked as if he'd sucked on a lemon. The wall clock would tick away the hours until she found herself and her suitcase pounding the pavements, knocking on doors in a desperate search for somewhere to stay.

Word of Violet's dire situation soon spread and at half past twelve that day Marjorie popped her head around the door of the grocery shop to commiserate.

'Here's a nice scone for your tea tonight,' she told Violet, bringing with her the sweet smell of baking. Her dumpy figure and flour-coated overall were matched by an old-fashioned cottage-loaf hairstyle. All aspects of Marjorie's appearance gave away the fact that she lived and breathed the bread, teacakes and Victoria sponges that made up her daily routine.

Violet took the proffered paper bag and thanked her.

'I'm surprised at Donald Wheeler,' Marjorie confided with a disapproving shake of her head. 'Yes, he's always had the reputation of a straight-laced, dyed-in-the-wool chapel-goer, but I expected if you scratched the surface you'd find a soft heart in there somewhere.'

'He hasn't got over Aunty Winnie,' Violet explained. 'He's not been himself lately.'

'Good for you, love, for sticking up for him,' was

Marjorie's response. 'And I promise I'll keep my ears open for you. If I hear of a room going begging I'll be sure to let you know.'

This was the pattern throughout the afternoon – customers coming in and offering sympathy, bad-mouthing money-grabbing landlords and telling Violet that a similar thing had happened to a cousin or a friend. 'Don't you worry, love, you may be out on your ear but people don't end up without a roof over their heads, not round here,' was the general opinion, which was some comfort to Violet but didn't bring her closer to a concrete solution.

'Cheer up,' Ben Hutchinson told her more than once as closing time drew near. 'With a face like that you'll curdle the milk.'

Forcing a smile for the mill workers who poured out of Calvert's and Kingsley's and called in for pork pies and cured ham for their teas, Violet was relieved to stay busy. She served potted beef to Frank Bielby, Wensleydale cheese to Kathy and Jacob's Cream Crackers to Alf Shipley, dressed in the pale grey uniform that the Barlows provided, with black gloves tucked into his belt and peaked hat under his arm. Out on the street she caught a glimpse of Colin Barlow himself ensconced on the back seat of his gleaming car, the window wound down to allow him to flick cigarette ash onto the pavement.

'That'll be nine pence halfpenny,' Violet told the chauffeur after he'd added more items. He was her last customer and when she followed him out of the shop to raise the awning with the long pole kept by the door, she found herself skewered by the sharp gaze of his boss who had stepped out of the car to grind the stub of his cigarette into the pavement.

From under the brim of his fawn trilby hat Barlow looked her up and down, taking in her blue apron and rolled-up sleeves, clearly not concerned that his scrutiny made her uncomfortable. 'Weren't you this year's Gala Queen?'

'I was,' she answered, red in the face and awkwardly holding the pole in both hands.

'Hmm,' the shop owner concluded with a shake of his head. Alf Shipley held open the door and Barlow got back in the car.

What did he mean by 'hmm'? Violet wanted to know. Did he mean that he was disappointed to see that the glamorous Whitsuntide Queen turned out to be a lowly shop girl, because that's what she'd read into it. Anyway, who was Colin Barlow to lord it over people, or any of the mill bosses and shop owners round here, for that matter? Violet hadn't been brought up to kowtow and just because she served cream crackers and Colman's mustard to the man's chauffeur, she wasn't about to start.

Still tetchy over the Barlow incident, Violet was inside the shop taking off her apron when Muriel rapped her knuckles against the glass panel and Violet unbolted the door. 'I'm sorry, we're closed – it's gone half five,' she began but Muriel breezed in and spoke over her.

'Eddie told us what's been going on so I went and had a word with Wilf Fullerton down at the brewery. He's promised to line up the horses and cart ready for your removals.'

'When?' Violet asked, taken aback by Muriel's energetic manner.

'Tomorrow teatime, of course. That's when you have to be out of number eleven, isn't it? Wilf says the best thing is to take the furniture straight down to Manby's on Canal Road. He reckons it should fetch a few pounds at auction.'

'Hadn't I better ask Uncle Donald first?' Violet put in. 'He might have other ideas.'

'I doubt it,' Muriel said abruptly, letting her low opinion of Violet's uncle show through. 'But yes, you should probably check. Anyway, we'll have Wilf standing by. And now I want you to come down to Jubilee with me. Is that all right with you, Ben?'

Huffing, puffing and chuntering his way towards the storeroom to hang up his brown shopkeeper's overall, Hutchinson gave his permission for Violet to leave work. 'I want you here at half past eight sharp, though,' he reminded her. 'Move or no move.'

'I'll be here,' she promised, flying out of the shop after an eager Muriel.

The heat of the late-afternoon sun hung heavy over the grey terraced houses and seemed to radiate from the stone pavement as the two young women hurried down the hill. They passed three girls chanting a rhyme and playing a skipping game, then Arthur Briggs and another boy, both in school caps and short trousers, dragging a go-cart out of the alley. Muriel almost tripped over the cart in her haste to reach Jubilee.

And there was Ida waiting in the shop doorway and beckoning them inside. The shop bell tinkled as Muriel pushed Violet through the door then closed it, shutting out the noise from the street. 'Don't worry, it's nothing bad,' Ida promised, her lively features showing that she was scarcely able to hold back the surprise that lay in store.

Her new short haircut added to her boyish air, Violet decided, yet there was still a girlish slimness and elegance to her figure that men must find attractive. Beside the more conventional Muriel, Ida looked very modern indeed.

'Come on, Violet, have you lost your tongue?' Ida urged. 'Don't you want to know what this is about?'

'Muriel already told me that Wilf is willing to lend a hand with clearing the furniture,' Violet explained.

'And Eddie,' Ida added. 'He'll be there to lift the heavy things – wardrobes and such like. But that's not why Muriel dragged you down here.'

'It isn't?' Despite the confusion, Violet kept in mind how much she had to do at home – packing ornaments and household items such as the iron, kettle, crockery, cutlery and last but not least her sewing machine, though what she would do with them she had as yet no idea.

'No. We've been chewing things over, Muriel and

I, ever since Eddie put us in the picture first thing this morning.' Ida smiled from ear to ear and practically hugged herself over the secret she was about to divulge.

'Let me put the poor girl out of her misery,' Muriel broke in, looking almost as pleased as Ida.

'No, it was my idea. I'll tell her.'

Violet looked from one to the other then at the fabric stacked on the shelf by the door, then at the white kid gloves and lace hankies on the counter and finally at the plaster bust in the corner wearing the latest style of hat – a Garbo 'Empress Eugenie', fitting close to the head and tilted over one eye. *They want to give me more to do*, she decided. *Perhaps they'll try me out on millinery work, sewing feathers onto hat bands, that kind of thing.*

'As I say, Muriel and I have talked this through carefully,' Ida continued. 'We've considered the pitfalls. It would make things quite crowded for a start and we'd have to be careful not to tread on each other's toes.'

'What would?' Violet didn't understand.

'And we could only afford to go without rent if you agreed to carry on doing extra sewing work for us whenever we happen to need it.'

Without rent? Violet thought she must be being especially stupid but she still couldn't work out exactly what was on offer.

'Come upstairs,' Ida said, seizing her by the hand. She led the way, with Violet in the middle and

Muriel close behind, up the narrow stairs and along the landing, turning left at the bottom of the attic stairs and arriving in a tiny room with just enough space for a single bed with a bare mattress and a wicker chair.

'Yours if you want it,' Muriel told an astonished Violet.

'Mine?' Violet queried.

'Yes or no?' Ida asked.

It took Violet a little while to take in the bare boards and faded sprigged wallpaper, the rickety legs of the chair, the mattress that was sunk in the middle. She saw that the iron fireplace-surround needed black-leading to bring it back to life and that the window overlooking the cobbled brewery yard was dim with cobwebs and grime. 'Are you saying I can live here?' she asked uncertainly.

'It's not much, I agree,' Muriel conceded, doubt entering her mind. 'But you could soon freshen it up with curtains and a pretty bedspread.'

Impatient for an answer, Ida paced the landing then peered back into the room.

It struck Violet like a lightning bolt – this meant there would be no knocking at doors on the worst stretches of Canal Road, no heart-sinking viewing of cellar rooms shared with rats and spiders, no bumping into strangers in the dark on the way to an outside toilet. Instead she, Violet Wheeler, would be living above her favourite shop, a close neighbour to satin ribbons and silk stockings, Lastex girdles and hat mannequins. And all this was thanks to Eddie, Ida and Muriel.

She took a deep breath. 'It's smashing,' she murmured in a choked voice.

'You'll take it?' A beaming Ida linked arms with Muriel and together they waited for Violet's reply.

'Like a shot,' she told them through her tears. 'Thank you, Ida. Thank you, Muriel. I can't wait to move in!'

CHAPTER TEN

Violet arrived home to find that an empty tea chest had miraculously arrived on the doorstep of number 11, much to the delight of a small boy with curly red hair who had decided to climb inside and hide.

'Hop it,' she told him when he peered out to check the whereabouts of his fellow hide-and-seekers.

The lad scrambled out and took to his heels, leaving Violet to unlock the door and cart the tea chest into the corridor. It could stay there, she decided, while she had a bite to eat then began to collect together Winnie's ornaments and framed photographs, ready for moving. She would wrap everything carefully in newspaper then pack items she wanted to take with her in the chest – whatever would fit in, including the blue and white crockery, the linen tablecloth and if possible the clock from the kitchen mantelpiece.

She set about her task methodically, trying to ignore sharp pangs of regret and the sensation that a loved one's life didn't add up to much when it came to it – just a pair of Staffordshire dogs, a Minton vase and a couple of photos in silver frames. It was only when she came to Winnie's sewing box in the front room and opened it to find the embroidery silks she'd bought for her still wrapped in their white tissue paper that she could fend off the sadness no longer and she sat down and wept.

I'll take the two sewing boxes – Aunty Winnie's and mine – with me to Chapel Street, she decided as she blew her nose and pulled herself together. *I'm sure the needles and scissors will come in handy for a start.* Then she turned on the wireless, hoping for cheerful tunes to brighten up an evening that had turned to grey skies and drizzle. She was so absorbed in her task that she didn't notice her Uncle Donald appear in the doorway. He stood there a while without speaking and startled her when she came out into the corridor with more ornaments for the chest.

'You look done in,' she said, taking in his dishevelled appearance. His jacket was rain soaked and his shirt collarless, his moustache badly in need of a trim. 'Where on earth have you been?'

'Out,' he said as he edged past the tea chest. It was obvious that there was no more to be said.

'Would you like me to make you a cup of tea?' Violet offered. 'I haven't packed the kitchen things yet and there's milk in the pantry.'

Donald shook his head and trudged on down the corridor.

Violet followed him to the foot of the stairs. 'Have you found somewhere to live?'

He stopped with one foot on the bottom step. 'What if I have?'

'I'm glad, that's all. I expect you'll want to take pans and the kettle with you, and some plates and knives and forks.'

'I don't want anything,' he insisted, taking two more steps before halting again. 'You can keep the lot.'

'Why? Won't you need the basics wherever it is you're going?' Worrying on his behalf, Violet couldn't fathom this display of apathy. It was so unlike him to let himself go and not to bother about practical things.

'I said no, didn't I?' He went on up the stairs and into his bedroom, where Violet found him at the window, staring down into the yard.

'Muriel and Ida have offered me their spare room above the drapers,' she informed him. 'It's not very big so there won't be room for much apart from the sewing machine and my personal bits and bobs. Are you sure you won't want Aunty Winnie's ornaments, for instance?'

Slowly Donald turned to look at her. 'What would I do with ornaments?' The question came out not as a bad-tempered objection but as a weary appeal from a man worn down by events.

Violet moved towards him. 'They might help you remember better times,' she suggested softly.

He shook his head but said nothing.

'Uncle Donald, it'll be all right in a little while, you'll see. We both have to get used to things and try to carry on, don't we?'

'Carry on?' he echoed.

'Without Aunty Winnie.' There was a pause and a thought struck her. 'The barber's shop is still empty. Why not take that up where you left off?'

He rebuffed the suggestion with a wave of his hand. 'I'm not going back to that. What's the point?'

'It's better than nothing, surely.'

'No.' Donald was adamant. 'Not without Win, it's not.'

It was a simple, short sentence but Violet saw in it the full reason behind her uncle's disintegration. It was Winnie's strength that had supported him and sent him digging on the allotment all those years ago, after he'd lost his job at Welby. And Winnie's optimism that had seen him through the dark days – her chatter that had sustained him and her faith in him that had kept him on the straight and narrow. She had shored him up and given him a reason to polish his shoes on a morning, put on collar and tie and go out to work. Without her, everything had collapsed.

'I'm sorry,' Violet whispered.

Donald made a strange sound – a choked sob that turned into a dry cough and once more he batted her away. 'I knew I wouldn't cope,' he said. 'I begged her not to leave me even though I could see what

141

was happening in front of me. Dr Moss realized it as well, the minute he got here, but I still clutched at straws. And Winnie saw it in my eyes. She squeezed my hand and said she was sorry.'

Pinned to the spot and hardly able to breathe, Violet knew she had to let her uncle have his say.

'You know it was Winnie's idea to take you on. I was against it from the start.'

At the sudden switch of topic, Violet took in a sharp breath and pressed her lips together. *I'm your brother's child*, she wanted to cry. *Not a stranger, but flesh and blood.*

'It was too much to ask of me and she knew it. But she did it anyway.' Speaking in a low voice, Donald's gaze was unwavering as he got off his chest what he'd felt for going on twenty years.

'But you agreed,' she reminded him, desperate for a drop of comfort.

'No, I never did – not in my heart of hearts.'

The full force of her uncle's rejection struck Violet like a blow to the chest but in a strange way she felt relieved. 'I won't be a burden to you,' she promised. 'I'll make my own way in life from now on, don't you worry.'

Donald gave a dismissive nod and remained silent.

'From tomorrow I'm a free agent. Wilf Fullerton is coming at teatime to cart the furniture away to Manby's. They'll need an address to send you any money it makes.'

'Tell them I'll call in and collect it when I'm ready.'

The practical arrangements over and done with, neither Donald nor Violet found anything more to say. 'Goodnight then,' she murmured, backing out across the landing to her own room.

He didn't reply.

Violet shut her door and lay down on her bed. She stared up at the ceiling, convinced that she wouldn't rest. Misery settled over her like a pall on this, her last night on Brewery Road. Rain splashed against the window panes, the house creaked as if ghostly footsteps trod up the stairs and along the landing. At three o'clock in the morning her eyes closed and she drifted into a dream-filled sleep.

It was already light when Violet awoke with a start. She knew in an instant that Donald was gone.

Good riddance, she told herself. At least there would be no awkward goodbyes.

Up and dressed by the time the knocker-up for Calvert's Mill came down the street rattling mill workers' window panes, she spent the time before work placing items in the chest then methodically folding her clothes and packing them in her aunt's brown suitcase, which she found under the bed in the front bedroom. At quarter past eight she was ready to leave the house.

Nine hours of stacking and weighing, sweeping and wiping later, Violet finished work and returned to the house on Brewery Road for the last time. She found two Clydesdales standing patiently at the kerb, with Wilf, Harold and Eddie perched on the back of the empty cart.

'Here she is with the key at last,' Wilf grumbled. 'We've been here ages, twiddling our thumbs.'

While Violet unlocked the door, the blinkered horses stamped their heavy feet and ignored a small group of children who had gathered to pet and admire them. 'Ta for doing this, Wilf,' she told the brewery man, whose grumpiness hid a heart of gold. 'And Harold, ta very much.'

'We don't mind, do we, Eddie?' Ida's fiancé was the first to follow Violet over the threshold. 'Not if it gets us off painting scenery for the evening. Where do you want this tea chest, then? Is it going to Manby's with the rest?'

'No. You can drop it off at Jubilee, along with the sewing machine, ta.'

'Rightio, we'll put them at the back of the cart, ready to drop off first.' Harold and Wilf sprang into action while Eddie stayed in the hallway to have a quiet word with Violet.

'I see that the chest came in handy,' he said with a smile.

'I might have known it was you who organized that,' she replied, smiling back and giving his cheek a quick peck. 'Thank you!'

'Mind out, you two love birds!' Harold cried, backing towards them carrying the kitchen table with Wilf at the other end.

They blushed and made room, then joined in

with the loading work. Out of the front door and down the three worn steps went kitchen chairs and the food-safe from the pantry, the fireside chair and mangle, all bound for the auction. From the front room they took the horsehair sofa, the set of shelves and two framed pictures, then they moved upstairs for the bed frames and mattresses, the chests of drawers and the wash stand with the old-fashioned pitcher and ewer. This left only the wardrobe in Winnie and Donald's room, which would require all three men to manhandle down the stairs.

'We're on the last lap, thank heavens,' Harold grunted as he, Wilf and Eddie took the weight of the wardrobe between them. 'Violet, are you ready to lock up after us?'

'Let me fetch my suitcase. I'll be with you in two ticks.' She felt she needed a few seconds to look around the empty rooms and say her goodbyes, going first into Winnie and Donald's bedroom then into her own, lingering longer than she'd intended until she heard footsteps on the stairs and turned to see Eddie holding a dark brown wooden box between both hands.

'This was hidden away at the back of the wardrobe,' he told her. 'We would've missed it except that it slid forward and tipped off the top shelf. It just missed Wilf's head.'

Violet had never seen the box before but it looked like something you would use to contain letters, writing materials and important documents – birth certificates, wills, and such like. She took it from Eddie and set it on the window sill, opening it carefully to find a small, leather-bound prayer book with an inscription written in copperplate on the fly leaf: *Joseph Wheeler, 1892*. Under this was a marriage certificate dated 3 July 1908 for Donald Wheeler and Winifred Craven and beside it a small blue box fashioned in the shape of a heart.

Violet took out the box and ran her fingertips over its velvet surface. She pressed a small silver button to release the catch. Inside there was a cushioned, cream satin lining and a gold bracelet. 'Well, I never. I had no idea this was hidden away in here,' she breathed.

It was a heavy chain bracelet with a fastener in the shape of a padlock, which bore an inscription almost too small for her to read.

'Can you make it out?' Eddie asked, resting his chin on her shoulder and sliding his arm around her waist to share in the unexpected discovery.

Violet read with difficulty. 'It says "Xmas 1914" and there's a hallmark on the back.'

'It's lucky we didn't send it to Manby's without realizing it was there. It might be worth something,' Eddie remarked.

She handed him the bracelet to let him feel its weight then spotted a small envelope about three inches square, tucked underneath the cushion. She drew it out, opened it, then took out a piece of yellowed paper bearing a short note. *To dearest Flo, as a token of my lifelong affection. Keep this bracelet for my sake.*

The note was unsigned but Violet knew that Flo must stand for Florence. 'Florence was my mother's name. And the inscription was done the year before I was born. Thank you, Eddie,' she whispered as with clumsy fingers he replaced the chain bracelet in its box. Then she slipped the loving note into her skirt pocket.

A heart-shaped case, a tiny envelope and a note . . . It was a link with Violet's past that might have been broken for ever, if not for the man she loved.

CHAPTER ELEVEN

Trying her best to put the bracelet to the back of her mind and concentrate on the task in hand, it took Violet no time at all to settle in above Jubilee. She moved in late on Wednesday and by the weekend she had scrubbed every corner, crevice and surface of her tiny new lodgings. Eddie set aside the Saturday afternoon to go in with stepladder, paint and wallpaper and when Violet came home from work, the room was transformed.

'It's perfect!' she sighed, gazing round at the pretty pink and white walls and breathing in the smell of fresh paint that disguised the odour of fermenting hops drifting in through the open window from the brewery. Her bed was tucked neatly into a corner, leaving space for a chest of drawers under the window, and an alcove next to the chimney breast was identified by Eddie as the ideal place to put up a hanging rail for her clothes. Her precious Singer sewing machine had been carried upstairs to the attic workroom. 'Honestly, Eddie. I can't thank you enough.'

'Think nothing of it.' His modest reply couldn't conceal the fact that he enjoyed basking in Violet's gratitude. 'You're easy to please – you know that?'

'I am – it's true, at least as far as you're concerned. Now, what do I owe you for the paper and paint?'

'Don't be daft. They were left over from a job we did at Thomas Kingsley's house.'

'For your time, then?'

'Violet, you don't owe me anything,' Eddie insisted, suddenly feeling self-conscious about his mucky overalls and the need to get home for a wash and shave before he clocked on at the Victory. 'Seeing you smile is good enough for me.'

Violet sidled close and put her arm around his waist – an embrace more chummy than romantic to both their minds so they soon turned to face each other and he slipped his arms around her and placed his hands on the small of her back. They kissed for a long time until she broke away.

'I'm sorry,' he murmured. But he wasn't really. Holding her and kissing her was what he dreamed about, day in, day out.

She shook her head. 'I didn't want you to think . . .' She'd almost floated off, then a warning thought had entered her head and she'd pulled back.

'No, it was my fault. I'm rushing things.'

You have to keep your feet on the ground. It was Aunty

149

Winnie's voice that gave Violet a clear, timely reminder and she felt hot with embarrassment. After that, Eddie left in a hurry, giving her the rest of the evening to make the room more homely until she was interrupted by Muriel who had stayed late in the shop to stocktake and who came upstairs at eight o'clock to check that all was well with their new lodger.

'My head's buzzing with lists and figures,' Muriel complained once she'd complimented Violet on her home-making skills. 'Making sure I know what we're running low on and deciding how much to re-order isn't an easy job.'

'Doesn't Ida lend a hand with that?' Violet asked.

Muriel laughed. 'Stocktaking isn't her strong point. She says she doesn't have the patience. Anyway, she's out on the town with Harold tonight and I really don't mind doing it myself.'

'I could help.' Violet's offer was accompanied by an eager smile. 'You know what they say – many hands make light work.' Without waiting for an answer she led the way downstairs into the shop then asked Muriel where she should start.

'Buttons,' Muriel decided, showing Violet the boxes stacked neatly on a shelf behind the counter. 'Each one has a code written on the front, next to a sample of the button that the box contains – these mother-of-pearl ones, for example. The code for that type is A34.'

'So you'd like me to count the loose buttons inside

150

each box then write down the total?'

Muriel nodded and showed her a notebook with ruled columns and neatly written figures. 'You're sure you don't mind?' she checked.

'Mind – after what you and Ida have done for me? I should say not.' Violet opened a box and started her task while Muriel concentrated on the stock of zips kept on the stand by the door then moved on to hooks and eyes. They wrote down their totals, knowing not to interrupt each other in mid-count and working in companionable silence until Muriel decided it was time for another break. She took Violet into the kitchen at the back of the shop.

'There's nothing like a good cup of tea,' she declared, sitting Violet down at a table piled high with pattern books by Butterick and McCall. 'You're up to date with your fashions, aren't you?' she said as the kettle boiled. 'What are your thoughts about this summer's dresses for girls of your age?'

'They should be nipped in tight at the waist to give a womanly look,' Violet told her without hesitation. 'And they should have cap sleeves with shoulder pads – that's all the rage.'

Muriel gave her the tea and sat down opposite. 'I'm all ears. Tell me, which designers are in favour?'

'Norman Hartnell because his dresses are soft and pretty.' Violet was in her element, ideas tripping off her tongue. 'And nobody does bias-cut skirts better than Madeleine Vionnet in gay Paree. But if you're talking tailored evening gowns, I'd go for

Schiaparelli and her man-made fabrics that cling to a girl's figure. You only have to look at pictures in the magazines to see that you can't beat them.'

'Slow down!' Muriel laughed. 'That's a lot to take in. And I'm only asking because Ida and I are seriously considering going ahead with our new idea to set up as dressmakers.'

'So you want to hear my opinions?' Flattered and excited, Violet's thoughts raced on. 'Now, the house dress is really what we should be talking about. It should have a scalloped neckline and a tailored bodice, in rayon or nylon.'

'Bold colours?' Muriel asked.

'Yes, nice and bright, with a row of small bows down the front. And if you really want to push the boat out this summer, how about the harem pants that Joan Blondell wears in her films?'

'Wide, like pyjama bottoms?'

'Yes, the wider the better in rayon or silk, worn with a halter-neck top.'

'Brr!' Muriel pretended to shiver then she laughed at herself. 'I must be getting old.'

'You can cover up with a little bolero jacket if it's chilly.' Seeing the amused twinkle in Muriel's eyes, Violet blushed. 'I'm sorry if I'm getting carried away.'

'Don't be sorry for dragging me and my starchy ideas into the nineteen thirties. It's exactly what Ida and I need to think about if we're to branch out. The trick will be to adapt the patterns from these catalogues and bring them up to the minute at a cost people can afford to pay. That's going to take some doing.'

'The money part of it is over my head,' Violet decided, taking the cups to the sink and rinsing them out.

Drying them off with a tea towel, she realized that this conversation had boosted her spirits more than Muriel knew, perhaps because it took her back to topics she used to cover at home with Winnie – ruffles and bows, the best way to gather material evenly to fit a skirt to a bodice. Happy days. 'I'll see you back in the shop,' she told Muriel with a grateful smile. 'I don't know about you but I've got twelve more boxes of buttons to count before I go to bed tonight!'

After the catastrophe of losing not only her beloved Aunty Winnie but also the house she'd lived in all her life, the miracle was how quickly Violet learned to look forward and not back. Her one concession was to carry in the pocket of whatever she was wearing the precious love letter from her father to her mother. She worked hard, both at the grocer's and at Jubilee, managing to squeeze in an hour or two at Brinkley Baths, and, under pressure from Ida, even agreeing to resume her connection with the Hadley Players.

'It's grand to see you looking cheerful again,' Marjorie said on one of her frequent drop-ins at Hutchinson's. Today it was for a tin of sardines and three slices of ham off the bone.

153

'I love my new digs – that's why,' Violet confided. 'I've made curtains to match the wallpaper and I'm saving up for a brand-new mattress. I couldn't be happier.'

'So it's got nothing to do with a certain young man?' Marjorie teased. 'You get those roses in your cheeks just from thinking about curtains and mattresses, do you?'

'That and helping Muriel and Ida with their new venture into dressmaking,' she protested, then realized in an instant that she shouldn't have let on. Knowing Marjorie, the news would spread up and down Chapel Street like wildfire.

'That's what they're up to, is it?' Like a dog at a bone, she tussled to draw more information out of a chastened Violet, asking why and when and for how long the owners of Jubilee had been planning to set up as rivals to Chapel Street Costumiers at the top of the hill.

'Please don't say anything,' Violet begged.

'Why – is it a secret?'

'Yes. Muriel and Ida aren't sure they're going to go ahead yet.'

The bakery owner placed her purchases in her wicker basket. 'Right you are. Mum's the word!'

Marjorie's exaggerated wink as she left the shop didn't inspire confidence in Violet and, aware that Ben Hutchinson had overheard the conversation, her fears mounted. That same teatime she confessed her mistake to Eddie when he dropped by at Jubilee

154

to find her working on her own after Muriel and Ida had both gone home.

'Still busy stocktaking?' he asked, sauntering in after parking his bike outside. Without waiting for a reply, he came round the back of the counter to steal a kiss. 'Shouldn't you have shut up shop by now?'

'Yes. What do you mean by coming in bang on half five?' she kidded, pretending to fend him off. 'Don't think I'm going to drop everything and serve you after hours.'

'What would I want with silk stockings?' His raised eyebrow suggested the cheeky answer to his own question and made Violet colour up.

Luckily she was diverted by a rap at the door and the bustling entrance of Lizzie Turner, the funeral director's daughter.

'Phew, I'm glad I caught you,' Lizzie began. 'I need some knicker elastic and it can't wait.'

'Don't mind me,' Eddie said, beating a hasty retreat. 'I'll call back in half an hour,' he told Violet. 'It's Wednesday. I can give you a lift over to Hadley on the Norton if you like.'

Despite the late hour, Violet brought out rolls of elastic of various widths for Lizzie, whom Violet had known since their school days. Lizzie, who was the same age as Evie, was waif-like, with long red hair and pale skin, but despite her elfin beauty she was down to earth and easy to get along with. 'It's not really for knickers,' she explained as she chose the half-inch-wide version. 'I just wanted to see the look on Eddie's face. As a matter of fact, it's for my little brother Jimmy's garters. He used the last ones to make catapults for himself and Arthur Briggs and now he wonders why his socks keep falling down.'

Laughing and chatting, Violet served her last-minute customer and awaited Eddie's return. Seeing him strolling down the hill, she dashed upstairs for her coat then down again and out onto the pavement to meet him.

The next minute they were on the bike and on their way to rehearsal and they arrived just in time to see Kathy walking from the bus stop beside the tall figure of Stan Tankard.

'Yes, I know – look what the cat dragged in!' Kathy gestured towards Stan then laughed to see Eddie and Violet's surprised expressions.

'What are you doing here?' Eddie wanted to know as he let Violet dismount then parked his bike by the entrance.

'Aww, what's wrong, Eddie? Can't I play too?' Stan grabbed the two girls by the waist and swept them through the open door. 'I heard there was a part going spare for a good-looking fellow and I thought I'd be a natural, so here I am, girls, ready and willing to play the romantic lead!'

'No, really, Stan – why aren't you at work?' Violet wondered, catching Evie's eye across the hall and noticing that she turned away awkwardly without signalling hello. It gave Violet the nasty feeling that either Ben or Marjorie had already spread the word about Muriel and Ida's proposed new venture into dressmaking.

'The corporation altered my hours.' Stan's answer reclaimed Violet's attention and she grew aware of Eddie's frown as he followed them in. She quickly broke away from Stan and took her place next to Eddie as the interloper developed his story. 'They don't want me to work on Wednesday nights any more, so I thought to myself, What's to stop me from joining in the fun with the Players over in Hadley? You know what they say, Eddie – if you can't beat 'em . . . !'

'Oh well,' Eddie said to Violet as Ida spotted Stan and pounced on him as another potential bit-part player, 'I suppose it doesn't do any harm.'

'Quite right,' she agreed valiantly. 'Stan can come and go as he pleases – it's no skin off our noses.'

And so they settled into the rehearsal – Eddie was soon up the ladder painting another backdrop and Violet was being herded here and there for her new non-speaking part. Then Ida called for a tea break and Violet took the chance to nip outside for a breath of fresh air. It wasn't until she was out in the yard that she realized, too late, that Stan had snuck out after her.

'Great minds think alike,' he said pleasantly. 'Don't worry, Violet. I don't mean any harm. I only want to have a bit of fun at Eddie's expense.'

'Your following me isn't funny,' she protested. 'Not in Eddie's eyes, anyway.'

'What about in yours?' he insisted. Opposite the Institute there was the vicarage next to a pub called the Miners' Arms. Behind them, rising like a mechanical giant from slag heaps and other spoil from the recently disused colliery, a tall pit wheel still presided over village life. 'I always had you down as a girl who liked to have fun.'

'Stan!' Violet protested as he slid an arm around her waist and she side-stepped out of reach. 'I mean it, this isn't funny!'

'Steady on.' Stan came up against some iron railings and almost overbalanced. The loss of dignity changed his mood. 'You shouldn't have led me on the way you did,' he grumbled as he straightened his tie. 'Giving me the wrong idea.'

'I never led you on.' Violet turned back towards the Institute. 'We went to the flicks together, that's all.'

'Without you letting on that you were already walking out with Eddie.' Winding himself up into a seriously bad mood, Stan pursued her and stepped across her path to stop her from re-entering the building.

'That's because I wasn't at the time,' she insisted. Trying to push past him was a waste of effort, she decided, he was too tall and strong for that. 'Eddie didn't ask me out until *afterwards*.'

'Then you dropped me like a hot cake.' Unaware that a solitary figure was crossing the yard, Stan towered over Violet and continued to block her way.

'I'm sick of this, Stan.' Shaking with anger, she backed away, only to bump into the down-at-heel old man heading round the side of the building. 'Uncle Donald!' she cried, completely taken aback.

He frowned then cast a troubled glance from her to Stan and back again.

'It's me – Violet!' she said, having failed to elicit a response.

'You don't have to spell it out; I know who you are.'

Seeing him trudge on, Violet ran after him. 'What are you doing here?'

'What's it to you?'

'Uncle Donald, don't be like that. I'm surprised to see you, that's all. Is this where you're living now – out here in Hadley?'

He took a deep breath. 'The vicar gave me a job as caretaker,' he informed her grudgingly. 'I look after the church and the Institute – it comes with a house attached.'

'That's smashing. Isn't it, Stan?' She looked round for support, only to find that he'd disappeared inside. 'That means you have room for some of the things I took from Brewery Road – the clock and pictures, and such like. You know you only have to ask.'

'I thought I made it clear I didn't want any of it.'

Realizing that he was thinner and more miserable than last time she'd seen him – if that were possible – Violet became all too aware of his razor-sharp way of cutting her off, yet still she risked one more try.

'I found a wooden box with your brother's prayer book and other bits and pieces inside. Surely there's something there that you'd like.'

'What bits and pieces?' Donald spat out.

'Your marriage certificate. And a gold bracelet in a blue box.'

Suddenly Donald staggered as if he'd been punched in the stomach. His face was stricken and he had to lean against the wall for support. As Violet reached out to help him, he thrust her away. Then he pulled himself upright and began to walk away without looking back, through a narrow gate at the back of the Institute.

Violet watched him go, fear clutching at her heart. What had she said to provoke this reaction? What was it about a marriage certificate and a bracelet that had almost floored him?

Donald walked on, head down, clutching the lapels of his jacket and leaning forward as if against a strong wind when in fact there was not even a breeze. He was so thin it looked as if he might break in two.

Violet recalled the blue velvet box, and with trembling fingers she pulled out of her pocket the tiny note that she always kept with her. She slid it from its envelope and read it again: *To dearest Flo, as a token of my lifelong affection. Keep this bracelet for my sake.*

On the point of slipping it back into its envelope, she lifted the small flap and noticed something that she'd overlooked until now. The sender had drawn a heart pierced by an arrow on the inside of the flap and inside the heart he'd written two letters – an 'F' intertwined with a 'D'.

'D' not 'J'.

A chill ran through Violet as a new version of events rushed in. 'D' not 'J' – Donald, not Joe.

At the end of 1914, Florence Shaw and Donald Wheeler had been in love! In the autumn of the following year, she, Violet, had been born.

CHAPTER TWELVE

The last thing Violet planned to do was to share her shocking discovery with anyone – not even Eddie. Instead, her instinct was to bury it deep.

If Uncle Donald really is my father – and it's a big 'if' – he would deny it, she told herself during the days that followed. What then was the point of pursuing it further? So she did her best to put on a brave face and carry on as normal. Yet she didn't feel brave on the inside – rather she was weak and trembling, nursing afresh the hurt of being rejected and wondering whether or not Aunty Winnie had been in on the secret from the start.

When Violet wasn't weak, she was angry. Donald was a sanctimonious prig, hammering away at the difference between right and wrong, making Violet's small, innocent self feel disobedient and unworthy when all the time it was him who'd committed a much worse sin than she could ever have imagined. Though Violet tried to keep busy in the grocery shop, Donald's sour face with its sunken cheeks and clipped moustache intruded on her tasks and she couldn't help bitterly re-enacting the unending, petty chastisements of her childhood – *wash your hands*; *tidy your toys away*; *don't speak with your mouth full*.

'What's wrong, Violet? You don't seem yourself to-day,' Ida remarked at the end of the working week when their new lodger trailed in from the street.

A weary Violet had just come away from Hutchinson's and was trying to cheer herself up with the prospect of a ride out to the moors with Eddie next day. 'It's nothing that a good night's sleep won't put right,' she assured Ida and Muriel, who had appeared from the back kitchen. Something about their manner was different, she thought.

They stood together behind the counter, smiles playing across their features – Ida with her short hair combed back from her lively face, Muriel looking excited and younger than her thirty years for once.

'Shall you tell her or shall I?' Ida asked, as if keeping their secret might cause her to burst.

'Let me guess – you and Harold have set a date to get married?' Violet chipped in.

Ida gave a loud laugh. 'Not on your Nelly! We haven't saved up enough for a kitchen table yet, let alone chairs to sit on or a bed to lie in.'

Violet managed a smile. 'Then it must be that the two of you have decided to go full steam ahead with the Jubilee dressmaking business.'

The clever guess did nothing to dent the pair's excitement – Ida's, in particular. 'We thought it would be a nice surprise for you to end the week on – before you had a chance to read the advertisement we're putting in the *Herald* next week.'

A faint smile flickered across Violet's serious features. 'I knew something was afoot when Muriel started quizzing me about the latest fashions.'

'That's right, but what I didn't tell you was an idea that came to me last night when I was in the library.' Muriel took up the thread. 'I looked at adverts in the local paper and it struck me that a lot of people these days are happy to buy things on hire purchase, so I asked myself why not set up an arrangement for customers to do the same with our dresses? They could order a blouse or a dress, we would accept a down payment and make it for them straight away then they could pay us in instalments of threepence or sixpence a week over the next ten weeks.'

'It makes sense,' Ida insisted. 'Some girls I'm friendly with do the same thing when they want to have a permanent wave for their hair. They call it the never-never. The hairdresser on Canal Road charges them a week at a time. The girl gets her hair done and the hairdresser gets her money in dribs and drabs. Everyone's happy.'

Violet quickly agreed. 'I don't need convincing. I think it's the right thing to do.'

'*And* . . .' Ida's sense of drama made her pause and hold her breath.

'What?' Violet wondered. Muriel and Ida's excitement was contagious and she let it bubble up through her recent worries.

'*If* we can get this off the ground . . .' Muriel began.

'There's no ifs about it,' Ida declared then concluded without more ado. 'So, Violet, what we're building up to saying is that we'd like you to come in with us.'

Violet's eyes lit up. 'You mean you'd want me to leave Hutchinson's and work for you full time?'

'That's exactly what we mean,' Muriel assured her. 'Not just mending and putting in zips, but helping us with the cutting out and sewing.'

'You wouldn't have far to go to work,' Ida pointed out. 'Just step out of your room and up one flight of stairs to the attic.'

'And we'd be able to pay you a fair wage, once we get properly started.' Muriel joined Ida in looking eagerly across the counter at Violet to judge her reaction. 'What do you say?'

'I say yes!' Violet declared without a second's hesitation and in a rush of pure delight. 'Yes, please – I'd love to. If you must know, it's a dream come true!'

'Goodbye to groceries!' Eddie declared when Violet shared her good news with him on a ride out to Little Brimstone.

It was a warm, cloudy Sunday with the threat of showers but this didn't deter the romantic pair from going out on the Norton as planned – Violet in bottle-green corduroy trousers and a cream pullover, Eddie in sports jacket and his favourite 'ratting cap' – a flat, checked cap that matched his jacket. They whizzed out of town and up onto the moors, Violet holding on tight as Eddie eased open the throttle and they soared up hill and down dale.

'Farewell, self-raising flour!' Violet laughed at having to raise her voice above the roar of the engine. 'Ta-ta, Ringtons tea!'

'What will old man Hutchinson say?'

'Not much, I shouldn't think. He'll soon find another slave to weigh out his sugar and slice his ham.' She had no regrets on that score, and no sentimental loyalty towards the old curmudgeon.

Eddie slowed down and leaned the bike into a sharp bend then he stuck out his right hand to indicate that he was pulling across the road to enter the small lay-by. From here there was a sign directing visitors towards the footpath that led to the local beauty spot famed for its spectacular outcrops of odd-shaped, weather-worn boulders. Eddie parked the bike and they set off on foot, feeling the first spots of cool rain on their faces.

'I know – we'll call in at the café for toasted tea-cakes.' Violet hit upon a plan for them to stay dry. 'It's along here a little way. I used to come here with Aunty Winnie.'

They pressed on in single file down a narrow path bordered by wet ferns towards the largest of the rocks and a flat, grassy area where there was a hut selling refreshments, with a view of the valley below.

'I can picture her face now.' Violet sighed. 'She used to tell me the tale of how a giant called Brimstone carried these rocks in his leather apron. He scattered them across the hillside while he was running away from his scolding wife and they've lain here ever since.'

'You've done your aunty proud.' Feeling a rush of warm affection, Eddie stopped to take Violet's hand as they came out into the clearing where the café stood.

'Yes. She'd have been pleased with my latest news,' Violet agreed. She grimaced then laughed as he leaned forward to kiss her and drips from the peak of his cap splashed onto her face.

Inside they ordered tea and teacakes from Kitty, an ancient lady who had served refreshments there since the year dot. 'Or at least ever since I've been coming here,' Violet pointed out. Kitty invariably wore a dark brown dress with leg-of-mutton sleeves and a high, cream lace collar and her hair was pinned up in a style that hadn't been in fashion for thirty or forty years. She showed no more interest in her customers than if they had been flies buzzing and crawling across the window pane.

'Ta very much,' Eddie said with exaggerated politeness as he carried two teas to a table by the window. It seemed they were the only customers Kitty was likely to have until the rain eased. 'Just so you know –

167

you're not the only one with prospects,' he told Violet as he sat down opposite. 'It seems I'm getting on well at the Victory, according to my boss, Mr Ambler.'

'You mean you've managed to play the reels in the right order so far?' Violet enjoyed teasing Eddie, just to see him colour up. 'You haven't shown the ending before the beginning?'

'All in the right order at the right time, with a fifteen-minute interval for ice creams and pop.' He winked then took a loud sip of his tea. 'We're not doing too badly, you and I. Not when you think I have to show the Pathé News before the feature film and on it I see hundreds of poor blokes joining hunger marches and standing in dole queues that stretch further than you can see. Then there are little kiddies picking over the slag heaps looking for handfuls of coal to keep their families warm of a night and women having to pawn their wedding rings. Between you and me, it makes me wonder what the world is coming to.'

'I know. We're well off compared to some.' Their conversation turned serious, and it was a chance for Violet to see where Eddie's sympathies lay.

'I back the unions against Ramsay MacDonald every day of the week, even though he calls himself a Labour man,' he confided. 'I say a working man deserves a decent wage for his blood, sweat and tears, whatever the bosses tell us about gaps in their order books and the cost of keeping machinery running. And without a union, look what happens: my dad scrapes by with his painting and decorating but he has no one to back him up if customers don't stump up the money on time.'

'I don't know what the answer is – it's beyond me,' Violet confessed. 'All I know is, I'm glad to move on from Hutchinson's into something I'm bound to enjoy.'

'And you'll be good at it, too.' Eddie felt it was time to lighten the mood. 'Watch out for Ida, though, she can be a right little tyrant.'

'Don't worry – I'll join a shop workers' union if there is one, and they'll back me up. I'll go to the library with Muriel and learn my rights!'

'That's the ticket,' he said with a grin. 'Now where's that teacake? Do I have to go behind the counter and toast it myself?'

Since the discovery of the heart inside the flap of the tiny envelope, Violet had stopped carrying the note with her and stored it back in its blue case in the writing box under her bed. Out of sight, out of mind, had been the intention behind this as she'd hastily tucked it away.

On the last Monday in July, she handed in her notice at the grocer's shop and offered to work out the week until Ben Hutchinson found someone new. On the Tuesday, however, she arrived to find Lizzie Turner already behind the counter with her red hair pinned back and a new, outsized blue apron wrapped around her slim waist.

'Now, Missy, you can be on your way and good riddance,' Ben Hutchinson told Violet.

Lizzie looked embarrassed until Violet gave her a reassuring wink. 'You're sure you don't want me to show Lizzie the ropes?' she asked.

'I'm obliged to you, but I can do that myself.' Without a word of farewell Hutchinson shuffled off into his lair – the stockroom stacked with cardboard boxes, barrels and sacks – and Violet stopped only long enough to wish Lizzie good luck.

'Stick up for yourself when he's in a bad mood,' she recommended quietly. 'And don't let him push you around.'

Lizzie squared her shoulders and tried not to sound as apprehensive as she felt. 'Rightio.'

'And remember, his bark is worse than his bite,' was Violet's parting shot.

Hutchinson's was in the past and Jubilee was Violet's future. She launched with gusto into the sultry days of August – opening up the attic window to let in some fresh air while she worked at her sewing machine alongside Ida or Muriel, the small workroom humming to the sounds of wheels turning to drive needles through fabric and of treadles rhythmically rocking back and forth. Down below, the shop bell tinkled as customers came in and out.

'Ida has asked for two shop mannequins to be delivered before we close today,' Muriel informed Violet during one of their spells working together to finish an order for a summer dress for Alice Barlow.

'One will go in the window to show off our work. The other will stand in the corner next to the rack of zips. Ida thinks there's room for it to fit in there.'

'We can dress them up in the latest fashions so customers will want to buy what we make,' Violet said, her heart lifting at the prospect.

'You know we're relying on you for that part.' Muriel snipped and carefully trimmed a shoulder seam.

Bending over her machine, Violet worked her treadle and steered the cornflower-blue fabric under the rapidly jabbing needle. 'I think we should make a house dress for the mannequin in the window.'

'I like the sound of that,' Muriel agreed. 'You choose the pattern and the material then Ida and I will help you make it.'

Downstairs the doorbell sounded then Ida came to the foot of the stairs. 'Violet, will you come down and lend a hand with this delivery?' she called up to the attic. 'The mannequins have arrived.'

Violet sped eagerly downstairs to find Ida un-wrapping two life-sized, plaster-of-Paris models with the longest necks and legs imaginable and, packed separately, two heads with beautiful, snub-nosed, blank faces painted in the style of Greta Garbo, all arched eyebrows and pouting lips.

'We'll stash them away in the kitchen until we're ready to dress them.' Ida, too, was excited as she took hold of a headless torso and carried it out of sight.

Violet followed her with the second mannequin, describing to Ida a style of dress she had in mind for the window. 'Sleeveless, with a V neckline, tailored at the waist and with a wrap-over skirt ending mid-calf.'

'Something slinky, that moves when you walk?' Ida asked.

'Yes, but not shiny – that would be for the evening, not for daytime. A lightweight jersey knit would be more like it, in orange and yellow or pink and green – something summery.'

The lively discussion was cut short by the sound of the shop bell. 'Could you see to that for me?' Ida asked, busy fixing heads to torsos.

Violet rushed into the shop to find Alice Barlow tapping her fingers impatiently on the counter-top, accompanied by a woman of roughly the same age dressed in a lilac costume with a scalloped neckline and elaborately pin-tucked bodice. Both women wore straw cloche hats that Violet privately thought looked rather outdated.

'Good afternoon, Mrs Barlow, how can I help you?' Violet asked, nervous in case she was obliged to tell this short-tempered customer that her dress wasn't ready.

But it turned out that Alice Barlow had a different objective. 'This is my friend, Mrs Ella Kingsley, in case you didn't know.'

A second quick glance told Violet that this was true. She recognized the mill owner's wife, though she'd never seen her at close quarters before. Taller than her companion, with a slimmer figure, she had chin-length dark hair styled into regimented waves beneath the cloche hat and a manner that seemed quieter and less overbearing than Alice Barlow's. 'How can I help?' Violet asked again.

'Mrs Kingsley is looking for a new dressmaker,' Alice explained. 'She's grown dissatisfied with the standard of service provided by Sybil Dacre higher up the street. I mentioned Jubilee because I know you will offer reasonable rates.'

Violet smiled and nodded, trying not to let her objection to Alice Barlow's hoity-toity manner show, though there was definitely something about the woman's voice, with its over-careful pronunciation and nasal twang that set her teeth on edge. 'We do our best to work satisfactorily,' she assured Ella Kingsley.

'That's good to hear.' The mill owner's wife studied Violet for a while, as if trying to solve a puzzle. 'I know – you were the Whitsuntide Gala Queen!' she said at last. 'And very pretty you were, too.'

Violet dipped her head and smiled modestly, thinking it was time to bring in Ida from the kitchen. 'Would you like me to fetch Miss Thomson?' she offered. 'She can tell you about our prices, and so on.'

'No need – I'm here.' Ida announced her appearance, allowing Violet the opportunity to slope off to the workroom. 'It was decent of you to recommend

173

us, Mrs Barlow. We're much obliged. Now, Mrs Kingsley, what exactly did you have in mind?'

'Flattery is the key,' Muriel informed Violet as they sewed in the attic, putting the finishing touches to the dress for the window mannequin, whom Violet had dubbed Maud. It was two days after the visit from Alice Barlow and Ella Kingsley, which had resulted in a firm order for an autumn tweed jacket and matching skirt from the mill owner's wife.

'That's right. We have to make them feel special,' Ida agreed. 'And whatever they say and do, you have to remember that the customer is always right.'

Violet was as eager as ever to take advice from her new employers. 'Even when they're not?' she queried.

'*Especially* when they're not,' Muriel insisted. 'The trick is to listen then steer them gently to what you know will work – a slightly longer skirt if the customer's legs are nothing to write home about, a couple of extra darts inserted into the bodice to flatter the – ahem – shall we say, fuller figure?'

'And then, of course, a dress-shop girl needs the patience of a saint,' Ida reminded Violet as they dressed 'Maud' and got her ready for display later that day. Muriel had gone out to the bank to start an account that would take weekly payments from customers who chose to buy garments on the never-never. 'Remember – yes, madam; no madam; three bags full, madam – that's the road we have to go down, come what may.'

174

Violet helped draw the mannequin's dress down over its head then pull it straight.

'Patience may not be my strong point,' Ida admitted, turning down the corners of her mouth and warning Violet not to comment.

Violet giggled and did up the zip on the dress. Together they lifted Maud into the window and out of the corner of her eye she caught sight of a slight figure running down the street. She frowned as Evie stopped outside and gestured to her. 'I won't be a sec,' she told Ida, stepping down from the window and out into the street. 'What is it?' she whispered.

'Sybil's read the Jubilee advertisement in the *Herald*. She's on the war path,' Evie blurted out, only stopping to glance anxiously up the street before hurrying on out of sight.

Violet went back inside, but before she had time to warn Ida what was afoot, a stern-faced Sybil appeared.

'What's this I read?' the newcomer demanded, brandishing a copy of the local newspaper as she thrust open the door.

Violet needn't have worried – Ida was ready for her. 'I take it that you mean our advertisement?' she asked coyly as she stepped out of the window.

'Come off it, Ida. You know very well that's what I mean.' Face to face with her adversary, Sybil Dacre was an imposing figure. She was equally tall for a start, with a natural dignity and she seemed fired up for a confrontation. 'What do you mean by setting

175

up in competition with us – and behind our backs, too?'

Ida wasn't intimidated, however. 'Oh, so you're the only ones who can work as costumiers round here – is that what you're saying?'

'I'm not saying that.' Sybil drew herself up to full height, her face flushed and locks of auburn hair escaping from a neatly pinned French pleat. 'But if I were in your place, I'd at least have had the decency to mention it before I put the announcement in the paper. And you know very well that two dressmakers on the same street can't be good for business – not for either of us.'

'Ah, you see – that's where you're wrong,' Ida argued. 'Muriel and I reckon we're going after a different type of customer – girls with less money to spend, not your average factory or shop owner's wife, which is who you deal with.'

'And that's why Mrs Kingsley has come to you, is it?' Sybil asked with scarcely suppressed anger. 'There's no point denying it – Alice Barlow enjoyed telling me all about it when I ran into her earlier in the week.'

Ida struggled to find an answer to this. 'You're probably well rid of Ella Kingsley, if Alice Barlow is anything to go by,' she advised Sybil.

'Come on – you can do better than that. We both know that any customer is better than no customer, however demanding they may be.'

'Not if they don't pay their bills on time, it isn't,'

Ida said, expecting Sybil to read between the lines.

It was the first either Violet or Sybil had heard about Alice Barlow's tardiness over payment and it took them aback.

'You don't say,' Sybil murmured, while Violet's opinion of the difficult-to-please customer dropped even lower. 'In any case, if I find out that you're setting out to steal custom away from us, you'll have me to answer to,' Sybil warned.

'Look, Sybil,' Ida spoke more quietly than before, 'I'm being honest with you when I say that isn't our plan. Jubilee will keep on with the drapery business as usual. As for the dressmaking part, we'll concentrate on customers like Violet here – young girls who will scrape by on bread and jam to save up their pennies in order to splash out on a summer dress every now and then. That will still leave room for you to attract the well-heeled customer.'

Sybil listened then sighed. 'It's taken us three years to get where we are,' she confided. 'And it's not been straightforward – not with Annie and Lily both leaving to get married and have their babies. Evie and I have had to work our socks off, I can tell you.'

'Likewise,' Ida told her. 'There's not much money to be made from selling small items of drapery – not any more. The world's changing and that's why we're branching out from knicker elastic and hooks and eyes into dressmaking.'

Watching from the sidelines, Violet judged that

the two women were evenly matched and she could see it from both points of view. She was glad that Sybil's frayed temper seemed to be subsiding.

'I came out of a steady job at Calvert's not knowing if I could make a go of sewing for a living,' Sybil went on. 'But I love the work and I'm good at what I do. And sure enough, we've built up a reputation for being quick and reliable – enough to buck the trend for women going into the town centre and buying their clothes off the peg from the big department stores, at least for the time being.'

'Quick, reliable and *costly*,' Ida reminded her. 'That's not a criticism – it's the truth. You do excellent work for those who can pay higher prices and in a funny way your customers don't mind paying the premium. They enjoy boasting to their friends that they go to Sybil Dacre on Chapel Street for the very reason that you're expensive.'

'Still,' Sybil sighed as she grudgingly accepted Ida's argument, 'there was no need to go behind my back.'

'I agree and I'm sorry,' Ida conceded. 'Muriel and I have been so busy making our plans that we didn't stop to think.'

Ida apologizing was something Violet hadn't expected and she looked from one to the other with growing relief.

'Apology accepted,' Sybil said, rolling up her newspaper and tucking it under her arm.

'And do you agree that there might be room for

both of us on the street after all?' Ida asked tentatively.

Sybil looked her in the eye for a long time before she nodded and made her final pronouncement as she departed. 'May the best man win,' she said.

'*Woman*.' Ida followed Sybil out onto the street and offered to shake her hand while Violet stayed inside to watch the rivals make up. 'All's fair in love and shop work, so may the best *woman* win!'

CHAPTER THIRTEEN

At the end of the rehearsal the following night Violet made a big point of waiting for Eddie to clear away his paints and clean his brushes while others went on their way.

'Ta-ta, Stan,' she said with a cheery wave. 'Goodbye, Evie. Don't do anything I wouldn't do.'

She and Eddie were the last to leave and it was poor timing on their part that they happened to bump into, of all people, Donald Wheeler, ready with his big bunch of keys to lock up the building for the night. Violet's heart skipped a beat and she took a step backwards.

He too seemed dismayed. 'A change is as good as a rest, eh?' he said with heavy innuendo and a curl of his lip, together with a nod in Eddie's direction as Violet squeezed by.

'Now, Donald, that's not very nice, especially since Violet has done nothing to warrant it.' Eddie jumped to her defence. 'I won't have you upsetting her like that.'

'It's all right, Eddie. Take no notice.' Intent on hurrying off, Violet didn't look back.

But Eddie stood his ground and glared at her uncle. 'No, it's not all right. The way you've treated Violet since Winnie died isn't fair. In fact, your rotten behaviour is the talk of Chapel Street.'

'Is it now?' Donald sneered.

'Yes. And what's the reason behind it? That's what we'd all like to know.'

'What goes on between me and Violet is our business, nobody else's,' Donald muttered, thrusting Eddie to one side and inserting the key into the lock. 'And if, as you say, you don't want me upsetting her, I'd warn her to steer clear of Hadley in future if I was you.'

The push incensed Eddie, who grabbed the older man by the back of his collar and spun him round.

'Don't, it's not worth it,' Violet pleaded from a distance of ten yards. She saw how grey and ill her uncle looked and had an overwhelming desire to put as big a distance as possible between them. 'Come on, Eddie – please!'

'Count yourself lucky,' Eddie said as he let Donald go. He leaned in and spoke in an angry whisper that he hoped Violet couldn't overhear. 'You're a bully, Donald Wheeler. If it was left to me, I'd stay and teach you a lesson you wouldn't forget.'

Violet's uncle squared up as if for a fight. 'You and whose army?'

The schoolboy bravado made Eddie laugh then

181

he shook his head. 'Violet's right. It's not worth it.' He unlocked his gaze from Donald's and backed off, striding to join Violet. Then he kick-started his bike and waited for her to climb on behind him. They rode out of the yard and onto the main street, leaving Donald Wheeler to secure the building and return to his lonely lodgings.

Violet was still upset when they arrived at Chapel Street so Eddie went into Jubilee with her, through to the back kitchen where he sat her down at the table and made them both a cup of tea.

'No sugar, ta,' she said when she saw him dip the spoon into the bowl.

'One won't hurt,' he argued as he went ahead. 'You turned white as a sheet back there. I was worried about you.'

'I'm all right,' she insisted, though she couldn't stop her hand from shaking as she raised the cup.

'You don't look it.' Deciding to stay where he was until he was sure she was better, Eddie settled into a seat across the table. 'Come on, why don't you tell me what's wrong? It'll do you good to get it off your chest.'

Everything's wrong, she wanted to say. But her hidden suspicion about her mother and Uncle Donald was still too shocking for her to share.

Eddie reached across the table to clasp her hand, which reminded him of a trembling baby bird discovered in its nest. 'This is about your mother's bracelet, isn't it?'

182

She gasped and tried to jerk her hand free. 'Please, Eddie. I don't want to talk about it.'

'I knew it,' he persisted. 'I saw how much it meant to you when you found it in its box and yet you haven't said a word about it since. There's got to be a reason for that.'

The initials inside the heart had wormed their way into every twist and turn of her brain. She woke up thinking about it and went through each day bowed by the suspicion that her uncle was, in fact, her father and that her whole life thus far had been based on a lie.

'There is a reason.' Hurriedly she took her hand away and rushed from the room. 'Wait here,' she pleaded, taking the stairs two at a time and returning with the blue box. 'I haven't mentioned it but it's been preying on my mind and now I think it's time to show you this.' She gave Eddie the box.

'Do you want me to open it?' he asked.

Violet nodded. 'Don't look at the bracelet, look at the note.'

'"To dearest Flo . . ."' he read with a puzzled frown. 'Do you mean the fact that there's no signature?'

'Yes – that set me off thinking. Then, later, when I happened to mention the bracelet to Uncle Donald, he stormed off.'

'That's par for the course these days, isn't it?'

'Yes, but it upset me and made me take another

look.' Violet leaned over Eddie's shoulder to open the flap of the envelope and point to the initials inside the heart.

Eddie pursed his lips. 'F and D,' he said gently. 'Christmas 1914.'

'I'll be nineteen in September.' Violet's voice was scarcely audible as she shared with Eddie her deepest fears.

'The D here stands for your Uncle Donald – is that what you think?'

'Yes.' The secret was out and there was no getting away from the shameful fact that her mother had betrayed her husband while he was away at war. She had slept with her husband's brother. The bracelet and the heart were proof.

'We can't be sure,' Eddie cautioned. He saw how much Violet suffered and wanted to wipe away the tears.

'No,' she sobbed. 'Let's not kid ourselves, Eddie. I know in my heart it's true.'

Eddie came round the table and raised Violet to her feet. He held her so close she felt his strong heartbeat and the warmth of him, breathed him in and clung to him to stop herself from falling down a deep hole into despair, into a dark, empty pit that had no bottom.

'It doesn't make any difference now,' he murmured. 'It's all in the past.'

Safe in his arms, Violet's resistance broke down and she started to sob in earnest. 'But it still matters.

Don't you see? I'm not who I thought I was. I'm a different girl.'

'Why do you say that?'

'I've discovered a past that I'm ashamed of. I can't even bear to think about it. And – what do I call him now, "Uncle" Donald? – he can't even look me in the eye. You saw what he was like.'

'Because he's in the wrong and he knows it.' All Eddie wanted was to console Violet and hold her until she stopped crying. He stroked her hair and planted soft kisses on the top of her head.

'It makes a difference, though, doesn't it?' Violet raised her tear-stained face to read the answer in his expression.

'Not to me, it doesn't,' he whispered, looking deep into her pleading eyes. 'Whatever's gone on in the past, you're still the girl for me.'

Once more Violet rode the rough seas of her feelings about her origins – up and down the giant breaking waves of regret, shame and disappointment. Somehow, though, it seemed easier with Eddie's help to banish the hurt and carry on ignoring the note hidden inside the velvet case, tucked away in the box under her bed.

Then there was work that she loved to raise her spirits – pinning and cutting material that smelled of fresh cotton and starch, using scissors to shear through layers of crisp fabric, placing raw edges together then pinning, tacking, gathering and sewing until a finished garment emerged.

In general, as the days went by, Violet found that she preferred being in the attic workshop to serving in the increasingly busy shop, but she dutifully took her turn downstairs, remembering to stick to the two main commandments of shop work – thou shalt not lose thy temper and thou shalt smile and flatter at all times.

'We need a new outfit for Gertie,' Ida decided on the Friday afternoon of their first week in business, standing behind the counter with Violet as they got ready to close for the day. 'Gertie' was companion to Maud whose blank gaze dominated the window of the recently re-titled 'Jubilee Drapers and Dressmakers'. 'She needs to be wearing something that will really brighten the place up.'

'We could make a wedding dress for her,' Violet suggested almost immediately. 'White silk with a dropped waist and a scalloped hem, decorated with tiny artificial pearls.'

'We could change them round and put Gertie in the window. We'd make quite a splash with that,' Ida agreed and straight away they went to the pattern books and were so taken up by the plan that they ignored the tinkle of the shop bell and instead kept their heads buried in their fashion bible.

'Shop!' Colin Barlow's loud voice and the rap of his silver-tipped cane against the counter startled them. He brought with him the stale smell of tobacco smoke, which overwhelmed the cologne that he must have applied after shaving first thing that morning. He wore a panama hat, a linen blazer over a pale blue shirt and striped silk tie – as usual, quite the dapper man about town.

'Good afternoon, ladies. I take it you're still open for business?'

Violet jumped to attention. 'Certainly, Mr Barlow. How can I help?'

'My wife asked me to call in on my way home. What was it for now? Let me think.' Running a gloved hand along the counter until he reached the stand that displayed sheer silk stockings, he cast a salacious eye over Violet, from her stylishly bobbed hair, down her wary face, on to her long, slender neck and down again to the flowered, flimsy crêpe de Chine blouse which she'd chosen for its lightness and coolness on this hot August day. 'What did Mrs Barlow require from Jubilee, I wonder?'

'Perhaps she wanted to know how we were getting on with her latest garments,' Violet suggested, refraining out of shyness from giving an exact description of Alice Barlow's recent order for pink silk lingerie consisting of petticoat and camiknickers edged with Belgian lace.

'Ah yes, that was it – her under-things!' Colin Barlow smiled to see the blush that crept up Violet's neck and over her cheeks. 'She'd like to know – are they finished?'

Violet clung to the second commandment – thou shalt smile. She swallowed hard and tried to ignore her customer's wandering eye. 'I'm not sure, sir. Shall I go upstairs and see?'

'No need,' Ida interrupted. 'It so happens that I spoke to Muriel half an hour ago. She thought we'd have the work finished by Monday, as promised.'

'Alice will be disappointed – and so will I.' Appearing disgruntled, but with a smile hovering on his lips, Colin Barlow seemed in no hurry to leave. 'Perhaps I should buy her some stockings to make up for it.'

'Shall I go upstairs and check again?' Violet asked Ida, by this time so embarrassed by the blatant way that Colin Barlow was undressing her with his eyes that she felt her palms begin to sweat. She rushed up to the attic without waiting for an answer, only to find that the earliest, revised deadline Muriel could meet for Alice Barlow's under-things was in two hours' time.

Violet went back downstairs and reported accordingly. 'Miss Beanland says she will do her best to finish the work and get the garments delivered to you at Bilton Grange later this evening.'

'Will she now?' Everything about Violet – her words, her appearance, and especially her embarrassment – seemed to amuse the chemist-shop owner. 'That's very good of her. And who will deliver it? Will it be the good-looking young man on the motorbike as before?'

Ida looked up from her pattern book. 'No, I'm afraid Eddie's working at the picture house this evening.'

A frown appeared on Colin Barlow's brow, but Violet could tell that it was for theatrical effect. He pretended to be at a loss. 'Oh, dearie me.'

'I'm holding an extra rehearsal for my principal players in Hadley tonight and Muriel will have to go to her St John Ambulance meeting once she's finished here,' Ida went on. 'But, Violet, you could borrow my bike and cycle out there with Mrs Barlow's order.'

Violet's heart sank at the same time as a fresh smirk appeared on Colin Barlow's face. 'Are you sure it would be all right for you to cycle all the way out to my house with the parcel for my wife?'

Sweating in earnest now, Violet knew she had to agree. 'Of course, it would be no trouble at all.'

'Smashing!' came the quick rejoinder followed by an equally rapid exit. 'Now that, ladies – and I speak from the point of view of one who recognizes a well-run shop when I see one – is what I call excellent customer service!'

'I could have done without this,' Violet grumbled to Dick Thomson after she'd caught the bus up to Valley Road and knocked on the door of number 20 to borrow Ida's bike, propped in its usual place against the front of the house. She deposited Alice Barlow's carefully wrapped petticoat and camiknickers in the wicker basket attached to the handlebars while Dick sat in his overalls on the doorstep and smoked his pipe.

'What's the rush?' he asked.

'Don't ask me. But when the Barlows say jump, we jump – that's all I know.'

Violet would have stopped for a longer conversation with Eddie's dad, who seemed to her more approachable than Eddie's mum. Though at fifty-four he was worn down by the years of hand-to-mouth existence that had followed on from the war, he usually managed a smile and a joke and Violet enjoyed the similarities between father and son – they had the same loose-limbed, easy gait, for instance, and the same thick hair, though Dick's was now grey and dull whereas Eddie's was a glossy dark brown.

'I'd better get a move on,' she told him as he turned the bowl of his pipe and tapped it against the step. 'Say hello to Eddie from me when he gets home from work. Tell him I hope to catch him later.'

'Rightio,' Dick promised, watching her manoeuvre the pushbike out onto the road. 'And mind you take care on that moor road. The dynamo is broken so you'll have no lights once it gets dark.'

'I will,' Violet promised. 'I want to get this over and done with long before dusk, believe me.'

CHAPTER FOURTEEN

The approach to the Barlows' showy, modern house was down a wide gravel drive flanked by horse chestnut trees that had been there much longer than the house they sheltered. Violet was hot and out of breath from the long ride and the tyres of Ida's bike spat up pebbles as she cycled down the drive. She stopped outside the front entrance, took Alice Barlow's parcel from the basket and hurried to push the doorbell. Hearing the melodious chime, she waited for what felt like an age.

Eventually there were footsteps crossing a tiled hallway and the door was opened by Colin Barlow in black trousers, shirtsleeves and braces. Resting one hand against the door jamb, he surveyed Violet's windswept appearance.

Violet filled the silence by thrusting the package at him without ceremony. 'This is for Mrs Barlow, as promised.'

'It's certainly not for me,' he agreed in his usual mocking tone. 'Not unless I've taken to wearing ladies' under-garments on the sly. And I'm not that sort of chap, believe me.'

Violet's eyes flashed wide in distaste. 'The bill for the work is inside the parcel,' she went on. 'Miss Beanland said it would be all right for Mrs Barlow to call into the shop with the money whenever it's convenient.'

'It's not Alice who's paying and it's convenient for me to pay now,' Barlow insisted as he methodically untied the string and unwrapped the petticoat and camiknickers. He took out the envelope containing the bill. 'So this is what it costs me to keep my wife in nice new under-things,' he mused, deliberately taking his time in order to better enjoy Violet's discomfort. 'Two shillings and sixpence, including materials.'

'It's Belgian lace, the best we can lay our hands on.' Violet tried to account for the expense. 'And the work is fiddly, so it takes time.'

Colin Barlow felt in his trouser pockets. 'Well, it turns out I don't have the money on me. That means I'll have to call in at the shop to pay my dues.'

'Any time you happen to be passing,' she said, glad to be let off the hook for now and eager to beat a retreat.

But before she had a chance to escape, Alice Barlow swanned down the wide stairs and across the hall, dressed for dinner in a sleeveless, silvery gown with a slim belt and a corsage made up of a crimson silk rose and dainty sprays of lily of the valley. 'My petticoat!' she exclaimed crossly when she saw it draped over her husband's arm. 'Really, Colin, was it necessary to unwrap it on the spot? Your hands are so rough – they'll snag the silk.'

He shrugged carelessly as his wife snatched the flimsy garments from him. Then he winked at Violet. 'See – that's all the thanks I get.'

Violet repeated Muriel's message about payment to Alice Barlow then fled. She was back on the bike, high on the moor road, with dusk quickly drawing in, when a car came up behind, its headlights raking across the mounds of heather, its engine roaring. Cresting the hill, Violet kept close to the grass verge as the Barlows' Daimler cruised by with Alf Shipley at the wheel. She wobbled in its slipstream, aware that Mrs Barlow had stared studiously ahead as they passed, while Mr Barlow had wound down his window and called out a remark that she hadn't caught.

Good riddance to bad rubbish, she thought as the car sped away. *I hope they have a rotten evening, wherever they're headed.*

Violet returned Ida's bike to Valley Road and was pleased to run into Eddie, who had just got home from work. He was in high spirits, telling her all about a swashbuckling film from the old, silent days with Douglas Fairbanks he'd been showing at the Victory.

'There's always a rope handy for our hero to swing from in an emergency,' he said wryly. 'And there's never a hair out of place when he finishes off the enemy with his trusty cutlass.'

'Lord knows who does his laundry,' Violet agreed.

They sat in the Thomsons' untidy kitchen, with Emily doing some crochet by the unlit fire and Dick scraping out his pipe at the table. A ginger cat sat on the window sill, licking his paws to clean his ears.

'That cat – he's been fishing for tiddlers in the quarry pond again,' Dick remarked when Violet went to stroke him. 'It's thirty feet deep. One of these days he's going to lose his footing and fall in. Splash! That'll be the last of his nine lives used up.'

Violet picked up the cat and cuddled him. She liked the higgledy-piggledy nature of the Thomson household – Ida's theatre books piled on the window sill next to the cat, dishes left to dry on the draining board, the threadbare hearth rug and some oily nuts and bolts from Eddie's bike resting on newspaper on a shelf meant for crockery. 'What's his name?' she asked, resting her cheek against the tom's soft fur.

'Crackers,' Emily said, crochet hook poised over her work.

Violet laughed. 'Why's that?'

'Because that's what he is – crackers.' Eddie slid his arm around Violet's waist and walked her out into the front yard. 'Barmy, like the rest of us in this house. Take me for a start – I'm crackers about you, Violet Wheeler!'

The cat wriggled and escaped as Eddie moved in for a kiss. Violet surrendered willingly, putting her arms around Eddie's neck and tilting her head back to let him press his lips against hers then take small nibbling bites down the side of her neck. 'That tickles,' she said with a low laugh.

'I'll stop if you want me to.' His breath was warm on her skin.

Violet shook her head and felt his lips on hers again. She heard a noise in the doorway and opened her eyes to see Eddie's dad knocking his empty pipe against the jamb.

'Time to take the young lady back home,' Dick told his son in a gruff voice. 'At this rate you'll have the neighbours tittle-tattling.'

Eddie cleared his throat and stepped away. 'Rightio, Father.'

'The sooner the better,' Dick commented, disappearing back inside.

'You should have seen your face when your dad came out,' Violet teased once she and Eddie were on the motorbike and threading through the cobbled streets, past shops and schools, churches, chapels and row after row of identical houses running downhill towards Chapel Street. She had her arms around his waist as usual and her cheek pressed to the rough tweed jacket he wore to keep out the wind. 'And the second you heard his voice, you dropped me like a hot potato.'

Eddie chuckled and patted her hand. 'Good job Dad came out when he did. Otherwise I might've got carried away.'

When he dropped her off at Jubilee, he planted an almost chaste kiss on her cheek before saying a quick goodbye. Violet waved him off and went inside, up to her clean, orderly bedroom with its smell of fresh paint and the scent of lavender from the linen sachet she kept under her pillow.

Lavender was supposed to calm you down and help you sleep, but tonight it wasn't working as Violet changed into her nightdress and slipped into bed. Her heart was beating too fast at the memory of Eddie's kisses and she could still feel the touch of his lips.

Maybe Uncle Donald is right, she reflected uncomfortably as she lay wide awake, reliving the thrill of her time with Eddie and conjuring up the picture of what he meant by getting carried away. *Maybe I am a bad girl after all*.

She slept at last and was up with the lark, in the workshop before either Ida or Muriel arrived. The day went by in a flurry of cutting and stitching, trotting down to the shop to serve a customer whenever the bell rang, boiling a kettle for their tea breaks and spending her dinner time with Evie when they ran into each other in Sykes' bakery.

'Fancy a stroll up to the Common?' Evie suggested as they emerged from the shop with a warm sausage-roll apiece. 'We could sit on a bench and eat these.'

Violet was glad of the company and happier still when they encountered Eddie, Stan and the rest of

196

the Canal Road Rovers putting up the goalposts and preparing for the afternoon's local derby against the Hadley Town eleven.

Eddie said he was too busy to stop and sit with them, worse luck, though Stan was his usual cocky self, strutting up to the girls to steal a bite of sausage-roll and finding time to arrange a meeting with Evie at the Assembly Rooms later that evening. 'I've given up on Violet,' he admitted with a comical wink.

'But I'll do instead?' Evie laughed at his bare-faced cheek and told him she might see him there if he was lucky.

The girls left soon after, with Violet blowing a kiss at Eddie, saying goodbye to Evie at the top of the street then walking down to Jubilee to discover with a sinking heart that the Barlows' limousine was parked outside the shop, although the 'Closed for Lunch' sign was clearly on display.

Colin Barlow opened the car door and stepped out in front of her, blocking her way. 'Fresh as a daisy as usual,' he commented, a lightweight over-coat slung around his shoulders and his panama hat set at a rakish angle. He nodded towards the sign on the door. 'You're an obliging girl. I'm sure you'll open up for me.'

'Of course, Mr Barlow. Come in, please,' Violet squeezed past and drew out the key to unlock the door. She quickly took refuge behind the counter, lifted a slip of paper off a spike and adopted her best shop-girl manner. 'We were expecting you to drop by so I have a receipt here ready for you.'

'I'm sorry, I don't have any change.' Colin Barlow handed her a ten-shilling note, not sounding sorry at all.

Violet took the money and opened the till. Then she counted the change into his outstretched hand.

Barlow closed his fingers over hers and squeezed – an action so quick and smooth that it left her flustered and confused. 'I happen to have a little something in my pocket that I thought you might like,' he said with a tilt of his head and a knowing smile.

Alarm flashed through Violet, making her step backwards against the shelf piled high with boxes of buttons. Suddenly the shop felt too small for comfort.

'All girls like scent, don't they?' Barlow drew a miniature bottle from his pocket and put it on the counter. It had a gold and turquoise label which read, *No. 4711 Eau de Cologne*.

'Oh no, Mr Barlow, I couldn't!' Violet gasped.

'Don't be silly – of course you could. I keep it in stock in all of my shops. It's a very popular line.' Brisk and matter-of-fact, he pocketed his change and headed for the door, bumping into Ida who had popped to the market during her dinner break and had come back bearing meat and vegetables for the Sunday dinner. Barlow tipped the brim of his hat and said good afternoon. Then he was gone.

'What's this?' Ida spotted the cologne and picked it up to examine it. '"Glockengasse, Cologne on

Rhine".' Squinting to read the small print out loud, she rapped the bottle back down on the counter. Then she frowned, took a quick, suspicious look at Violet and went upstairs without another word.

The day was spoiled after this. Though Violet hid the perfume out of sight and made up her mind to donate the unwanted gift to a church raffle or some other good cause, there was an awkward atmosphere in the workroom. Ida seemed to sew with extra vigour and made hardly any small talk before going home early without explanation.

'What's got into her?' Muriel wondered as she and Violet worked on into the evening.

'She's upset with me for something that happened earlier,' Violet confessed. She felt she could confide in Muriel without her flying off the handle the way Ida might.

Muriel snipped a thread to free the fabric she was sewing from the spool of her machine. She shook it then folded it and set it aside ready to continue on the Monday morning. Her face was calm as she listened to a troubled Violet.

'Ida saw some scent that Mr Barlow gave me as a present. I tried not to accept it but he caught me off guard then he left the shop without me having time to hand it back.'

'Scent?' Muriel repeated slowly.

'Eau de cologne.'

'And he sprang it on you? You're certain you didn't do anything to lead him on?'

'No!' Violet felt a pang of guilt that came from nowhere and for no reason. Perhaps she had encouraged Colin Barlow without even realizing it?

'Don't worry. I don't have a high opinion of Mr Barlow, given the way he treats his poor wife. So I believe you,' Muriel said kindly. 'But you're worried that Ida doesn't?'

Violet nodded. 'What if she goes home and tells Eddie?'

'She won't do that. Ida may be a hot head over some things, but she doesn't tell tales.'

The reassurance calmed Violet and she went on to explain the various ways in which she'd tried to keep Colin Barlow at bay. 'It's the same with Stan Tankard,' she told Muriel. 'I try my best to put him off but sometimes he just won't leave me alone.'

'I wouldn't compare Stan with Mr Barlow,' Muriel pointed out. 'That man's a different kettle of fish altogether, what with his chemist shops and fancy house and car. Are you sure you're not even a little bit tempted?'

'Not in the least.' Violet thought about it then shuddered. 'As a matter of fact, I dreaded him calling into the shop today and with good reason, as it turns out.'

'The trouble is, you're not a plain girl,' Muriel commented with typical understatement. 'It's bound to happen to you a lot – men running after you, whispering sweet nothings and giving you presents. The trick is not to let it go to your head, especially now that Winnie's not around to keep an eye on you.'

'I won't let it,' Violet promised. 'They can say what they like, it won't make any difference. I'm walking out with Eddie and I'm not interested in anyone else.'

'That's good to hear.' Taking a soft broom from the corner of the room, Muriel swept under the tables – her final task before closing the workshop for the day. 'But I know from my own experience that a person can swear something like that and still get led astray.'

Tidying pins into their round tin, Violet ventured into unknown territory with Muriel, whom she had learned to respect more and more. 'Do you mean your fiancé?'

Muriel propped her broom against the table. 'Yes, Ron. He courted me and promised me the world. We would get married and rent our own little house. We would have a family. I would stay at home to look after the children and Ron would carry on working as an overseer at Kingsley's to look after us. Or so he told me.'

'Is that what you would have liked?' Violet asked.

'Maybe not the staying at home part. I'm not sure that being a mother would have been enough for me, but who can tell? Anyway, that's not the way it turned out. Ron was very handsome – that's what I'm getting round to. The type who couldn't walk down a street without attracting the girls' attention, the sort you see in films – tall with thick, wavy hair and clear blue eyes that took your breath away.'

In her mind's eye Violet pictured the two of them together – Ron walking arm in arm with Muriel, her having to put up with other girls' flirtatious advances, him resisting their flattery until the one time when he didn't, it seemed. Her heart went out to Muriel when she remembered the way it had ended – a bride at the altar without a groom.

'The woman he took up with wasn't from round here, so I never met her. She was married to a doctor in Harrogate, apparently. Ron wrote me the note saying he was sorry and he hoped I would soon find someone else. I didn't keep it – I read it then threw it straight in the fire. And I never knew what happened to him and his precious doctor's wife after that. As for finding someone else to get hitched to – I'd had my fingers burned once so I never fancied giving it another go.'

'Honestly and truly?' Violet found this hard to believe. Muriel was still a good-looking woman. Besides, she was clever in all sorts of ways and kind with it.

'Hand on my heart,' Muriel said, acting out the sentiment by crossing one arm over her chest. She stood with a halo of warm sunlight behind her and smiled at Violet. 'As far as I can see there's nothing wrong with being an old maid sitting by the fire with cats for company. At least that way your heart isn't broken and you can call your life your own.'

CHAPTER FIFTEEN

For days Violet and Eddie contained their suspicions about Donald Wheeler and went on without further upsets until the good weather broke on the third Tuesday of August. It broke with one of the worst thunderstorms for years, presaged by purple clouds gathering over the moor and turning the sultry summer daylight into eerie, early dusk.

'I don't like the look of that lot,' Marjorie said, nodding in the direction of the lowering clouds. She'd come into Jubilee for a yard of lace trim for a christening gown she was making for a great-niece.

'No, we'd better batten down the hatches,' Violet agreed. She happened to be alone in the building and she judged that Marjorie would be her last customer of the afternoon. 'Anyone with any sense will stay indoors until it passes.'

'I've shut up shop a few minutes early,' Marjorie admitted. 'There was nothing much left on the shelves anyway, so I thought I'd pop down for the lace before the rain started. That way I've got something to keep me busy while it gets it out of its system.'

She'd no sooner left the shop than fat, dark splashes of rain began to fall on the pavement and Violet likewise closed the shop then went upstairs to wait for the deluge. First there was a rumble of thunder in the far distance but as yet no lightning. Next jagged forks of blinding light pierced the clouds, then more thunder, closer now and strong enough to rattle the window panes in Violet's tiny room. Then the rain came down in sheets. It pounded onto the cobbled courtyard of Thornley's brewery, and caused the gutter to run in fast rivulets, soon flooding the drains which regurgitated water back into the yard and across the cobbles in a wider stream until it ran down the alleyway onto Brewery Road and on from there down the hill towards the canal.

Violet sat on the bed, as far away from the window as possible. A childhood fear of thunder and lightning came back to her, and she adopted the old habit of counting the seconds between lightning and the sound of thunder to judge how many miles she was from the eye of the storm.

One . . . two . . . three. Three miles. Another electric flash. One . . . two. Two miles. Then another, accompanied by a simultaneous battering of noise loud enough to make her put her hands over her ears. She cowered on the bed, waiting for it to pass.

And of course it was soon over, because storms

as violent as this never lasted long. The clouds blew away and the sky lightened, the rain eased so that when Violet ventured downstairs and looked out onto the street, all she saw was clear water running in the gutter and steam beginning to rise from the rapidly drying pavements. And to her surprise, here was Eddie, on foot and soaked to the skin, coming to knock on her door to make sure she was all right.

She was, she assured him, inviting him into the shop but not up to her room. 'Wait there while I fetch my coat.'

'Why – where are we going?' he wanted to know. Water dripped from the peak of his cap onto the floor.

'Down to the Green Cross – a shandy for me and whatever you fancy for yourself,' she told him boldly. 'My treat.'

'Why's that?'

'Because you thought about me and got soaked to the skin for my sake – that's why.'

'I'll always think about you,' he vowed as she slipped upstairs. He wasn't sure that she'd heard, but it was true – Violet was never far from his thoughts and slowly but surely he would go out of his way to make sure she knew it.

The storm broke the normal rhythm of Violet's days – an early rise to have breakfast in the kitchen then up to the attic to work before Ida and Muriel arrived. Conscientious as ever, she would serve in the shop or stitch like a demon, whirring away at her machine to complete the ever-mounting orders for dresses, trousers, jackets and costumes, looking forward to evening treats – a lovely ride out on Eddie's motorbike alternating with the occasional trip to the cinema, and if not that, quiet nights in with the Thomsons on Valley Road. Then, of course, there was the Wednesday rehearsal with the Hadley Players.

'Are you sure you need me tonight?' Violet's tentative question to Ida broke the silence in the workroom towards the end of a busy afternoon. All day she'd felt the usual small knot of anxiety about the evening, building to a level where she felt she must ask to be excused. 'Only, I feel like I might need an early night.'

'Oh, dearie me!' Ida mimicked the quavery voice of an ancient crone. 'What's the youth of today coming to, finding excuses to stay indoors instead of going out to enjoy themselves.'

Violet had the grace to blush and smile. 'But seriously, would you miss me?'

'We would!' Ida declared. 'Tonight we're learning the moves for the dance hall scene in Act Five where the murderer is finally unmasked. I need all members of the cast to be present.'

'Hard luck,' Muriel commiserated when she saw Violet's dejected expression. 'But no doubt Eddie being there will help cheer you up.'

'He's working late tonight,' Violet said. 'But all

right, Ida, I give in – anything for a quiet life.'

Which was how, despite her qualms about running into her Uncle Donald again, she came to take the bus out to Hadley with Peggy, Evie and Kathy. Then it was just her luck to have an empty seat next to her when Stan got on halfway along Overcliffe Road, and what should he do but sit down there and take the liberty of putting his arm along the back of Violet's seat and leaving his hand resting on her shoulder all the way to their destination?

'Now, now, don't you two go putting my other passengers off their suppers,' the bluff conductor teased when he took Stan's fare. He winked at Violet as he clicked his ticket machine and tore off a ticket. 'Don't worry, I'm only kidding. You don't look like that kind of girl to me.'

Mortified, Violet tried to shake Stan off as soon as they got off the bus, but he stayed close by her side as they made their way into the Institute and waited for the rehearsal to begin. Then who should Ida partner Violet with during the dance scene but Stan again, eager to get into waltz hold and whiz her around the stage, oblivious to Ida's directions?

'Ouch, Stan – that's my foot!' Kathy complained.

'Watch where you're going, Stan!' Peggy protested.

'Stan, stop clod-hopping around. I want you and Violet to finish upstage left when the music ends,' an exasperated Ida called. 'You do know your left from your right, I take it?'

Nothing dented Stan's confidence. He simply

charged on at more of a polka than a waltz, blundering into the backdrop or almost falling off the front of the stage and taking Violet with him.

Kathy for one couldn't stop laughing. 'You're a hoot, Stan,' she cried. 'He's a hoot, isn't he, Evie? Poor Violet is going to end up covered in bruises if he's not careful.'

At least Stan's antics kept Violet's mind on the task in hand and off the risk of bumping into Donald Wheeler, so that by the end of the rehearsal she felt more relaxed and ready to hold her own on the bus trip home.

'What happened between you and Evie at the Assembly Rooms that time?' she challenged as Stan walked her to the bus stop ahead of the other girls. 'Did you manage to sweep her off her feet as planned?'

'Evie's a hard nut to crack,' he confessed, his jacket slung carelessly over one shoulder and his shirt open at the neck. 'Just like you, Violet.'

'Oh, I see.'

'What do you see?'

'I take it that Evie refused to dance with you?'

'As it happens, she never gave me an opening. She was either tripping the light fantastic with someone else or disappearing into the cloakroom to powder her nose.'

'Poor Stan,' Violet commiserated. 'Look, she's coming up behind us with Kathy and Peggy. Why not work your charms on her now while you have the chance?'

Instead of following her advice, Stan unexpectedly flung his arms wide and dropped onto one knee – right there at the bus stop, in full view of everyone. 'Because I have eyes for no one but you, Violet Wheeler!'

'Good Lord above!' she cried, glancing up and down the street. There was a group of men outside the Miners' Arms and a woman wheeling a bike down the pavement towards the post office at the start of the row of stone cottages.

'Hold on, you know I'm only teasing.' Stan jumped up with a grin.

But it was too late – Donald Wheeler, keys in hand, had come out of his house next to the post office and spotted them. He stopped in his tracks, shook his head and stayed rooted to the spot.

'Now look what you've done!' Violet told Stan in real distress. Her stomach churned as she prepared herself for a fresh volley of insults.

'Why, what's the matter?' As the other girls arrived at the bus stop, Stan was suddenly serious. 'It's always just a bit of fun between us, isn't it?'

'Are you all right, Violet?' Evie asked, while Kathy and Peggy remonstrated with Stan for overstepping the mark.

'You've upset her,' Kathy remonstrated. 'She's turned white as a sheet, poor girl.'

Violet took a deep breath and wished for the ground to swallow her up, or at least for the brown and yellow number 15 bus to arrive. Where was it?

Would it reach the stop and whisk her away before the enemy had time to make his way up the street?

Sure enough, the bus turned the corner and Stan waved it down. Kathy bundled Violet up the step ahead of the others. The conductor rang the bell and the driver set off as they found their seats.

Still holding her breath, Violet glanced out of the window to see Donald fixed to the spot outside his house. He glared at the bus as it passed, seeking Violet out and spotting her next to Stan on the back seat. His gaze followed them along the main street until the bus turned the next corner onto the moor road.

'Someone's not happy,' Stan commented with a backwards glance at the solitary figure.

'Yes – what has got into your Uncle Donald lately?' Kathy asked with her usual lack of tact. 'He's turned into a right sourpuss.'

Violet didn't reply but she was glad of her narrow escape and relieved to be surrounded by her friends. She was even nice to Stan and agreed to let him walk her home from the bus stop, as long as he behaved himself.

'Ta-ta, you two!' Kathy called after them as the bus drew away from the kerb.

Taking his tone from a serious Violet, Stan saw her to her door in respectful silence. 'I meant it earlier,' he said as she took out her key. 'The last thing I want is for us to fall out.'

'No, in the end I was glad you and the girls were

210

with me,' she replied with a grateful smile. 'You helped me out of a tight spot.'

'So we're still pals?' he checked.

Violet smiled. 'Pals,' she confirmed, turning the key in the lock. That would do, she told herself as they said goodbye. She went through the shop and up the stairs. She and the irrepressible Stan had known each other a long time and from now on she hoped he would hold himself in check and be just that – a pal and nothing more.

'I'd like cod and chips, please,' Evie told Albert Pennington behind his high counter at the top of Regent Street.

'Salt and vinegar?' The fish shop owner predicted a yes and shook condiments over Evie's purchase without waiting for an answer. 'The same for you?' he asked Violet, who was standing behind Evie in the long Thursday-evening queue.

'Yes, please.' Violet's stomach was rumbling after another busy day at Jubilee.

Evie waited while Albert wrapped Violet's supper in newspaper then the two girls walked out into the street together. 'I hear you're run off your feet down at number one,' she commented. 'Kathy says she was thrilled with the dress you made for her so she's been passing the word around.'

'We are busy, thank goodness,' Violet agreed. 'I think it's partly word of mouth but it's Maud and Gertie as much as anything.'

Evie was nonplussed. 'Who?' she asked.

'Our two new mannequins. They attract attention and bring people in. Tell Sybil she should think about buying one for your window.'

'Ta – I'll pass it on.' Happy to stroll down Chapel Street with Violet, though it meant she would have to take the long way home to Albion Lane, Evie chatted on. 'We're kept on the go, too. We've hung on to all our old customers except for Mrs Barlow and her friend, Mrs Kingsley.'

'We thought you would.' Violet opened up the newspaper parcel and dug into her fish and chip supper. 'I'm starving,' she explained. 'Anyway, we can both keep our fingers crossed and say so far so good. It turns out Ida and Muriel were right – there is room for two dressmaking shops on Chapel Street.'

'Thank goodness.' Outside Sykes' bakery, Evie seemed to hesitate then decided to venture on. 'Violet, can I ask you a question?'

Expecting more along the lines of what had gone before, Violet nodded and was taken aback by what came next.

'About Stan,' Evie said.

'What about Stan?'

'What would you think if I went to the pictures with him?'

Violet raised her eyebrows. 'Why – has he asked you to?'

'Yes. He was waiting for me outside work half an

hour ago. He wants to take me to see an adventure film next week.'

'He doesn't waste much time, I'll say that for him.' Violet stared at Evie, pretty as a picture in a pink and white day dress with three-quarter-length sleeves and darts at the waistline and across the bust that flattered her sylph-like figure. Her short fair hair showed off her slender neck and slight shoulders. 'Did you tell him yes?'

'I didn't give him an answer straight away. I said I would let him know tomorrow, after I'd talked to you about it – not that I told Stan that last little bit,' Evie added hastily.

A puzzled frown appeared on Violet's face. 'Surely you're not asking my permission to go to the Victory with Stan? You know that I've got nothing to do with him, not in a romantic way.'

'Oh, now I've upset you,' Evie said with a sigh. 'All I know is, Stan has been keen on you for ages and I wanted to make it all right with you before I said yes to the pictures.'

'Feel free,' Violet insisted more forcefully than Evie expected. 'I'm walking out with Eddie, remember.'

'I know you are. Still, I thought I'd better check.' There was a long pause then another question. 'So you think I should go?'

Violet cocked her head to one side. 'How old are you now, Evie?'

'I'm seventeen.'

'And Stan's twenty-three, remember. And shall we say he's not backwards in coming forward.'

Evie managed a brief smile. 'So you think I should say no?'

'I don't know. Do you like him?'

'He makes me laugh,' came the doubtful reply.

'Well, that's a start.' Now that she'd cleared up the misunderstanding, Violet relaxed into giving the younger girl what she hoped would be good advice. 'Stan's a card – that's what everyone says about him. But underneath it all he's a decent sort. That's my opinion, anyway.'

'So I should say yes?'

Realizing they were in danger of going around in circles, Violet gave Evie her final verdict. 'Go ahead and give it a try,' she advised. 'And if Stan puts so much as a foot wrong – you come and tell me about it. I'll soon set him straight.'

The fish supper was eaten and Violet had taken its newspaper wrapping down to the ash pit in the back yard shared with the brewery and with numbers 3, 5 and 7 Chapel Street. She was back inside, ready to go upstairs again, when the outline of a figure in the shop doorway, obscured by the lowered blind, made her hesitate. It was probably a local chap hanging about, waiting for a friend, she thought – nothing she should worry about. Then again, perhaps she should go and see.

She was still in two minds when there was an insistent rap on the door and Violet hurried to answer it, astonished to be confronted by, of all people, Donald Wheeler.

'Don't worry, I'm not coming in,' he began in what could only be described as a surly manner. 'I can say what I have to say out here on the doorstep.'

'You look terrible,' she gasped. It was true – his chin was unshaven, his hair uncombed and the lapel of his jacket was ripped as though he'd been in a brawl. A closer look at his lined, sallow face revealed a recent bruise under his right eye.

'I saw you with Stan last night, don't think I didn't.' He spoke as if this was a sin that would send her careering straight to hell.

'What of it?' Violet said wearily. She was tired of going down the same old track, of not being listened to and being treated like a criminal. 'I wish to goodness you'd mind your own business.' Almost adding 'Uncle Donald' to the end of her complaint, she remembered what the note inside the bracelet box had revealed and stopped herself just in time.

'This *is* my business, and you'll thank me in the end,' he insisted. 'Listen to me. I've already had words with him and now I'm telling you once and for all to steer clear of Stan Tankard.'

So that was where the bruise had come from, Violet decided. Donald had tried giving orders to Stan and got a punch in the face for his pains. It served him right. 'And my answer is I don't need advice from you, ta very much.'

'I mean it, Violet.' Suddenly there was a new note in his voice – the tone was urgent but not bullying for a change. 'You have to listen to me: Stan isn't the one for you.'

'And I suppose you'd say that about every young man I took up with, wouldn't you? It would be the same thing – don't do this, don't do that – on and on until I was sick of hearing it.' Exasperation rose from deep inside. Here was the man who should have taken a father's responsibility from day one, who had hidden the truth and thrust the burden and the joy of Violet's upbringing onto Winnie, standing to one side and interfering only to issue orders about the way she led her life. 'You're nothing but a lousy, rotten hypocrite,' she said in a raised voice, aware of spying eyes and ears behind net curtains at front-room windows. 'I don't know how you have the nerve to come here and tell me what to do.'

'He isn't the one for you,' he repeated, as if oblivious to Violet's anger. 'You have to tell him to leave you alone, you hear me?'

'And if I don't do as I'm told?' she asked defiantly.

'For once in your life, you have to.' He stared at her with great intensity, refusing to budge an inch:

'Oh, I could throttle you!' she cried, her voice breaking down as her feelings swept her along like storm water in the gutter. 'Tell me one thing before I slam this door in your face – why have you been so nasty to me? I don't mean just lately, but all my life, ever since I can remember – giving me sour looks and tut-tutting and always making me feel I was in the wrong. Why couldn't you have . . . loved me?'

Violet's halting plea affected Donald more than either had expected. He lowered his gaze and his lips quivered as tears welled up. Violet felt her own eyes water and she put a hand over her mouth to stifle a sob.

'I tried my best,' he attempted to say, but the words fell half-formed from his mouth. 'But you were wilful and your Aunty Winnie didn't help – she spared the rod and spoiled the child.'

'Wilful?' she echoed in a faint voice, realizing with a shudder that he blamed her even now. 'That's not fair. I was only tiny – too young to understand what I had to do to please you.'

'We won't go into it now,' he said, regaining control. 'I came here with a final warning and now I've done all I can to make you steer clear of a certain person.'

'Well, there was no need.' Violet's frustration receded and gave room for a different picture of Donald Wheeler to form in her mind. He had become an old, broken, lonely man who couldn't take care of himself let alone anyone else. 'You can rest assured that I'm not walking out with Stan. I never have and I never will.'

'Then my conscience is clear.' Donald stepped back onto the pavement. 'It's the last conversation I wanted to have with you before I cleared off.'

The finality of this last remark panicked Violet

into joining him on the pavement and asking more questions. 'Cleared off where? Are you leaving your job and house in Hadley?'

'I am and that's that.' He lifted his hand, forefinger raised in a peculiar reminder of a priest giving a blessing. 'Don't ask me where I'm going because I won't tell you.'

'Then I won't ask,' she decided. 'If that's what you want.'

He met her gaze for another instant then looked down again. 'It is,' he said. Then, without looking back Donald Wheeler shuffled down Chapel Street and turned onto Brewery Road, out of sight.

That's the last I'll ever see of him, Violet decided. Her thoughts flew to her beloved aunt. 'I'm sorry, Aunty Winnie,' she whispered with a final pull on her heart strings; sorry that the only solid link with her past had ended this way in bitter regret.

CHAPTER SIXTEEN

Violet was in the shop window, putting the finishing touches to Gertie's wedding dress that she, Ida and Muriel had slaved over for weeks. She spread the full skirt as wide as the small space allowed then tweaked the gathering at the shoulders, puffing out the sleeves for maximum width. Having arranged things to her satisfaction, she went outside to judge the effect.

'Not bad,' was Sybil's comment as she rounded the corner from Brewery Road and cast an appraising eye over the satin confection in the window.

'Is that all?' Violet prompted with a secret smile. *I hope Aunty Winnie's up there listening to this echo from the past*, she thought.

The practised seamstress gave her professional verdict. 'You've overdone the pearl trim around the cuffs for my liking, otherwise you've made a good job of it.'

'Thank you, I'm glad you like it.'

'Tell Muriel and Ida they'd better be on their toes, though.' Sybil was ready to walk on but not before she'd delivered a lively parting shot. 'We're putting new adverts in the *Herald* next week.'

'I'll let them know,' Violet promised.

'And *two* mannequins in our window.' On Sybil went without waiting for a reaction, head held high, humming a tune.

'Good – the race is hotting up,' Ida said when Violet passed on the latest development. She was like Boudicca at the head of her small female army, holding a sewing machine aloft and marching on.

'I'll make posters to put in Hutchinson's and Sykes' windows,' Muriel decided. 'And we can pin one up on the noticeboard in the entrance to the library if they'll let us.'

This was a Friday in early September and Muriel had an appointment with the bank manager. She would be back before dinner, she said. Meanwhile, Ida decided she would man the shop while Violet made a few deliveries.

'My bike's in the back yard,' she told her. 'I want you to go to Hutchinson's with the blouse Lizzie ordered and then on to the Victory to drop off that bolero jacket with George Ambler – it's a surprise birthday present for his wife. Last but not least, there's the evening dress for Ella Kingsley. She's asked us to leave it in the mill office for Mr Kingsley to take home later on today.'

Violet took the bike and set off willingly up Chapel Street. By the time she reached the mill, her hair was flyaway and her cheeks flushed.

Doubting that she looked her best, she tucked her blouse more firmly into the waistband of her skirt and patted her hair as she approached the wide stone entrance to Kingsley's Mill, where overpowering noises and smells told her that spinning and weaving machines were going full tilt.

Tall buildings to either side of the street formed a wind tunnel down which thick smoke billowed from two tall chimneys that dominated the skyline – acrid, dirty stuff that clogged up the lungs, adding to other unhealthy conditions surrounding mill work. For a start, in the yard behind the elaborate stone façade there were insatiable, roaring furnaces that powered steam engines to drive the giant machines. Then there were the notorious spinning and weaving sheds – cavernous spaces that were so cold in winter that ice formed on the insides of the window panes and so stifling in summer that young loom cleaners and reaching-in workers fresh from school would often collapse from heat exhaustion.

Grateful as always that she didn't have to endure this kind of daily grind, Violet took her last delivery from the basket then ventured under the archway where the stench of raw wool hit her and the sound of pounding engines overwhelmed her.

'Who are you looking for, love?' a boiler man in grubby grey overalls shouted across the yard.

'Mr Kingsley,' she called back.

'Try the General Office. They'll know where to find him.'

Violet thanked the man and followed the direction of his pointing hand. She knocked on the office door and heard a faint, 'Come in.'

Violet turned the handle and entered to find a homely, middle-aged woman wearing horn-rimmed glasses seated at a desk. 'I've brought a parcel for Mr Kingsley,' she explained.

'He's out. Try the chemist's next to Brinkley Baths,' the secretary suggested, giving short shrift as she tapped busily at her typewriter.

Violet's heart sank to hear that her errand was taking her to a branch of Barlow's, but what else could she do other than carry on with her task? She went back out onto the street to wheel her bike a hundred yards further on until gold lettering on a shiny black background told her that she'd arrived at one of Colin Barlow's five shops.

Propping the bike against a lamp post, she squared her shoulders and entered an unfamiliar scene. Hundreds of glass jars lined the shelves behind the counter, each with a gold-edged label inscribed with an abbreviated Latin name: P:SANG:DRACON, TAB:SODA.MINT and PULV:BISMUTH:CO. Below the jars were small drawers with more mysterious chemical ingredients for the medicines made up by the dark-haired female pharmacist working intently in a glass booth to one side of the shop. Then there were shelves reaching the ceiling to all sides, stacked with tooth powders and toothbrushes, shaving soaps and talcum powder, razor blades, tweezers and Brilliantine and in the centre of the shop a stand displaying Max Factor face powders and rouge.

The pharmacist, who was young, fashionable and evidently short tempered, glanced up from her work rolling out a thin white paste from which to make prescription pills. 'Yes?'

'Is Mr Kingsley here, by any chance?'

'In the back,' was the snappish reply.

Violet spotted a door to one side of the counter. 'Shall I knock?' she asked tentatively.

But just then the door opened and Thomas Kingsley emerged, followed by his wife, Ella. 'No need,' he said, taking in the sight of a confused Violet holding a parcel wrapped in tissue paper and tied with white ribbon that could only be for his wife. 'For you,' he told Ella before saying he had important things to do and quickly departing.

Ella Kingsley took delivery of her evening dress with a pleasant smile and a sincere thank-you. 'It was clever of you to track us down,' she told Violet. 'We called in here to finalize arrangements with Mr Barlow for an outing to the theatre.'

'And lo, speak of the devil!' Colin Barlow announced as he emerged from the back storeroom, dressed in a dark business suit with a grey silk tie. 'And if it isn't our shrinking violet,' he smirked.

'I'll love you and leave you,' Ella Kingsley told him, pretending not to notice Violet's blushes. 'Thank you again for finishing my order in good time for our night out,' she said as she followed her husband onto the street.

Violet hurried after her but haste made her clumsy and she knocked Ida's bike sideways from the lamp post onto the road where it was almost run over by a tram. Violet watched helplessly and with frayed nerves as the tall tram rattled by.

'By Jove, that was a close shave.' Colin Barlow came rushing out of the shop and pulled Violet back from the kerb. Then he made a big show of dusting her down and picking up the bike. 'Why not come back in and sit down until you've got over the shock?'

Violet shook her head and took the bike from him. 'No, thank you. I'll be getting back to the shop.'

'This is a busy road. You have to watch your step.' As Violet crossed the road then got on the bike and started to pedal towards Kingsley's Mill, Colin Barlow strode alongside her. 'Look out for the drain cover. And there's a stray dog ahead. Mind he doesn't bite.'

Barlow's solicitations made Violet wobble unsteadily, giving him time to step out in front of her and lay one hand on her handlebars, the other on her shoulder. 'You see – I was right to be worried about you. You should have let me look after you, as I suggested.'

Without saying a word, Violet shook his hand from her shoulder then waited for him to step aside.

He stood firm and smiled. 'Little Violet – has anyone told you how beautiful you are when you're angry?'

His nonsense rendered her speechless though inwardly she seethed. Who did Colin Barlow think he was, standing in her way and doling out compliments willy-nilly? Did he suppose she would be taken in, even for a second?

'Because you are a truly lovely specimen in anyone's book,' he went on, shamelessly disregarding the curious glances of passengers in a double-decker bus and of the girl running to catch the stray dog. 'You know, Violet, your looks could be your fortune if you play your cards right.'

This was enough! Violet wrenched the handlebars free and launched out into the middle of the road before pedalling full steam ahead past Kingsley's. She was too furious to glance back to see what Barlow was up to now or to notice Ella Kingsley standing with a puzzled expression under the imposing portico entrance to her husband's mill.

If it happens again I'll be good and ready for him, she swore to herself, cycling furiously up Canal Road. *No more perfume, no more compliments – I'll give Colin Barlow a piece of my mind and let him know exactly where he stands.*

For a change the next evening, Violet agreed to meet up with Kathy at the Green Cross on Ghyll Road, where they would have one drink then catch the late evening showing of a new film at the Victory.

'Two birds with one stone,' Kathy said with a wink as they sat at a copper-topped table sipping at their cold ginger ales. 'You can watch the picture then enjoy a tryst with Eddie afterwards.'

'That's the plan,' Violet agreed brightly.

'Is that why you've come out in your best bib and tucker?' Kathy teased. She was the sort of girl who could chat with a friend at the same time as staying alert to the possibility of flirting with any likely lad who happened to catch her eye. This included Stan, drinking at the bar with a couple of football team-mates, and Harold Gibson, sitting at a table near the window with Dick Thomson.

'I thought I'd make an effort.' Violet admitted that getting ready for her evening out had entailed extra time in front of the mirror. She wore a new red dress with cap sleeves and a skirt cut on the bias, with canvas, wedge-heeled sandals that she'd Blancoed a pristine white for the occasion. Her hair too was looking especially nice – glossy and groomed to frame her oval face with its touch of lipstick and rouge.

'Stan, come over here,' Kathy called with a devilish air. She too had dressed up for the girls' night out in a flowery summer dress, nipped in at the waist by a thin white belt. Her hair was swept up at the back and waved on top, tumbling forward over one side of her forehead. 'Tell Violet how pretty she looks. Come on – it's not like you to be shy.'

'Stop it, Kathy.' Violet's protest was mild and un-worried. 'Let poor Stan drink his beer in peace.'

Unable to resist the invitation, Stan and his two

pals joined Violet and Kathy at their table, drawing up stools and bantering loudly.

'Blimey – it looks like you picked the whole blooming garden for that outfit,' Stan told Kathy as he sat close to Violet, backing her into a corner in order to make room. He nudged her with his elbow. 'This is snug, isn't it?'

'But not for long,' she told him, still confident that their last talk had set new ground rules which Stan would keep to. 'We're off to the Victory in two ticks.'

'And we're off to the Assembly Rooms, aren't we, lads?' Stan's high spirits made him the centre of attention as usual. He raised his glass at Harold and Dick, who were crossing the bar to begin a game of darts. 'Where's Ida tonight, Harold? Has she let you off the lead for once?'

'Ha-ha, very funny, Stan.' Harold knew better than to rise to the bait, though he gave Violet a long stare as he and his prospective father-in-law passed by. Soon the thud of darts into the board in the far corner told Violet that the game had begun.

'We have to go,' she reminded Kathy, who by this time was perched on the knees of Les Craven, a tall, gangly lad who was learning to be an electrical engineer and who played goalkeeper in Eddie and Stan's team.

'You see – we have to love you and leave you,' Kathy cooed at Les. 'But you can look out for me later at the Assembly Rooms if you like.'

'Will you be there too?' Stan asked Violet, who

had stood up and was waiting patiently by the door.

She shook her head. 'Have a nice time without me.'

'And don't forget to save me the last waltz,' Kathy called to Les as she followed Violet on to the street.

The chat with the lads had left them short of time so they hurried along Ghyll Road towards the cinema on Canal Road. When they passed Barlow's, Violet saw fit to recount her recent close shave with the tram. 'Another second and Ida's bike would have fallen clean under the tram wheels, then what would I have done?'

'Better that the bike had got flattened than you,' Kathy reckoned. She had her money ready for her ticket and went ahead up the steps and into the shiny, well-lit foyer of the Victory. 'And you mean to say, Mr Barlow saved your bacon?'

Violet put her right. 'No. He likes to think he did. But little did he know that he was the one who made me all fingers and thumbs in the first place. I was in such a rush to get away from him that I lost my balance and that's how it happened.'

Kathy slid her money across the desk to the cashier and took her ticket. 'I don't blame you for keeping Colin Barlow at arm's length,' she sympathized. 'He's a nasty piece of work. I've heard he tries it on with a lot of the girls who work for him – usually the best looking ones. And lo – if they turn him down, they're out of a job before you can say Jack Robinson!'

'And if they say yes, their name is ruined.' At least Violet wasn't in that unenviable position, she realized.

'Let's hope Eddie doesn't get to hear about it, though. He might get the wrong end of the stick,' were Kathy's last words as they made their way through to the darkened theatre with its raked seats and giant screen, revealed by a slowly opening velvet curtain.

'Hush!' a nearby usher warned, waving her torch towards two empty seats.

Sitting down, Violet lowered her voice to a whisper. 'He won't. I'm safe on that score. There was nobody around to tell Eddie – only a few strangers on a bus.'

Still, Kathy's warning rankled throughout the picture that featured Clark Gable and Violet's favourite actress, the chic and cheeky Claudette Colbert. What if Eddie did learn about Colin Barlow's unwanted attentions – the eau de cologne, for instance? *I'll make a clean breast later tonight*, she decided before the violins reached a crescendo and the final credits rolled up the screen.

'The road to hell is paved with good intentions' had been one of Donald Wheeler's trite sayings whenever Violet had used the excuse of not meaning any harm. Her protestations would fall flat and he would trot out the aphorism so that in the end Violet stopped trying to explain. After all, it was easier not to say anything and go on living in the shadow of her uncle's disapproval.

Later, this not-saying-anything was part of Violet's logic when she examined why she hadn't tackled the thorny problem of Colin Barlow with Eddie after she met him out of work. The other reason was that she didn't want to spoil his good mood and drag him down to earth.

'"I'll be loving you – always,"' he crooned as he hugged her then swept her down the steps of the cinema and waltzed her along the pavement. '"With a love that's true – always."'

'Eddie, stop, you're making me dizzy!'

'"When the things we planned need a helping hand . . ."'

'You are – my head's spinning. Stop!'

He laughed and ran with her down the street. 'I didn't come on the Norton tonight. I'll have to walk you home instead.'

'Walk, not run,' she pleaded, skipping after him down some steps leading to the canal side.

He stopped on the towpath and kissed her. Then when they came to a damp, dripping tunnel running under the railway line, he took her by the hand and ran up the steps two at a time, pausing under a street lamp to kiss her again. 'Or we could stop out all night and not bother going home. How does that sound?'

'That would set tongues wagging good and proper,' she murmured. 'Anyway, can you slow down a bit?'

'What's wrong – are you out of breath?'

'No,' she lied. 'All right then – yes, a little bit.'

'Shall I give you a piggyback?'

As Eddie offered to hoist Violet onto his back, she laughed and hitched up her skirt then changed her mind. 'If we're not careful we'll end up in the canal.'

'What's wrong with that? Stan tells me you're a good little swimmer.'

'Not in these clothes, I'm not.' It was Violet's turn to lead the way, over the railway crossing and back down some steps to the towpath with only a black cat for company and no lamps to light their way. Laughing and walking arm in arm by the dark water, they went on until Eddie sat her down beside a lock gate.

'We have a fine time together, the two of us,' he said in a more thoughtful tone.

'We do,' she agreed. Sliding her arm around his waist, she rested her head on his shoulder.

'That's nice, Vi – I'm glad we're agreed on that.'

She lingered over this shortened version of her name and decided she liked it.

'Sorry,' he said in a low voice, 'I'm not used to putting things into words the way they do in the songs.'

'No, it doesn't sit easily with me either.'

'Honestly and truly?' Leaning away from her, Eddie looked tenderly into her eyes then hit upon a comparison for how he was feeling. 'When we're together, it's as if I've won the football pools, only a hundred times better.'

She smiled at the comparison that was typical and

funny and said everything she needed to know about Eddie's view of the world, if he did but know it.

'I'm serious. I mean it.'

'Well, I'm glad I'm better than a prize in a sweep-stake, at any rate.'

'You know what I'm getting at.' He moved in for a long kiss, drawing Violet close as they sat, overlooking the still water. 'When I'm with you I know what they mean by being in seventh heaven.'

That was more like it – the romantic phrase pleased her and she responded lovingly. 'And I'm happier now, here with you, than I ever thought I could be.' Violet's voice was so low that Eddie had to ask her to repeat it.

'I couldn't be happier,' was all she said before she kissed him again. On the street above them, a late tram trundled by and men coming out of a pub shouted cheerio. Canal water lapped gently against the lock gates while, enfolded in each other's arms, Violet and Eddie were perfectly happy to let the world go by.

Next day, Sunday, brought an invitation from Eddie for Violet to go to dinner with the Thomsons.

'Are you sure your mother won't mind?' Violet asked when she heard a knock at the shop door and she ran downstairs to answer it.

'No, Ida's doing the cooking – a roast with York-shire pud and baked potatoes. There'll be plenty to go round.' Eddie waited for her while she fetched her coat then they walked up to Valley Road. He strolled with her round the quarry pond while Ida put the finishing touches to the dinner. It was a warm day with mellow sunlight reflecting off the water and Eddie's mood became thoughtful, as on the previous night. This time, however, he put the focus on Violet rather than his own feelings for her.

'I've been wondering,' he began as they reached a rock backed by straggly willows where they could sit for a while. 'Now that your Uncle Donald has performed his vanishing act, what are you going to do about the bracelet and the note that you found?'

'I'd rather not talk about it, ta.' It was best where it was, stashed away under the bed.

'Are you sure you're not just bottling things up instead of bringing them out in the open?' Eddie asked.

He was spot on, Violet realized, but still she persisted. 'Yes. I've decided not to bother about it any more,' Violet answered without conviction. In fact, the question made her feel weary and hopeless. 'If he's turned his back on me, what good would it do to drag everything into the open?'

Eddie put a comforting arm around her shoulder. 'I'm sorry, Vi, I shouldn't have brought it up.'

'No, don't say that. I know you mean well. But I can't do anything about how Uncle Donald feels about me or the fact that he's vanished into thin air. So I've tried to put it to the back of my mind as best I can.' To the back of her mind, tucked away in a

233

box in the corner of the room under her bed. *Keep this bracelet for my sake.*

'You could let me help,' Eddie suggested, picking up a flat stone and flinging it so that it skimmed across the murky, yellowish water and bounced three times before it sank.

'How?' She sighed, touched that he cared enough about her to solve the mystery, but still reluctant to open up the wound.

Eddie skimmed another stone across the pond. 'Donald isn't the only person you could ask about the bracelet, is he?'

'My mother's dead. Who else is there?'

'Other people who were around in 1914. *My* mother for a start. She might remember a few things from that time.'

'No, Eddie, I don't want to drag her in. Anyway, it's a long time ago. She's probably forgotten.'

'The thing is—' He stopped halfway through his sentence, not knowing how to go on, but staring intently at Violet.

'What?'

'Don't take this the wrong way – I'm sure that, like me, you made out the letter "D" alongside the "F" and straight away jumped to the conclusion that it stood for your Uncle Donald. But what if it didn't?'

'You mean, the "D" could stand for someone else?' Violet murmured and shook her head.

'I'm not saying it does – not for definite. But what if . . . ?'

234

Slowly Violet let the possibility enter her mind.

'In a way, that would turn out better, wouldn't it?' Eddie persisted. 'If the bracelet was a present from someone other than your uncle?'

'Maybe.'

'Which would make it worthwhile asking a few questions to see what answers we came up with.' Flinging a last stone into the pond, Eddie stood up and dusted himself down. Then he offered Violet a hand and led her back towards the house. 'Only if you wanted to, mind you.'

'Let me think about it,' she decided. Eddie had opened a door that she wasn't quite ready to step through – one which let Donald Wheeler off the hook and led in a different direction altogether.

'That's fine – you take your time.' He squeezed her hand then stepped aside for her to enter the kitchen, topsy-turvy with dirty pans and smelling of roast meat. 'I don't know about anyone else but I could eat a horse.'

Try as she might over the meal, Violet couldn't get rid of the notion that there was a bad atmosphere in the room.

Dick Thomson stood at the head of the table, carving the joint of beef. Eddie sat to his right, with Violet beside him and Ida perched awkwardly on a corner of Emily's chair at the far end. Meanwhile, Harold had plenty of elbow room on the side opposite to Violet and Eddie.

'Squeeze in here,' Harold told his fiancée when everyone's plates were piled high. He'd avoided looking at Eddie and Violet ever since they'd arrived and seemed ill at ease, darting glances at Ida and Emily instead of tucking into his dinner.

'This cabbage isn't cooked through,' Emily complained as Ida sat beside Harold.

'Oh Mother,' Ida muttered, 'you only like it when it's boiled down to a pulp. But everyone knows cabbage should be a bit crunchy.'

The bickering continued, with Ida complaining to Eddie about being woken up the night before. 'It was gone midnight when you finally remembered you had a bed to come back to,' she said, looking pointedly at Violet. 'You could at least have shut the front door quietly without waking the whole house.'

'Anyway, I thought you were meant to be working,' Dick chipped in.

'That's right, I was.' So far Eddie hadn't picked up anything amiss and happily made inroads into his meat and gravy.

'And didn't I see you in the Green Cross?' Harold asked Violet pointedly.

With all eyes on her, Violet's discomfort grew. 'Yes – I was with Kathy Land. We went on to the Victory to see the Clark Gable picture, then after that I met Eddie and we went for a walk by the canal.'

'What's wrong with that?' Eddie wanted to know. 'I had to see Vi home, didn't I? My bike's blown a gasket so I was on foot. That's why I was late back

236

and why Ida lost her beauty sleep.'

'And you don't mind Violet gadding about town without you?' Ida insinuated.

'What's got into Ida all of a sudden?' Eddie retaliated, knife and fork poised as he addressed the whole company. 'Isn't she the one who's always going on about women being equal with men ever since they got the vote? Don't they have the right to do what they like, go where they want and so forth?'

Violet's stomach churned. What flashed through her mind was that the episode outside Barlow's had somehow got back to Eddie's family, who had talked about it among themselves. It had made Ida recall the shop owner's earlier gift of eau de cologne and this had fuelled their growing suspicions. *I should have gone ahead and told Eddie all about it much sooner,* she thought. *Then he would know there was nothing to worry about.*

'I wasn't gadding.' Desperate to defend herself, Violet mouthed the only protest she could muster.

'That's what it looked like to me,' Harold argued stolidly.

They've all been talking about me behind my back and made two and two add up to five! The realization struck Violet like a ton of bricks. *They haven't even had the decency to hear what I have to say before they made up their minds.* 'When? What did you see?' she demanded, looking from Harold to Ida and back again.

'Yes, Harold – what are you going on about?' His

attention claimed at last, Eddie's knife and fork clattered onto his plate and he scraped his chair back from the table. 'Come on – out with it.'

Violet wanted to shut her ears and close her eyes to pretend it wasn't happening but she forced herself to speak up. 'Everybody, stop talking and listen to me. If this is about Mr Barlow, I can explain everything.'

There was an astonished silence. Emily stared down the table at her husband, who, it seemed, was the only one determined to finish his dinner. Harold looked to Ida for guidance.

'You mean Colin Barlow from Bilton Grange?' Eddie asked at last, as if he had no idea how the shop owner's name had suddenly entered into things. His eyes were filled with uncertainty as he turned to Violet for an explanation.

'What's he got to do with anything?' Dick interrupted laconically. 'I thought we were meant to be finding out about Violet and Stan Tankard.'

'Stan?' Violet echoed faintly. The name confounded her and left her speechless.

Ida took up the reins. 'Come along, Violet, don't play the innocent. We've all seen the way Stan is with you – he can't keep his hands to himself. Isn't that right, Harold?'

Reluctantly Harold nodded. 'I'm sorry, Eddie, but I did see Stan and Violet together in the Green Cross.'

Eddie rose uncertainly to his feet. 'When?'

'Last night.'

'But I was with Kathy!' Violet protested, her heart fluttering as she fought the urge to run away and hide.

'And what about at rehearsals when Eddie isn't there, or even if he is sometimes?' Ida reminded her.

'And at the baths, behind Eddie's back,' Emily added. 'I've seen it with my own eyes.'

Eddie pressed his lips together, sat down as if his legs were about to give way then shot straight back up. 'Everybody, sit tight,' he said before rushing out of the house.

Violet ran after him onto the street and seized his arm. 'Where are you going?'

'To find Stan and have it out.'

'Stop – you have to believe me, it isn't true!' The world had tipped off its axis and was spinning out of control. In one mad leap of events, it seemed that Violet was in danger of losing the man she loved.

'Then you've got nothing to worry about,' Eddie shot back, breaking free and hurrying on. 'Let go of me, Violet. Either stay here or go on home and wait for me there.'

Rooted to the spot as Eddie ran down Valley Road, Violet's pleas had fallen on deaf ears and she was helpless to stop him from seeking Stan out. Suddenly, out of nowhere, her world was in danger of falling apart.

CHAPTER SEVENTEEN

Are you going to stand by and let that happen? It was Winnie's voice that spurred Violet into action. *You'll lose Eddie if you don't watch out. And what for? For nothing, when all's said and done.*

'That's right – nothing,' Violet echoed out loud as she pulled herself together then hastened after Eddie through the sleepy Sunday-afternoon streets. But he ran faster than her down the hill and onto Canal Road, past the mills and the shops, swimming baths, chemist's shop and the picture house where he worked and on, in spite of Violet's pleas for him to stop, towards the grimy and overcrowded tenements next to the railway arch where he knew Stan had his lodgings. Eddie paused at the railings outside the second house in the row then disappeared down some steps leading to the cellar.

Violet followed hard on his heels, her heart pounding, her throat dry from the effort of running and shouting. She reached the railings in time to hear Eddie yelling Stan's name through an open window and to see Stan himself emerge.

'Now then, Eddie – what's all the racket?' Stan grumbled as he swept his tousled hair back from his forehead. He was barefoot and in his shirtsleeves, with braces dangling, as if awakening from an afternoon nap.

'Out with it!' Eddie yelled, slamming both hands against Stan's chest and thrusting him back against the window sill. The two men faced each other in a dank, cramped space about six feet by three. It was littered with empty crates and a broken stepladder, which crashed sideways as Eddie grabbed the front of his rival's shirt. 'You've been seeing Violet behind my back. Come on, admit it!'

At the head of the cellar steps, Violet grasped the railings until her knuckles turned white. Two bystanders dressed in worn tweed jackets and caps crossed the road in the hope of some small entertainment to liven up the sultry afternoon, while a woman flung open a window on the first floor and shouted down that the noise had wakened her baby and the two of them would pay for it if they didn't pipe down.

'Keep your hair on,' Stan grunted at Eddie as he tried to free himself but only succeeded in putting a foot through one of the crates. Angered by this, he lowered his head and butted Eddie in the chest, knocking the air out of him and sending him back against the cellar steps.

'Stop it, both of you!' Violet pleaded. 'Tell him,

Stan. Tell Eddie that there's nothing going on between us.'

Too late – Eddie was back on his feet and charging Stan, catching him with such force that his adversary staggered back inside his lodgings and disappeared from view, crate and all.

Eddie piled into the cellar room after him, leaving the onlookers bemused.

'What have you been up to, you naughty girl?' the mother of the baby asked Violet with a knowing wink.

'Fighting over you, are they?' one of the men asked, casting an appreciative eye over Violet. 'I can't say I blame them. Can you, Jack?'

Still breathless and with her head starting to spin, Violet ran down the steps. Her aim was to separate Eddie and Stan before either of them did the other serious harm, but when she entered Stan's room she found them still going at it hammer and tongs, landing punches to jaw and chest then grappling at close quarters. Finally, Eddie succeeded in getting Stan down onto the stone-flagged floor. He knelt over him and raised his fist to deal another blow. Just in time Violet grabbed his wrist with both hands and pulled with all her weight, dragging Eddie off balance and giving Stan the chance to roll sideways and spring back up. She darted between them and raised both hands to keep them apart like a referee in a boxing match.

'Oh no, you don't,' she told Stan, whose head was

already lowered ready for another charge. 'And, Eddie – if you carry on like this, cross my heart I'll never speak to you again!'

It was enough to make them lower their fists and take a moment to consider. Eddie saw that Stan's foot was still stuck in the ridiculous crate and Stan noticed that blood trickled from a cut on Eddie's cheek. Standing between them, Violet's face was pale and her hair tangled. Her chest heaved, her eyes flashed with anger.

'I mean it, Eddie. You can't go flying off the handle just because Ida and the rest of them got hold of the wrong end of the stick. And, Stan, this is what happens when you don't take no for an answer. Whatever I do to try to put you off your stride, people notice what you get up to and they *talk*!'

Bending to pull the crate apart and extricate his foot, Stan was the first to admit he was wrong. 'Violet's right – I took things too far. You know what I'm like, Eddie.'

'Yes, you're a blithering idiot,' Eddie muttered as Stan stood up straight again. 'But I also happen to know you'd take up with Violet at the drop of a hat and you wouldn't care about anybody else – only yourself.'

'And what does that say about me, you two talking about me as if I was a piece of property to be passed between you?' Violet intervened again. 'Eddie, do you think that Stan can whisper sweet nothings behind your back and that I'll fall for them, even after I've told you that you're the one I'm interested in?' She was angry now and didn't care that the cut on her beloved's face was bleeding or that a swelling had appeared under his eye. 'I told you there was nothing in it but you didn't even let me explain my side of the story before you dashed off. And now this is what happens.'

'I saw red,' Eddie admitted. 'I didn't stop to think.'

'Well, you should have.'

'You're right – I should.' He wiped the blood from his cheek with the back of his hand then began to set straight some of the furniture that had been disturbed during the brief scuffle. An upturned kitchen chair had suffered a broken leg and the cast-iron kettle was up-skittled from its hob on the open range.

'See!' Stan chided. 'I may be a blithering idiot, but you're the hot head here.'

'Stan!' Violet warned against his latest challenge.

'He is – he woke me up and had a go at me for nothing – just like your Uncle Donald.'

She shook her head and glared at him until he backed down.

'All right then – for me having a bit of fun, that's all . . . What? That's just me, isn't it? And you can't blame me for trying . . . Oh, all right, if it's an apology that you're after . . .'

'It is,' Violet said calmly. Now that she knew exactly what she had to say and do, her breathing grew more even and she felt strangely calm.

'Then I'm sorry, Eddie,' Stan mumbled, shame-faced and rubbing the elbow that he'd grazed during his fall onto the stone floor.

She tugged at his shirtsleeve. 'Don't apologize to him, you simpleton – say it to me!'

Stan turned to face her. 'I'm sorry, Violet. It won't happen again.'

'Apology accepted,' she declared, head held high as she made for the open door and climbed the cellar steps.

Eddie followed soon after. 'I'll walk you home,' he offered humbly, catching her by the hand when she reached the railings.

'I can walk myself home, thank you,' she said loud and clear, freeing her hand and walking boldly on.

'Good for you, love,' the first-floor mother called down. 'That'll show him.'

'Go on, go after her,' one of the tweed jackets advised Eddie.

'I wouldn't if I were you,' the other countered. 'Not until she's calmed down a bit.'

Violet ignored them all. She walked up Canal Road without a backward glance, leaving Eddie stranded and floundering.

Good for you, Violet. She heard Winnie echo the stranger's praise. *Eddie Thomson will soon come knocking on your door cap in hand – just you wait and see.*

True enough, straight after work on Monday Eddie appeared at Jubilee with a bunch of pink roses. He

245

shuffled sheepishly into the shop as Muriel was pulling down the blinds and Ida was cashing up the day's takings. From the back kitchen where she was re-stacking catalogues, Violet heard his voice asking for her but she didn't immediately go through.

'What are the flowers for?' Muriel asked dubiously. 'I thought roses were for Valentine's Day and that was months ago.'

'They're to say sorry to Violet for being such a clown yesterday,' Ida informed her with a knowing look.

'And whose fault was that?' Eddie retorted. 'If you lot hadn't ganged up on her around the dinner table, none of this would have happened.'

'I've already said sorry, haven't I?' Ida said with her usual jauntiness.

'None of what?' Muriel was bemused by the bad feeling between Eddie and Ida who normally got on so well. 'No, don't tell me – I've a feeling I'd rather not know. Eddie, wait here while I find out if Violet wants to see you.'

Bustling from the shop into the kitchen, Muriel found there was no need to bring Violet up to speed with what was happening because she'd overheard every word.

'How many roses has he brought me?' Violet asked in a whisper, drawing Muriel into the furthest corner.

'Twelve, I think. Nicely wrapped in paper from Blamey's florists on Ghyll Road. Why?'

'Because I want to know how sorry he is.'

'Very, by the look of him.'

Violet took her time to decide what to do. 'All right, listen to me. I want you to ask Eddie to leave the roses on the counter for me.'

'Are you sure? Wouldn't you rather speak to him face to face?'

'Not yet. Tell him I'll be in touch when I'm ready.'

Muriel shook her head and sighed. 'Poor Eddie.'

'"Poor Eddie" nothing! He has to realize how much he hurt my feelings before I see fit to forgive him. I will, of course, but don't tell him that.'

So Muriel took Violet's stern message back to a hangdog Eddie, who left the flowers on the counter and traipsed out of the shop.

'The course of true love . . .' Muriel muttered as Violet brought a jug of water from the kitchen and arranged the roses in it before carrying them upstairs to her room.

'I'm not altogether to blame,' Ida claimed. 'Yes, I'm sorry to have stirred up a hornets' nest, but anyone could have made the same mistake, the way Stan carries on.'

'Ah!' Muriel put two and two together. 'So that's where Eddie got that nasty cut on his cheek.'

For a while after this, Violet sewed in the attic workroom and served behind the counter, her confidence in both roles growing as she proved her worth.

'A yard of red taffeta ribbon, two yards of elastic,

247

half a dozen mother of pearl buttons . . .' She totted up items on the list that Lizzie Turner had brought in on the Thursday dinner time.

'Make it snappy,' Lizzie said with an anxious eye on the clock. 'Old Man Hutchinson will dock my pay if I'm late back.'

'Yes, a leopard never changes his spots,' Violet sympathized as she showed Lizzie the total and took the exact money.

'Ta very much,' Lizzie said as she hurried off.

Three yards of cream lampshade trimming . . . Size 8 knitting needles . . . Five yards of pink rayon . . . Butterick pattern number 568. Violet was kept busy in the shop all afternoon while Muriel and Ida sewed upstairs.

At half past five, when she was ready to lock up, she saw with a sinking heart that a familiar car had pulled up outside and knew that this meant she had one last – and unwelcome – customer to deal with.

Preparing herself, Violet retreated behind the counter. 'Good afternoon, Mrs Barlow,' she said above the tinkling of the bell. 'How can I help you?'

Alice Barlow, dressed in a dove-grey costume and matching hat with a dainty veil that came down over her eyes, looked all around the shop before she settled her critical gaze on Violet. 'I was hoping to speak to someone more senior.'

'Of course. Please wait a moment while I fetch Miss Thomson.'

'No, no, I don't have time. My husband's waiting

in the car and all I need from you is a lace doily for my dressing-table. I suppose you know the sort I mean.'

Violet went straight to the doily drawer. 'Certainly, Mrs Barlow. What size would you like? We have round doilies, crocheted by hand – five or seven inches in diameter, or an oval one that measures four inches across by six inches in length—'

'Oh, good heavens, how would I know the size? Do you think I spend my time measuring things?'

'Perhaps you could take a sample of each home with you, try them and then return those you don't need,' Violet suggested, trying not to be distracted by the sight of Colin Barlow emerging from the Daimler and crossing the pavement.

'Yes, wrap them as quickly as you can.' Imperious as ever, Alice Barlow's powdered face creased into a frown as the bell rang and her husband came in.

'Well, if it isn't our little hedgerow flower,' he said the moment he spied Violet. 'Growing more beautiful with each day that passes, I see.'

'Really, Colin, there was no need for you to follow me in,' his wife remonstrated. Deeply irritated by his opening gambit, she automatically turned her anger on Violet. 'If you weren't all fingers and thumbs, I'd have been in and out of here without having to keep my husband waiting.'

'Leave the poor girl alone,' he objected with a sly wink behind his wife's back. 'She's doing her best. And besides, I'm enjoying the view.'

Luckily for Violet, Ida chose this moment to come downstairs and take Colin Barlow discreetly to one side. There was an amount outstanding on the latest alterations they'd carried out on Mrs Barlow's dresses, plus an unpaid bill for more lingerie items and Ida wondered, since he was here, if she could trouble him for the money he owed.

'It's not convenient,' he replied, unabashed.

'And when would be convenient?' Ida asked, bright as one of the buttons she stocked.

'The next time I'm passing, whenever that happens to be. Why – you don't think I'll abscond without paying my debts, do you?'

Ida bristled at the cavalier reply. She looked him in the eye, one shopkeeper to another. 'Of course not. But here at Jubilee we like to keep our books in order. Would you rather I sent you a reminder in a letter?'

'No need, I assure you.' Colin Barlow tipped the brim of his panama and held open the door for his wife, who was ready to leave. '*Au revoir, ma cherie*, as the French say,' he told Violet with a flourish.

The door closed. Ida and Violet grimaced. Violet pulled down the blind.

'I'll give him until the end of the month to pay up,' Ida decided. 'After that, the Barlows will get nothing else on tick – not a single button or a reel of cotton until they've paid us what they owe.'

*

250

The roses had wilted in their jug and Stan had taken an excited Evie to the Victory a second time before Eddie finally plucked up the courage to seek Violet out again.

'What are you waiting for?' Ida had asked during one of the evenings that she'd found her brother sitting aimlessly by the quarry pond, staring into its murky depths. 'Why don't you find out where you stand with Violet once and for all?'

He'd given her the main reason why not – that Violet might send him away again with a flea in his ear. 'Then what do I do?'

'She won't,' Ida had predicted.

He'd picked up a stone and thrown it into the water. 'Why, has she said something to you?'

'No – I can just tell. Call it women's intuition.'

The conversation nudged Eddie into action so that on Friday after work he rode his newly repaired bike down Chapel Street and parked it outside Jubilee.

Up in the workroom, Violet's heart missed a beat when she heard the engine cut out.

'It's him.' Ida gave Violet an encouraging smile.

'Violet!' Muriel soon called from the bottom of the stairs. 'Eddie's here.'

Take a deep breath, Violet told herself. *Don't rush.*

'Shall I ask him to wait?' Muriel asked.

'No need. I'm on my way.' *Put down scissors, brush white thread from skirt.* Though Violet's heart was racing, she went down slowly and sedately. Muriel passed her on the first-floor landing, giving her the same kind of smile as Ida, accompanied by a re-assuring pat on the arm.

'Don't you dare say "poor Eddie"!' Violet whispered, gliding on down the stairs. Her nervous beau stood marooned in a sea of buttons and lace, ribbon and yarn. The cut on his cheek was healed, his tweed jacket unbuttoned.

'Hello, Eddie,' she said as calmly as she could.

'Hello, Vi. Have you clocked off work?' He saw that her face was flushed and there was still a thread of cotton clinging to the front of her red dress. 'If you have, I wondered if you fancied walking up to the Common with me.'

'That would be nice,' she agreed primly.

So far, so good. Eddie took a deep breath and held open the door. Violet walked through and he caught a whiff of her flowery perfume. What was it again? That's right – lily of the valley.

'Are you working tonight?' Violet asked nonchalantly as they made their way up the hill past Sykes' and Hutchinson's. Children played the usual hopscotch and skipping games, or else kicked a ball against a wall. Mothers called them in for their teas.

'Yes. I have to be at the Victory by seven.'

They passed Chapel Street Costumiers then the chapel itself before reaching the junction with Overcliffe Road. Men and women from the mills cycled home in droves, dodging in between cars and buses, shouting their goodbyes. At last there was a gap for

Eddie and Violet to link arms and make their way across.

'We could have picked a better evening for a walk,' Violet remarked. A cool wind blew from the exposed moors onto the Common and a bank of bruise-blue clouds gathered on the horizon. She kept her arm linked through his, he noticed.

'Would you like my jacket?' Breaking free and slipping it off without waiting for an answer, Eddie draped it around Violet's shoulders. They shared their walk with a man and his dog and then a girl pushing a pram. Otherwise the Common was deserted except for the dray horses from Thornley's, left out to graze overnight.

'Did you see Stan and Evie at the Victory the other night?' Violet dropped the subject into the conversation as if it was the most natural thing in the world rather than her trying to prove a point.

'I ran into them afterwards,' Eddie said. Here was the topic of Stan raising its ugly head again, he thought uneasily.

'Evie said they had a nice time.'

Eddie stopped and drew her arm through his again then anchored it firmly in the crook of his arm. He didn't say anything – only looked deep into her eyes. His beseeching gaze melted the last scrap of Violet's intention to maintain the upper hand. She'd kept it up long enough, she decided, as she stopped to run her fingertips over the mark on his cheek. 'That cut could have spoiled your good looks. I'm glad it didn't.'

'You think this is bad? You should see Stan's face,' he quipped.

'And he was no oil painting to start with.'

They laughed and walked on.

'Joking aside,' Violet continued, 'it was never Stan I was bothered about – it was you. You do know that, don't you?'

'I do now.' Eddie kept his hand over Violet's. The anxiety that had built up inside his chest over the last few days slowly began to ease. 'I've been an idiot but thank you for sticking with me.'

'In a way, I was flattered,' Violet admitted. 'I've never had two men fighting over me before. But, remember, Eddie, I'd given you my word.'

'I know. I should've listened to your side of the story before I lost my rag. I'm sorry.' The wind on the Common took their words and blew the difficulties clean away, making Violet wonder if now was the time to come clean over her problems with Colin Barlow. But Eddie moved on too quickly for her. 'I've been doing a lot of thinking lately, wondering how I could make things right between us.'

'There's no need,' she said simply, moving closer and matching her steps to his.

He felt the sway of her walk and the warmth of her body encased in his jacket. 'I went round in circles and kept coming back to the same topic.'

'Not Stan again,' she broke in. 'I thought we'd got past that.'

'No, not Stan this time. It's the bracelet I'm talk-

254

ing about. I thought if you still didn't want to do anything about it, then perhaps I could do it for you.'

'Do what?' Violet felt a small shock run through her. 'Eddie, you haven't mentioned it to your mother . . .'

'Don't worry – no, I didn't do anything you might not like. I just kept on thinking about it.'

'And?'

'I worked out that there were definitely two or three other people we could ask to find out who else the "D" might stand for.'

'Who?' A dozen roses was the easy way to say sorry, Violet thought. This showed something different and deeper – for Eddie to hold her in his thoughts even after they'd argued. It made her more pre-pared to tackle this other thorn in her side and so she wound her arm around his waist and asked him to go on.

'How about Marjorie Sykes for a start? Her mem-ory goes way back and she's the sort who knows every-thing about everyone.'

'Not Marjorie,' was Violet's first reaction. Asking her would be like opening the flood gates. 'We'd never hear the end of it.'

'Someone else, then.'

'Yes – someone else.'

On they walked, to the far edge of the Common, where they let their conversation drift into incon-clusive silence. Instead, they stood arm in arm and looked out across the moors.

Actually, Eddie thought, *I don't mind who we go to for information about what happened in 1914. Right now I'm here with Violet, turning for home as rain drops begin to fall. That's all that matters.*

CHAPTER EIGHTEEN

Once Eddie's idea of asking Marjorie for help had settled in Violet's mind, she got over her first nervous reaction and began to consider it more carefully. For a start, it was true that Marjorie was the fount of all knowledge in the neighbourhood and that her memory stretched back to the time when her mother would have been a young woman. Secondly, though she was a natural gossip, she was warm hearted and had kept a close eye on Violet ever since Winnie's untimely demise, so there was no doubting her desire to help if she could.

Sitting on her bed early on Sunday morning, Violet opened the blue velvet box that nestled in her lap. She took out the small envelope and studied the name and address written in faded black ink – Florence Wheeler, 25 Railway Road, Hadley. Then she took out the note and reread the message.

Puzzling over each word, Violet could see that the use of the word 'Wheeler' on the envelope meant for certain that the gift of the bracelet had been made after her mother's wedding to Donald's brother, Joe.

Violet turned her attention to the bracelet itself, taking it up and draping it across her fingers so that the rose-gold padlock swayed like a pendulum. The details on it were finely executed, she realized – especially the inscription, 'Xmas 1914'. This was careful workmanship, down to the miniature key-hole and the slender safety chain – a gift that she supposed must have cost more than a working man's weekly wage in those days.

The longer Violet studied the bracelet and held it between her fingers, the greater the urge to solve the mystery grew.

It was only the sound of Eddie's bike chugging down the alleyway beside number 1 that roused her from her reverie and made her return the bracelet to its box. Forgetting that she was in her petticoat, she dashed to the window and slid it open, leaning out to wave at him as he parked the machine in the yard. 'What are you doing here, Eddie? I wasn't expecting you.'

Eddie looked up at the radiant, bare-shouldered girl calling from the upstairs window. 'You'll catch your death if you're not careful!'

'Hold on!' Violet disappeared from view and minutes later she came downstairs dressed in her favourite red frock. 'Have you come to take me out for a ride?' she beamed.

'Get your coat. You're invited to my house for dinner,' he explained, with a smile.

'Again? Are you sure? Don't forget what happened last time.'

'That's why Mother especially wants you to come. She and Ida have made a slap-up meal to show you how sorry they are.'

'Right you are.' This was all the invitation Violet needed. She ran back upstairs to fling on her coat and very soon she and Eddie were threading their way through the streets to Valley Road, arriving at the Thomsons' house just as Ida took a leg of lamb from the oven. Emily was turning roast potatoes in their fat and prodding them to see if they were ready, while Dick and Harold kept out of the way in the front yard.

'Now then, young lady.' Dick's greeting to Violet was phlegmatic as ever.

'Hello, Mr Thomson.' She responded cheerily to let him know that what had happened last time was all water under the bridge. Inside the kitchen she encountered the usual, cheerful domestic chaos – a dinner table only half laid out with mismatched cutlery, Crackers the ginger cat prowling perilously close to the joint of meat, which had been perched on the window sill to rest, and Ida suddenly exclaiming that she'd forgotten to make the gravy.

'Here you are, Violet.' Emily sank into the nearest chair and fanned her flushed face with Dick's folded newspaper.

'Yes – here I am!'

'Just in time to set the table,' Ida told her. 'The

259

dinner plates are on the draining board. Pass me that colander for the peas, while you're over there. Shoo, Crackers – get away, you naughty cat!'

Smilingly Violet lent a hand and by the time they all sat down to dinner, there were no clouds of embarrassment left over to spoil their enjoyment.

'Harold's knocking up a kitchen cupboard from some pine floorboards he rescued from Bradley's rag and bone yard,' Ida informed them. 'If there's any wood left over, he'll put it towards a blanket chest for bed linen and such like.'

'Have you even got a bed yet?' Emily wanted to know.

'I picked up two iron bed ends from Bradley's while I was there.' Harold's face reddened but he ploughed on. 'I asked them to be on the lookout for a frame to go with it.'

'But not a mattress, I hope.' Emily grimaced at the thought of scrap-yard fleas and tics. 'You'll need to save up for a new one of those.'

'Yes and at this rate we'll be drawing our old age pensions before we're wed,' Ida joked. She'd made room at the beginning of the meal for Violet to sit next to her and ensured that she got first choice of peas and potatoes.

'Ida, this gravy's got lumps in,' Emily complained.

'No it hasn't, Mam.'

'Yes, it has.' She scooped thick gravy onto her fork. 'What's this if it's not a lump?'

'A pea,' Eddie told her with a laugh.

After dinner the cat chose Violet's lap to sit on as she and Ida relaxed by the pond while Emily dozed by the unmade fire and the men tinkered with Eddie's motorbike in the front yard.

'I wasn't joking earlier,' Ida confessed, kicking off her shoes, rolling up her trousers and dangling her legs over the edge of the rock. 'I'm tired of trying to save up enough money to buy furniture and so on, not to mention a deposit on any house we might be able to afford to rent. Oh and then there's the cost of the wedding on top of that.'

'It can't be easy,' Violet acknowledged then thought for a while. The cat settled down for a nap. 'Have you and Muriel considered charging more for the dress-making work?'

Ida shook her head. 'That would defeat the object, remember. We keep the orders rolling in because we deliberately pin our prices down lower than Chapel Street Costumiers. That way it works for both parties.'

'So we have to work faster and put in longer hours if we want to earn more,' Violet decided.

'But then you know what they say: all work and no play makes Jack a dull boy. Harold and I are still young. We need to have fun.'

'I suppose so.' In that case, Violet could see no way to help Ida save enough money to marry.

'Besides,' Ida went on in a confidential tone, 'I'm not sure I'm quite ready to give up my freedom just yet. I'm in love with Harold, of course I am. But I love my work, too. If I marry and have babies, bang goes my dressmaking time. Then how do I make my own way in the world?'

'I'm not sure,' Violet murmured as she stroked the cat's soft fur. 'Surely your mother would be able to help you?'

The comment made Ida laugh. 'I can't imagine her getting involved in changing nappies again, can you? She'd tell you herself that she wasn't the best mother in the world when Eddie and I were little. She was too busy gallivanting with her friends – your mother and aunty included.'

'Did your mother really go about with my mother?' Violet turned to Ida so sharply that the cat started from his sleep and jumped from her lap.

'I expect she did,' Ida replied. 'Why?'

Violet thought better of it and frowned. 'Oh, nothing.'

'Come on, Violet, what's eating you all of a sudden?'

Something about the warm isolation of the cosy nook they'd chosen and the confessional tone of the conversation made Violet open up to Ida in a way that she hadn't expected and explain to her all about the mystery of the bracelet and her search for her family.

'You don't say.' For once Ida was at a loss after hearing Violet's story, but she soon rallied. 'I see!' she said with fresh energy. 'You're hoping that Mam will have some of the answers.'

'Or someone who was part of the young crowd

back then. But honestly, Ida, I don't want to upset anybody by asking awkward questions.'

'Nonsense,' Ida decided, springing to her feet and hauling Violet up with her. 'Mam won't mind. She loves a gossip as much as the next person.'

'Wait – I'm still not sure,' Violet protested.

'But I am,' Ida argued, marching Violet around the edge of the pond, through the yard and into the house to rouse her mother. 'Wake up, Mam, and get your thinking cap on. Violet wants to talk to you about the old days.'

'What was my mother like?' Violet asked Emily once they'd furnished her with a reviving cuppa and Ida had provided a rapid preamble to the questions that Violet needed an answer to.

Ida and Eddie's mother sipped her tea and strolled willingly down memory lane. 'Florence was just like you to look at – the same hazel eyes and her hair had your auburn tint, though it was long and she wore it up – as we all did in those days. She knew how to make the best of herself too, did Florence Shaw . . . You'll have seen pictures of her, I reckon?'

'As a matter of fact, no. Aunty Winnie was never big on photographs. There was no family album or anything like that.' Fascinated by Emily's snap-shot description, Violet was eager to hear more. 'What was she like?'

'She loved the music hall, if I remember rightly. She had a nice singing voice too.' Emily turned to

Ida. 'You know the album I keep in the pine chest of drawers?'

'In your bedroom? Yes. Do you want me to fetch it?'

'Yes. There's a photograph there of a group of us, including Florence, performing in a Christmas pantomime for the Hadley Players.'

Violet smiled at the odd coincidence and waited for Ida to bring the dog-eared album down. She watched Emily open it at the right page then leaned in for the first ever view of her mother.

'This is her in 1913.' Emily pointed to a figure in the front row of a group of around a dozen women dressed in pale satin tunics and matching trousers, wearing elaborate stage make-up and with their hair tied back in pigtails. 'We were in *Aladdin*, singing and dancing in the chorus. We had fun and games that year, I can tell you.'

Violet peered closely at the photograph, taken just two years before she was born. Her mother was taller than the others, her smile not quite so broad for the camera and her head was tilted at a shy angle.

'My – even under all that make-up you can see how lovely she was,' Ida said in an admiring tone.

'That was the trouble,' Emily commented. 'She could have had the pick of the bunch, could Florence.'

As they looked and talked, Violet was aware that Eddie had come quietly into the kitchen. He stayed in the background while the talk continued.

'What kind of trouble?' Ida wanted to know.

'That's what I mean by fun and games. Joe Wheeler was falling over himself to ask Florence out, getting into scraps after rehearsal with Ben Hutchinson over who had first claim on her.'

'Why does that sound familiar, I wonder?' Ida said with a meaningful look at Violet and Eddie.

'Ben Hutchinson?' Violet echoed in disbelief, her gaze still fixed on the figure in the photograph.

'Yes. Believe it or not, he was a smart young fellow about town back then, before he buried himself in dusty ledgers and stocktaking. There were others, too – I forget exactly who.'

'So why did she plump for Joe Wheeler in the end?' Ida wanted to know.

'Don't ask me.' Emily shrugged and closed the album with a dull thud. 'Why does anyone plump for anyone? The war came along soon after that picture was taken and the two of them married quickly, just as so many people did. Kitchener was pointing his finger from bill boards in every railway station and outside every town hall, telling us that our country needed us and Joe, Donald, Ben and the rest of them – they all went off like lambs to the slaughter.'

A chill ran through Violet and she shuddered. 'What about Joe?' she asked. 'What do you remember about him?'

'Not much. Only that he was the opposite to his brother, Donald. Not so po-faced and holier than thou. And he was handsome with it, so I could see

265

why a girl might fall for him, except that he had a bit of a bad reputation.'

'In what way?' Ida saved Violet the embarrassment of asking the obvious question, taking the empty teacup from her mother and refilling it from the brown pot on the hob.

Emily narrowed her eyes. 'Joe had lost his steady job down the mine in Hadley for bad time-keeping. After that he went from one place to another, just scraping by. They seemed to think he wasn't reliable. That's why we were all a bit taken aback when Florence upped and married him.'

Saddened by the picture Ida's mother had painted and by how short and troubled the marriage seemed to have been, Violet felt it was time to draw the conversation to an end. She had one last question but she hesitated over how to frame it without giving too much away. 'Was there anyone else my mother might have been interested in at that time?' she asked cautiously.

'Besides Joe and Ben?' Emily racked her tired brain. 'There was Walter Briggs for a little while, when he was renting a cellar room on Canal Road. But he was married to Rhoda Preston by the time I'm talking about. And there was a friend of Ben's – the two of them fell out over it. I forget his name. Oh, there must have been half a dozen others when I think about it.'

'Anyone whose name began with a D?' Ida said, blunt as you like.

Violet's stomach churned and she glanced across at Eddie.

'D?' Tiring of the subject and with her interest visibly waning, Emily gave over her second cup of tea to Ida and sat back in her chair. 'Not that I can remember. Why?'

'Vi was just wondering,' Eddie said quickly. He'd stood by with the intention of plucking Violet out of the situation as soon as it became uncomfortable. 'Evie and Stan are here,' he told her. 'They want to know if we fancy an afternoon ramble out to Little Brimstone. They're outside in the yard waiting for an answer.'

The impromptu hike out of town and into the countryside was just what Violet needed.

Stan was on his best behaviour with Evie, who took his arm and laughed at his jokes and seemed pleased as Punch to have a young man with whom she could walk out on a sunny September afternoon.

'I'm building up a thirst,' Stan complained as they tramped the moor road on the way to the beauty spot.

'Don't worry – we'll stop for tea when we get to Kitty's,' Eddie promised.

By this time, the two girls walked behind while the men strode ahead. For a while they chatted about Violet's upcoming birthday then the latest dress patterns and types of sewing thread before moving on to how Evie and Stan were getting along.

'I like him,' Evie confessed cautiously. 'When we're together he's not brash and pushy the way I thought he might be. I think that's all an act. Beneath it all he's a little bit shy.'

'So he's quite the gentleman?' Violet asked.

'Yes. He holds doors open for me and sees me home properly. He's polite to Father and funny with Arthur. To tell you the truth, I couldn't ask for more.'

'Blimey, don't tell me he's turned over a new leaf.' Violet laughed. 'Is this really Stan Tankard we're talking about?'

'Should my ears be burning?' Stan turned and enquired. 'I'm sure I heard my name mentioned.'

'Evie's telling me what a gentleman you turn out to be.' Violet hurried to catch up.

'That's because I know you'd tear me off a strip if I stepped out of line,' he said with the old bravado.

However, Violet caught the genuine, gentle smile that Stan gave Evie behind her back and she decided not to tease him any more. Instead, she seized Eddie by the hand and pulled him along. 'Come on, slow coaches – I'll race you to the café!'

They hurried the final mile on tired legs until they came to the track leading to the tea-rooms-with-a-view where Eddie, Violet and Evie chose a bench to sit on while Stan went inside to order tea.

'Eddie, you're the pantomime dame between two leading ladies,' Stan quipped on his return with the tray of refreshments. 'Move along, Evie, make some room.'

They drank tea and ate fruit scones from plates balanced on their knees, taking in the panoramic view of the boulder-strewn, steep-sided valley until Violet and Eddie took a stroll to their favourite spot overlooking the waterfall while the other two polished off the last of the refreshments.

'Let's sit for a while.' Eddie cleared early-autumn leaves from a ledge.

'Yes, I'm happy as Larry here,' she said, edging close to Eddie and smiling up at him.

'And it's good just to see you wearing a smile after Mother's stroll down memory lane,' he told her.

'Yes. Well, I'm glad she showed me the picture.' The rush of water over worn stone almost drowned the sound of Violet's voice. 'I thought it might upset me but it didn't. It was nice hearing about my mother but we didn't get far with what I'm really after, did we?'

Eddie squeezed her hand. He pulled at a grass stalk and chewed on the juicy end, keeping it hanging between his teeth as he went on. 'What we need is a Sherlock Holmes type – someone with a razor-sharp memory and more of a bloodhound instinct to pick up clues. That's not Mother, unluckily for us.'

'Perhaps I should have been more truthful about the reason behind it all.' Violet sighed, resting her head on Eddie's shoulder.

'Not unless you felt up to it,' he consoled and they sat a while enjoying the green, secret place. Eventually he stood up and offered her his hand.

'Are you ready to go back and see if Stan is still behaving himself?'

'He'd better be.' Violet grinned, brushing herself down and leading the way. She and Eddie emerged from the leafy glen into the sunlit clearing to hear Stan render an out of tune version of 'Daisy' in front of an embarrassed Evie while a small bunch of fellow ramblers laughed and generally encouraged him.

'Dai-sy, Dai-sy, give me your answer, do . . .'

Violet ran to the rescue. 'Shy my foot!' she exclaimed, knocking Stan out of the way and pulling Evie to her feet. 'Stan Tankard, behave yourself. We've got a long walk home and Eddie and I will be keeping an eye on you every step of the way.'

CHAPTER NINETEEN

Against the grimy bustle of mills and factories, of trams and buses loaded with their cargos of workers, of women shopping in Clifton Street market and children playing in the cobbled streets, the rich colours of late September shone forth. Leaves on the horse chestnut trees at the entrance to Linton Park turned to gold and in the distance, bracken on the moors showed russet brown. Early mornings brought silvery mist to the Common.

'They say we're in for a hard winter,' Emily Thomson grumbled to Muriel on Monday morning when she called in at Jubilee with a message for Ida. 'They can tell by the berries. When the trees are laden at this time of year, you can bet we're in for weeks of snow in December and January. Anyway, where's Ida got to? I haven't got all day.'

'She's upstairs in the workroom,' Violet reported. 'I told her you were here.'

'We could pass on the message for you if you like,' Muriel offered. Lately she'd taken to wearing glasses for close work and she had them perched on top of her bobbed, fair hair. The prim effect was countered by a soft, flowered blouse and a shiny belt around her trim waist.

'I'll wait, thank you.' Contrary as ever and with half an eye on Violet until the customer had paid and left the shop, Emily examined embroidery silks. 'I hear your birthday's coming up soon,' she mentioned in the lull that followed.

'At the end of the month,' Violet confirmed. 'I'll be nineteen years young.'

'And I expect you're glad to be away from slicing bacon and weighing out butter?'

'I truly am,' Violet said with a laugh. 'Give me silk stockings and kid gloves any day of the week.'

'Violet, this order for Mrs Kingsley is ready to go out,' Muriel informed her. 'Why not have your dinner early then you can ride out with it straight afterwards?'

The arrangement suited Violet. 'My tummy's rumbling. I think I'll nip up to Hutchinson's for a pork pie.'

'That's what comes of not having any breakfast,' Emily tutted. She opened the door for Violet and followed her out onto the street. 'Tell Ida I couldn't wait any longer – I need to buy flour and sugar before I catch the bus home,' she called to Muriel.

'I can buy your groceries for you and send them up with Ida,' Violet offered as Emily started up Chapel Street.

'No, but you can give me your arm, thank you. You'll have to slow down a bit, though. You youngsters don't know what it's like, making your way up these steep hills when you get to my age.'

Violet knew that Eddie's mother couldn't be more than fifty-two or -three but she took into consideration Emily's cup-half-empty outlook and slowed down to a snail's pace. The two of them together made an interesting contrast – Emily Thomson was stooped and dour, her wispy grey hair untidily brushed back and held in place by a gap-toothed tortoiseshell comb while Violet walked with a spring in her stride and a smile on her face, shoulders back, her hair as glossy as one of the horse chestnuts nestled inside their green, spiked shells.

'By the way, I was thinking that Ben Hutchinson is the man you need to talk to,' Emily told Violet, seemingly apropos of nothing as they passed under the shade of Sykes' striped canopy.

Violet was taken by surprise. 'What about?'

'About the old days and that mother of yours. He's got a memory like an elephant, has Ben.' Putting on an uncharacteristic burst of speed, Emily led the way into the grocer's shop before Violet had time to object, up the black-and-white, mosaic-patterned step into the cool interior with its strong smell of smoked bacon. 'Come along, slow coach. There's no time like the present.'

*

'What's the good of raking up the past?' was Ben Hutchinson's first response when Emily collared him in his storeroom and demanded to hear everything he could remember about Violet's mother, Florence Wheeler, née Shaw. At that moment Violet felt ready to agree. Backed up against boxes of cornflakes and with the door of the cluttered, airless room shut tight, she viewed her old boss with the usual trepidation.

'Wouldn't you want to find out as much as you could if you were in Violet's shoes?' Emily challenged. 'The poor soul's just getting over losing her Aunty Winnie, not to mention her Uncle Donald jiggering off. That's enough to unsettle anyone, I should think.'

'Where's he jiggered off to, as you put it?' Ben seemed more interested in this than in Violet's plight. 'No one's seen hide nor hair of him at Chapel lately.'

'Never mind Donald Wheeler – it's Florence, his sister-in-law, who we want to hear about. Tell us what you remember about her carryings-on.'

For someone who lacked the bloodhound quality, Eddie's mother was doing a good job of sinking her teeth into a reluctant Ben Hutchinson, Violet realized. Though Emily was small and skinny, she seemed to have forgotten her frailties and cornered him against a high stack of cardboard boxes with no chance of escape.

'Carryings-on is right,' he muttered, pressing his silver-rimmed glasses higher onto the bridge of his nose. 'What if little missy doesn't like what she hears?'

'"Little missy", meaning me?' His dismissive tone made Violet stand up for herself, even though she felt the familiar rising panic when on the brink of revelations about times gone by. Then she recalled the weeks and months she spent under the mean-minded grocer's thumb and it brought out her stubborn, independent streak. 'You can tell me the truth – it won't bother me.'

'And think on – none of us were angels,' Emily warned. 'Not with the country about to go to war. You least of all, Ben Hutchinson.'

'Pots and kettles, Emily Thomson,' he grumbled with another tap at his glasses and a loud sniff.

'I'm ready,' Violet vowed, as though preparing to face the firing squad.

'The truth?' Ben repeated. 'The fact is we were no different to anybody else back in those days. We worked hard and we played hard, those of us who had roofs over our heads and steady jobs – either down the mines or in the mills, you took your pick. If you were lucky, like me, you went into shop work, starting at the bottom and gradually working your way up.'

'What about my mother in particular?' Violet prompted.

'Mill girl over in Welby,' came the quick, abbreviated reply. 'Not from these parts. And if you must know, no better than she should be.'

Thinking about the shy, serious face she'd seen in

the old photograph, Violet instinctively rose to her mother's defence. 'What do you mean by that?'

'I mean, she had men swarming about her like wasps around a jam pot.'

'Including you, and she turned you down flat.' Emily reminded him that his opinion of Florence Shaw might be no more than sour grapes.

'All right, then. Even if she couldn't help being popular because of the way she looked, when it came to it she didn't do herself any favours. Right from the start, soon after she'd joined the Hadley Players, she played us all off against one another – me and Joe Wheeler, and a few others. And the women didn't take to her either, apart from Winnie Craven – your Aunty Winnie – who never had a bad word to say about anybody.'

'I didn't mind Florence – I could take her or leave her.' Emily defended herself in her usual laconic fashion. 'And she was good friends for a while with Gladys Sowden, as was, until all that went wrong.'

'That's what I mean,' Ben insisted. 'Wherever Florence Shaw went, trouble was bound to follow. She left Welby Mill and came to live on Westgate Road to be near her new job at Calvert's. Gladys was already married and she was an overseer in the weaving shed – a good-looker in her own right, but no competition for Florence. She found out that being friendly with the new girl put her in the shade and she didn't like it one bit. They soon fell out.'

'I'd overlooked poor Gladys,' Emily admitted as

she turned to Violet. 'That's what I mean about Ben – he never forgets.'

'Are you going to let me out of here, or not?' he demanded crossly. 'I have customers to serve, as if you didn't know.'

'Lizzie's doing a grand job out there, don't you worry. Explain to Violet who or what Florence and Gladys argued over.'

Grudgingly Ben took the only way out of the cramped storeroom and back to work. 'It was after Florence got married to Joe Wheeler and they set up house on Railway Road in Hadley. The argument was over a pal of mine – the chap who Gladys was already married to. They had a little boy between them – about three or four years old. Gladys was sure that Florence was set on stealing her husband away from her, even though she'd recently settled down with Joe.'

'And was that really my mother's plan?' Violet wanted to know, turning uneasily from Ben to Emily and back again.

'Some said it was, some said it wasn't.' He shrugged. 'I once took the bull by the horns and asked Douglas about his fling with Florence. He wouldn't give me a straight answer.'

'Douglas?' Violet echoed. A shudder of alarm ran through her.

'Ah yes, I'd left him out of the picture too,' Emily murmured with pursed lips and an apprehensive look at her young companion.

'Douglas who?' Violet insisted. This then was the Pandora's box that she had been afraid of, and it turned out that the key was not with Emily Thomson or Marjorie Sykes, but was held in the unlikely hands of Ben Hutchinson – open the lid and out would fly a horde of dark secrets that could never be put back.

'Douglas Tankard,' he told her straight out. 'You probably know Gladys and Douglas's son, Stan – everybody does.'

That's why! Violet said to herself over and over as she set off on Ida's sit-up-and-beg bike. When Ben had dropped his bombshell, she'd felt the blood drain from her face and had run from the shop. No wonder Uncle Donald was so much against her walking out with Stan and had done his utmost to prevent it – with good reason if what Ben had said was true.

Almost without realizing it, she found herself cycling along Canal Road, work, parcel and deliveries all forgotten in her shaken state of mind. It was too hard to keep this to herself, she realized. She had to find Stan and speak to him. Knowing that he usually worked mornings at Kingsley's, she decided that the best place to track him down during a weekday afternoon was at Brinkley Baths.

Along the wide, flat road she pedalled with the wind in her hair, bombarded with new thoughts and fears that she had no control over.

Her mother had entered into a love affair with a

married man. She had deceived her new husband, the ne'er-do-well Joe Wheeler. Douglas Tankard had wooed her by sending her the gift of a gold bracelet in a blue velvet box shaped like a heart. *Keep this bracelet for my sake.*

Or else it was all a lie, made up by gossips – men who had been turned down by Florence and women who were jealous of her. But that didn't explain the initials on the inside of the envelope or the lack of other keepsakes and photographs in Aunty Winnie's possessions. It was as if there was something to be kept secret and to feel ashamed of surrounding Florence's marriage to Joe.

Ideas flitted like moths in and out of Violet's head. She could almost hear dry wings beating, the faint brush of them before they veered off and were replaced by new ones, even more unwelcome than those preceding them. That's the real reason why Uncle Donald didn't want me. He knew I was nothing to do with his brother Joe. I was a cuckoo in the Wheelers' nest. *Like mother, like daughter*, he'd said with savage anger. It made sense now – a mother, Florence, who had enjoyed the company of men too much and had gone astray. A daughter, Violet, whom he suspected of stringing men along, whose looks reminded him daily of the wrong that had been done to his brother.

Violet's heart beat fast as she reached the swimming baths, flung down her bike and mounted the broad steps. She strode through the tiled entrance and towards the ticket office to ask for Stan.

'We're not open yet,' the man behind the desk informed her – a diminutive, portly stranger with a florid complexion and a bald head. 'Stan's due in any time now to start his shift.'

An exasperated Violet considered what to do. Should she ride out to Ash Tree House with the Kingsley delivery then catch Stan on her return? No, she would rather wait here then explain later to Muriel why she'd taken so long, because in this current state of mind she couldn't trust herself to cycle safely without ignoring traffic lights or crossing the path of an oncoming tram. So she went outside and paced the pavement, all the time keeping watch for Stan.

He came at last, full pelt on his bike down Ghyll Road and onto Canal Road, jacket flying open and cap tilted forward over his forehead, screeching to a halt outside the baths then leaping off and wheeling his bike down the side of the building.

'No time to talk – I'm running late!' he yelled when he spotted Violet rushing towards him.

At the thought of him vanishing without her having a chance to talk to him, suddenly and without warning she broke down in tears.

Startled, he drew her to one side. 'There, there, don't cry,' he said, offering her his crumpled handkerchief. 'Tell me what's up.'

'No, you haven't got time. You'll get the sack if you're not careful.'

'So what if I do? Have you and Eddie had a fight, or is that too much for me to hope for?'

'Stan, this is serious.' His flippancy was good for her. It made her dry her tears. 'Besides, you promised.'

'Yes, take no notice.' Leaning his bike against the wall, he kept his distance, folded his arms and waited for her to go on.

'I've found out something important that affects us both. It's to do with my mother and your father.'

'What kind of thing?'

Violet paused and studied the sudden look of bewilderment on Stan's face. It made him seem younger than his years and vulnerable. So, with her own feelings back under control, she proceeded more cautiously. 'How long have we known each other – you and me?'

'Since you were knee-high to a grasshopper. Why?'

'And in all that time you've never mentioned your family and I've never thought to ask about them.'

'That's because there's nothing to say. You know I lost my dad in the war, like you did.'

'But . . . No, carry on.' Violet stopped herself from interrupting.

'Then ten years ago, in March 1924, my mother took ill with TB. She died in the November.'

'I'm sorry, Stan – I didn't know that.'

'I was thirteen. They wanted me to go into an orphanage but I said no, ta very much. Instead, I left school early and managed to make my own way, doing odd jobs – cleaning windows, cutting hedges, and so on, until I landed the job at Kingsley's.'

'I didn't know that either,' Violet said gently.

'I wasn't going to be cooped up in an institution after Mam died, was I?'

'No, I can see that wouldn't have suited you. But what affects us is to do with your father, not your mother – if what I heard turns out to be true.'

'Not that devil,' Stan said with a grimace. He thrust his hands in his pockets, scuffed at a stone with the toe of his boot then looked up at Violet as if half anticipating what she was about to say.

'There's a rumour,' she said softly.

'Just one? You're kidding me. From what I know, you could take your pick from at least a dozen.'

'Such as?'

'Such as, my father, Douglas Tankard, managed to get the sack from at least three different jobs – one as a miner down Hadley pit, one in a pawnbroker's shop in Welby and another here as a boiler man at Calvert's – and after that it was downhill all the way. Such as, he was a regular propping up the bar at the Green Cross when he should have been out looking for work. Oh, and not forgetting that he was well known as a ladies' man, which is something my poor mother had to put up with until the day he enlisted and disappeared out of our lives for good.'

Emboldened, Violet drew breath before going on to divulge what Ben had told her. 'The rumour I'm interested in is that in 1914 your father, Douglas, had a love affair with my mother, Florence.'

Stan stared. Still with his hands deep in his pockets, he turned away then spun back towards her.

'He gave her a bracelet.' She met his gaze and held it, along with her breath.

'You don't say,' he murmured, his brain racing.

'I don't know anything for certain, Stan. But I thought it was only fair to tell you.'

'That there's a chance . . . they had a kid?'

'It looks like it – yes.'

'We could be brother and sister?'

'*Half*-brother and *half*-sister,' she corrected, fixing him with a hopeful gaze.

Stan scarcely paused to consider Violet's startling news. 'By Jove,' he said, a grin lighting up his puzzled face. 'You and me could end up related. Blimey, Violet, that really would be a turn-up for the books!'

'Seriously, you're pleased?' she asked uncertainly.

'You bet! You're the nicest kid sister anyone could wish to have.'

'Don't say anything about it – not yet,' Violet pleaded. 'Wait until we're sure.'

'When will that be?' Stan asked. He spotted his boss stepping off the bus at the stop outside the baths and making his way into work.

'When we're sure of everything. It happened a long time ago, but I still don't want people calling my mother names she might not deserve, not until we have all of the facts.'

283

'Will you tell Eddie?'

'Yes, but only him. He'll help us sort it all out and with a bit of luck we'll be able to prove that the situation wasn't as bad as it seems at first glance.'

'All right, cross my heart and hope to die – I won't breathe a word,' Stan promised before hurrying away to receive the expected telling-off from his boss.

CHAPTER TWENTY

After leaving Stan, Violet had no choice but to go back to work and deliver the package Ida had given her. She pedalled hard to the Kingsleys' house, forcing herself to concentrate on the task in hand and forget about her conversation with Stan. She arrived out of breath, and looked up at the Kingsleys' imposing, stone-built mansion set back behind privet hedges and overlooking a small tarn at the edge of the moor. *I only hope Mrs Kingsley is in*, she thought as she freewheeled down the drive. *Otherwise I've had a wasted journey.*

The front door was firmly closed, but Violet followed an arrow indicating the tradesmen's entrance round the side. She dismounted then wheeled her bike into a cobbled yard with an old-fashioned coach house that had recently been converted into a garage for the Kingsleys' car. She could see through the open door that the car was missing, however, and once more prepared herself to return to Jubilee with Mrs Kingsley's new dress undelivered.

Then she caught sight of a figure looking out from a downstairs window in the main house and soon after that the side door opened and out stepped Colin Barlow. He was dressed for pheasant shooting in plus-fours and a checked, tweed jacket and he wore a look of eager expectation as he bore down on Violet.

'If it isn't my favourite dressmaker!' he exclaimed, striding towards her. 'Don't look so surprised, my dear. Monday is Kingsley's and my day for taking pot shots at a few innocent birds up on Brimstone Moor, followed by a couple of fine whiskies before supper.'

'Good afternoon.' Violet hoped that her politeness, though stiff, would mask her increasing dislike for Barlow and her shock at finding him here. 'I have a parcel for Mrs Kingsley.'

'Not in, I'm afraid. And Thomas is busy with a telephone call at present.'

Boxing Violet into a corner of the yard, the mill owner's guest breathed whisky fumes into her face and she noticed that his speech was slurred. 'Of course, I could do you a favour and take the parcel for you.'

'Thank you.' Violet made an attempt to slip sideways out of the man's reach, intending to take the dress from the wicker basket attached to her front handlebars and hand it to him.

He blocked her way. 'But then you would have to do me a favour in return.'

'Please let me by, Mr Barlow.' Dislike slid into disgust, but still Violet had no clear sense of what he meant. What did he want from her?

'Don't play the innocent,' he mocked, pressing in on her. Then, before she had a chance to realize what was happening, he pushed her back into the darkness of the garage, up against a brace of dead birds hanging from a hook to the left of the door. There were two guns propped against the wall and three more pairs of pheasants hanging from similar hooks.

Recoiling from a splash of cold blood that dripped from the head of one of the pheasants onto her raised hand, Violet retreated further into the garage with its smell of dirty engine oil and petrol from cans lined up against the back wall. Disgust swiftly became fear.

'You understand me well enough – you know exactly what I mean,' Barlow sneered. His usually handsome face was shadowy and distorted by a crude eagerness to lay hands on his prize.

'Don't you dare touch me,' she warned, her back to the wall as she slowly edged sideways away from him towards the daylight. Her foot caught one of the cans and it tipped onto its side with a loud metallic clatter.

Startled, Barlow lunged swiftly at the door and banged it shut. As he did so, he caught his cheek on one of the hooks, giving it a small nick. He yelped and swore, but was quickly calm again. 'Don't make a fuss, Violet. We both know what has to happen here.'

She was trapped. They were in total darkness. 'I've told you – leave me alone,' she insisted.

Recognizing that Violet was not going to willingly give in to him, Barlow dropped his attempts at persuasion and turned to brute force. He lurched at her and seized her by the shoulders, pressing her backwards with his forearm against her throat until they collided with the hanging birds that swung violently against her face, their feathers sticky with blood. His mouth made contact with her cheek then her mouth, lips on lips, his hands mauling her.

Violet recoiled and managed to place her palms on his chest, gaining leverage to push him off. Then she twisted and felt for the shotguns, took hold of one and instantly aimed it towards him.

'You wouldn't . . .' he challenged, swaying unsteadily in the murk and hesitating to wrest the gun away.

'I will!' she swore, though her hands trembled and her voice was faint. *I could shoot him through the heart*, she thought, *and the world would be rid of him. Good riddance.*

'No, you couldn't.' Sure of himself again, he laughed as he moved in towards her again.

He was right – Violet would never pull the trigger. Instead, she slid her hands down the long barrel and swung the gun at him like a club, catching him heavily in the ribs as he lurched towards her.

Barlow made a winded, groaning noise then bent

double while Violet dropped the gun and fumbled at the door, searching for a handle. Finding none, she shoved against the door with all her might. It swung open and daylight flooded in. She fled from the garage, running for her bike and setting off across the yard with blood streaking her face and hands. Barlow stumbled from the garage behind her then he watched her gather speed up the drive. He stooped forward with one arm holding his side.

Inside the house, Thomas Kingsley came to the window of his study to watch Violet's hurried departure. Wondering what had caused the commotion, he quickly went in search of his shooting companion and, to his surprise, found him carrying the day's spoils out of the garage.

'Where can I put these out of harm's way?' Barlow overcame the pain in his ribs to smile and hold the birds aloft. 'We don't want them to scare the living daylights out of any more visitors, do we?'

So that was it, Kingsley thought. Or at least that's what Colin wanted him to think and he was prepared to leave it at that. 'Hang them in the keeping cellar, then clean yourself up and find me in my study,' he told his guest. 'I have a very nice single malt that I'd like you to try – aged in an oak barrel on the Isle of Skye for fifteen years.'

Violet suspected there were some women who would have rushed straight to the police after what had happened at Ash Tree House, but she wasn't one of them. It would feel too much like a scene from one of Ida's murder mysteries and she couldn't stand having to answer questions or see the look of cynical disbelief on the policeman's face when she brought up Colin Barlow's name. And perhaps she was building it up in her own mind to more than it was. A man finds himself attracted to a young woman and naturally tries to follow it through. It happens all the time in pictures made in Hollywood – Clark Gable holds Claudette Colbert in his arms, she swoons, they kiss . . .

Even when she says no, as Violet had, it turns out she might not mean it. Sick to the stomach and confused by each turn of thought, she made slow progress through the streets. The incident in the garage dislodged everything else from her thoughts – the failed delivery of Mrs Kingsley's dress, even the family secret that Stan had sworn to keep earlier that afternoon. No – what she couldn't shift from her mind was the sense of Barlow's rough hands pawing at her and the feel of his lips pressed hard against hers.

'A penny for them,' Marjorie called from her bakery-shop door.

Violet raised her hand and waved feebly without offering a riposte. Almost back at Jubilee, she steeled herself to act normally – to explain why she still had Ella Kingsley's dress in her basket and why it had taken her so long to fail to deliver it.

Stay calm. Pretend nothing happened. That's the ticket.

The shop bell rang. Clutching the parcel, Violet stepped into her warm cocoon of buttons and silks.

'You took your time,' Ida said from behind the counter with hardly a glance at Violet.

'Sorry – I was held up.' Violet's plan was to offer a bland explanation then retreat into the kitchen until her heartbeat returned to normal and she could tidy herself up. 'Mrs Kingsley wasn't at home so I rode over to the mill to try to find her. She wasn't there either—'

'Good heavens above, Violet!' Ida interrupted as she finished counting buttons and looked up at last. 'You're covered in blood.'

Violet looked down at her hands. The pheasants' blood had dried darkest crimson, almost black on her fair skin. 'I had an accident.'

'Your face, too.' Ida came out from behind the counter and took the parcel from her.

'It's nothing.'

'Go into the kitchen and sit down. Let me make you a cup of tea.'

'Honestly, it's not as bad as it looks. I'm not even hurt.'

'And I'm not listening,' Ida insisted. Standing at the bottom of the stairs, she called up to Muriel. 'Violet's back. She's had an accident. She says it's nothing but the poor thing looks as if she's seen a ghost.'

Within seconds Muriel had flown down from the workroom and both she and Ida began fussing over

Violet, telling her not to mind about the undelivered parcel, making her sit down, giving her tea and fetching a warm cloth to wipe away the blood.

'There are no scratches or cuts but you're shaking from head to foot,' Muriel murmured. 'Are you sure you're all right?' She crouched beside Violet and gazed up at her as she sponged stains from her skirt.

'I've had a shock,' Violet confessed, but what fell from her lips was not the name of Colin Barlow but that of Stan Tankard, even though she'd planned to keep their secret and intended only to tell Eddie when the time was right. 'It turns out that Stan and I could be related.'

'How? In what way?' Ida demanded.

'Hush. Don't upset yourself,' Muriel said softly.

It all came out in a rush – about the bracelet and the note, Uncle Donald's warnings against taking up with Stan, the reasons behind him walking out on her after Winnie died. With the words came tears. They coursed down Violet's face, welled up and choked her until her confession was reduced to sobs and it was Muriel who put her arms around her and held her until she stopped.

'There must be a birth certificate somewhere with the father's name on it,' was Eddie's first thought after Ida had found him working with his father on Ghyll Road and fetched him back to Jubilee to listen to Violet's news. He was calm and practical in the face of this latest crisis, though inwardly he was rattled by how close Violet had come to pairing up with Stan.

'Not that I know of,' Violet said. 'If it existed, it would've been in the wooden box in Aunty Winnie's wardrobe.'

'And it wasn't?' Muriel checked. She'd left Ida to serve in the shop and sat with Eddie and Violet in the kitchen.

Violet shook her head.

'It must be somewhere,' Eddie insisted. 'You don't think there's any chance that someone gave it to Douglas Tankard for safe keeping, do you?'

'It couldn't have been my mother, because my birth couldn't have been registered until after . . .' Violet's voice faded into a sigh.

'Perhaps Tankard himself?' Muriel suggested.

'But then again, no.' Violet ignored Muriel and took her time to think things through. 'Stan's father never came back from the war.'

The new mystery defeated them and they lapsed into silence. 'There's nothing we can do at the present so I'll leave you two to it,' Muriel decided, going upstairs and back to her sewing machine.

Eddie too knew that he couldn't stay long. 'I left Dad wallpapering a ceiling,' he told Violet apologetically. 'It's a two-man job.'

'Yes – you go. We can talk about this later.'

He hovered by the door. 'Ida mentioned something about you falling off your bike. How did that happen?'

'It was nothing – I didn't hurt myself. I wasn't concentrating on what I was doing, that's all.'

'That's not like you.' There was something in the air – an awkward barrier between them that made Eddie uneasy.

'It's been a hard day,' Violet told him. She felt it too – a need to keep up her defences and hold Eddie at a distance even though he'd left his work and rushed across to help her. 'I need a rest.'

'Shall I tell Ida that you're taking a nap on my way out?'

'Yes – could you?' *Go now. Please don't come near me until I've scrubbed my body from head to toe. Don't smell Barlow's whisky-soured breath on my clothes and skin.*

'Rightio,' Eddie said with deep uncertainty. 'I'm working tonight and tomorrow. Will I see you at rehearsal on Wednesday?'

'Wednesday – yes.'

'I'll give you a lift over,' he promised as he left and Violet crept upstairs to hide under her bedclothes, pretending to be asleep until Muriel and Ida had shut up shop and gone home.

She knew that soap wouldn't be enough to wash away the stains of the day. Still, she tried, feeling her way downstairs in the dark to the kitchen and rubbing until her skin was red, examining one by one the bruises on her shoulders where Barlow had seized her and pushed her against the garage wall. At last she went back to bed, not to sleep but to lie awake and relive the attack, trying to contain it and give it a shape that she could bear and move forward from.

I stood up to him, she told herself time and again. *It was soon over. It could have been much worse.*

CHAPTER TWENTY-ONE

Violet managed to get through the routine of the next day and the one after that without telling a soul what had happened at Ash Tree House. On Wednesday morning she even delivered Ella Kingsley's dress, parking her bike in the same cobbled yard and knocking on the side door before handing over the delivery to a handyman working there for the day without betraying her discomfort. He was about thirty-five years old – small and stocky, dressed in crisp blue overalls, with a hinged metal ruler and a screwdriver protruding from a top pocket.

'You mean to say you rode all the way up here without breaking sweat?' The handyman's friendly question threw Violet off balance and she fumbled for a reply. 'There's no need to look at me like that – I won't bite. I'm only saying you still look fresh as a daisy after your bike ride.'

'I'm in a rush,' she explained. 'Could you tell Mrs Kingsley that she can drop in at Jubilee and pay us what she owes whenever she's passing.'

'That's trusting of you,' the man said with a wry smile. 'My name's Kenneth, by the way. Kenneth Leach. What's yours?'

'Violet Wheeler.'

'Well, Violet Wheeler, I bet you're new to the business of supplying goods. In future, I'd always demand payment on the spot if I was you. I learned that lesson early on in my trade – never let customers owe you money because they'll always find an excuse not to pay. The longer they leave it, the harder it gets to squeeze it out of them.'

'I really am in a hurry,' Violet repeated, all too aware of the garage door yawning open behind her and of the memories that came flooding back.

'Yes and Mr Kingsley doesn't pay me for standing here chatting,' Kenneth acknowledged. 'I've got a sink to unblock and a couple of door hinges to mend.'

Violet said a hasty goodbye then got back on her bike and was gone before anyone could stop her, out onto the road and past the splendid houses built at the turn of the century by mill owners and colliery bosses when it looked as if the good times would last for ever. Carved stone lions stood guard on gate posts, curving driveways were swept clear of falling leaves and decorative gables were newly painted. All stood to attention, present and correct.

That night, soon after Eddie and Violet had arrived at Hadley Village Institute for rehearsal, Ida made a beeline towards her. 'Good, Violet – you're early. We've just got time to carry out my secret plan.'

'Why? Where are we going?' Violet asked as Ida frogmarched her out of the hall and across the yard onto the main street. They passed Stan chatting with Kathy, Peggy and Evie in the pleasant evening air, crossed the road and hurried on towards the row of houses where Donald Wheeler had briefly lodged.

'Oh no you don't!' Violet protested when she saw what was afoot. 'Anyway, it's no use. Uncle Donald doesn't live here any more, and even if he did I wouldn't have anything to say to him.'

'That's my point – you might not want to talk to him, but that doesn't mean he doesn't have plenty he could tell us about Douglas Tankard and your mother if he wanted to.' By this time Ida was knocking on the door and peering through the downstairs window. 'It seems you were right – the place is empty. Look.'

Taking Ida's place and pressing her nose to the dirty window pane, Violet saw nothing but bare floorboards and cobwebs. There wasn't a stick of furniture in the room or any other sign that it had recently been occupied.

'But my plan doesn't end here,' Ida declared. She was dressed as usual for the night's theatre business in practical trousers and a light, short-sleeved sweater, with rouge and lipstick to lend a softer touch to her cropped fair hair. 'Our next stop is the vicarage.'

'I'm sure you're on the wrong track,' Violet told her. Nevertheless, she marched up the street with Ida then followed her through a tall iron gate into a tidy front garden with lawns and flower beds leading to a substantial house next to the church. 'Uncle Donald's lips have been sealed on the subject of my mother for nearly twenty years,' she reminded her. 'What's going to alter things all of a sudden?'

'Coming out with the name – Douglas Tankard – to your uncle's face – that's what's going to make him buck up his ideas. You wait and see.' Ida knocked on the vicarage door and waited impatiently until it was opened by a tall, upright man in a clerical collar.

'What can I do for you?' The vicar's opening remark was delivered in a guarded tone. His face was unusually worn, his skin pale and criss-crossed with wrinkles, with tufts of white hair sprouting sparsely from the top of his head.

'We're looking for Donald Wheeler,' Ida announced, bold as brass.

'Not here.' The elderly vicar was already closing the door on them, going back to his tea of tinned-salmon sandwiches and a well-deserved rest from parish business.

'This is his niece,' Ida explained, thrusting Violet forward for inspection. 'She's bothered about losing touch with her only living relation – and who wouldn't be? Surely that deserves five minutes of your time, Vicar.'

The door stayed open as the clergyman's conscience

pushed itself to the fore. 'I'm afraid your uncle didn't leave a forwarding address,' he told Violet in a kinder voice. 'In fact, his leaving left me rather in the lurch.'

'My aunty died and he took it hard.' Violet gave the explanation she felt the vicar would understand but without going into details.

'Are you sure you can't give us a clue as to where he went?' Ida persisted. 'He didn't mention anything to anyone here in the village?'

'I did hear that Donald Wheeler had links with Welby in his youth,' he said abruptly. 'Perhaps that's where he went back to now that his wife has passed away.'

'Maybe,' Violet said doubtfully.

'Welby's a big place.' Ida was eager for more details while with a sinking heart Violet pictured the tall chimneys and dark, maze-like terraces, the thousands of mill workers and the gangs of un-employed miners on the steps of Public Assistance offices, women in wash houses and children in rags sent out with rough carts to scavenge coal from the old slag heaps.

'I'm sorry not to be of more help,' the vicar said, his duty done. He prepared to close the door on his visitors. 'But when a man like Donald Wheeler chooses to drop out of sight, there's very little any-one can do.'

An hour later, Ida was throwing her energy into rehearsing her leading players for a section in the final scene where the police inspector revealed the identity of the murderer. Violet sat in a corner with Kathy and Peggy, quietly hemming costumes until they were called onto the stage. Stan was in a side room making tea with Evie, while Eddie and Harold had slipped out to the Miners' Arms for a swift pint, returning just as Ida called a halt and Stan announced that refreshments were ready.

Kathy left off sewing and jumped up with alacrity to reach the head of the queue. 'Where's the sugar, Stan?'

'Not sweet enough, eh?' he teased from behind the trestle table laden with teacups and biscuits.

Kathy gave as good as she got, delving a spoon into the sugar bowl once, twice then three times. 'No, not like Evie, as I'm sure you know better than anyone else by now. Evie, you don't take sugar in your tea, do you? You're sweet enough already.'

Though Evie blushed at Kathy's cheek, she kept on steadily pouring out the tea. 'Who's next?' she asked.

'I'll take two cups,' Eddie told her. 'One for Violet, one for me.'

'Always the gent,' Stan commented, noticing that Violet had found a quiet spot behind the tea urn and seeing that Eddie was carrying the cups in the wrong direction. 'Violet's over there, Eddie.'

His friend changed course and thanked him as he went by.

'Take care of her,' Stan told him without lowering

his voice. 'She's looking a bit peaky tonight. And I'm not surprised after what she told me.'

Eddie sat down next to Violet. 'Are you feeling all right? Stan hit the nail on the head – you do look under the weather.'

'I'm tired, that's all,' Violet admitted as she balanced her cup and saucer on her knees. 'Ta for the tea, Eddie. I really need a pick-me-up.'

'I saw Ida get you into an arm lock and march you down the street earlier. What was that for?'

'Nothing – just one of her madcap ideas.'

'To do with your Uncle Donald?'

'Yes, but it didn't come to anything.'

Violet's short answers made Eddie feel that he was trying to squeeze blood out of a stone and he took it personally. 'Look, Vi, if I've done something wrong, you'd tell me, wouldn't you? Then I could try to put it right.'

'You haven't.' The effort of holding herself to-gether for the last two days was taking its toll and Violet felt close to tears.

'You're sure it's not something I said after you had the accident on Ida's bike? Wait a second – the brakes didn't pack up on you, did they? They shouldn't have because I only put new pads on the front two weeks ago.'

Violet shook her head miserably then stared down at her lap.

Feeling the distance between them grow every time he opened his mouth, Eddie frantically cast around for another subject. 'Stan and Evie are getting on like a house on fire over there. Look, she's sending him out to collect the empties. Have you finished yours? Give it to me and let me save Stan a job.'

Taking the cup from Violet, he gave the steaming tea urn a wide berth then disappeared from view, returning empty-handed to arrange to take Violet home on the Norton as usual. 'Unless you'd rather go home on the bus with Kathy and the others tonight,' he added abjectly.

Violet swallowed hard. What was she thinking, behaving so badly towards Eddie and shutting him out when all she wanted, deep down, was for him to put his arms around her and for her to lay her head against his chest? But the memory of Colin Barlow's sour breath, his hands and lips and the secret she was keeping from Eddie seemed to get in the way of a comforting embrace. She swallowed again and with an effort she pushed the memories to one side. 'No, I'd like a lift home with you,' she said above the hiss of the urn, the hurt in her heart starting to heal as she saw Eddie's brown eyes light up with relief. 'I wouldn't miss our ride along the moor road – not for the world.'

It would take time, but in the end Violet vowed to herself that she would put the Ash Tree House incident behind her and never need to mention it to anyone. Eddie would be by her side.

That night, after the ride home, she slept longer and woke up refreshed. On Thursday she busied herself with work. At the end of the day Evie dropped by for a chat, bringing reports that Sybil's recent adverts had attracted some new customers, but not as many as she'd expected.

'It's to be hoped that things pick up again towards Christmas,' Evie said knowledgeably. After all, she'd watched Lily, Sybil and Annie set up the business and knew it inside out.

'Yes. Here at Jubilee we have to hope orders coming into the mills buck up. That way the girls will hang onto their jobs and be able to save up for new dance dresses.'

'Fingers crossed,' Evie agreed, stepping to one side to let Violet see the arrival of Alice Barlow's Daimler. 'Here comes trouble,' she warned.

'No – she's probably here to pay her dues at last.' Violet said goodbye to Evie, who slipped out as Mrs Barlow entered, but one look at her customer's angry face soon told her that her guess was wrong.

The bell shook violently as Alice Barlow slammed the door behind her, producing a jangling noise that echoed throughout the building. She looked wild eyed and in disarray – her hair dishevelled and the buttons of her mauve jacket wrongly fastened.

'Good afternoon, Mrs Barlow, how can I—' Violet began.

'Hark at you!' Alice Barlow raised her voice to a high, scornful pitch. 'To look at you, butter wouldn't melt. But you can drop the act right now, you sly customer!'

Violet steadied herself against the counter. 'I'm sorry . . . ?'

'I'm telling you – it's a waste of time pretending not to know what this is about.' Alice Barlow advanced quickly and slammed her handbag down. 'How long did you imagine you could keep it a secret – this carrying-on behind my back?'

'Mrs Barlow, please—'

'Did you honestly believe that it wouldn't get back to me – the perfume and the excuses, the secret assignations?'

Assignations? The word seemed ridiculously over-blown and at last Violet found her voice. 'Mrs Barlow, if you want to know the truth about the eau de cologne – believe me, I didn't want to take it. It's at the back of a drawer ready to be given to a raffle. And I've never made any arrangement with Mr Barlow, secret or otherwise – quite the opposite.'

'That's right – I knew you'd try to blame Colin.' Alice Barlow's fury seemed to roll like a high wave over the counter towards Violet. 'That's what girls like you do, isn't it? You lead a man on and wheedle presents out of him then you turn the tables by threatening to go to his wife. What is it that you're after now? Is it money? Well, I can see straight through you and your nasty ways.'

'It's not true.' Violet sensed that the wave was about to break and crash down on her and she braced herself. 'I haven't done anything.'

Eyes bulging, Alice Barlow leaned heavily on the counter and ignored the fact that her raised voice had brought Ida and Muriel hurrying down from the workshop. 'Three words,' she hissed at Violet. 'Listen carefully: Ash Tree House.'

A cold shudder ran through Violet. 'Mrs Barlow, please—'

'There! What's your answer to that? You don't have one. Ash Tree House on Monday afternoon. You set a trap by enticing my husband out of sight into the Kingsleys' garage but luckily he realized what you were up to and managed to escape your clutches.'

Outrage threatened to choke Violet. 'No. That's not how it was.'

'He didn't want to tell me at first but I got it out of him eventually – the reason why he came home with a cut on his face that evening.'

There was no reasoning with the woman. Violet sensed she would be swept off her feet and dragged under by a strong current and there was nothing she could do about it. Ida and Muriel stood at the bottom of the stairs, trying to take it all in.

'Do you deny it?' Alice shouted.

'I do.' Violet's answer was faint and her chest tightened with fear.

'Which is why I made sure to find a witness,' her accuser went on triumphantly. 'Guttersnipes always twist things around, but you won't get away with it this time.'

'Mrs Barlow, please calm down.' With a worried glance at Violet, Muriel stepped in. 'We need to talk this through. I'm sure there's a perfectly good explanation.'

Alice turned on her with a vengeance. 'Miss Beanland, did you or did you not send this girl out to Ash Tree House on Monday afternoon?'

'I did.' Muriel accepted that this much was true. 'I asked Violet to deliver a dress to Mrs Kingsley.'

'And did she do it promptly?'

'No, indeed. Violet was delayed.' Muriel fell silent and Ida took her turn to intervene.

'There was an accident. Violet had blood all over her,' Ida explained.

Alice Barlow puffed out her chest and the triumphant expression took over her whole body. 'Her blood or my husband's?'

'Mr Barlow's name wasn't mentioned,' Ida admitted as she turned towards Violet, who simply shook her head.

'You see – she has no answer. What does she say to Colin's injuries? That happened when he resisted her advances and she couldn't get her own way.'

'That doesn't sound like Violet,' Muriel insisted. 'You mentioned a witness, Mrs Barlow. May I ask who it is?'

'Violet, will you tell them who else was there, or shall I?' Alice Barlow prompted, a glint of triumph in her eyes.

'No one,' Violet whispered. She'd been alone and

terrified out of her wits – Barlow had made sure of that.

'Wrong!' The stinging contradiction preceded the breaking of the wave and the deluge. 'Colin had been out shooting with a companion. Unbeknown to you, Violet Wheeler, Thomas Kingsley was present throughout, watching every sly move you made.'

CHAPTER TWENTY-TWO

'Typical!' Ida bustled around the shop, rearranging stock that didn't need to be moved, trying to get her thoughts back in order. 'Who does Alice Barlow think she is, throwing her weight around and flinging accusations here, there and everywhere?'

'Without a scrap of real evidence,' Muriel added. She kept a wary eye on Violet who stood transfixed behind the counter like a rabbit caught in car headlights, trying to piece together the sentences she should have said to Alice Barlow and the truths she should have told. Too late, as it turned out.

'That's what they do, these people,' Ida fumed. 'They gang up on us, knowing we can't answer back.'

'She's a woman who's never satisfied with her lot in life and in a way who can blame her? She's had a lot to put up with being married to Colin Barlow.' Sad rather than angry, Muriel judged it best not to address Violet directly until she'd come out of her trance of her own accord.

Ida displayed the Closed sign on the shop door then gave the window blind a vicious tug. 'Can you believe it – she actually told us to send Violet packing on the strength of her husband's rotten lies? As if we'd do that!'

'We wouldn't,' Muriel agreed.

'No, we sent *her* packing instead. And who cares if we never get another penny out of her? Not me, for one. She doesn't pay her bills anyway. We can do without her.'

Violet heard Ida and Muriel's spirited defence as if through a thick pane of glass – faint and oddly disembodied. She was still too overwhelmed by the look of hatred that her adversary had thrown at her as she'd stormed from the premises to make sense of what was going on around her.

'Can we, though? That's the question.' Muriel knew that a lost customer – even one as slow to pay as Alice Barlow – could affect them badly. 'I can just picture her at her tea dances and soirées, recommending a new dressmaker and telling lies about us to Ella Kingsley and such like. That could be very bad for Jubilee in the long run.'

'Don't worry – I'll leave Jubilee and find another job, somewhere a long way away, where nobody knows me.' Violet broke out of her daze and rashly volunteered the first solution that came to mind.

'You will not!'

'Don't be daft!' Muriel and Ida spoke simultaneously.

'No, you're staying here with us,' Ida insisted. 'We won't be bullied by Alice Barlow.'

'Or done down by her lies,' Muriel added.

'Lies that she'll no doubt spread far and wide, but eventually people will see them for what they are and everyone will take your side just as we have.'

Ida indicated that this was the end of the matter, but Violet wasn't so sure. She dreaded being the centre of such a scandal, even with Ida and Muriel's support, especially the sideways, salacious glances from men in the street and girls whispering gleefully behind her back. 'I'm not sure I can face it,' she confessed tremulously.

'It's either that or run away,' Ida pointed out. 'And how would that help? It would only add fuel to Alice Barlow's fire. She'd win hands down.'

It was Muriel who, after a short pause, offered a temporary answer. 'Listen to this, Violet. What do you say to staying out of the shop for the time being and spending your days in the workroom? There's plenty for you to do up there and that way you wouldn't have to face customers until this has all blown over.'

Ida disagreed. 'I say go on as usual,' she argued. 'You know the old saying, "Sticks and stones may break my bones."'

This is more than words that I have to overcome, Violet thought miserably. *This is a deliberate attempt to ruin me.* She remembered again Alice Barlow's uncontrolled fury, trying to imagine what version

311

of Monday's events her husband had seen fit to give her and how it had come to light in the first place.

'I'll sleep on it,' she told Ida and Muriel, feeling the weight of the world sink onto her shoulders. 'In the morning I'll decide what to do for the best.'

Within hours, Violet's fears had come true and word had got around. Alf Shipley knocked off from work that evening and went down to the Green Cross with his friend, Kenneth Leach. There, in the cosy confines of the snug, with its dartboard in the corner and men playing dominoes on copper-topped tables, Les Craven and the others overheard the tale of Colin Barlow having to fight off Violet Wheeler's unwanted advances. Les sloped off from the pub to meet Stan outside Brinkley Baths and pass on the story soon after. Stan blew his top then cycled up to Valley Road to find Eddie and warn him before the rumours got out of hand.

'Eddie's not here – he's working tonight,' Ida informed Stan warily. She invited him in and sat him down at the kitchen table to find out what was the matter.

'Violet's got herself into hot water,' he explained, out of hearing of Ida and Eddie's parents. 'They say she's fallen for Colin Barlow's fancy promises and his missis got wind of it. Eddie should know there's bound to be trouble.'

'This is Violet we're talking about,' Ida reminded him, fizzing like a bottle of shaken lemonade when the cap is taken off. 'Anyway, it's old news. Muriel and I were there when Alice Barlow blew her top.'

'Fancy that. Anyway, I didn't believe a word of it,' Stan said stoutly. 'I gave Les a box around the ears for spreading lies and warned him we wouldn't pick him for tomorrow's match if he wasn't careful.'

'Good, I'm glad.'

'You know how these things get passed around, though. Before too long, Barlow's the hero and Violet's the villain of the piece.'

'Yes,' Ida agreed as she got to her feet. She was already forming a plan to prove Alice Barlow wrong. 'Violet doesn't deserve any of this. If something bad happened at Ash Tree House, there's not a shadow of doubt in my mind that Colin Barlow was the real culprit. Just you wait and see.'

The jetsam of Violet's life was flung here and there inside her own head. Foremost amongst the wreckage was the hot shame she felt that Colin Barlow saw her as the sort of girl who would fall for his charms. Was it the way she acted, she wondered, or the way she dressed? How might she have behaved differently to give him the clear message to leave her alone?

Perhaps Uncle Donald had been right all along. She recalled his dry, clipped voice warning her that her carryings on with Stan would get her name dragged into the mud and that she was heading for the gutter where she belonged. Well, his prophesy had come true and she couldn't rid herself of the conclusion that she should have followed his advice and chosen hymn singing and Bible study over lipstick and nice clothes.

There is only one thing for it, Violet decided, alone in her room and without anyone to help her see sense. *I will pack up and leave after all. Whatever Ida and Muriel say, I know that Jubilee will be better off without me.*

She took dresses from the rail in the niche beside the chimney breast and began to fold them and place them in a pile on her bed until an urgent knocking on the shop door interrupted her and she went down to open it.

'You need to watch out – Alice Barlow barged into our shop spreading nasty rumours about you,' Evie began breathlessly and without preliminaries as she pushed past Violet and stumbled inside. 'Sybil couldn't get a word in edgeways.'

As Muriel's predictions flickered into life and quickly flared out of control, Violet felt a jolt in the pit of her stomach. 'That happened faster than I expected,' she murmured. 'Mrs Barlow must have come up to you straight after leaving here.'

'We know it's not true,' Evie went on, chin up and with her young, innocent face set in determined lines. 'Sybil tried to say as much, but you know what Mrs Barlow is like. She claims she has a witness and that she'll turn all your customers against you if Muriel and Ida decide to keep you on.'

'She can't do that if I pack up and leave,' Violet

said, her mind more firmly made up.

'You can't do that!' Evie gasped in alarm. 'Jubilee is where you belong.'

They gazed around the dimly lit shop at the shelves stacked with haberdashery goods – cards of lace, spools of ribbon, boxes of buttons, Maud in her colourful house dress in the far corner – and at Gertie in the window, resplendent in her beautiful wedding gown, every stitch lovingly sewn. For a moment Violet felt dizzy and she leaned against the wall.

'You can't go,' Evie repeated.

'What else did Mrs Barlow say?' Violet asked faintly.

Seeing the drastic effect she was having, Violet's informant was reluctant to go on. 'It doesn't matter. It was all lies.'

'Tell me, please.'

'Well then, she used a word you read in the newspapers and in books. She said you "seduced" Mr Barlow.'

'That sounds like her,' Violet said grimly. 'What else?'

'Like I said, she'll make sure to tell her friends about the shoddy work you do here. She'll "recommend" – that was the other word – that everyone brings their business back to us.'

Violet frowned and brought her hand up to her mouth.

'Do you want to know what Sybil said back to her?'

315

With a slight nod of the head, Violet allowed Evie to continue.

'She said, "Thank you very much, Mrs Barlow, but we prefer to build up our business on the quality of the work we do here, not on the back of lies." That was it – word for word. It was how Sybil put Mrs Barlow in her place. To tell you the truth, I've never seen her so angry.'

'That's all very well,' Violet whispered, 'but Chapel Street Costumiers won't turn down new orders, not when it comes to it.'

'That's up to Sybil and nobody else,' Evie pointed out. 'And you know her – she sticks to her word through thick and thin. In fact, she told Mrs Barlow that she wouldn't accept any more orders for sewing work from her in the future.'

Violet pictured the scene: Alice Barlow face to face with Sybil Dacre, the one red faced and incensed, the other calm and cool. 'How did that go down?'

'There was a lot of shouting,' Evie recalled with a shudder.

'About me or about Jubilee?'

'Both. But I've given you the gist.'

'And I'm grateful,' Violet told her. 'It doesn't change anything, though, and the matter won't end with Sybil showing Mrs Barlow the door. That woman will want to get back at me in all sorts of other ways.'

'But you can't up and leave,' Evie protested, gesturing around the shop and looking on the verge of tears.

'It's true – I don't want to,' Violet admitted. She knew the finely stitched gloves and gauzy stockings, the silky camisoles and petticoats, neat zips and tiny press studs like the back of her hand. She loved the sound of the till ringing, the cool feel of silver sixpences and angular three-penny bits in the palm of her hand. 'But, whatever anyone says, Evie, it's time to move on.'

Eddie had never felt fury like it after Stan had turned up at the Victory to tell him about the latest attack on Violet's good name. In a fit of rage he jumped on his motorbike and without a moment's hesitation headed straight out to Bilton Grange.

I'll knock Barlow's block off! was the phrase he repeated over and over as he sped through the dark streets and up onto the moor top.

He arrived at the house to find it in darkness. Half past nine on a Friday night was early for people like the Barlows to be in bed, but in any case Eddie hammered at the door to rouse them. He peered in through windows, knocked again and yelled Colin Barlow's name. 'Come outside, you rotten bugger. Say what you have to say to my face, man to man!'

There was no answer, even when Eddie pushed open the letter box and issued his challenge, and at last he had to admit that the Barlows had gone out.

What next? Should he ride back into town and scour the streets, looking for their car? What were the chances of him tracking down the Daimler outside City Varieties or perhaps the new Odeon cinema at this time of night? Mightn't they be out to dinner at a friend's house instead?

Eventually Eddie decided against a wild-goose chase and satisfied himself for the moment by giving the Barlows' front door a hefty kick before turning his back on the Grange. Then he rode like the devil along the moor road that he and Violet loved, only dimly aware of the sprinkling of house lights – magical specks of white lights glimmering in the blackness of the valley bottom – before sweeping down into town, engine racing, heart beating fast and hands gripping the handlebars until he reached Chapel Street.

Once more the house he drew up at was in darkness but he didn't hesitate to run down the alley, stand in the yard and call Violet's name. 'Vi – it's me, Eddie. Open the door!'

An upstairs light went on then there was a long pause before Violet drew back the curtain and appeared at the window. Her face was bathed in the moon's pale light as she raised one hand to cut out her reflection and peer down onto the street. 'Eddie!' she whispered.

'Open the door!' he repeated.

She shook her head in alarm and retreated from view.

'Open it!' he yelled.

After what seemed like an age, he heard sounds

from inside the shop and ran back along the alley. There was the noise of the bolt being drawn back. He pushed open the door and rushed inside.

Violet, in only her silky nightdress, stepped backwards, clutching her hands to her chest.

'I'll knock him down dead, I swear I will!' Eddie ranted, dragging off his gauntlets and flinging them on the counter. His cap and goggles followed suit then he turned to seize her and draw her to him.

Her head spinning and almost unable to breathe, Violet resisted. 'Eddie, you're hurting me.'

'Why didn't you tell me?' he asked wildly, his fingers pressing into her flesh.

'How could I?' She felt the cold night air on his cheeks, breathed in the smell of autumn heather and damp bracken on his jacket.

'You should've told me. Why didn't you?'

Pulling herself free and trembling violently, she backed away. 'I couldn't find the words. I didn't want to see the look in your eyes when I told you what had gone on.'

'Did he . . . harm you?' Eddie hesitated mid sentence, looking for the right word.

'There – that's the look!' she cried. 'It's when you dwell on what went on – Barlow with his hands all over me.'

Eddie steadied himself with a deep breath. 'But now you have to tell me straight. How bad was it?'

A note of defiance entered Violet's voice as she recalled specifics. 'Bad enough but I didn't give in

319

to him. I managed to fight him off. There was a shotgun leaning against the wall. I let bid with it.'

'You shot him?' Eddie was aghast.

'No. I wanted to, but I thought better of it and cracked him in the ribs instead.'

'Bloody hell, Violet.'

'What? Did I do wrong?' Looking like a ghost in her white nightdress and with her pale skin and dark eyes hardly visible in the darkness, she was desperate to hear what he thought.

'You say you hit him with the butt of the gun?'

'Hard,' she confessed.

Eddie's troubled face lightened. He raised his eyebrows and there was a shadow of a smile on his lips. 'By Jove, Vi. Hard enough to make him fall down?'

'I knocked him sideways. I wasn't thinking what I was doing.'

'That's the spirit. Good for you for sticking up for yourself.'

Violet took a deep breath. 'The trouble is, though, that they're saying Mr Kingsley was looking on. It's my word against theirs.'

'All the more reason you should have told me straight away.' Though Eddie felt proud of the spirit Violet had shown, he was sorry she'd had to cope alone. 'I'd have gone and beaten the living daylights out of Barlow before that nasty wife of his could start spreading lies.'

'Evie came to see me earlier and that's when I

realized everyone on Chapel Street had already got wind of it. Now I see the whole town knows.' She lowered her head then sighed.

Gently Eddie moved towards her, his rage against Barlow subsiding and concern for Violet taking its place. He put his hand under her chin and tilted it until she was looking directly at him. 'I haven't said this before – not to anyone . . .' he began.

Violet raised her hand and cupped it over his. The only light came from the street lamp, shining in through chinks in the blind – just enough for her to make out his features and see that he was looking deep into her eyes.

'You know what I want to tell you,' he murmured.

It was as if she was floating free of the ground – a dizzying, delicious sensation. 'What?'

The low, soft words came from deep in his throat. 'I don't want it to sound daft. You won't laugh at me?'

A slender thread of common sense tied Violet to the ground when she spoke through scarcely opened lips. 'Does it look like it? I'm standing here shivering and catching my death, waiting for you to spit it out.'

'I love you,' he said in a rush of emotion that almost knocked him off his feet. 'And whatever happens, I'll be here by your side.'

'For better or for worse?' she murmured.

'Yes, if you'll have me.'

'I will, Eddie. And I love you too.' She was too

happy to say any more, too dizzy to think, lost in his arms.

'I'll do anything for you,' he promised, breathing the loving words against the soft skin of Violet's lips and neck.

CHAPTER TWENTY-THREE

In bed that night, Violet remembered a solitary childhood game where she'd sat on the grass on the Common, picking dandelion seed heads then pursing her lips and blowing on them to the chant of 'He loves me, he loves me not', until every feathered seed had blown free and floated off.

He loves me! Eddie Thomson had told her that he loved her and would stay with her through thick and thin. His kisses had made her believe that it was true. *He loves me. He loves me.*

Eddie had said what she'd been longing to hear but hadn't dared to hope for and still she could hardly believe the thrill of those words drawing her out of the depths, the perfection of his dark brown eyes, the feel of his lips on hers and the strength of his arms wrapped around her – Violet Wheeler – the once lonely child who had looked out across the Common towards the moors, wondering what her life would hold.

She got up next morning and set to work in the

clean, cool attic. Unless recent events brought about a change of mind in Ella Kingsley, as it very well might, an order from her was due for delivery. It was a tasteful eau-de-Nil, crêpe de Chine blouse with a Peter Pan collar and pearl buttons, just needing finishing touches. Violet sat eagerly to hand-sew the facings in place and was humming a tune when Ida arrived.

'There'll be no more talk of leaving Jubilee, I gather?' Ida observed in her forthright way.

'No,' Violet agreed. 'I've decided to stick it out.'

'Tra-la!' Tilting her head thoughtfully to one side as she sat down to thread her machine, Ida judged that teasing was the order of the day. 'I caught Eddie humming away before he buzzed off to work this morning. Is it a coincidence, or could there be more to it than that?'

'I didn't know there was a law against humming all of a sudden,' Violet responded with a secretive smile.

'There isn't – not that I know of.' Ida started to unpin pieces of paper pattern from a dress she'd cut out the day before. 'How long will you be with Mrs Kingsley's blouse?'

'Finished!' Violet declared, snipping the final thread.

'Fingers crossed she still wants it,' Ida commented, hearing the ring of the shop bell. 'If that's her, come up and let me know.'

Violet followed orders and it was only when she

came to the first-floor landing that she remembered Muriel's kindly meant advice about keeping her head below the parapet for a while. It might have been better for Ida to serve their customer, she realized as her stomach started to churn.

'Go on – what are you waiting for?' Ida called down, hearing Violet's light steps come to a halt.

Violet gave herself a shake and carried on down the stairs into the shop, surprised to find that it was Sybil who was examining price tags on the linen hankies displayed on the counter. Hatless and without a cardigan to protect her from the chilly autumn air, it was obvious from their rival's appearance that she had slipped out from her own shop on the spur of the moment. 'Good morning. How can I help?' Violet began uncertainly.

'I need a reel of pale blue sewing cotton to match this material,' Sybil replied, sliding a scrap of linen across the counter. 'I ran out and I don't have time to get the tram over to Cliff Street to buy another.'

'Certainly.' Violet took several reels from a shallow drawer and matched each against the fabric. 'This is the closest, I think.'

'Or this one.' Oddly, Sybil didn't seem to be in a hurry after all. She took her time to choose her shade then asked to see an example of the Lastex undergarments that had recently been gaining favour. 'I hear they're more comfortable than the old sort – according to Evie, anyway. You young ones know what's what better than me. Not that I have one foot in the grave just yet,' she added mischievously.

As Sybil browsed, she seemed to have something else on her mind and it was no surprise to Violet when she eventually changed tack.

'I'm glad to see you're none the worse for wear.' She looked directly at Violet. 'I'm not naming names, but a certain shop owner's reputation is well known to everyone but his wife, unfortunately.'

Violet swallowed hard. 'Thank you,' she said quietly.

'I hear you gave him more than a clip round the ear.' Sybil smiled then raised a hand to tuck a hairpin more firmly into place, seemingly pushing the thorny topic to one side. 'It's windy out there – I almost got blown away.'

'I haven't been out yet.' Gamely Violet carried on with the everyday topic. Showing Sybil more of the brassieres that they had in stock and conscientiously pointing out the various lace trims, she was relieved to hear the bell ring once more and see that Muriel had arrived.

'Hello, Violet. Hello, Sybil,' Muriel said breezily, removing her hatpin and taking off the brimless, crimson hat that coordinated well with her dark grey jacket, broad at the shoulders and with wide lapels. 'What brings you down to this end of Chapel Street?'

Sybil showed her the reel of blue thread. 'Don't get carried away. It's not enough to help you out of your tight spot – not by a long chalk.'

'Who says we're in a tight spot?' Muriel demanded,

turning her back to busily rearrange items in the window.

'Ah, but you will be, if a certain person carries on spreading rumours about your shoddy workmanship. I take it you've heard?'

Frowning, Muriel turned to face Sybil. 'Yes, along with everyone and his aunt, apparently. But it's not like you to gloat.'

'I'm not gloating – far from it,' Sybil assured her. 'In fact, I came here especially to tip Violet the wink about Alice Barlow's latest sneaky move. And, seeing as you're here, Muriel, I'd like us to put our cards on the table, once and for all.'

'Shall I tidy these things away now?' Violet was apprehensive about a row breaking out and had decided to make herself scarce. Swiftly she began to clear the counter.

'Why not write down what these brassieres cost on a slip of paper?' Sybil's suggestion delayed her. 'I mean, Muriel, that these rumours will do Jubilee harm unless you manage to scotch them.'

'Thank you, Sybil. I'm well aware of that.'

Muriel's stiff response succeeded in putting Sybil's back up. 'Have it your own way,' she sniffed. 'I'm only trying to help, though Lord knows why.'

'Yes – why?' Muriel wondered. 'If we end up losing business to you over this, surely you'll be pleased.'

'I'll be over the moon, I can assure you.' Sybil's sarcasm widened the gap between the two shopkeepers and for a while there was stalemate.

'Here are the prices, Miss Dacre.' Violet broke the silence. She saw that Muriel and Sybil were alike – both were single women who stood too much on their dignity and, though clever, they had difficulty saying what they really meant. Yet they were both honest and kind, with hearts of gold.

In the end it was Muriel who cut through the awkwardness to the quick of the matter. 'Listen, Sybil, let's get to the point. We both know that Jubilee's work isn't inferior.'

'Quite,' Sybil acknowledged with a curt nod.

'And the criticism comes from a customer whose opinion nobody admires.'

'Not to mention her taste in fashion.' The uncharacteristically sly remark, delivered deadpan and with a raised eyebrow, broke the tension and made both Violet and Muriel smile.

'Neither of us can do anything about that,' Muriel acknowledged. 'Cards on the table, as you say – I'd be the first to admit that we run things on a knife edge here at Jubilee, wondering if our customers can keep up with their weekly instalments, being prepared to run back to the bank manager if they can't. But, touch wood, so far, so good.'

'Unless Mrs Barlow continues to set the cat among the pigeons and you lose your loyal band of mill girls and factory workers,' Sybil reminded her. 'Then what?'

'Then we go out again and find new ones, maybe further afield.'

'Hmm.' Sybil felt the force of Muriel's determination. 'That's good to hear. But in that case, I'd better be on my toes.'

'Yes, you'd better.' Taking the cotton reel and popping it into a bag, Muriel left the challenge hanging between them. 'That'll be tuppence you owe me.'

'Two pence.' Sybil took the worn copper coins from her purse and slid them across the counter. 'You and Ida can't say I didn't warn you.'

'And you can't expect us to roll over and admit defeat,' Muriel argued, ringing up the purchase and following Sybil's exit with a gimlet eye. 'Can she, Violet?' she added.

'No. We live to fight another day.' Violet had come full circle since her low point of the night before. *We hold our heads up and walk shoulder to shoulder like the suffragettes of old in their purple and green sashes. We don't give in to the likes of Colin and Alice Barlow.*

That night, the day before Violet's birthday, she and Eddie braved the Overcliffe Assembly Rooms on Cliff Street for the first time. It was his special treat and Violet felt a mounting excitement as they approached the grand Edwardian building.

'Best foot forward, birthday girl,' Eddie advised, guiding her past a crowd gathered on the entrance steps, underneath blank-eyed stone caryatids into a wide foyer where they joined the queue for tickets.

'I forgot to ask, Eddie, are you any good at dancing or have you got two left feet?' Violet covered up her nerves with a light-hearted tone. She'd felt curious eyes upon her as they'd mounted the steps, especially those of Alf Shipley and Kenneth Leach, both dressed up to the nines in navy chalk-stripe suits for a night out together. She suspected that she'd read something unpleasant in their expressions, but she tried to dismiss them from her thoughts.

'Wait and see,' Eddie replied. He came to the front of the queue and paid for two tickets then waited while Violet took her coat to the cloakroom. 'All set?' he asked on her return.

'Ready as I'll ever be.' A deep breath was needed prior to their entrance, and the support of Eddie's arm, which she leaned on as they walked together into a large hall with polished floor and raised plat-form at the far end.

'The place could do with a lick of paint,' Eddie noticed, casting a professional eye over the dull cream walls and flaking ceiling. 'I doubt if it's been done in the twenty-odd years since it was built.'

Violet didn't reply. She was concentrating instead on the band tuning up onstage – a lady in black evening dress at the piano, with two violinists in penguin suits and a second woman drawing a bow over the strings of her double bass. There was a lot of squeaking and squawking, scraping and practising of scales that made her wonder whether or not the musicians would ever be able to produce a decent tune.

'Look who it isn't,' a cheerful voice said and both

Eddie and Violet turned to see Stan approaching with Evie. 'How did you get here?' Stan asked as a way of passing the time. 'Did he bring you on the bike, Violet, or was it Shanks's pony?'

'The bike – in this dress?' Violet gave a twirl of her flimsy, emerald-green skirt – part of a dress with cap sleeves and a crossover bodice that she wore with her white, wedge-heeled sandals.

'You walked,' Stan decided with a what-do-I-know-about-women's-clothes shrug followed by a long, meaningful look that Violet chose to ignore. She drew Evie to one side as the men struck up conversation. 'This is a nice treat from Eddie for my birthday,' she confided. 'And since you're here, even if it turns out that he and Stan don't know their left foot from their right, it means I'll still have someone to do the quickstep with.'

'You kept that quiet. Anyway, happy birthday – you look better than when I last saw you,' Evie told Violet, while admiring the cut of her skirt and the shape of her neckline.

'I *feel* better, ta. Did you know that Sybil paid us a visit?'

Evie nodded. 'I knew something must have got under her skin. She left meek and mild and came back roaring like a lion about how she would print more leaflets and push them through letter boxes in the centre of town and out in Hadley, not just in our neck of the woods.'

'That was Muriel's fault.' Violet explained. 'When

331

Sybil and Muriel lock horns, it's best to stay out of their way. Anyway, we're not here to talk about work – we're here to dance. Come on, Eddie – put out that cigarette and show a girl how to foxtrot the night away.'

When, an hour later, Violet and Evie bumped into each other again in the ladies' cloakroom, Violet had to admit that Eddie's fleetness of foot on the football pitch carried over to not only the foxtrot but the waltz and the quickstep too. 'He's danced me off my feet.'

'Count yourself lucky.' Evie eased her bruised toes inside her satin dancing shoes. 'I'm ready for this break. Stan was like a baby elephant back there.'

'You poor thing.' Violet glanced sideways at Evie's flushed reflection in the mirror over the wash basins. 'How are you two getting along these days?'

'Like a house on fire,' Evie replied with a small smile as she dried her hands.

'Honestly?' Since listening to Ben Hutchinson's possible explanation of the mystery behind her mother's bracelet, Violet had had little time to think about the next step. Mainly she was relieved that she'd always kept Stan at a safe distance and hoped that he felt the same way. She also wanted to know that he was sincere with Evie and treating her well.

'Cross my heart,' Evie assured her. 'He came to tea with us this afternoon at Albion Lane.'

'That's a big step.'

'I know. Can you believe it? Father invited him.'

'And did Stan behave himself?' Patting her hair into place, Violet was ready for round two on the dance floor.

'Yes. He played a game of dominoes with Arthur while I made egg sandwiches and Father read his *Herald*. Then Father took Arthur down to Newby's for his sweets and Stan kissed me.'

'Oh.' For a second Violet was taken aback. 'And how was that?'

'Very nice,' Evie said, blushing slightly. 'He had his arm around my waist but it was only a kiss on the cheek. That was all right, wasn't it?'

'Tickety-boo,' Violet agreed, linking arms with Evie in a jolly fashion. 'As long as Stan didn't overstep the mark – that's the main thing.'

The evening went on and the band played slow waltz tunes from popular musicals – 'I'll Be Loving You Always', 'What Is This Thing Called Love?' and others.

'"Love flew in through my window",' Eddie murmured as he held Violet close. She smiled and let herself enjoy the final moments on the dance floor, scarcely noticing that the crowd was thinning out.

'Still tripping the light fantastic, I see,' Stan called out. He was lolling back in his seat with his arm around Evie's shoulder, his tie knot loosened and jacket hanging open.

'Yes – what's up with you two?' Eddie asked. 'Can't you take the pace?'

'It's my big clodhoppers that are the problem,' Stan admitted.

'Evie's poor feet are black and blue,' Violet explained, breaking hold and leading Eddie off the floor to sit down next to them. 'I hope you're not expecting her to walk all the way home, Stan.'

'No, I'll splash out on a taxi if she's good.'

'Blimey.' Eddie gave him a good-natured jab with his elbow.

'If she's good!' Violet echoed, while Evie huffed and puffed, pretending to be offended.

The evening was winding down when a group of lads sauntered in from the bar set up in a small side room beside the ticket office. There were half a dozen of them, some carrying glasses of beer, all smoking and joking as they surveyed the hall.

'They've left it a bit late to find a dance partner,' Stan commented.

'Oops-a-daisy – someone's tiddly.' Evie saw Les Craven split from the group and start to make his way towards them. Then he staggered to a halt as if forgetting what he'd set out to do. Luckily Alf and Kenneth were standing by to rescue him and steer him towards a nearby chair where he sat down heavily, long legs splayed wide.

'Are we ready to go?' Violet asked.

'Yes. Give me your cloakroom tickets,' Stan said to her and Evie. 'You three wait here while I go and fetch the coats.'

To get to the cloakroom he had to pass Les and

334

other members of the football team. Smiling and stopping for a friendly word about the day's match, Stan slowly made his way out while Les struggled to his feet, found his balance and continued to walk with a swaying gait towards Eddie, Violet and Evie.

'Bottoms up,' he said, sinking the last of his pint and dropping onto Stan's empty chair.

Dying strains of the last waltz drifted from the stage, followed by a smattering of applause then laughter as two of Les's burly pals got into a dance hold then drunkenly lurched onto the empty floor. Once more, Alf and Kenneth left their post by the exit and strolled towards Les, who by this time had closed his eyes and was starting to snore.

'I'm sorry, ladies,' Alf apologized to Violet and Evie. He seemed sober enough, carrying himself upright in a way that conveyed his years in the army. His dark moustache and short back and sides added the finishing touches. 'Young Les here has obviously had one over the eight. Kenneth, give us a hand to get him back up on his hind legs.'

Kenneth quickly obliged and between them they managed to get Les upright while Evie and Violet felt embarrassed that the lanky goalkeeper had shown himself up.

'What? . . . Where?' Still swaying, Les broke free and looked around in a daze. He rocked forward as his gaze rested on Violet. 'Hell-oo!' he cried, swaying backwards then lurching forwards towards her with what was a definite leer. 'Who'd have thought it, eh?'

Quickly interpreting Les's lecherous look, Violet sprang to her feet and tried to push past him.

'Steady on!' Eddie too was on his feet, though he hadn't caught the look and was left wondering why Violet had reacted the way she had.

'Not me, for a start – I wouldn't have credited it,' Les blundered on, pushing Eddie off balance. He flailed his arms to left and right and ignored warning looks from Alf and Kenneth. 'I had her down as a good little chapel-goer, didn't you, Eddie?'

Trapped in the narrow gap between Les and a row of chairs, Violet closed her eyes and held her breath.

'Well, Ed – we were all wrong,' Les crowed. 'Not that you've got any complaints on that score, I take it?'

The insult to Violet hit Eddie hard and he didn't stop to think. He seized Les by the shoulder and spun him round then lashed out with his fist. The blow landed right on Les's chin and made his teeth chatter. Blindly Les launched himself back at Eddie. He swung a punch but failed to make contact then toppled forward and landed flat on his face. He lay groaning until Eddie hauled him onto his feet, backed him against the wall and held him there.

'Don't say another word or I'll flatten you,' he hissed through gritted teeth, one warning finger raised to within an inch of his opponent's eyes.

'I'm only . . . I didn't . . .' An incoherent Les hardly seemed to know what was happening. With clumsy movements he tried to wrest himself free until Kenneth stepped in to pull them apart.

'All right, sonny, let's get you out of here while you're still in one piece.' The older man took charge of Les just as Stan came back with the coats. 'There's been a bit of bother,' he explained.

'What about?' Stan looked at Violet and saw that she was trembling, then at Eddie, speechless with anger.

Alf helped Kenneth to take hold of Les by the scruff of the neck. 'Ask them,' he advised, brows knotted as he took note of Violet's shaky state.

'I don't have to,' Stan muttered. 'I've had this out with Les once already.'

'Yes, well, some people never learn.' Alf turned Les towards the door and started to march him away, then he had second thoughts and addressed Stan once more. 'Your pal back there – Eddie Thomson?'

'What about him?' Stan's belligerent tone was his way of sticking up for his friend but it rattled Alf Shipley.

'Tell him to keep his hair on in future. And don't look at me like that. I'm not the enemy round here.'

'Who is?' Stan demanded.

'You can work that out for yourselves.' The Barlows' driver felt he'd said enough, and anyway Les was trying to wriggle free, lashing out with his

337

fists again. He and Kenneth Leach dragged him out of the hall and had him propped up against the cloakroom counter when Kenneth felt a tap on his shoulder and they both turned to see Evie standing there – fair haired and dressed in pale blue satin with frills and bows, five feet four inches of fierce determination.

'Eddie was only sticking up for Violet,' she pointed out.

'Yes, and I'd have done the same in his shoes,' Kenneth conceded. 'Stand up straight, Les, there's a good lad. The trouble is if the wrong people hear about Eddie losing his temper and lashing out, that'll be one more black mark against your troublemaker friend – the one with the dark hair – the Jubilee girl.'

'Violet!' Evie gasped.

'They'll say she put him up to it, that it's her fault.'

'Even when it isn't?'

'It makes no difference.' Alf stepped in to explain. 'Not if they've got it in for someone. The Barlows and the Kingsleys – they're the ones who shout the loudest, not the likes of Violet and Eddie. You hear?'

Frowning, Evie understood and accepted what Alf and Kenneth said. 'Thank you. I'll pass it on.'

With a curt nod, Alf turned away. 'Make sure to leave our names out of it,' he mumbled, helping

Kenneth to keep Les upright and reaching for his coat.

'I will,' Evie promised.

'Otherwise we'll all be out of a job. And what good would that do?'

CHAPTER TWENTY-FOUR

'There goes another order down the Swanee,' Muriel said glumly as she entered the shop. 'That's the fifth cancellation this week and it's only Wednesday.'

Behind the counter, Violet and Ida exchanged worried glances.

'Who is it this time?' Ida wanted to know.

'It's Eunice Shackleton – Lizzie Turner's married sister. She put in an order for a christening gown for her first baby but I popped into Hutchinson's for biscuits and while I was there Lizzie let on that Eunice has changed her mind.'

'Why would she do that?' Ida asked, while Violet stayed quietly in the background.

'Lizzie said that Eunice can't find the money for it after all, but reading between the lines, I worked out the real reason.'

'Which is?' Ida prompted.

'Which is that Eunice does ten hours per week scrubbing floors and polishing furniture for none other than – guess who.'

'Alice Barlow,' Ida said without hesitating.

'Bingo! The truth is, she's warned Eunice off using us. At this rate we'll be out of business by the end of the week.' Too upset for once to put on a brave face, Muriel shook her head and went upstairs. Violet too was cast down by this latest cancellation.

Ida was more resilient. 'Not if I have anything to do with it,' she decided as she unbuttoned her coat. 'Sybil isn't the only one who can advertise further afield – out as far as Hadley and even Welby if we feel like it. In fact, Violet, why not get Eddie to bring you to rehearsal half an hour early tonight – that'll give us time to pop our leaflets through letter boxes.'

'Eddie's working at the Victory so I'll have to catch the bus. And do you really think it's worthwhile?' Violet wondered.

'What are you talking about?' Ida demanded. 'Of course it's worthwhile.'

'I only mean that Alice Barlow is like an octopus. Her tentacles spread everywhere you look.'

'Squeezing us to death?' Ida's lively imagination took up the idea.

'This is serious,' Violet protested. Shaken by the latest cancellation, her heart sank and she felt boxed into a familiar corner. 'Perhaps we need to think again about me leaving Jubilee, at least for a little while.'

'And then what?' Ida demanded, bustling through to the kitchen and carrying on the conversation from there.

341

'Then I could find new lodgings and look for a job.'

'Violet, I've said it before and I'll say it again, Alice Barlow can squeeze all she likes – she won't throttle the life out of us, not while I have anything to do with it.'

At the end of the afternoon, while Muriel was out collecting new leaflets from the printer's, a customer came to Jubilee to collect an order that helped put the fight back into Violet.

'I take it my blouse is ready.' Ella Kingsley addressed her with an open, friendly smile, altogether different from what might have been expected.

'Yes, Mrs Kingsley.' Violet's heart skipped a beat. 'If you wouldn't mind waiting a moment, I'll tell Miss Thomson you're here to collect it.'

'Finally!' was Ida's reaction when Violet raced upstairs to pass on the news. She rapped down her scissors and took the finished blouse from a tailor's dummy in the corner of the room. 'Come with me,' she told Violet with an eager smile. 'I've been waiting days to have this conversation with Ella Kingsley.'

Ida hurried downstairs to greet her customer and show her the finished article, laying it flat on the counter. 'Violet managed to find the exact buttons to match the shade of the material,' she said proudly. 'She's the one who did the finishing touches – the buttonholes and facings, and suchlike. Violet is painstaking over details, I hope you'll agree.'

342

'I do.' Ella Kingsley examined her purchase before glancing up at Violet who hovered nervously behind the counter, bewildered and a little embarrassed by Ida's lavish praise. 'I certainly can't fault the workmanship.'

'No. We jumped at the chance of employing her the minute we saw what she could do with a needle and thread. And, despite what some people are saying, we haven't regretted it, not for a second.'

Mrs Kingsley received the thinly disguised challenge and let an awkward pause develop. She looked uncertainly from Violet to Ida and back again.

'I'm glad to have the chance to speak plainly,' Ida went on in her courageous way. 'We were very upset here at Jubilee to hear what went on last week.'

'At my house,' Ella Kingsley acknowledged, deep frown lines appearing on her unmarked brow. As if to distract herself, she carefully peeled off her grey leather gloves and ran her fingers over the crêpe de Chine blouse. She sighed. 'It's a bad business. I wish I'd been there to prevent it.'

'Luckily for Violet, Mr Kingsley *was* there,' Ida said pointedly. 'He did see what happened.'

Violet swallowed hard at the risk Ida was taking and wished the floor would swallow her up. Her heart beat loud and fast.

The frown deepened. 'Thomas was there, certainly. Inside the house, I believe.'

'Ah!' Ida's exclamation spoke volumes.

'He told me he was in his study, speaking on the

343

telephone.' Quick to acknowledge the implications of what she was saying, Ella Kingsley continued nevertheless. 'I'm afraid Thomas couldn't possibly have anything useful to say about what went on outside.'

'No witnesses,' Ida confirmed with undisguised triumph. 'Then it comes down to who is to be believed – Violet or Mr Barlow.'

'Quite.' Ella Kingsley's expression was inscrutable, but she quickly turned the conversation in a new direction, one that proved without doubt where she stood.

'Now tell me, Violet, how hard would it be for you to copy a house dress I've seen in the latest copy of *Harper's Bazaar*?' Sliding the magazine from her handbag, she showed her a picture and together with Ida they pored over details about hemlines and ruffled collars, tailored bodices, shoulder pads and three-quarter length sleeves.

'I'm sure we can do it.' Violet smiled in relief. She felt in a small way that the octopus's tentacles had begun to loosen. 'It would look best in a bright colour, perhaps in rayon or nylon, which is nice and shiny.'

Ida added her ideas. 'Violet could make it in royal blue trimmed with white, or perhaps a warm red for winter.'

'Both!' Their customer threw caution to the winds. 'A blue one and a red one, with contrasting piping around the neckline.'

There was more enthusiastic discussion. Should the dresses be lined? Should the shoulder pads be quite so wide?

'That all sounds satisfactory,' Ella Kingsley said pleasantly, once the decisions were made. Then she gave Violet a direct look and a reassuring smile before she put her gloves back on.

Everything was agreed at last with smiles then handshakes all round. 'Thank you, Mrs Kingsley,' Ida said.

'Thank *you*,' came the calm, confident reply.

'Well I never!' Violet exclaimed to the jangle of the shop bell and the sight of their loyal customer crossing the street.

'Hallelujah!' Ida grinned, her chest puffed out. 'Unless I'm mistaken, Ella Kingsley has reached her own conclusions about the Barlows.'

'She's broken ranks.' Violet's smile was like the sun coming out from behind clouds.

'You can say that again. Now who says it's not worthwhile us handing out leaflets in Hadley tonight?'

That evening, Violet caught the double-decker bus to Hadley, climbing the metal stairs and positioning herself at the front to enjoy the sight of the glorious, heather-covered moors – a blanket of pale purple stretching as far as the eye could see. At the end of the journey she found Ida standing on the main street with Harold.

'About time too,' Ida grumbled when she saw Violet alighting.

'Why – I'm not late, am I?'

In a rush as always, Ida handed leaflets to Harold and Violet. 'We've got twenty minutes before the rehearsal is due to start. Harold, you can go up and down Railway Road. I'll do Minehead Terrace and Victoria Street. Violet, take this batch and drop one through every letter box on Main Street. Come along – chop-chop!'

Taking the yellow leaflets, Violet pretended not to notice long-suffering Harold's raised eyebrows and hurried off to deliver to the post office with its lowered blinds, then to the mean-looking terraced cottages that fronted straight onto the road. Hurriedly she delivered to the blacksmith's forge then crossed the street and carried on with her task, up garden paths, getting her fingers caught in letter boxes with vicious hinges and avoiding a dog – a snappy Yorkshire terrier with a yapping bark. At last she came to the final house – the stately vicarage with its neat lawns and leaded windows. As she walked up the path she became aware of the vicar himself, complete with dog collar and worn grey jacket, standing in the doorway.

'Good evening,' he said, stretching out a hand to take a leaflet then reading the top line. '"Jubilee Drapers and Dressmakers – Good quality, Reasonable rates." I'm afraid it's a waste of time leaving one of these with me,' he pointed out. 'There's no call for

346

dresses here, unless you include church vestments and altar cloths.'

'I'm sorry, I didn't think.' Violet was ready to take the leaflet back and hurry off but tonight the formerly aloof vicar seemed in chatty mood.

'Yes, but you weren't to know that I lived alone. Most people suppose that a clergyman has the support of a loyal and loving wife but that's not so in my case, unfortunately. I can only suppose it's God's will.'

To Violet, it seemed that the well-worn phrase drew attention to the vicar's loneliness and her heart unexpectedly went out to him. True, he wasn't one to attract sympathy – he was too stiff and formal for that, with an artificial, sing-song voice and with those odd tufts of white hair so sparsely spread over the dome of his head. Strangely this made her think of her Uncle Donald and his barber's scissors, which once upon a time would have made short work of the straggly locks.

'Donald Wheeler,' the vicar said suddenly and with such concurrence of thought that Violet's hand shook as she received back the unwanted leaflet. 'Your uncle, I believe?'

She looked in alarm at the clergyman. 'Yes, sir.'

'And Donald's late wife, Winifred – she would have been your aunt?'

'Yes, sir. She was.' For Violet, the reminder brought on a rush of grief almost as fresh as the day when her Aunty Winnie had passed away.

'I'm sorry.' The vicar's sympathy was gentle and sincere. 'She was a good woman, by all accounts.'

A nod was all Violet could manage as a lump rose in her throat and she fought back tears.

'You said your uncle found it hard to go on without her. I did my best to reach out and offer the hand of kindness.'

'Yes. Thank you for that.'

'Since we last spoke, I happen to have received notification of your uncle's whereabouts.'

The revelation, delivered hesitatingly, rocked Violet back on her heels.

'When? How?' she exclaimed.

'Hadley is a small parish but my duties reach further afield,' the vicar explained carefully. 'Among other things, I act as chaplain to parishioners who are admitted to hospital in Welby. The doctors there take care of their bodily ailments. Their spiritual welfare is left to me.'

'Hospital, you say?' Violet was slow to absorb the information. 'In Welby?'

'Donald's last known address is noted as Main Street, Hadley. The hospital contacted me yesterday to say that he'd been admitted as a patient. I decided that I would try to speak to you tonight when you came to the Institute.'

'Why? What's wrong with him?'

'I'm afraid he has a bad case of pneumonia. This morning I went to visit him, as I'm bound to do. Unfortunately, your uncle refused to see me.'

Slowly Violet nodded.

'I'm sure this has been a shock. Would you like to come in and sit down?' the vicar asked.

'No, thank you. I can't stay. Is he . . . is he very ill?'

The answer, when it came, was cautious. 'The hospital thought it was wise for me to visit him sooner rather than later. That's all I can tell you.'

'I see.' Seized by panic, Violet backed away from the door. 'I do have to go now. Thank you.'

'If there's anything else I can do . . .'

'No.' Shaking her head, she reached the gate and blindly made her way to the Institute where she sank onto a chair in the anteroom, her head in her hands. Uncle Donald was dying, or had already died – the thought hammered away inside her head. He was departing this world and leaving her behind, taking with him everything he'd kept secret about her mother's past. *I might never know for certain who my father was*, she thought with chilling finality. *And now Uncle Donald and I might never get the chance to say goodbye.*

'Where are you going?' Ida bumped into Violet as she flew, white faced, out of the building and across the yard.

'To see Uncle Donald,' she gasped, seeing the bus appear at the corner. 'He's in hospital in Welby. I'm sorry I can't stay for rehearsal, Ida. I'll see you to-morrow, all being well.'

349

CHAPTER TWENTY-FIVE

The Queen Victoria Hospital in Welby was the largest
building Violet had ever approached. Built around
a courtyard along the lines of a medieval castle,
with arched windows and castellated ramparts, it
stood back from a busy thoroughfare criss-crossed
by tramlines and blocked by buses that lurched out
from pavements to join the ranks of slow-moving
black cars. Horns hooted, draymen in charge of
wooden carts drove heavy-footed horses down
narrow side streets and ambulances fought through
traffic to deliver patients to the wide hospital door.

Bracing herself to enter, she found a large, well-
lit hallway leading to a daunting maze of corridors
peopled by porters pushing trolleys and what looked
like groups of bewildered relatives trying to follow
signs to wards identified only by letters – Ward A,
Ward B, and so on, through to the letter H. She
walked uncertainly past an empty office furnished
with metal filing cabinets and banks of black type-
writers towards the open window of a booth where a

dour-looking woman sat at a high desk.

'Please could you help me?' she began. 'I'm looking for a patient here by the name of Donald Wheeler.'

'Ward?' the woman barked without looking up from the ledger she was scribbling in.

'I don't know. He was brought in with pneumonia.'

The clerk sighed and began to flick through the pages of her ledger. 'Date of admission?'

'I don't know that either.'

'Address? Date of birth? Next of kin?'

'Me – I'm his niece.' Violet pounced on the one question she could readily answer.

'W-H-E-E-L-E-R.' Spelling out the name, the woman searched then finally stabbed her pencil onto the page. 'Admitted on the twenty-ninth of September. Ward C.'

Thanking her, Violet hurried down the corridor, its green walls and russet-coloured linoleum floor stretching on before her, the hushed atmosphere and disinfected smell designed to cow even the boldest of visitors. She kept her head down to avoid exchanging glances with the people she met along the way – an old lady in a wheelchair with wispy white hair trailing over her shoulders, a young lad with a bandaged head and sallow complexion – until she came to the ward she was looking for.

'Yes?' The nurse stationed at a desk inside the swing-doors at least looked up when Violet entered.

'I've come to visit Donald Wheeler.'

'Are you a relative?'

'He's my uncle.'

The nurse pointed to a chair. 'Wait there.'

She disappeared through another set of doors and didn't return. Violet was kept in suspense, watching the hands of the clock above the nurse's desk jerk forward. Visitors came and went, and occasionally a nurse in starched cap and apron, but not the one she'd first spoken to.

At last she stood up and approached a porter – a heavily built man in a brown cotton coat with a receding hairline and an old scar stretching from his eye to the corner of his mouth. 'Excuse me. I'm waiting to see my uncle. I asked a nurse about him but she hasn't got back to me.'

The porter tutted. 'Was she tall with a snooty air? That's Edith. You'll wait forever for her if you're not careful. What's your uncle's name, love?'

Listening to Violet's answer, he went behind the desk and was calling out that her Uncle Donald was in bed number eleven when the tardy nurse re-turned and caught sight of Violet sitting where she'd left her.

'Are you still here?' she said sharply. 'I told your uncle you were here. His answer was that he didn't want to see anybody.'

Violet heaved a sigh. The long wait had deflated her and she was stung afresh by this latest rejection. Ah well, she'd made the last-ditch attempt at putting right the wrongs of the past, but she'd failed and that was that, it seemed.

Then out of the blue came a mental picture of Aunty Winnie in a shaft of sunlight in the corridor, standing full-square with arms folded, an unshake-able presence. *Don't take no for an answer* was the clear message in the loving, down-to-earth voice that Violet remembered so well.

'The poor lass came all this way,' the porter pointed out to the sharp-tongued nurse. 'Why not try again – see if he's changed his mind?'

Edith frowned but then relented. She disappeared again. There was another, shorter wait until she came back. 'Your uncle says you can go in after all,' she reported. 'But if I were you, I wouldn't get my hopes up.'

Duly prepared, Violet thanked the porter for his help and entered the ward with mixed feelings. The last time she'd seen Uncle Donald, on the doorstep of Jubilee, she'd felt sure their paths would never cross again. Looking back to that moment, she realized she hadn't even been sorry. Part of the reason was that she now had people who cared for her – Ida, Muriel, Evie, Stan, to name but a few, and, of course, Eddie above all. She didn't have to rely on Donald any more. But if the vicar was to be believed, he was nearing the end here in this hospital bed.

Once more Violet imagined what Aunty Winnie would have said – that it would be cruel to leave Donald all on his own and that their little family had stuck together through thick and thin.

So Violet walked between rows of iron bedsteads,

eyes straight ahead out of respect for the sick people lying there, until she came to the bay marked 11. The shape under the green blanket was skeletal, the head on the pillow skull-like. Only the dark, sunken eyes moved – glittering in the pale face, papery skin drawn tight over the cheekbones, lips dry, breath loud and rasping. Pity and sadness drew her close to his bedside.

'Well?' Donald said when he saw her.

Violet swallowed her distress and tried to speak normally. 'Well, how are you?'

His eyes flickered shut. 'How do I look? I told them to let me get on with it – to leave me there and let me die, but they carted me in here instead.'

'Who's "they", Uncle Donald?'

'The Public Assistance busybodies. They found me collapsed on their doorstep.' Talking seemed hard. Words came in short snatches, in between painful attempts to drag air into his rattling lungs. 'Who told you I was here, anyway?'

'The vicar in Hadley. I came as soon as I heard. I'm sorry to see you in this fix, Uncle Donald, I really am.'

'I'm not – I'm glad. I'm on my way out and it's a blessing.'

Gradually, as she pulled a chair close to the bed, Violet once more mastered her feelings and came to terms with what she saw. 'But is there anything you need?' she asked gently.

'Like what?'

'The prayer book that I kept for you, for a start?'

'If you want,' he conceded after a long silence. 'It belonged to Joe. But fetch it anyway.'

'Tomorrow,' she promised. As if she could still hear the clock above the nurse's desk ticking and measuring out the short time that her uncle had left, she went to the heart of the matter. 'Uncle Donald . . . I've worked things out at last.'

'What things?' A flash of the old suspicion appeared in his glittering eyes.

'Why you were so dead set against me and Stan. It was because his father was my father too.'

'Douglas Tankard.' The dying man filled two simple words with a lifetime of bitterness. 'He was a married man, but that didn't stop him.'

'It's true, then?'

For a long time Donald struggled for air but he held Violet's gaze. 'Florence Shaw had got hitched to my brother but that didn't stop her either. The two of them were as bad as one another.'

'From what I can gather, Joe had already gone off to the Front?'

'He answered the call straight off, in late 1914. I went to the town hall and signed up with him.' There was pride in this and it set the memories flowing more freely. 'It's true Joe wasn't as steady as me when we were growing up, but he had a decent heart, not like Tankard. No one had a good word to say about him, not once they got wind of the way he treated Gladys Sowden and their little lad.'

Violet leaned forward. 'Mightn't there have been two sides to the story – especially if Joe wasn't a good husband either?'

'No. Right is right and wrong is wrong. Your mother broke a holy commandment when she went with him. Winnie suspected it and by promising not to tell a living soul she managed to winkle the truth out of her. Florence admitted that Tankard had got his feet under the table by Christmas and nine months later you were the result.'

So then, there was no room for doubt. The jigsaw of Violet's life, first broken apart by her discovery of the bracelet, was pieced together again to form a new picture, a new identity. 'What about Gladys and Stan?' she asked shakily.

'Winnie kept her word so they never found out. Anyhow, with another baby on the way, and out of wedlock this time, Tankard saw he was in a tight spot so in the spring of 1915 he upped and enlisted as well. He was never seen or heard of again.'

Listening to the halting words, Violet began truly to see what it must have cost Donald to agree to adopt her after he'd returned from the trenches. His brother and Florence – betrayed and betrayer – were both dead. There was an illegitimate child and every reason in the world to have nothing to do with her. Yet, out of love for Winnie, Donald had given in to her desire to nurture the baby. 'I see,' she said slowly, laying a hand on the cool bed cover.

'You see some of it . . .' A raw cough rattled in

356

Donald's throat and panicked Violet into calling for the tall nurse who came with more pillows to prop him up.

'He needs to rest.' Edith spoke to Violet more kindly than before, waiting at the bedside for her to leave.

'. . . but not all,' Donald carried on with difficulty, as if he hadn't been cut off.

Violet felt a shudder of apprehension. 'What else should I know?'

There was a grim silence while he dredged through ancient events. 'No last letter home, no personal effects – nothing. And there was never any telegram.'

'To say Tankard had been killed?'

'He didn't come home to Gladys and Stan – that's plain. But no – Gladys didn't get proper word of what happened to him in France.' Donald coughed again but as the nurse moved in to help, he pushed her away, seized Violet's hand and pulled her close. 'No telegram,' he repeated with an urgency that shocked her.

'Please,' the nurse murmured to Violet as she came between them. 'It's time to leave.'

'I have to go now, Uncle Donald.'

'Joe's prayer book,' he reminded her amidst a fit of violent coughing, falling back against the pillows.

'I'll bring it tomorrow,' Violet promised. She was glad that she'd come, if 'glad' was the right word. It showed Uncle Donald that she cared and that she'd won the chance to do this one last thing for him.

'Aye, do,' he gasped, letting his outstretched hand fall onto his chest.

'Goodnight, then,' she said softly.

'Aye and God bless,' he sighed, as if begging and not bestowing.

Shaken to her core, Violet backed away from the bed and turned to walk out of the ward, down the long green corridor, with Uncle Donald's pitiable gaze etched in her memory.

A sober mood hung over Violet during a visit from Eddie later that evening. They sat together over a cup of tea in Jubilee's small kitchen, Violet glad of Eddie's company while she thought out her next move.

'In my heart I can't help but believe that Douglas Tankard loved my mother, despite what Uncle Donald said.'

'Because of the bracelet?' Eddie quickly picked up her train of thought and saw how this might help Violet to feel better.

'Yes. In the note he calls her his dearest Flo. He asks her to keep the bracelet for his sake. That shows he did love her, doesn't it?'

'Let's hope so.' There was a note of caution mixed in with gentleness in Eddie's voice. 'We'll probably never know for certain.'

Weary from the day's events, Violet gripped his

hands more tightly across the table. She felt comforted by everyday things – the brown teapot and mismatched cups and saucers on the deal table, the flecks of white paint on Eddie's cheek. 'What if we could?' she ventured.

'Could what?'

'Find out for certain that what Douglas wrote in the note came from the heart. "Lifelong affection" – that says something about him, surely?' Shaking off her weariness, Violet's mind raced on. 'He never came back from France – we already knew that. But Uncle Donald told me there was a mystery about what actually happened to him out there.'

'That went on a lot,' Eddie cautioned. 'Sometimes a whole regiment was blown to smithereens and afterwards they couldn't put names to them.' Every schoolchild learned about the Tomb of the Unknown Soldier in Westminster Abbey and though men who had survived the trenches rarely talked about their experiences in the Great War, it was an accepted fact that they'd been offered up as cannon fodder, foot soldiers following orders to go over the top and slog it out over a few yards of muddy ground – lions led by donkeys.

'So what happened afterwards?' Violet wondered. 'If Gladys didn't learn for certain that Douglas had been killed and there was never any death certificate, what would she do next?'

'I expect she'd have to wait a certain while and see. After that they'd decide he'd been killed in action and sort out a widow's pension for her – that kind of thing.'

Violet freed her hands and stood up in sudden agitation. 'And there'd be a record of that, surely?'

'Somewhere.' Eddie was deliberately vague. 'But do you really want to go down that path? What if you end up banging your head against another brick wall?'

'I'm not saying I will try to find out for definite.' Violet reined herself back and reminded herself of the more pressing situation. 'For the time being I have to concentrate on Uncle Donald. I'll go up-stairs this minute and dig out Joe's prayer book. I promised to take it in tomorrow and I can't let him down.'

A male customer was a rarity in Jubilee, so Violet and Ida were surprised next morning to see Frank Bielby, the chapel preacher, come in through the door.

'Good morning, how can I help you?' Ida's greeting was wary as she took in the sturdy brogues, tweed suit and bald head.

The minister averted his gaze from the feminine frippery on display. 'Good morning, Miss Thomson. And Violet, how are you?'

'I'm all right, thank you.'

Pleasantries exchanged, there was an awkward pause during which Bielby shuffled and cleared his throat, Ida sorted through the morning's post and

Violet waited for him to state his business.

'I suppose you're wondering why I'm here,' he said at last, his eyes fixed on Violet in a way that made her nervous. 'I'm afraid it's because I've been the recipient of bad news.'

'About Uncle Donald.' Violet responded quickly in a quiet, flat voice that held no surprise.

Frank Bielby nodded then went on in measured tones. 'Donald succumbed to pneumonia during the night. The hospital chaplain, who, as you know, is also the Church of England vicar in Hadley, saw fit to inform me since he knows your uncle's past connection with Chapel Street. I promised I would pass on the bad tidings to you, his next of kin, at the first opportunity. I'm sorry, my dear – it's a sad end.'

Violet's first, irrational reaction was to regret that she had failed to take in Joe's prayer book in time. 'I broke my promise,' she murmured tearfully.

Seeing her sway and turn pale, Ida rushed to fetch a chair from the kitchen. 'Here, love – sit down. Are you all right?'

As a man who prided himself on his self-control, Bielby continued to concentrate on practical matters. 'Of course, if you'd like to hold the funeral here on Chapel Street, I'd be more than happy to lead the service. Mr Turner will be able to put the necessary arrangements in place.'

'Thank you, Mr Bielby.' Speaking over him, Ida shook his hand and led him to the door. 'We're very much obliged. Once Violet has had a little time to get over the shock, we'll be in touch.'

Violet was only dimly aware that the bell had rung and the door had closed. First Aunty Winnie, now Uncle Donald. *I'm adrift*, she thought. *Lost at sea*.

'Don't bother your head with the funeral details.' Ida crouched at Violet's side. 'There'll be time for that later.'

'I think he had regrets,' Violet said faintly.

'Who – Bielby?'

'No, Uncle Donald. About the way he treated me.'

'There, there,' said Ida, stroking Violet's arm.

'He didn't come right out and say sorry, but I know he was.'

'Hush, Violet. Don't cry.'

'He told me "God bless". Those were his last words, just like Aunty Winnie's. You should have seen him, Ida, he was skin and bone.'

'Hush.'

'He was lying there and he gave me the story, chapter and verse – how Douglas Tankard was Stan's father and mine too, which is what we suspected. But I learned something new.'

Violet's distress brought tears to Ida's eyes. She held her hand tight.

'They couldn't say for sure that Douglas . . . my father . . . died in France. That's what Uncle Donald said – that there was no death certificate.'

'Hush. Don't go on.' Wanting to stem the flow of

362

Violet's distress, Ida helped her to her feet. 'Can you manage? Come upstairs and tell Muriel all about it,' she murmured. 'We'll sort out the rest later.'

CHAPTER TWENTY-SIX

'You know what they say – there's nothing we can do for the dead, so let's concentrate on the living.' Muriel's wise advice when she heard the sad news about Donald Wheeler was put into action before his funeral took place on the following Tuesday.

Monday morning was cold and damp and she and Violet walked briskly into town from Chapel Street, leaving Ida to man the fort. 'I mean you, Violet. If this business about Douglas Tankard is still bothering you, we can drop in at the library to find out more.'

'I won't rest until I know what happened to him,' Violet confessed. Though Eddie had tried to keep her chin up over the weekend by inviting her to Valley Road for Sunday dinner, her head had been filled with endless, worrying questions about her father.

'And Eddie's guess is that he went missing in action – is that it?' Emerging from Brewery Road onto Canal Road, Muriel gathered what she could from Violet before their proposed trawl through records in the reference department of the central library.

'I'm thinking about the look on Uncle Donald's face when he was telling me about it.' In fact, Violet couldn't get rid of the memory of his dark eyes glittering as he gripped her hand and drew her towards him. *No last letter, no death certificate. Nothing.* 'I'm certain he wanted to tell me more but the nurse stepped in and he didn't have time.'

'Half an hour in the library should clear it up.'

'What will we be looking for in the library?' Violet asked Muriel as they walked under the railway bridge and turned a corner onto St David's Street where the clean, curved façade of the new Odeon dominated the older Victorian buildings. A stiff breeze swept down the steep hill, raising autumn leaves and litter from the gutters and blowing cold drizzle in their faces.

'We'll go upstairs into the reference section.' Muriel knew her way around the library and she had a clear strategy. 'All the men from round here who enlisted for the Great War joined the Yorkshire Warriors – that was their nickname. It was really the Yorkshire Regiment. The Second Battalion went to the Western Front in October 1914 then the Fourth and Fifth Battalions followed in spring the next year. But before we make our way upstairs to read the records we'll be checking the names on the Roll of Honour inside the main entrance.'

As she and Muriel reached the entrance to the library, they came face to face with a group of chattering schoolchildren with satchels and books, surging down the wide steps onto the pavement.

'Let's wait until the coast is clear,' Muriel suggested, standing to one side. Her slim-fitting grey coat and maroon cloche hat, handbag and gloves gave her a sophisticated air that wouldn't have made her seem out of place on the fashionable streets of much larger cities. 'The Roll of Honour gives the names of infantrymen with the Yorkshire Warriors who fell in battle. They should be in alphabetical order,' she told Violet.

Violet felt small and inexperienced beside Muriel. If she'd been prepared for coming into town she would have dressed more smartly. As it was, she was in her second-best, navy blue coat, threadbare around the collar and cuffs, which had been made for her by Aunty Winnie when Violet was fifteen.

The children flowed past, full of laughter and excited chatter.

'Ready?' Without waiting for Violet's answer, Muriel went up the steps, between fat, fluted stone columns, through hefty doors with brass handles into the library.

The peculiar smell of old books – a mixture of leather bindings, musty paper, glue and ink – hit Violet immediately, together with lavender furniture polish and linoleum. There in front of them was a turnstile entrance into the lending section – a high-ceilinged room lined with thousands of brown, black and red volumes, many too high to reach without the use of a special stepladder. And to their right was the Roll of Honour for the Yorkshire Regiment, printed in gold on a varnished oak panel – name after name of privates, corporals, sergeants and captains who marched into battle and never returned. Sons, husbands, fathers.

'Watson, West, Weatherly . . . Wheeler.' It took Muriel no time at all to find Joe's name on the list. 'Savage, Selkirk, Swinson, Taylor . . .'

Violet could see for herself that Douglas Tankard did not appear.

'What did happen to him, I wonder?' Muriel's curiosity took her up some wide stairs ahead of Violet until they came to another turnstile manned by a smart young woman with neatly waved hair and a dark brown blouse with cream collar and cuffs. Muriel showed her membership card and signed Violet in as a visitor. They went through the waist-high turnstile into another vast room filled with a maze of bookcases separated by narrow walkways. Straight ahead was a counter with a large sign above it. The sign read, *Reference Stacks. No Books to be Taken Away.*

A second attendant, less well turned out than the first, stood behind the desk, pencil poised. 'Good morning. What is the name of the book or document that you wish me to fetch?'

'We want to look at the military records of men

who joined the Yorkshire Warriors in the spring of 1915, please.' Muriel kept her voice low so as not to disturb other readers in the vicinity. 'I take it you keep a copy for the general public to consult?'

'We certainly do. Wait here please.'

The woman glided off and soon returned bearing a slim foolscap volume bound in green cloth and decorated with a gold regimental insignia. She put it down on a table to the side of the counter then invited Muriel and Violet to sit down and peruse it at leisure.

'Alphabetical again,' Muriel murmured, opening the volume at the letter R and turning pages until she came to names beginning with S. She traced her finger down the page and they read in silence.

Pte Tankard, Douglas, 4th Battalion, 12 March 1915 – 3 May 1915, AWOL.

Muriel's finger hovered. She looked in alarm at Violet then closed the book with a faint thud.

'AWOL?' Disconcerted, Violet shook her head.

The woman behind the desk cast a quick, curious glance in their direction.

'Hush!' Muriel slid her arm through Violet's and walked her away, back through the turnstile, down the stairs and past the painting of the mayoral dignitary.

Outside on the steps Violet asked again: 'What does it mean?'

'AWOL is "absent without leave". It means Douglas Tankard abandoned his post without permission.'

'Not injured?'

'No, and not necessarily dead either,' Muriel confirmed, wondering whether Violet could stand another shock after all she'd been through. 'As far as the army is concerned, Tankard was the lowest of the low. He was a deserter.'

From their vantage point at the top of the hill, Violet stared down towards the railway bridge at the bottom, her shoulders slumped. People hurried heads down about their Monday-morning business – in and out of shops, on and off buses and trams, crossing the street. 'They executed men like that, didn't they?' She knew this much from her history lessons.

'Yes. They put them in front of a firing squad and shot them at dawn as an example to others.'

Violet shivered.

'But that's not what the record is telling us,' Muriel said, slowly piecing together her own knowledge about such things. 'It doesn't show a date for a court martial, for instance, let alone an execution.'

'Then what does it tell us?' Confirmation of the suspicions that Violet had harboured since her last talk with Uncle Donald put her mind in a spin.

'That Tankard ran away and they never managed to recapture him,' Muriel explained. 'He left his comrades on the field of battle. I'm afraid that's a big black mark against him in anybody's book.'

*

That evening Violet arranged with Eddie for him to bring Stan up to Overcliffe Common to meet her there.

'What's wrong with the Green Cross?' a mystified Stan had asked when Eddie had met him outside Kingsley's. 'I've put in a full day today. A man works up a thirst after ten hours of fine-tuning looms.'

'Violet wants a word in private,' Eddie had explained. 'We can call in at the Cross later, if you like.'

So at half past six in what was left of the daylight, the threesome embarked on a walk across the rough grass towards the far boundary of the Common, with a view of Little Brimstone and the moor beyond.

'Sorry to drag you out here, Stan, but this won't take long,' she assured him. 'It's just . . . I've taken the trouble to find out more about our father.'

'Who art in heaven,' Stan quipped uneasily. He used his tried-and-tested weapon of flippancy to hide the storm of conflicting emotions that Violet's recent revelation had awakened.

Eddie frowned and gave him a warning look.

'It's bad news but Eddie and I talked it through and we thought you ought to know,' Violet continued. 'He is your father as well as mine, when all's said and done.'

'Is or was?' Stan quibbled over the detail. He slowed his pace and gave a quick shake of his head, as if a fly was bothering him.

'*Is*,' Eddie confirmed. 'It turns out he wasn't killed by the Germans, Stan.'

'Come off it,' Stan muttered resentfully as he thrust his hands in his trouser pockets.

'We're serious. I went with Muriel to the library. She helped me look up the army records. They showed that Douglas Tankard went absent without leave.'

'When?' Stan demanded more details.

'In May 1915, just a couple of months after he joined up.'

Stan's frown deepened. 'Running away was what the bastard was best at,' he said savagely.

'We knew you wouldn't like it and I don't blame you,' Eddie said. 'But when you stop to think about it, absent without leave could mean a few things. Sometimes they were men who got captured by the enemy but then they would show up later as prisoners of war and that would be entered on the record. Others were wounded and were carted off to field hospitals, but likewise that would be written up afterwards.'

'That's how we can be sure that he ran off on purpose,' Violet added.

'So for all we know he skedaddled and could still be alive.' Stan gritted his teeth and kicked aimlessly at a rough piece of turf. He thought back to the years of hand-to-mouth struggle when he was a small, skinny schoolboy – the one at the back of the class with holes in his shoes, no coat and an empty belly, who ran errands after school for the halfpenny that would buy him two bread buns to take home – one each for him and his mother.

'He could,' Violet acknowledged. More than anything, she felt sorry now for upsetting Stan. 'Maybe I should've kept it to myself.'

Stan stared at the ground. 'Bastard,' he said again. Then, still shaking his head, he took his hands from his pockets and turned his back on the emptiness of the moor. 'Come on, you two – how about that drink? It's on me.'

The Green Cross was busy as usual. Chalky White stood behind the bar with sleeves rolled up, pulling pints as fast as he could. While Stan elbowed his way through the noisy crowd, Eddie and Violet found a corner table to sit at.

'I should have kept quiet,' Violet muttered. She'd spent the time during the walk down to Ghyll Road regretting her decision to involve her half-brother.

'You know Stan – he won't stay down in the dumps for long. And he deserved to know,' Eddie reassured her. 'Look at him now, chatting ten to the dozen with Alf Shipley and Kenneth Leach.'

Sure enough, Stan was deep in conversation and when he brought the drinks across to Violet and Eddie, he dragged the Barlows' driver and the local handyman with him.

'What now?' From the lively expression on his

pal's face, Eddie sensed a fresh turn of events.

Stan settled the glasses on the table then nudged Alf. 'Tell 'em.'

Even out of uniform, Alf Shipley retained his military air. Head tilted to emphasize the square set of his jaw and with shoulders back, he could have stepped straight off the parade ground. 'You're looking at a man fresh out of work,' he announced without any lead in, while Kenneth stood by shaking his head. 'That's right – Barlow gave me my marching orders.'

'Or, to be more accurate, it was Mrs Barlow who blew her top,' Kenneth added. 'I was there to change a washer on the kitchen tap so I saw what happened.'

'Blow me down.' Eddie made room for the two men to sit at the table. 'When was that?'

'Earlier today.' Alf seemed philosophical. 'She near as damn it tore the uniform off my back and sent me packing.'

'All over nothing.' Kenneth made a good witness to events. 'She'd had a barney with her friend Ella Kingsley. I was in the kitchen. They were next door in the breakfast room and I heard Mrs Barlow weeping and wailing like she does then screaming her head off. I don't know the ins and outs but it ended with Mrs Kingsley driving off and Mrs B storming into the kitchen, yelling for Alf to bring the car to the door.'

Alf took up the story. 'It was in the garage and by the time I'd brought the Daimler round to the front of the house she was beside herself, calling me all the names under the sun for slacking. I was sacked on the spot. Kenneth was caught in the cross fire and she sent him packing too.'

'So here we are.' A gloomy Kenneth drowned his sorrows in his pint glass.

Eddie and Stan commiserated while Violet pictured the scene at Bilton Grange and wondered what had caused the argument between Ella Kingsley and Alice Barlow, tuning in again when Alf offered his opinion.

'If you ask me, it's what happens when problems between a man and his wife run out of control. Everyone else takes the flak.'

At the mention of Colin Barlow, Violet was suddenly alert, but she held back from drawing attention to herself. Luckily, Eddie stepped in and asked questions for her.

'Why, what's Colin Barlow up to now?'

'Word is that he's taken up with another of the young lasses that works for him.' The hitherto inscrutable Alf made no bones about his ex-boss's philandering. 'Someone must have let the cat out of the bag. My guess is that the reason for Mrs Kingsley's visit earlier today was to put Mrs Barlow in the picture.'

Violet felt her stomach lurch but neither she nor Eddie passed comment. It was Stan who said what they all felt. 'You'd feel more sorry for Alice Barlow if she wasn't such a nasty piece of work.'

'It's hard to have any sympathy,' Alf agreed. 'I've been on the sharp end of her tongue once too often. *Do it this way. No, do it that way.* Job or no job, I'm glad to be free of the woman, believe you me.'

CHAPTER TWENTY-SEVEN

As was the way with the mill workers and labourers who lived, worked and loved in the rabbit warren of terraced streets nearby, the mourners at Donald Wheeler's funeral chose to remember the man in his prime. They overlooked the last few months of his life and were sincere in talking about him as a faithful husband and an honest, reliable neighbour.

'In the good old days you could always go to Donald for a favour,' Marjorie reminded Ben Hutchinson after the service. There were fifty people gathered in the room behind the chapel where, with Violet's agreement, Marjorie had laid on a spread at her own expense – sandwiches, scones and cake. 'He'd let you have anything from the loan of a cup of sugar to a free haircut if you'd had a bad week money-wise. Donald knew from experience what that was like.'

'He never touched a drop of alcohol, even at Christmas,' Ben recalled. 'He was a man who held to his principles, was Donald.'

Violet heard more along the same lines as she

mingled with familiar faces, always making sure that she knew whereabouts Eddie was in the room as a kind of anchor for her own movements. She would glance over at him and he would smile.

Teaspoons clinked against saucers, the urn hissed, the afternoon drifted on.

'I'm proud of you – you've got through today with flying colours,' Stan told her when he joined her. He and Eddie had volunteered to act as pall bearers and his dark suit and crisp white collar showed that he'd made an effort for the occasion.

'Thank you.' She was in a daze and scarcely took in what he said. From across the room, Eddie smiled again and nodded. He was close to the door, speaking to a lad in a grey jacket and old school cap that had seen better days. The lad was wearing bicycle clips around his trouser bottoms and was handing a small package to Eddie. Eddie beckoned Violet to join him.

'It's from the hospital,' he explained, giving the lad a sixpence and sending him on his way.

It was a brown paper parcel tied with coarse string. A white label was gummed to one corner: *Donald Wheeler – personal effects.*

Violet read the label and shuddered.

'Come next door where it's quiet,' Eddie suggested. He led the way back into the empty chapel and sat Violet down on the nearest bench.

She took a deep breath and looked up at the high ceiling then at the white walls and clear, leaded windows. Sunlight flowed in. It fell across rows of plain chairs, each with its red hymn book slotted into a compartment on the back of the seat, onto polished pine floorboards, bringing up the intricate, swirling grain of the wood.

Eddie placed the parcel on her knee. She untied the knotted string with shaking fingers then methodically folded back the paper.

Inside was an old-fashioned watch on a chain that Uncle Donald had hardly ever worn. There was an oblong metal box containing a razor and razor blades, a shaving brush and small, pointed scissors to trim moustaches. It lay on top of clothes that he'd been wearing on his admission to hospital – shabby jacket and trousers, black shoes that had taken on the shape of their wearer's feet, a grey knitted scarf and a cap whose peak was bent and shiny from fingering. A letter without an envelope slipped from Violet's lap and fluttered onto the floor.

Eddie stooped to pick up the flimsy paper.

'Read it out,' Violet whispered, steeling herself to hear what she knew must be her uncle's last message.

'"Dear Violet, a word before I go. The nurse wants me to rest but there'll be plenty of time for that where I'm headed." You're sure you want me to go on?' Eddie asked.

A word before I go. Typical Uncle Donald, to be at death's door and writing as if he's taking his cap from the hook and leaving for work. 'Yes, please,' she told Eddie.

'"To set the record straight – yes, Joe's marrying Florence Shaw was a mistake. I should have made more of that when you visited. It was done on the spur of the moment and both regretted it. Joe wasn't ready to settle down but he was dazzled by your mother's looks. He asked her and she said yes – don't ask me why. From what I gathered she had no one to advise her." The writing's in pencil – it's hard to make out.' Eddie explained the reason why he read so slowly.

'"Joe was in and out of work and what spare money he had went on having a good time. Florence was soon in the family way but it wasn't to be – the baby was early and stillborn. By that time, Joe had enlisted and left for the Front. She coped with that by herself."'

Imagine that. Getting married and knowing that you've made a mistake. Your husband seems not to care about you. You hope for a baby to heal the rift but the baby dies in the womb. You're alone in the world.

Eddie read on: '"There's more to tell you about Tankard, too. I'm writing it down, just in case. There was a reason that there was no telegram from the War Office and this is it. It's true that Tankard stepped into Joe's shoes as far as Florence was concerned. She got pregnant again but it turned out that he didn't take to the idea of being a father any better than Joe had, so he enlisted but didn't take to military life either. He lasted a few weeks then he deserted his regiment."'

'Yes. Go on,' Violet pleaded when Eddie paused to ask if she was all right.

'"I found this out straight after Winnie died. She wouldn't let me pry into things while she was alive, but the question ate away at me all those years – what had happened to Tankard? I got my answer by coming into Welby in the days after Winnie's funeral and making enquiries. I found out where his family was from, the house he'd been brought up in and if anyone was still alive who knew him. A man can desert the army and hope to vanish for good, but it's not that easy. So, Violet – I found an address."'

She took the letter from Eddie. The faint, scrawled words swam in front of her eyes. *Wesley House, Albert Road, Welby.* She handed it back. 'Read me the rest,' she pleaded.

'"The odd thing is, curiosity drove me to track Tankard down but when it came to it I didn't follow it through. Don't ask me why. I kept putting it off, telling myself maybe tomorrow or the day after. But now there are no more tomorrows for me, Violet, so I hand it over to you – for you to decide.

'"One more thing: if I haven't been fair to you in your life, I'm sorry. If I've hurt you, I hope you can forgive me. The truth is Winnie was the only one who mattered to me. Sharing her with you was sometimes more than I could manage. She is the one you have to thank for all the good things in your life. Goodbye now and God bless again. Love from Uncle Donald."'

*

Without a moment's hesitation Muriel and Ida agreed to Violet's request to take the next morning off work.

'I know you won't rest until you've followed this up,' Ida acknowledged when Violet showed her Donald's letter. 'We can manage without you for a few hours.'

'Why not wait until Eddie is free to go with you?' Muriel suggested. 'I'm worried about you going all the way over to Welby on your own.'

'He did offer but I've asked Stan to come with me instead,' Violet replied as steadily as she could. Though it was only eight o'clock and the Jubilee blinds were still down, she was ready in her smart red dress, green jacket and hat.

Ida was dubious. 'Was Eddie happy about you doing that?'

'Yes. He sees that this is more to do with Stan than him.'

'And what about Stan?' Muriel asked. 'I can't imagine him champing at the bit to track down a man who left him and his mother high and dry.'

'He wasn't keen at first but he says he'll do it for my sake.'

Violet was anxious to leave. With a hurried goodbye, she stepped out of the shop and turned left onto Brewery Road. From there she wove through the back streets onto Canal Road, hurrying to reach Stan's lodgings by half past, as arranged.

The main road was busy as always with trams, cars, bicycles and buses, and the roar and clatter from Kingsley's Mill in full swing made her press on even more quickly. Then came the Victory, its doors closed, with a caretaker mopping the steps, next to Barlow's, where the familiar maroon Daimler was parked at the kerb.

Violet's heart lurched at the unlucky coincidence. She made a snap decision to cross the road to escape notice but hadn't found a gap in the traffic before the passenger door opened and Alice Barlow stepped out and ran towards her.

'You again!' Mrs Barlow took hold of Violet by the wrist and pulled her away from the kerb. 'I might have known.'

Held in a tight grip, Violet tried to wrench herself free. 'Let go of me,' she pleaded.

'I *knew* he was up to something. He was in a hurry to leave the house without me and now I see why. But I wasn't having it.'

'Mrs Barlow, I've no idea what you're talking about.' Violet wrenched free and rubbed the skin on her wrist. Close up, she saw that Alice Barlow's eyes were red and puffy and that she was without make-up.

'Not so fast. I know your game.'

'Please – I'm not playing any games. I've arranged to meet someone.'

'Yes, and don't I know who!' There was wild triumph in Alice Barlow's expression. 'Caught red-

382

handed – you and my husband. Why else would you come trotting down here first thing in the morning? He's cowering in there now, hoping you'd have the gumption to make yourself scarce as soon as you spotted me. But I was too quick for you both!'

Shamed by the tawdriness of the situation, Violet let out a groan. 'Once and for all, Mrs Barlow, I've never gone near your husband of my own free will. He's been in the wrong from start to finish and if you must know, after that time at Ash Tree House he's lucky that I didn't go to the police.'

Violet's retaliation sent Alice Barlow into an even greater frenzy. 'You think you're special,' she screeched. 'You suppose you're so good-looking that no man can resist you; well, let me tell you – you're just the latest in a long line.'

'I am not in anyone's line,' Violet insisted, trying both to keep her dignity and to push her adversary out of the way but finding that she was trapped in the shop doorway.

'The latest and the last,' Alice Barlow vowed. 'I've told Colin it has to stop. No more cheap flings. Do you know his reply? He said that if I knew what was good for me I would keep quiet and count myself lucky. Lucky!'

'I'm sorry, this is nothing to do with me.' Summoning her strength, Violet succeeded in pushing free, just as the door behind her opened and Colin Barlow emerged.

His wife flew at him. She barged past Violet and

pummelled his chest, letting out infuriated grunts while he let the ineffectual punches rain down.

'You see what I have to put up with,' he said to Violet, eyebrows raised and with a smile hovering on his lips.

His hateful expression turned Violet's stomach. Instead of walking away as she should have done, she challenged him. 'You ought to be ashamed. Look what you're doing to her. Your lies are making her think things that aren't true.'

'Goodness gracious.' Undaunted, Barlow thrust Alice to one side and stepped down onto the pavement. 'Between the two of you, you're making quite a scene.'

Anger fired Violet up and she decided that she would continue to stand up to him, not let him win. 'You enjoy making women miserable but in the end it's you who will suffer. People watch you. They know what you get up to.'

'I couldn't care less,' he laughed, taking his wife by the wrists and shoving her across the pavement towards the car. He thrust her inside and slammed the door. 'She knows she'll end up back where I found her if she's not careful.'

The effort had made him red in the face. 'As for you, Violet – who really listens to what you say? You're a grocer's girl with ideas above your station. A queen for the day, maybe. But in truth no one takes any notice of you.'

'It's not true. You'll see!' Anger against him

choked her and she lost the ability to say more, but still she wouldn't back down.

'See what?' Turning the key in the lock, Barlow trapped Alice inside the car. 'Here I am, dining out with the Kingsleys as usual, driving my car and counting up my takings. There you are – a nobody with no one.'

'That's not true!' she declared. *I am someone in my own right. I have Eddie and Stan, Ida and Muriel to back me up.* 'I'd rather be me than you any day of the week.'

Alice Barlow hammered her fist against the car window, mouthing desperate words that couldn't be heard.

'And that's why you are where you are in life, and I am where I am.' Case proven. Barlow turned away from Violet to find his dark-haired assistant standing in the doorway, her expression wary. 'Take no notice, Glenda,' he instructed, deliberately and brazenly brushing against her as he strode past. 'Miaow – they were clawing each other's eyes out, the pair of them.'

The dispenser frowned at Violet and closed the door. Alice Barlow sobbed and subsided into the passenger seat. In silent anguish, Violet walked on.

CHAPTER TWENTY-EIGHT

Sitting on the train to Welby with Stan and with the blue velvet box in her handbag, Violet forced herself to concentrate on the task in hand. Swaying to the steady rhythm of steel wheels clicking over wooden sleepers, she looked out of the window at the weed-strewn banks, at fields opening up ahead of them, with three enormous, newly built cooling towers on the horizon billowing clouds of steam into the dismal sky.

'Here comes the rain and we didn't bring a brolly, worse luck,' Stan said as the first spots streaked the window panes. He was dressed for work at the baths in his old jacket and cap, having managed to swap shifts at the last minute with another lifeguard. That gave him three hours flat to hop on the train with Violet, find the address on Albert Road that Donald Wheeler had written down and make their next move in Violet's mission to find their father. Then back on the train in time to man the afternoon session at the baths.

Violet continued to stare out at the gloomy scene until a tunnel cut off her view. As the carriage filled with the acrid smell of smoke, she turned gratefully to Stan. 'I'm glad you're with me.'

'Anything for you, Violet.' Beneath the usual bravado, he was sincere. Yes, things had turned on their heads and it had taken a lot of getting used to, to all of a sudden regard Violet as his little sister. But Stan had risen to the occasion and drawn a line under past flirtations and flattery. 'You've been through a lot lately. This is the least I can do.' That in a nutshell was why he was here on the train to Welby with Violet, doing something that he'd rather not do.

'Thank you.' She smiled at him. 'All I want to do is find our father and hear his side of things. Then I'll be satisfied. That's all right, isn't it?'

'Easier said than done,' he warned. The rain came down hard now, running in rivulets across the glass and distorting the maze of grey terraced streets that came into view at the end of the tunnel. *The man's a coward. His whole life is a lie.* Stan kept these thoughts to himself as the train ran clickety-click along the rails.

'I wonder how he'll behave.' Violet imagined the moment when the three of them came face to face and she showed Douglas Tankard the gold bracelet. It would be a shock at first, but after that there would be facts to be filled in, new pieces of the jigsaw to slot into place. Then, who knew what would happen? Her heart raced at future possibilities.

'Here we are,' Stan said as the train slowed down under a vast canopy of glass and ironwork. The brakes squealed and steam hissed and obscured the platform as they jerked to a halt.

They stood up and filed out of the carriage.

'Lead on, Macduff,' Violet said as bravely as she could, though the huge station and busy platforms unnerved her so much that she didn't take much in as they emerged onto a wide square with a soot-stained statue of Queen Victoria on a high plinth in the middle and with roads heading off in all directions.

Stan hurried her across the square onto Wellington Street, across wide Gladstone Street onto the road they were seeking, which was narrower and less busy than the main thoroughfare behind them. 'Mind the puddles,' he warned as they crossed the road.

And mind the trams and buses, the delivery boys on bicycles and the Model T Fords and Morris Oxfords. Concentrating on not getting run over helped Violet to overcome her nerves at the prospect of what they would find on Albert Road. It began with three-storey detached buildings, housing solicitors and city offices for the county's wool merchants, manufacturers of steel and importers of sugar and tea. As it dipped steeply towards the canal, the buildings grew less grand – an ironmonger's and a greengrocer's, a pawnbroker's displaying gold jewellery in its small window. Across the street from this row was an old chapel, squashed between a corn merchant's and a low, plain-fronted building with its name carved in stone above the door.

'Brace yourself – this is it,' Stan told Violet, pointing it out.

She studied the worn stonework and unadorned frontage of Wesley House. It had two storeys, a wide door with plain pillars supporting a triangular pediment and four tall windows to either side. From this distance there seemed to be no movement inside the building.

'What is it – a kind of hostel?' she asked, hanging back with a disconcerted frown.

'That's what it looks like,' Stan confirmed. 'It's run by Methodists, to judge by the name of Wesley over the door.'

'This isn't what I expected.'

'Nor me. A disease-ridden, rat-infested cellar – that would've been more like it.' And more what Tankard deserved, his tone suggested.

'We were wrong,' she pointed out. 'Well, at least this is better than we thought.' She glanced at a disgruntled Stan. 'What's wrong, are you having second thoughts?'

'No, I said I'd come with you, didn't I? Let's go.'

Soaked through from the rain and wondering what Uncle Donald would have made of Douglas Tankard being reliant on the charity of Methodists of all people, Violet gathered her courage and crossed the street. She pulled at the old-fashioned bell to the right of the blue door and waited. After a long time the handle turned and the door was opened by a small, thin man with exceptionally bushy eyebrows and a flattened, crooked nose.

'Yes?' he enquired in a light voice that was neither hostile nor friendly. He cast an impartial eye over Violet and Stan while he waited for them to state their business.

'We're looking for Douglas Tankard,' Violet explained, her heart skipping erratically inside her chest. Behind them the rain fell steadily, streaming along gutters and gurgling down a nearby drain.

'There's no one of that name here,' the door-keeper replied.

Stan said nothing but was evidently ready to turn away. He wasn't surprised – a man with Tankard's past wouldn't stick to his real name anyway.

'But we've been given this address,' Violet protested. 'Wesley House on Albert Road. I'm sure this is the right place.'

Picking up the urgency in her voice, the man cocked his head to one side. 'We look after twelve men here and I know the names of each and every one. None of them is called Tankard.'

'You say you look after them?' Stan was quick on the uptake as usual. 'Why can't they fend for themselves?'

'Either they're too old to manage,' the man replied in the same impartial tone, 'or else they've been injured.'

390

'Injured – how?' Stan interrupted.

'At work or in the army. That throws them on the mercy of charities like us. We take them in and provide food and shelter.'

'Do you have anyone called Douglas staying here?' Violet asked. Frustrated by the apparent dead end, she strained to see inside the hostel but could make out only a shadowy entrance area with a low bench set against the far wall. 'We don't know much about him – what he looks like or what would bring him here – only that he was born in Welby then moved out to Hadley where he went from job to job before he got married then went to fight in France in 1915. We heard recently that he'd moved back here.'

'I'm sorry – Tankard is not a name I recognize.' Still showing little sign of curiosity, the man, who was wiry and agile-looking, prepared to close the door.

'I'm his daughter, Violet Wheeler. Stan is his son,' Violet blurted out.

Stan cleared his throat and took a step backwards. Trust Violet to get straight to the point.

The man blinked and cocked his head sharply to the other side, as if dodging an uppercut. 'I'm Jack Towers, the superintendent here. We do have a resident called Douglas – a man in his fifties who has been living with us since 1926,' he admitted. 'There are things in common with the person you describe. We know him as Douglas Thornton, though, not

Tankard. Please wait.' Leaving the door ajar, he disappeared from view.

'It's him – I'm certain it is,' Violet whispered to Stan, her eyes alive with hope.

'Steady on,' came the reply. 'We don't know anything yet.'

'It *is* him.' A man who had chosen to live incognito, injured either at work or in the army, living here for the past eight years. She prepared herself for the moment she'd envisaged in her dreams. An exchange of information followed by an embrace. A doorway into a happier future.

Five minutes later the superintendent returned. 'Follow me,' he directed. He led them across the dark hallway and down a wide corridor at the back of the house into a small room with a scrubbed table and painted pine chairs. There were framed religious tracts on the cream walls and one small window overlooking a yard.

'Sit down.' Towers pulled two of the chairs from under the table. 'I've told Douglas you're here.'

'Did you explain who we were? What did he say?' Violet demanded of the superintendent. Her skipping heartbeat had turned to a heavy thumping as she put down her handbag and gripped the edge of the table.

'I did tell him. He didn't say anything but I could see it was a shock.'

'You can say that again,' Stan muttered, hanging back in a corner of the room and looking ill at ease.

'I'm not thrilled to be here myself.'

Violet and Stan heard slow footsteps coming down the corridor towards them. Stan prepared himself by fixing his gaze on the flat stone roofs of the out-houses across the yard, watching two grey pigeons squat there in the rain. Violet stared straight at the door.

The footsteps stopped outside. The superintendent darted nimbly to open the door then stood to one side. 'Here they are, Douglas – your visitors,' he announced before sliding out of the room.

A tall man shuffled forward. His hair was thick and white. A shapeless grey jacket hung loosely over his stooped frame and deep lines on his spare face gave him a permanently miserable look. A pair of steel-rimmed glasses with black lenses obscured his eyes.

Violet's heart lurched and she sprang to her feet. 'This way,' she murmured, taking hold of his arm and leading him to the nearest chair.

Douglas Tankard ran his fingers along the edge of the table then bent to feel the seat of the chair. He sat cautiously with a quick movement of his head towards Violet. 'Who's here?' he asked.

'Violet and Stan – your daughter and your son. We think.'

There was a pause but no attempt at denial. 'Flo named you after her favourite flower, did she?'

'I didn't know that. She died when I was born.' Violet fell silent, pressing her lips together to bring herself back under control.

There was a long sigh followed by silence. Then, 'Yes – violets were her favourites. Never mind that; how did you two track me down?'

'Uncle Donald wrote the address in a letter before he passed away.'

'Dead then.' The blind man's voice didn't express regret. It was low and rich – perhaps the last vestige of the attractive man he must once have been. 'Stan, where are you?'

'Here in the corner.' Stan emerged from his first shock and saw in the wreckage of his father's face and frame himself as an older man – they shared the same long limbs and prominent Adam's apple, the same beak-like nose. He resisted a strong urge to run from the room and slam the door behind him.

'Are you expecting me to say sorry?' Tankard addressed Stan in a sharper tone. 'Would it make any difference if I did?'

'Not to me. I'm here to look after Violet, that's all,' Stan assured him, feeling muscles at the corners of his jaw twitch and jump.

Tankard tapped the table with his fingertips. There was a tremor in his hand that he couldn't control. 'What about you, Violet? Why are you here?'

'I found the bracelet and the note,' she began before her feelings overwhelmed her – astonishment at what she saw and heard, followed by sadness wrenching at her heart and stinging disappointment that her father was not the man she'd hoped he would be. Words were not enough – she had to give the blind, broken man sitting at the hostel table time to work out for himself what had brought her here.

'You want answers,' Tankard guessed. 'For a start, why I took up with Florence in the first place and why I ditched her.'

'Yes.' Struggling against the tide of feelings that washed over her, Violet fixed on the one question that mattered. 'I want to know – did you love her?'

In the corner of the room, Stan banged his fist against the wall. Then he strode towards the door. 'I'm not staying to hear this,' he vowed.

Violet jumped up but was too late to stop him leaving. 'Stan, I'm sorry,' she called after him.

'I'll wait outside,' he muttered over his shoulder.

'Leave him. He's sticking up for his mother and I don't blame him.' Tankard sighed. 'For what it's worth, you can tell him afterwards that I loved them both – Gladys and Florence. Is that what *you* want to hear?'

'Only if it's true.' She sat back down to face the blind man and hear him out.

Tankard leaned his elbows on the table and let his head hang low. 'As far as I could, I loved them. But the lad is right to be angry – I was young and callow back then and the type of love I could offer wasn't enough.'

'As far as you could, you loved them,' Violet echoed. She let his answer settle like autumn leaves drifting from trees.

'Anyway, I paid a high price,' Tankard said bitterly.

'Yes – what happened to your eyesight?' Violet asked once she'd gained mastery over her voice.

'Gas – that's what happened.' Tankard kept on tapping the table with an uncertain, drum-like beat. 'Gravenstafel, the twenty-second of April, 1915. You understand me?'

Violet dug deep into her memory of the accounts she'd read of war on the Western Front. 'That's when the Germans used gas against the allies.'

'That's right – at Wipers. The French were on the front line. We stood back and watched the green mist creep towards them. It killed thousands. They hadn't got a clue what was happening so they breathed it in, started foaming at the mouth and choking to death. We saw them retreat, falling like flies. Then the wind changed direction and the gas came straight at us. I saw fellow Tommies a few yards ahead of me struck blind in a flash. As soon as I felt the sting of it, I ran.'

Tankard relived the battle with his head still bowed. 'I couldn't see a bloody thing. I was down in the mud, crawling on my hands and knees, trying to stay ahead of the worst of it, right into a barrage of ack-ack guns from my own side. In the end, I found a crater made by a shell, dropped into it and stopped where I was until it died down. My eyes and lungs felt on fire. All I could hear was men screaming and bodies thudding down on top of me.'

Violet closed her eyes at the horror of what he described. 'And when it was all over?' she queried.

'Silence – I remember that. And darkness. I won't tell you what I had to do to claw my way out of there. Up on the surface, there was still no sound, no sign of anyone. Then I made out a light in the distance and staggered towards it. The light came from a farmhouse half a mile behind the Front. I found a barn with hay in it. I crept in there and curled up like an animal.'

'Still blinded by the gas?'

Tankard nodded. 'In the morning I crawled outside to find a water butt to cool the raging fire in my eyes. The farmer's wife found me and bandaged me up. She kept me in that barn and never said a word about me going back to my regiment, even when the blisters started to heal. She'd lost her own son to the Germans in the first battle of Ypres and found me in the second so she nursed me and gave me the clothes and food I needed to get out of it for good.'

'Which you managed to do for the rest of the war?' The army record was proof of this and now Violet swung from any blame she might have felt to pure pity. 'And your poor eyes – how much of your sight did you get back?'

'The damage was done. For a few years I could see enough to get by – shapes and colours, that kind of thing. Then gradually it went completely. Right from the start I knew I wasn't much good to anyone – not to Gladys or Florence, or to you and Stan, especially since it was me who'd buggered off in the first place. No, the best thing was for me to get back to the area I knew best, change my name and lie low here in Welby. Besides, the army was after me, remember. Gas or not, I ran the risk of being lined up in front of a firing squad for hiding in that barn.'

'And all this time I've been living less than half an hour's train ride away with Aunty Winnie and Uncle Donald, without any of us knowing the first thing about you.' Even though the reasons had begun to take shape, Violet still felt the abandonment keenly. In her mind's eye she was five years old again, smarting from Donald's harsh criticisms and wondering what in the world she could do to please him. 'Aunty Winnie was a mother to me – the best in the world – but I can't say the same for Uncle Donald. The truth is, I needed a father in my life and you weren't there.'

'You wouldn't have wanted me – not like this,' Tankard insisted as he left off drumming and rested his hand on the table. The tremor continued. 'I'm not asking for pity because I don't deserve it. It was me – I cut myself off because I didn't want anyone to see how low I'd fallen. That's pride for you. And if you want to know whether I've thought about you and Stan over the years, the honest answer is no, I haven't.'

Across the table from him, Violet felt the cherished dream of being loved by her father shrivel and die. She thought again of the note Tankard had written to her mother and the words, *lifelong affection*. Not undying love that came from deep in the heart –

only shallow affection that could be cauterized and cut out, despite Florence's forlorn longing for a man who would stand by her. Violet took the blue box from her handbag and slid it across the table. 'This is for you,' she murmured.

Tankard reached out and felt the velvet surface with trembling fingers. He seemed to recognize what it was but left it unopened. 'I haven't dwelt on the thought of you two growing up without me because there wouldn't be any point. I was never going to change my mind and come looking for you.'

'Why not? You must have known where to find us.'

'I could have done it,' he acknowledged. 'But I was Douglas Thornton by this time, remember. For one thing, your uncle would have had it in for me because of what I'd done to Joe. And if I'd come to claim you, I'd have had the army on my back thanks to him.'

It all made sense to Violet, who now had to swallow the bitter pill. Not enough love and a big helping of fear was the lethal combination that had kept her father away. 'The note you wrote to my mother is still in the box with the bracelet,' she told him, snapping her handbag shut.

He pressed the catch of the blue box then lifted the chain from its satin nest. The tiny padlock gleamed pinkish-gold as he looped it over his gnarled, trembling fingers. 'I got this from a pal of mine who worked in a pawnbroker's. He sold me it at a knock-down price and I had the engraving done especially for Flo – "Xmas 1914". She was pleased as Punch.'

Violet had heard enough. She stood up jerkily. 'Thank you,' she said in a voice that didn't seem to belong to her.

'For what?'

'For agreeing to see me after all these years.' *And for unlocking the padlock of the past, releasing me from false hope and setting my heart free.*

'You know where to find me.' Tankard raised his head and turned his face in Violet's direction – perhaps a sign of hope that she would visit again.

'I do.' Her voice more disembodied than ever, she made her way to the door without making any promises. 'And I do understand.'

She'd opened the door and was out in the corridor when her father issued a last request. 'Will you make sure the lad does too?'

'I will,' she agreed. She left without saying goodbye, only turning to glance over her shoulder at the blind man hunched at a table, carefully taking the note from the envelope, unfolding the heavily creased paper and with tremulous fingers tracing his long-ago, faint-hearted words to a woman he'd failed to love.

CHAPTER TWENTY-NINE

'Where was Stan while all this was going on?' In the workroom above the shop, Muriel sounded irritated. 'The idea was for him to go with you this morning to keep an eye on you, wasn't it?'

Violet pulled out some tacking stitches in a white blouse she was making for Kenneth Leach's wife, Avril. The order had come in while she was in Welby and she'd started work on it as soon as she got back. 'One look at Douglas Tankard was enough for him.'

'Was it that bad?' Muriel peered at Violet over the rim of her glasses, scissors poised.

'Yes, Stan wasn't in a mood to forgive. And I didn't help by asking if our father had ever loved my mother. I put my foot in it good and proper. Poor Stan didn't know where to put himself. That's why he stormed off.'

'But you're glad you stayed to hear the man out?'

'I wouldn't say glad was the right word.' The tacking thread slipped easily through the silky rayon material. Violet held up the half-finished garment and decided that it was time to start on the collar.

'Sad then?'

'No, not sad either.' On the train journey home, Violet had pulled herself together and done her best to explain to Stan what had led Tankard to desert them but Stan was having none of it.

'He was saving his own skin, that's the truth of it. I don't care if he was going blind – he should've been a man and owned up to what he'd done.'

'Then he'd have had the army to deal with,' Violet had reasoned.

Stan had shaken his head and stared truculently out of the window, refusing to say another word about his father – not just now but for ever. He'd done his best to back Violet and look after her, but for him the subject was now closed.

'Relieved?' Muriel steered a lightweight worsted fabric under the pounding needle of her sewing machine as she made a tailored jacket for Ella Kingsley.

'Yes, I suppose that's it.' Violet relived the moment when she'd handed over the bracelet and loosened the chains of the past. 'Honestly, though, it would break your heart to see Douglas Tankard and to hear what he had to say.'

'Your trouble is you're too soft,' Ida muttered.

'Really it would. As it was, he wouldn't let me pity him. But I can't help it when I think about what he had to go through – the mud and the guns and the gas. It was enough to make me cry, just listening.'

'Aren't you forgetting that he ran away from his comrades?'

'Crawled away,' Violet insisted. 'If you ask me, he only did what a lot of other men would have done given half a chance.'

The ring of the shop bell down below told them that they had a customer. 'I'll go,' Muriel said swiftly.

She left Violet sewing interfacing to the collar piece, reflecting on where the day's events had left her. Not glad, not sad. Relieved because she knew she was undergoing a sea change and what it boiled down to was this: it wasn't her, Violet Wheeler, who wasn't fit to be loved, but her father, Douglas Tankard, who couldn't love.

'It was the sight of him sitting there holding the bracelet that hurt the most,' Violet confided in Eddie when he came to the shop that evening to take her to the rehearsal in Hadley.

All day Eddie had been worried about her, hoping that Stan had been the right choice to go to Welby with her. Eddie had finished his decorating work early and arrived at Jubilee at half past five on the dot to find Violet pulling down the blind and putting up the Closed sign. 'You did the right thing by handing over the bracelet to him.'

'It belongs with him. But his hands were shaking and of course he's blind so he couldn't see to read the note he'd written to my mother.'

403

'I know how to take your mind off things. Come on, Vi – let's go for a spin.' Eddie's sudden suggestion was aimed at pulling her out of the past into the present. 'We've got time to stop at Little Brimstone if we set off now.'

'But it's raining.'

'No, it's nearly stopped. What are we waiting for?'

So they locked the door and climbed on the bike just as the clouds lifted and by the time they reached the moor road, the wind had swept them away completely.

'Do we have to stop?' Violet asked, her arms clasped around Eddie's waist as he pulled into the usual siding. 'Couldn't we just ride on like this for ever?'

He laughed and parked the bike. 'If we follow our noses in that direction we'd be in Morecambe and the Atlantic would stop us. The other way it's Scarborough and the North Sea.'

'We could get on a ferry and keep going all the way to America,' she said wistfully. 'You and me without a care in the world.'

Eddie kept hold of her hand as he led the way down the narrow path bordered by sodden bracken. 'And live on what – fresh air?'

'They need dressmakers in America, don't they? We could ride to sunny Hollywood and you could show the latest flicks in the picture palaces where they're made. I could sew costumes for Claudette Colbert.'

'And pigs might fly.' They arrived at the clearing to find Kitty's café closed and boarded up in readiness for winter. Eddie chose a bench to sit on and together they gazed out over the eruption of black boulders scattered across the steep hillside. In the background they heard the sound of their very own tumbling stream. 'I don't think we'd fit in,' he said with a smile.

'Where?'

'In Hollywood. We're Yorkshire born and bred. It's where we belong.' Rooted in the black earth of the open moors, treading the paved streets of the town shoulder to shoulder with mill girls and mechanics, shop workers, lamp lighters and delivery men.

'I know that.' Violet smiled back at him. 'I don't really care where we go.'

'As long as we're together?'

She nodded. Her heart swelled with love for Eddie – for his laughing brown eyes and the way his black hair refused to stay slicked back no matter how much Brylcreem he combed through it. She loved him for the way he sat, legs splayed and stretched out in front of him, his head tilted back and resting against the green wooden boards of the window shutters, looking at her through half-closed eyes. 'Yes, that's what I want.'

He sat up straight and drew his feet back under the bench. 'That's all right then. Listen – I want to say something but as usual it might not come out right.'

'Try,' she murmured, slipping an arm around his waist and nestling close.

'First off, I realize you're down in the dumps about Tankard. I know he wasn't what you hoped he might be.'

'No, I wasn't too surprised, just sad. And it was upsetting to find out that he can't see, and that makes me sorry for him.'

'But you're glum because you wanted to love him and now you can't – that's the heart of the matter.'

'Don't say that.' Even as Violet protested she knew he was right. Meeting her father had drawn attention to a lifelong space in her heart that he would never be able to fill.

'So if you want someone to love, why not try me?' Eddie held his breath, waiting for her reply.

'You already know I do. I told you,' Violet said softly, reaching up to touch his cold cheek.

'I mean I want to take it one step further,' he murmured, turning his head to kiss her palm. 'We love each other. We don't need anyone else.'

'That's right – we don't.'

'So we can get married.'

'Oh, Eddie!' Violet pulled free, stood up and walked across the clearing.

Eddie followed her, afraid that he'd picked the wrong time and so upset her. 'Not straight away. Not if you're not ready.'

'Stop. I wasn't . . . I don't . . .'

'I didn't say it right, I'm sorry.'

The doubt in his eyes made her take his hands between hers. 'What about Jubilee?' Could she marry Eddie and still sit at her sewing machine with Ida and Muriel? 'Getting married doesn't mean I have to stop work, does it? Only, that's the way Ida sees it – she says she can't marry Harold and expect to carry on working.'

Eddie gave a small shrug. 'Ida sees things in black and white, remember. Who's to say you can't do both?'

'That's right, I can!' Violet saw it in a flash – a white wedding in a dress made in the Jubilee workshop, a rented house on Brewery Road or Chapel Street that Eddie would decorate, with two bedrooms – one for her and Eddie, one for the baby that would arrive in due course. She ran ahead of herself so far and with such a dazzling smile that Eddie couldn't help wrapping his arms around her and drawing her close.

'Where there's a will there's a way,' he said, his lips touching her forehead.

She tilted her head back. They were so close that his features blurred. She closed her eyes and kissed his mouth.

After a while he drew back, still with his arms around her waist. 'I know you don't have any family left now, Vi,' he said gently, 'but I won't run away and leave you on your own – not ever.'

407

CHAPTER THIRTY

Despite the thrill of Eddie's proposal, Violet had agreed to keep it quiet for the time being. At rehearsal Stan had been back on form, accusing Violet of looking like the cat that got the cream. As Violet had fumbled for an explanation, Ida had come, blue pencil tucked behind her ear, and dragged him up onstage.

'Best not announce our engagement until I've had a chance to tell Mam and Dad,' Eddie had said.

'So we're engaged now, are we?' Violet had laughed.

'Aren't we?'

'Not until I've got a ring on my finger, we're not!' she'd declared, pulling him to his feet. 'Come on. Ida will be champing at the bit to start the rehearsal. We'd better get a move on.'

Then, next morning, after a night spent dreaming of wedding veils and bouquets, of 'Do you take this man?' and 'I do', Violet was charged by Ida with keeping secrets from her and Muriel.

'I don't know what you've got to smile about.

Didn't Douglas Tankard turn out to be a dead loss?'

'You could say that.' Violet didn't attempt to describe the mixed feelings she'd experienced in Welby. Instead, she went on unrolling and measuring out a yard of pale blue ribbon intended to adorn a baby boy's christening gown.

'Then why are you so blooming happy?'

'Leave her alone,' Muriel advised as she came into the shop and placed her wet umbrella in the stand by the door. 'She'll tell us when she's good and ready. Violet, will you be all right down here by yourself this morning? Ida and I need to get on with that rush job for Ella Kingsley.'

'We'll be upstairs if you need us,' Ida promised. 'By the way, I was chatting with Evie on my way here and she let slip that Sybil intends to put a card in the window advertising for more help in their workshop. That'll put her one step ahead of us if we're not careful.'

'We can't sew any faster than we already are,' Muriel pointed out. 'Anyway, even if Sybil does shell out for another dressmaker that still doesn't put her one step ahead. She'll have a total of three and we've already got three. That makes us even.'

As ever, the spirit of competition put wind in Muriel and Ida's sails and they bustled upstairs to begin work, leaving Violet to tidy the window display and await their first customer of the day.

It's time we put Gertie into something more suited to winter than a wedding dress, she reminded herself as she squeezed past the mannequin then crouched to rearrange the folds in the flowing train. *This will soon be me*, she thought with a smile to herself – *all dressed up in white and walking down the aisle with Eddie.*

In her happy daydream she was caught unawares by the jangle of the shop bell and couldn't conceal her panic at the sound of an agitated Alice Barlow announcing her arrival.

'Shop!' Mrs Barlow rapped her knuckles on the counter and when Violet stepped down from the window, she launched into a complaint about poor service. 'Never leave your counter unattended,' she told Violet. 'It's the first rule of shopkeeping.'

'Good morning. What can I do for you?' One look at her customer warned Violet that Alice Barlow was a loose cannon about to fire off yet another volley of accusations. She prepared herself for the attack.

'The second rule is to smile at your customer and show good manners at all times.' The challenge was issued in a high, strained voice and a closer study of her mottled skin and swollen eyes showed a woman on the verge of hysteria. With no umbrella to protect her from the rain, water dripped from her hair and soaked through the front of her light brown coat, making her shiver.

'Mrs Barlow, if you've come to buy something, I'll do my best to help.' Violet tried to overcome her uneasiness and to stand firm.

The patches on Alice Barlow's neck grew redder,

the shivering more pronounced. 'Can I help you or not?' Violet repeated.

Outstared by Violet, Alice Barlow let out a long breath, like a balloon deflating. She glanced nervously towards the door and the street beyond. 'Don't worry – you can relax. It's not your blood I'm after.' When she spoke, her voice had lost the narrow, nasal quality that Violet disliked. It was broader, more hesitant.

'No?'

'Not any more.' Pushing her wet hair from her forehead, she rushed to the door and looked down the street. 'If it's anyone's, it's that sly little minx who works for us on Canal Road.'

'Minx?' Violet echoed. It wasn't a word she was used to hearing except on the silver screen when well-dressed women in evening gowns argued and exchanged insults.

'Glenda Morris. Colin is rubbing my nose in the dirt by cavorting right under my nose.'

'Ah, yes.' Glenda, the unfriendly, dark-haired dispenser. Violet felt a stab of pity for the unhappy woman before her.

'No, don't say anything.' Alice Barlow closed the door and came back into the shop with a strained expression, her eyes flitting from the displays in the shop back to the rain-splashed pavement.

'Please, Mrs Barlow . . .' Thrown off balance, Violet struggled for a response.

'He likes to see me suffer, he takes pleasure in it.

A snide remark here, a public snub there – that's nothing to Colin.'

'Please don't talk like this.'

Alice Barlow put her hand to her mouth but it was an ineffectual gesture. She was incapable of holding back the confession that rose from deep within and in her despair had run straight to Violet. 'You've seen him. You know what he's like. Behind closed doors it's ten times worse. I've put up with his bullying and pushing me around for years – what else could I do? But now . . . now we've reached the point where Colin says he's sick of me and ready to throw me aside like – like a worn-out shoe.'

'Come through to the kitchen and sit down,' Violet offered. She thought tears would have been better than this wild-eyed, wailing torrent of words.

'No – I don't want your pity.' Alice Barlow resisted Violet's proffered hand. 'You heard him the other day – he says he'll chuck me in the gutter. Then what will I do?'

'Would that really be so bad?' Violet said earnestly, her true feelings about Barlow coming through. 'To stand up to him and be rid of him?'

'You don't understand. Where will I go? What will I do?'

Violet had no time to find an answer before the door was flung open and Colin Barlow himself strode in. 'Oh, very nice!' he mocked. 'I might have known – not only does my wife create another scene

412

in front of my dispenser but she high tails it over here to wash her dirty linen in public. I won't have it, Alice, do you hear me?'

Violet felt her loathing for every inch of the man – his sneering mouth beneath the trim moustache, his groomed hair, his swagger – boil up inside her. As he advanced towards his wife with a raised hand, she thrust herself between them. 'Stop that or I'll call the police,' she warned.

He laughed again as he shoved her aside. 'Showing your true colours now, eh, Violet?' Making a grab for Alice, he caught only the lapel of her coat, allowing her to twist free, duck under his arm and run towards the door. 'Damn and blast, girl, get out of my way!'

The bell jangled and Alice had escaped onto the wet pavement. She fled towards Thornley's, turned the corner and was soon out of sight.

'I said – get out of my way!' Barlow seized Violet by the shoulders and shoved her aside. She crashed against the counter and onto the floor, bringing display racks crashing down. Then he was gone from the shop, chasing after his wife, leaving Violet breathless and calling for help.

'What is it? What's happened?' Ida had flown downstairs at the sound of the fracas below. Muriel was close behind. They helped Violet to her feet.

'Lord knows what Barlow will do to her if he catches her – call the police!' Violet gasped. Without stopping to explain or to dust herself down, she too ran onto the street and set off after the warring couple.

She reached the entrance to Thornley's in time to see the back view of Colin Barlow disappear down a set of narrow steps leading to Canal Road. Violet followed and came out onto the thoroughfare opposite the Victory. Picking out Alice Barlow's brown raincoat amongst the hubbub of delivery boys, shoppers, taxi men and street cleaners, she realized that a desperate Alice was intent on reaching the empty Daimler parked outside the chemist's before her husband caught up with her. Violet paused. Surely someone would see what was happening and step in? But no – a butcher's boy moved aside for Colin Barlow to continue his pursuit and a woman at the bus stop merely shook her head at the sight of a drenched Alice wrenching at the handle of the car door.

This wasn't fair – she knew now that Barlow was a brute who wouldn't hesitate to use his fists against his wife. Sure enough, it only took a few seconds for him to reach the car and lay his hands on her, clamping a hand over her mouth as she began to scream.

'Steady on.' A car mechanic carrying a spare tyre was the first to intervene. He put down the tyre and tapped Barlow on the shoulder. Barlow used his elbow to shove the man off but stumbled backwards over the tyre.

The interruption gave Alice the chance to break

free. She hadn't been able to take refuge inside the locked car so now she darted down the alleyway beside Brinkley Baths. Barlow yelled at the mechanic then pushed him aside. Again he ran after his wife. Violet's heart was in her mouth as she reached the alley and followed them onto the deserted towpath.

A more miserable scene was hard to imagine. The narrow, overgrown path was littered with rusty tin cans and old newspapers. The canal water was slate grey and pocked by raindrops. A hundred yards to the right there was a lock gate and the sound of trickling water, to the left a dark tunnel under the main road. Violet searched frantically but at first saw no sign of the Barlows. They couldn't have gone towards the lock because they'd still be in view, she reasoned, so she chose the direction of the tunnel. As she ran she slipped on the slimy flagged surface, dislodging a can and sending it over the edge of the path into the murky, weed-choked water. She steadied herself against a wall that towered over her, glanced up at the traffic trundling across the road bridge and ran on into the tunnel.

Violet heard water dripping from the roof then muffled voices but it took a while for her eyes to get used to the gloom.

'I'm sick to death of you.'

'Colin, let go of me!'

'You hear me!'

'Let go!'

Violet made out two figures. Alice crouched against the wall of the tunnel. Barlow stood over her. A slap followed each word. 'Sick – to – death!' Then he pulled her upright.

'Stop that!' Violet edged forward. She lost her footing a second time.

Barlow held Alice by the wrist and swung her away from the wall. They stood on a ledge just wide enough for one person and the momentum brought Alice to the very edge. He held her teetering there. Her free arm flailed as she tried to keep her balance. Violet was ten yards away. Barlow used both hands to pull his wife back towards him so that their faces were an inch apart. There was no sound, only the dripping water and Violet's muffled footsteps. Then, without a word, Barlow thrust Alice backwards into the canal.

There was a loud splash, and Alice Barlow sank beneath the black surface. Seconds passed. Then, with a swift brushing together of his palms, Barlow passed by Violet, who pressed herself against the curved wall of the tunnel just out of his sight.

He was gone, striding back the way he'd come and Alice had floated to the surface, her face a pale blob, her mouth open and gasping for breath. She reached up towards Violet who had gone down onto her knees, but Alice failed to catch hold of Violet's outstretched arms then sank a second time.

Seeing that the gap between the towpath and the water was anyway too great for her to haul the drowning woman to safety, Violet knew there was only one way to save her.

Without thinking, she held her breath and plunged headfirst into the filthy canal, breaking its cold surface and groping her way underwater. It was impossible to see anything. Her fingertips touched the soft sludge at the bottom. She kicked and turned sideways, still reaching out. There was something square and solid – a metal frame, perhaps – then more slime and sludge. She must go up for breath. She'd turned her face upwards, ready to rise, when a soft weight drifted against her. Violet tried to catch hold of it. There was an arm, a hand clutching at her. She kicked her legs and swam deep enough to wrap her arms around a woman's body, raise it up and break the surface. She dragged air into her lungs, struggling to keep Alice afloat.

'Hold on tight, Vi – we're here!' a voice called.

Hands reached down.

'Lift her up towards us – that's right, higher!'

Alice was lifted clear of the water and it was only then that Violet recognized whose voice it was. 'Eddie – Barlow pushed her in!' she cried. 'He tried to drown his wife.'

'Explain later.' Eddie's grim face appeared at the edge of the towpath. He lay full length, reaching down for Violet. 'Come on, Vi – grab my hand. Hold tight.'

Eddie was strong enough to raise Violet onto the towpath. While Stan carried Alice from the tunnel,

Eddie gave Violet his jacket. The grey October light revealed two policemen running towards them, whistles blowing. On the bridge above their heads and on the steps from Canal Road, onlookers had gathered.

Eddie supported Violet towards the steps. 'Are you all right? Can you walk or shall I carry you?'

'Walk,' she insisted. With Eddie – one step in front of another to safety.

CHAPTER THIRTY-ONE

There was a flurry of activity on Canal Road. An ambulance stood by to take Alice Barlow to hospital. A policeman dressed in civvies arrived and spoke to his officers. He pointed to Barlow's shop then the two uniformed men hurried inside.

'Do you want me to take you to the King Edward's for them to check you over?' Eddie asked Violet.

She shook her head. 'I just want to go home,' she whispered.

But the senior policeman approached them and pinned them to the spot. 'I'm Detective Inspector Butterworth. We had an emergency call from Jubilee Dressmakers – a lady by the name of Muriel Beanland.'

'Yes. I work there. I asked them to ring you.' Wet and shivering, Violet clutched Eddie's jacket across her chest. 'He pushed her in the water. He must have known she couldn't swim.'

'You mean Mr Barlow?' The inspector ignored the hubbub that arose when the two policemen escorted

Colin Barlow out of his shop and concentrated on the facts.

'I saw him,' Violet insisted. 'He was beating her and then pushed her in. And just walked away.'

Barlow wrenched free of the escorting officers. 'That's a lie. Alice slipped and fell. Neither of us knows how to swim. I ran to fetch help.' He was still arguing, fending off the two officers with his elbows until one of them took firm hold of him again. 'This girl has a grudge against me.'

Violet noticed Glenda Morris standing stony faced in the shop doorway, watching the police trying to drag her boss towards a Black Maria. Her gaze flickered towards Violet and she gave an almost imperceptible nod. In that instant an agreement was reached and an alliance formed.

'I'm telling the truth,' Violet said. 'Mr Barlow chased Mrs Barlow out of Jubilee down Chapel Street. She was frightened out of her wits. That's why I asked Muriel to call the police.'

'It's a good job she did,' Eddie said stoutly. 'Then Ida rang me. She knew I was at the Baths with Stan. We dashed over here as fast as we could.'

'It's the girl's word against mine.' Barlow struggled with the officers until one brought out handcuffs and snapped them around his wrists. 'She's making all this up. My wife was hysterical. I tried to calm her down but she fell.'

'Take him to the station.' It was clear that the facts were falling into place and telling the inspector a different story. He turned his back as his men dragged Barlow away to their waiting car.

'And take this young lady home before she catches her death,' the inspector advised Eddie. 'There'll be time later on to make a formal statement.'

So Eddie and Stan pushed through the crowd, each with an arm around Violet's shoulder.

'Plenty of people saw what went on,' Violet murmured. She was so cold that her teeth chattered. Her legs felt heavy, the inside of her head light. 'A butcher's boy, a woman at the bus stop, a man with a car tyre . . .'

'You heard Inspector Butterworth – we'll concentrate on that later,' Stan insisted.

Eddie agreed. 'Right now we have to get you back to Jubilee.'

To Jubilee where Ida and Muriel were waiting with hot tea. Muriel ran upstairs to fetch a dry blanket from Violet's bed. Ida sat her down by the kitchen range.

'Stan, Eddie . . .' Muriel indicated with a meaningful look that it was time for them to make themselves scarce while she and Ida helped Violet undress, sponged her down and gave her clean clothes.

They were slow on the uptake – two tall, ungainly men getting in the women's way in the cramped kitchen.

'You've done your bit,' Ida insisted as she showed them the door. 'I take it Barlow's in clink?' she added.

'Where he belongs,' Stan vouchsafed.

'And between us we'll make sure that's where he stays,' Eddie swore.

All the next day the shop bell tinkled.

Lizzie called in during her dinner break to buy half a dozen horn buttons for her father's sports jacket but really to quiz Violet, the heroine of the hour.

'What was the water like? Was it freezing? Alice Barlow must have been a dead weight – how did you manage to drag her out? Goodness gracious, Violet, you're a blooming marvel.'

Lizzie had heard the story from Marjorie who had seen Stan and Eddie bring a dripping Violet back to Jubilee. Marjorie had waited all of two minutes before haring across Chapel Street to Sybil's shop to find out if Evie knew what Stan and Eddie had been up to. Evie ran to the telephone box on the corner of Cliff Street to speak to Emily Thomson in her box office at Brinkley Baths and so the cat was out of the bag – Violet had saved Mrs Barlow from drowning! And now everyone must call in to see if Violet had survived her dip in the canal unscathed. First Evie dropped by with a fresh sachet of sweet-smelling lavender to pop under Violet's pillow and take away the nasty, lingering smells of the canal. Then Marjorie herself sailed in, convinced that Violet needed building up with beef tea, marvelling that such a slip of a girl could drag Alice Barlow up from the murky depths single handed. In and out of the shop neighbours came to gossip and praise, to learn of the part that Eddie had played then criticize and condemn.

'Colin Barlow tried to kill his wife – fancy that.'

'I never liked the man. Nor her either, for that matter.'

'She can thank her lucky stars that you risked your life to save her. A lot of people wouldn't have bothered.'

Violet listened and smiled, sticking up for Alice Barlow when necessary. Though she was looked after by Muriel and Ida who fussed around like mother hens, by teatime she was worn out. After a short visit from Eddie to see how she was coping, she was in bed by eight o'clock, breathing in lavender and falling straight asleep.

On Friday she was asked to go to the police station to give her account. Inspector Butterworth, inscrutable as on the previous day behind a pair of silver-rimmed glasses, tapped a pencil on the table and listened carefully while a police constable wrote down every word Violet said. Afterwards Butterworth told her that Alice Barlow was still in the hospital but that she was on the mend.

'You've no need to worry – she's already backed up your version of events,' he told Violet calmly. 'We've charged Barlow with attempted murder for a start. There'll be other things to add to that, I shouldn't wonder.'

Violet left the police station with a spring in her

step. *At last*, she thought, *the man will get what's coming to him!*

Walking along Brewery Road, on her way back to work, Violet ran into Sybil, who insisted on shaking her by the hand.

'Winnie would have been proud,' she said with the warmest of smiles. 'I don't know the full story of what Colin Barlow got up to behind his wife's back – only what I've picked up here and there from Ella Kingsley and the like. But we all knew he was a bully and a cheat. It takes courage to stand up to a man like that.'

Violet thanked her and would have hurried on, but Sybil kept tight hold of her hand.

'Now, Violet.' She spoke with a mischievous twinkle in her eye. 'You've probably heard that I have room for a new seamstress at Chapel Street Costumiers.'

'I have.' Violet looked steadily at Ida and Muriel's inveterate rival.

'Whenever your name comes up, Evie never fails to sing your praises.'

'She does, does she?' Violet raised her eyebrows.

'Yes. And I know from past experience that you make a good job of hems, buttonholes and suchlike. So, I've been turning it over in my mind – well, let me get to the point. I don't suppose that you would think of applying for the vacant position?'

A smile appeared on Violet's lips and she spoke with confidence. 'You suppose right. I'm very happy where I am, thank you.'

Sybil released Violet's hand and smiled back. 'It was worth asking, at any rate,' she called over her shoulder as she walked on, heels clicking smartly along the pavement.

'She only did it to annoy us!' Ida exclaimed when Violet reached Jubilee and told her what had happened.

'You weren't tempted, were you?' Muriel gave Violet a searching look.

'Never!' Violet swore. 'I'm only just getting started as a dressmaker but believe me, I'm a Jubilee girl through and through.'

Saturday came and an invitation from Eddie via Ida for Violet to meet him at the Assembly Rooms at seven o'clock.

'He said I should tell you that he was sorry he couldn't pick you up as usual – and very mysterious he was about it too,' Ida commented as she closed up for the day.

Violet didn't mind. 'I'll walk,' she decided. 'It's a nice night. The fresh air will do me good.'

So she dressed warmly in her red hat and best coat over her green dress and set off at a sprightly pace up Chapel Street in time to see what was left of the sun sinking behind clouds on the far horizon. She faced the biting wind and walked along Undercliffe Road. On Violet went in the autumn evening, past the cemetery gates then the entrance to Linton Park, looking straight ahead along the busy road until she could see the lights of the Assembly Rooms and Eddie waiting for her on the steps outside.

Her heart quickened as the man she loved came to meet her, his hand in his jacket pocket, a nervous smile on his lips. Strains of music – the introduction to a waltz – drifted from the hall.

Eddie took a small red velvet box from his pocket and handed it to her, there in the middle of the pavement where couples brushed past in their eagerness to get inside the dance hall, where friends called to each other or gazed expectantly at passengers alighting from the tram.

Violet opened the box. Inside was a gold ring set with a small ruby, with two sparkling diamonds to either side.

'Do you want me to go down on one knee?' Eddie's heart was in his mouth until he got a response.

'No – people will stare!' The ring was beautiful, nestling in cream satin, glinting in the lamplight.

Trying to read the look on Violet's face, Eddie said the only thing he could think of. 'I rode into Welby after work to fetch it.'

'It's lovely,' she whispered, looking up at him with tears in her eyes.

'Is that a yes? Does that mean you'll definitely marry me?'

Voices washed around them.

'Yes I will,' Violet murmured.

Eddie breathed again. 'Try it on. Is it the right size? Do you like it?'

'I love it.' A ruby and four glittering diamonds seen through a blur of tears – five tiny stones signifying a life together. 'I love *you*, Eddie Thomson.'

The music began full swing. Stan and Evie stepped from a tram and strolled hand in hand towards Violet and Eddie.

'Hello, you two,' Stan said. 'I hope you've got your dancing shoes on.'

Violet held up her hand to show them the ring, her heart so full she thought it would overflow. 'You're the first to know – Eddie and I are getting married.'

Evie smiled and hugged her. Stan shook Eddie's hand. The band played 'Blue Skies'.

'That sounds like our tune.' Eddie spun Violet round and ran joyously up the steps with her into the dance hall.

Behind them, still visible, the moors formed a sweeping horizon against a sinking, melting sun. Tomorrow Eddie and Violet would announce their engagement then ride out on the bike. She would clasp her arms around his waist with a ruby ring glinting on her finger. They would swoop, swerve and sail along the moor road and not look back.

Acknowledgements

A huge thank-you to Francesca Best and the Transworld team for lighting the lonely road, providing signposts and pointing out the way ahead. You're the sat navs on this writer's journey.

If you enjoyed *The Shop Girls of Chapel Street*, look out for the next heartwarming tale from Jenny Holmes

The Midwives of Raglan Road

Summer 1936 – with the mill towns of Yorkshire still in the grip of the Great Depression, newly trained midwife Hazel Price returns to the streets of her childhood only to find that her modern methods and supposedly 'stuck-up' ways bring her into conflict with her mother, other family members and residents of Raglan Road.

Determined Hazel battles on. She knows that all eyes are on her as she assists in home deliveries and supports the local GP. The days are long and hard but Hazel brings knowledge and compassion to the work she loves. But then the inevitable happens: a complicated labour ends disastrously.

With accusations flying on Raglan Road, will Hazel's reputation survive the tragedy? And what of the widower, John Moxon, the man she is beginning to fall for – whose side will he take in the war between the old ways and the new?

The Midwives of Raglan Road
will be available in September 2016

Read on for an extract now!

CHAPTER ONE

'Wakey-wakey!' A voice in the street roused Hazel Price from a deep sleep. It was followed by an urgent knocking and a cry of 'It's Leonard Hollings here. Come quick – baby's on its way.'

Hazel jumped out of bed and slipped into the set of clothes laid out on her bedside chair – her underthings followed by a crisp white blouse and dark-blue skirt.

Down on the first-floor landing, Hazel's mother, Jinny, called up to make sure that her daughter had heard the call. 'Get a move on before Leonard wakes the whole street,' she grumbled.

It was six o'clock in the morning. Raglan Road was silent except for the raucous caller at number 18. Hurriedly slipping on her shoes and jacket, Hazel picked up her bag and flung open her attic door to find her bemused father standing alongside her mother in shirt sleeves, with braces dangling from his waist.

'Do you want me to go down and tell him you're

433

on your way?' Robert offered, his voice still thick with sleep.

'No, ta. I'm all set.' Rushing downstairs two at a time, Hazel brushed past her mother and father and then down again to open the front door just as a scrawny man raised his fist to knock a second time. His hair was prematurely grey and his figure small and permanently stooped as if in recognition that the life he'd been born into was hard and getting harder by the day.

'About time too,' Leonard grumbled, backing down the three stone steps and wheezing his way up Raglan Road until he reached the alleyway leading into Nelson Yard. Following close on his heels, Hazel almost bumped into him as he paused for breath. 'At this rate Betty will have gone ahead and done the job herself,' he complained.

'Let's hope not.' Hazel gave a shake of her head. She knew every crack of these stone pavements, the worn steps, rusty iron railings and lion-head knocker on each front door. Even the dank smell of the alley and beyond that the washing lines strung across the yard and the weeds pushing up between the cobbles were familiar to her. All details were the same as before – except for her, of course. She was the one who had changed.

Fumbling in his jacket pocket for his cigarettes, Leonard changed his mind then shuffled on across the yard that consisted of four rows of inward-facing dwellings, each row made up of eight terraced houses that even in their heyday had never offered local mill workers more than basic accommodation. Most were owned by absent landlords who shirked their responsibility to keep the houses in good order so it was no wonder that when roof tiles slipped and fell, they were left in the gutter, and when a window pane was shattered by boys at play, a wooden board was haphazardly nailed to the frame, never to be replaced. Hazel and Leonard passed a row of dustbins lined up against the wall of an outside privy and then a lean-to shelter that housed a dented pram with a broken hood and a bicycle frame without wheels. Beyond that, tucked away in the corner, was an open door.

'Home sweet home,' Leonard muttered sarcastically, standing aside to let Hazel cross the threshold into a cramped kitchen with a chipped pot sink piled high with dishes. She saw the heel of a stale loaf of bread on a bare table, from under which two grubby faces stared up at her. They belonged to Leonard and Betty Hollings' half-naked offspring – a grubby boy of three or four and a girl under two, sitting cross-legged, still and silent as little Buddhas amidst the chaos around them.

'The midwife is here,' Leonard yelled up the stairs.

'Take the kiddies to Doreen next door,' his wife called back, before a fresh wave of contractions gripped her and the sentence ended in a series of groans.

'I'll need hot water,' Hazel instructed the down-at-heel father. 'Plenty of it. Plus towels and some sheets of brown paper if you have them.' She hurried upstairs, following the sounds of a woman in labour into the first-floor bedroom where she found her patient prone on the bed. The grate in the small fireplace was empty and the only objects in the room besides the old-fashioned iron bedstead were a washstand with an enamel basin and a rack with a scrap of striped towel hanging over it.

'Hello, Betty. It seems your husband called for me in the nick of time,' Hazel remarked, as she put her bag on the washstand then picked up the frayed cloth. 'I take it this is the only towel you have?' It was straight down to business and no mistake.

Betty turned her head away and gripped the sides of the thin mattress. She was propped up on two pillows, their covers stained a nasty brown. A torn yellow eiderdown had slipped from the bed on to the bare floorboards.

Once the contractions were over, Betty looked wearily at Hazel. 'Do me a favour – make sure Len gets off to work in good time, there's a love.'

Hazel tilted her head to one side. 'Are you sure? Won't he want to stay until after the baby's born?' Quickly taking everything in, she grew concerned about the lack of hygiene and heat in the room. Still, she'd better lay out her instruments on the wash-stand – scissors, cord clamps, foetal stethoscope – and not act in any way that would cause alarm.

'Not Len – he's not interested in this end of the business,' Betty told her matter-of-factly. 'He'll be happy enough after baby makes his entrance, don't get me wrong. But for the time being, he's better off putting in his shift at Kingsley's.'

Hazel took out cotton swabs and forceps. Betty was as scrawny as her husband and her hips were narrow so it was best to be prepared. By the look of things there would be no brown paper provided to slide under her to absorb some of the mess. Hazel could manage without this, but not the hot water.

Approaching the bed, she put her stethoscope against Betty's swollen abdomen. 'I'm sorry – this will feel cold,' she murmured, counting carefully until she was satisfied that the baby's heartbeat was normal. She finished just in time, because Betty drew up her knees sharply and clenched her teeth at the start of yet more contractions. 'I'm afraid we've left it a bit late to give you something for the pain,' Hazel admitted.

'Not to worry. I never had anything for the last two either. They say it slows things down.'

Hazel patted Betty's hand and smiled. How was it that the ability to endure labour pains without chloral hydrate was still seen as a badge of courage in these parts, she wondered?

'I never went to the infirmary either – not once. You wouldn't catch me in one of those places, not even for a check-up. I stayed at home both times and I've got two healthy kiddies to show for it.'

Though ill-informed, Betty's pride in her own achievement drew a warm smile from Hazel. Then, hearing movement outside the room, she went out to find Doreen, the elderly next-door neighbour, struggling up the narrow stairs with a large pan of steaming water. 'Excellent,' she exclaimed, hurrying to relieve the stout woman of her burden. 'We'll need more of this. And towels if you have any to spare.'

Doreen nodded then bustled away while Hazel carried the water into the room. Maternity pads would have to do the mopping-up job of the more traditional brown paper, she decided. 'Would you like Doreen to send for your mother?' she asked as she prepared Betty for a further examination.

'No, ta. Mam and Len fell out soon after little Poll was born. Mam's gone to live with my sister over in Welby,' came the resigned reply.

'Is there anybody else – someone closer to hand?'

'There's no one.' Raising her head from the pillows, Betty attempted to look beyond the clean sheet that Hazel had draped over her crooked knees. 'How are things looking down there? Please tell me baby's ready to make his entrance.'

'I think so, Betty.' Gentle palpation of the lower abdomen and a rapid vaginal examination had confirmed that the cervix was fully dilated. 'Now, I want you to turn on to your left side and draw your right leg up towards your chin. That's good. Breathe deeply – in, out, now in again as deep as you can. Try not to push until I tell you to.'

There were more contractions and this time Betty did cry out – so loudly that Doreen came scuttling from next door.

'Why have you got her on her side, trussed up like a Christmas turkey?' she demanded as she burst into the room. 'What are you trying to do, finish the poor blighter off?'

'This is what's recommended,' Hazel calmly explained. 'We need to go nice and slowly now, Betty, so the head isn't forced out. Steady as we go.'

'Recommended?' Doreen echoed, her face aghast. 'By who?'

'By the Royal College, that's who.'

As Hazel and Doreen debated the pros and cons of the new method, Betty's free hand clutched at the rails of the bedstead. She cried again and pushed hard despite Hazel's warning.

'They never did this in my day,' Doreen muttered.

'More hot water, please.' Casting a firm glance in the old woman's direction until she backed out of the room, Hazel used her trumpet-shaped pinard stethoscope to listen again to the foetal heartbeat. Still regular, still normal which meant there were no complications with the cord, thank heavens, and really the only difficulty was the size of the head compared with the mother's narrow hips. 'Betty, you have to keep your knee up to your chin as high as you can,' she advised. 'More deep breaths . . . that's good. And now – now you can take short ones. That's right – pant as fast as you like. But don't push yet.'

Hazel saw the dark crown of the baby's head. The contractions were stronger than ever and now she must let Betty push down as hard as ever she could until the face appeared, bluish in colour, its mouth puckered. 'Push now. That's good, Betty – that's grand.'

Sooner than expected, Hazel saw a shoulder emerge and then part of a tiny torso covered in mucus and blood, then a second shoulder. After another moment or two she was able to clamp the cord in two places and make a clean cut then pick up the baby by the ankles and hold her upside down until she sucked the first vital breath of air into her lungs.

'It's a little girl,' she said gently, as an exhausted Betty rolled on to her back and held out imploring hands.

Quickly Hazel wiped the baby's head and face, swaddled her in a square of soft cotton fabric from her bag, then gave her to Betty.

The mother's job was done, the pain already put behind her and she was holding perfection in her arms, but Hazel must work on. She must follow the textbook and see to it in due course that the placenta was delivered whole and that haemorrhaging did not occur.

Meanwhile Betty cuddled her infant and cooed over her while Doreen ascended the stairs with more water and towels, together with further old wives' advice and grumbles about what it cost these days to have a baby, what with doctors' visits and medicines to stop morning sickness, not to mention the money that Hazel would charge. 'Believe me, you won't get much change out of a pound note,' the garrulous neighbour warned Betty. 'Not like in the good old days when you knocked on your fire-back with the end of a poker and someone like Rhoda Briggs, God rest her, or Mabel Jackson came running. That was all it took back then. Not college girls with certificates like Hazel Price here. Just nice and natural did it – flat on your back and with no one breathing down your neck telling you what to do.'

For a second or two Betty managed to tear her attention away from her newborn baby. She looked at Hazel with the sleeves of her white blouse rolled up waiting patiently at the bottom of the bed, then at Doreen standing hands on hips by the washstand. 'Pipe down,' she said sternly to the old woman. 'Do you think Len and me are wet behind the ears? No – everyone knows Hazel only came out of college last week so my Daisy is her first since she got qualified.'

Listening with half an ear as she dealt with the afterbirth, Hazel allowed herself a smile. She liked the name Daisy, and especially enjoyed the disgruntled frown that had appeared on Doreen's face.

'As soon as we heard she was back, Len went straight round to Raglan Road and haggled until she brought the price down to what we can mange,' Betty announced with a triumphant smile followed by a sly wink at Hazel. 'A pound note, my backside!

We're paying her ten shillings and sixpence for my lying-in, not a penny more. So tell Mabel Jackson to stick that in her pipe and smoke it.'

The Midwives of Raglan Road will be available in September 2016

The Mill Girls of Albion Lane

On the cobbled streets of a Yorkshire mill town in 1931, Lily Briggs does all she can to keep trouble at bay for her and her family.

She works hard at Calvert's Mill to make ends meet and take care of her parents and younger siblings. Saturday nights at the dance hall and dressmaking with her two best friends keep Lily upbeat, and now there's a blossoming romance with childhood friend Harry Bainbridge to put an extra spring in her step, too.

But then a run of misfortune threatens Lily's work, home and personal life, and she has to rely on the community at the mill to rally together for support. With so many others to worry about, will Lily always put them first or can she find her own happy ending?

Page TURNERS

· TRANSWORLD ·

Do you love talking about your favourite books?

From big tearjerkers to unforgettable love stories, to family dramas and feel-good chick lit, to something clever and thought-provoking, discover the very best **new fiction** around – and find your **next favourite read**.

See **new covers** before anyone else, and read **exclusive extracts** from the books everybody's talking about.

With plenty of **chat, gossip and news** about **the authors and stories you love**, you'll never be stuck for what to read next.

And with our **weekly giveaways**, you can **win** the latest laugh-out-loud romantic comedy or heart-breaking book club read before they hit the shops.

Curl up with another good book today.

Join the conversation at
www.facebook.com/ThePageTurners
And sign up to our free newsletter on
www.transworldbooks.co.uk